Deep Time

A novel by Peter Dingus

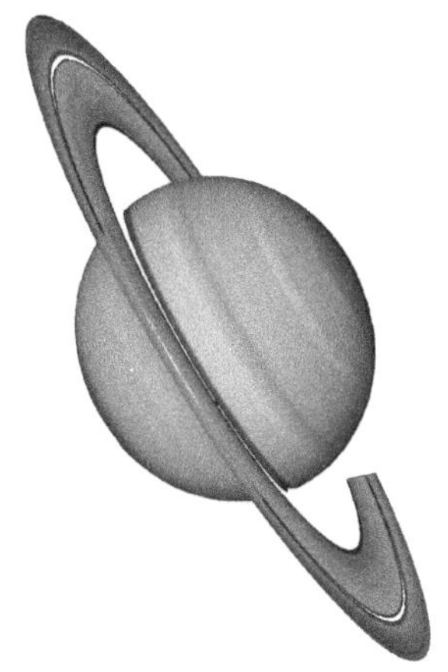

Published by SpeculativeFictionReview

Copyright © 2023 by Peter Dingus

ISBN 979-8-9892200-0-7

Cover Art by Eve H and Peter Dingus

Deep Time

SpeculativeFictionReview

In loving memory of my mother Marie Jeanne Degioanni

Chapter One

Titan, Drill Site, Lakeshore, 2240 AD

Serena stared into the blue glare of the robot's plasma arc. She was hypnotized by the rhythmic flashes marking the drill's encounter with an increasing density of dendritic metal veins in the ice, signaling the robot was getting closer to an iron-ore deposit. Magnetometers indicated something ferrous and large should be around here somewhere, probably a long-buried asteroid that had slammed into Titan millennia ago. She shook her head and blinked her eyes, trying to break the spell. She'd been at this for thirty-six hours and felt like her head was full of water, foggy and unresponsive. She thought about Dex, and her sensorium responded. A pinprick in her upper thigh signaled the suit had injected another dose of amphetamine into her leg, the third this period. She thought of the time and the chronometer appeared in her sensorium. A shift change should be happening within the hour.

Serena felt her head clear with a wiry buzz that meant she wouldn't be getting much sleep this coming rest period. Pushing off the robot, she straightened from a crouch and peered above its carapace into the gloom of the tunnel. Yellowish, methane-laden circular walls disappeared in thin dust clouds of ice, making the other robots in the distance look like dark spidery shadows manipulating the bright flashes of their drilling arcs like monstrous fireflies.

She walked around the robot toward the next one down the tunnel, her helmet visor becoming lighter now that she was away from the glare of the plasma arc. As her vision expanded into the infrared, its longer wavelengths penetrated the dust, clearing up the scene farther down. Robots were arrayed along the walls, some standing on the floor and some hanging from the walls and ceiling, eating away at the fabric of the moon, digesting metal into ingots, and excreting water-methane ice dust, which was constantly pulled from the shaft by powerful ventilators.

Walking toward the far-end tunnel exit, she visualized the status of each robot in her sensorium, scrolling through the units, looking for any anomalies as was her habit at the end of shift. The unit closest to the exit appeared to be registering an increased volume of oxygen in the atmosphere. She stopped and concentrated on that unit, going full telepresence, pivoting its sensor array, and trying to locate the oxygen. It was coming from the vent at the mouth of the tunnel.

Serena stiffened with panic, backed her mind out of the unit, and sensed the robots positioned farther down the tunnel, those coming closer to her registering increasing oxygen, like dominoes falling in her direction. She concentrated on the robot closest to her, ran toward it as fast as she could, then threw herself next to it, balling up and grabbing the floor as she slid beside it. It mimicked her crouch and anchored its legs into the icy floor as the tunnel went incandescent. She waited for the concussion in the shadow of the robot. A second later, she felt the ground shake violently and heard the deafening roar of an explosion cascading down the shaft, ignited by the plasma arcs and the methane-oxygen fuel. She felt the reactive lurch of the robot taking the brunt of the explosion, but its manipulators were sunk deep into the floor and it held fast. Her sensors registered a quickening rise of the outside temperature, from the normal minus two hundred ten Celsius to minus fifty and rising. Soon the cave walls would start melting.

As the tunnel continued to shake, she felt pieces of ice falling on her, punching her, burying her. She willed her suit fabric to stiffen. The temperature passed zero Celsius, then the ground started to liquefy as a chunk of ceiling slammed into her helmet and she lost consciousness.

She tried to open her eyes, but the lids were encrusted and stuck. She slowly pried them apart and red light blurred by dust obscured what little she could see through her helmet's faceplate. How long had she been out? She vaguely remembered the explosion, then being hit all over, then nothing. Serena queried her sensorium. Her heartbeat was way up at 140, body temperature down to 36.4 Celsius, and high adrenaline was coursing through her blood, but otherwise she was okay. She concentrated on calming down, then checked the chronometer. She estimated she'd been out for about 20 minutes. She knew from experience that panic and survival didn't usually mix. After a couple of deep breaths, she tried to sit up—she couldn't move. Suddenly, the panic returned; she felt sweat bead on her forehead, followed by a clammy chill all over her body. If she was paralyzed, she was dead. Again, she took a couple of deep breaths. Her arms and torso were pinned. She thought a moment and then wiggled her toes. That single distal point in her suit offered some free movement. It worked, she wasn't paralyzed, but why couldn't she move? She couldn't even turn her helmet, and the view through the faceplate wasn't enough to allow her to see her body.

She tried to project into the robot beside which she remembered hunkering down—no luck; it was inoperative. She tried the next one down the line. Bingo, she was in. She saw the tunnel through its visual array. The once clean bore of the shaft looked melted, the ice walls were sagging into the floor and stalactite-like protrusions were dripping down from the ceiling, ice dust everywhere. She checked the temperature, minus 100°C; *it's warm in here,* she thought. Serena swiveled the array in her direction and zoomed in. She saw herself covered with ice, stuck to the floor and to the side of the robot where she'd sought shelter. Now it was clear what had happened. The blast melted the tunnel walls, and while she was out cold, the puddle she remembered lying in just before passing out had refrozen, locking her up tight. Then, in the robot's peripheral vision, she sensed movement. She swiveled the array and centered on a dark shadowy figure making its way toward her from the far tunnel entrance. She switched to IR and saw a suited figure skirting around the melted obstructions, making its way to where she lay prone. She left the robot and reestablished herself in her sensorium, then to her normal senses.

The figure was looming over her, looking down at her.

"Hey, am I glad to see you," she croaked. No answer.

"Can you hear me?" Still no answer.

He just stood there, above her, face-plate darkened, just staring at her. She checked her suit status to see whether the com was working and saw all green indicators. It was clear she was transmitting, he just wasn't responding.

"Hey," she shouted. "What the hell's wrong with you? I need help."

He bent down, reached somewhere behind her left shoulder and she felt a tug, then heard a snap through the material of her suit. Instantly, she saw the suit com status go red. The son-of-a-bitch had snapped the com antenna. He straightened up and stared down at her again, *the black shadow of the angel of death*, she thought. Then he turned and vanished from sight, headed back toward the tunnel exit.

Serena lay there for a moment not moving. What just happened? It was hard to reach the obvious conclusion. *The son-of-a-bitch is trying to kill me*. This didn't make any sense. She was the only one in the tunnel at the time of the explosion. *Somebody wants me dead, me in particular*.

"Shit," she said out loud. If she was going to get out of this, she knew it was up to her now, no help was coming. The good news was the assassin didn't know her sensorium and suit com were on separate network channels. Whoever had tried to kill her didn't know much about miners. He must be someone from the outside, someone here for this specific purpose. She checked her air supply, no time to figure this out now. She had an hour of air left. Her first order of business was to get the hell out of here as soon as possible.

Back in the robot, she tried to stand. She felt it rise on its six legs, then stop. She swiveled the array and saw one of the legs was pinned by ice at the knee. She activated the ultrasound drill tip in the second left actuator and brought it to bear on the knee. The ice fractured and began falling away. She quickly worked the tip around the joint, and with a jerk, the knee came free. The robot bobbed up and down a few times to loosen its joints as she applied heat to them. Once everything was moving smoothly, she walked the robot to her immobile form.

Standing above her, Serena scanned the array across her suit in IR, the temperature difference establishing an exact profile of the ice gluing her to the floor. The robot's AI quickly developed a map of how to apply the ultrasonic head to her icy sarcophagus so as to free her without damaging the suit. She reviewed the plan, then shifted the robot to automatic and executed the program. She switched back to her senses.

Serena saw the large frame of the robot above her, straddling her. Then it descended on its six legs coming to rest about six centimeters above her, blotting out her view of the tunnel. It rotated on its waist joint several times, then in a blur of movement swiped the head across her suit. She could hear the whiney buzz and the ice cracking all around her, then suddenly all sound and motion ceased. The robot levitated into an upright stance above her, then stepped aside.

She sat up, the ice falling away in an avalanche of crystalline debris. She had raised the temperature of her suit heaters the whole time, making the de-icing job easier, especially for those areas beneath her where the sonic drill was less effective; but now it was hot in the suit and she felt faint. So she sat for a moment until nausea and dizziness passed, then she stood.

She stumbled toward the entrance, unsteady at first, leaning on the walls and the various melted structures in her way, but soon found her footing and quickly came to the lift at the tunnel mouth. Looking up, she spied the cyclops-eye of the surveillance camera looking her over. The realization made it even more puzzling. Explosions in the tunnels were rare and the equipment, at least, was valuable to the company, but no rescue had come even though the accident happened almost an hour ago. *The accident*, she thought and shook her head. She looked up at the camera again and wondered, *what the hell is going on.*

Inspecting the lift, it was clear this wasn't the way out. Blow-back from the cascading explosion had destroyed the lift's supporting composite trusses, and falling debris from above had blocked the lift channel. Serena checked her air—forty-five minutes. She exhaled and leaned against the wall. Then it hit her. The bastard who had tried to kill her, how did he get down here after the explosion, and more importantly, how did he get out? She straightened up, looked around, then cracked a smile. There were tracks in the ice dust leading off to somewhere behind the lift that must be hiding something out of sight. She followed the tracks to a crack in the wall behind the lift shaft. *What the hell?* She'd been around the lift more times than she could count and knew this hadn't been here. *This thing was planned.* There was just enough space to squeeze through. The crack led to a small space beneath a cramped shaft leading straight up, its summit out of sight. In front of her were footholds etched into the ice wall going up as far as she could see. She was a kilometer underground; this couldn't go to the surface. She started climbing, the fear of suffocating pushing her forward—*into what?* She didn't know, and at this point, she didn't care, as long as it was out of here.

Chapter Two

Titan, Lakeshore, 2240 AD

Serena climbed up the cramped shaft, pressing her boots securely into each foothold, stopping occasionally to rest by pressing her back against the opposing wall and taking a couple of relaxing breaths. Looking down the shaft past her feet, she could still see the bottom, but just barely. Looking up, she thought she saw a reflection from her helmet lights that could signal the end of this exhausting climb. *Twenty minutes of air left, it better be the top*, she thought. *But the top of what?* It wasn't the surface. If this was the top, it was barely a hundred meters above the tunnel from which she was ascending, and that meant it was at least nineteen hundred meters below the life-saving air supply she sought.

She reached the summit and peered over the lip of the shaft. A cramped horizontal tunnel crudely etched out of the ice, probably with a plasma torch, reached into the darkness. She hoisted herself up and stood straining to see. Her helmet lights made an Escherscape of odd orange-yellow patterns, reflections from the water-methane ice irregularities etched into the walls that stretched into the distance. She started walking at a brisk pace toward an uncertain destination.

As she approached the end, she saw a dim diffuse light coming from somewhere out of sight, somewhere to the side of the tunnel. She couldn't hear any voices since her suit com was inoperative, but she could hear noise indicative of activity being carried by the thick nitrogen-methane atmosphere and conducted through a resonance channel that was built into the side of her helmet. As she expected, when she got to the end of the tunnel, there was a cramped passage to the right. Following it, she finally emerged into the shadows of an immense staging area. She knew where she was.

There were many horizontal mining shafts in this area. Heavy equipment, air recyclers, reactors, robots, and items too big for personnel lifts were aggregated and distributed via large caverns like this one. But because she never used it, in her confusion, she'd forgotten about this area. Strangely, it was only a couple of hundred meters up and to the south of the tunnel lift where she'd started.

She stood there, the bright lights of the cavern ahead, people scrambling around unloading drilling and support equipment from a platform that had just descended from the surface. There were different colored suits, blue like hers signifying a miner, red a technician, and black a corporate security officer. Slowly, she walked out of the shadows. Nobody noticed at first since her transponder was dead along with her suit com, but slowly a couple of miners turned her way, drawn by her blue suit. Serena could see them talking through their faceplates, then turning to look at each other, confusion evident on their faces after realizing her com was dead. She quickly walked up to the nearest miner, held him by the forearms, pressed the resonant pad of her helmet against his, and said, "Serena-5786."

The miner broke away and nodded in recognition. Serena made a cutting motion beneath her helmet indicating no com. The miner nodded again. Then she pointed to the wrist pad on her suit that had various status displays and moved her finger to the air supply level indicator. He waved her to follow and quickly walked to a piece of equipment that had just been unloaded. It was a rectangular unit with tanks vertically tied together behind it and tubes and regulators connecting the tanks and the body of the device. He unhitched a tube attached to the front of the air recycler and snapped the male end of a connector to a port on the side of Serena's suit. Immediately, her suit's air indicator began to rise. She breathed in deeply, then sat at the base of the device, put her elbows on her knees, and cupped her helmet in her hands. She felt a hand on her shoulder, and for the first time in the past couple of hours, she felt the tension seep from her taut muscles.

On their way up to the surface, a technician replaced the broken com module on her suit. All at once, com chatter assaulted Serena's senses and she ordered the suit to switch to proximity connections only. Instantly, she was immersed in silence once again. She gave the technician a thumbs-up.

"Yeah, it works, thanks," she said, and the tech returned a thumbs-up.

"What happened down there?" the security man asked. He was standing next to her. She looked up at him and had an instant reaction to the black suit, the same type of black suit the person who tried to kill her wore. He caught the hesitation.

"You all right?" he asked, backing off a bit.

"Just a little shaken up, that's all, just give me a minute."

They spent the rest of the ascension in silence. She sensed him looking her over. Unlike the guy who had tried to kill her, his faceplate was clear. He was about eight centimeters taller than she was and had a light complexion. The shape of his face was hidden by the helmet coupling covering his cheeks and forehead. His eyes were close-set, dark, and looked right through her, conveying a lack of empathy. Knotted brow lines bearing down on a broad bridge of the nose seemed to suggest he regarded her with either suspicion or worry—she couldn't tell which. Whatever was happening, though, she decided not to offer anything until things cleared up. At this point, she didn't trust anybody, a habit reinforced by a long history of bad experiences.

It didn't take long to reach the top of the lift. She'd been down in the mine for nearly three and a half days and the sense of freedom she felt by being able to look up and see the sky through the dome gave her a sense of relief, some room to move.

The technician who accompanied them up from the tunnel walked off.

"Good luck," he said as he disappeared into the crowd.

"Yeah, thanks..."

Serena felt the security man put his hand around her upper left bicep in a firm grip, letting her know there would be a formal debrief, this wasn't over. They walked briskly to the tube hub in silence and waited on the platform for a couple of minutes before a private tube car appeared; its door slid silently open to reveal it was empty. *They have this thing perfectly orchestrated,* she thought, as she took a seat near a window. The security man sat beside her and just stared straight ahead as the silent acceleration of the car pressed her back into the seat.

The tube was transparent and mostly evacuated, with internal pressure orders of magnitude less than outside, enabling the car to reach speeds of hundreds of kilometers per hour, but less than the speed of sound in the tube. Cement-ice coupling structures supported the tube every couple of kilometers keeping the hundreds of kilometers of tube network stable and eternal like it had been there forever. The expanse beyond the window was mostly textured dark methane ice with a profuse scattering of heavily shadowed ice boulders ranging in size from pebbles to ice rocks larger than the tube car.

The flats continued for about a kilometer south until they reached the shores of Orion Lake, a large stretch of liquid methane bordered on the far side by rock-like ice spires reaching heights of more than fifteen kilometers. Above the mountains was an orange-yellow sky illuminated by both a distant sun and the reflection of light from the immensity of Saturn, resulting in twilight as compared to her distant memories of Earth. Large yellow-white clouds, moving fast enough to be noticed, cast shadows on the placid body of the lake in undulating dark changing shapes. Presently, it started raining methane, with wispy streaks flying past the window almost horizontally, but not sticking to the micro-Teflon coating on the silicate glass of the tube. Serena laughed to herself remembering the arid parched Earth of her youth, where it seldom rained. She had come more than a billion miles into the void to see rain. She shrugged and lost herself in the scene, forgetting about the security man and the game to come.

After a while, she saw the lights of the Citadel, the Commonwealth headquarters on this side of Titan. Silicate glass, titanium, and aluminum spires rose out of the distant ice mountain, looking like a futuristic medieval castle. To the right of the Citadel, Serena saw the landing lights of the spaceport that accommodated heavy shuttles from other points on Titan, the floating independent cities in Saturn's atmosphere, as well as landing crafts from transports coming from farther down the Sun's gravity well.

"So, we going to the mining office?" Serena asked.

The security man just sat there. "You asleep?" Serena prompted.

He turned to face her. "Not anymore," he replied.

"We going to the mining office?"

"Do I look like a mining supervisor? No, we're goin' to security."

"Why security, this is a mining accident, isn't it?"

"Look, we don't have explosions in the mines every day. I was told to bring you to security and that's where we're goin'," the security man said and turned forward again.

"Huh," Serena said. All she knew was somebody wearing a security suit had just tried to kill her, and if this guy was telling the truth, something was happening that probably involved some higher-ups freelancing. *But why?*, she wondered. *Best keep my mouth shut and see what develops, find out who I can trust.*

The tube turned toward the Citadel and Serena struggled to calm herself. She would have to look the part of an accident victim during the interrogation; let her assassins think she might not be the problem she knew she was. *Well, whatever's going on, it'll be good to get out of this suit and breathe some air that hasn't been breathed a hundred times before.* The thought helped her relax, and she sat back in her seat.

Chapter Three

Earth, 2222 AD

The storms had subsided, and the sky was clear and bright, with mild winds of no more than ten to fifteen knots. There wouldn't be any blinding dust storms today, which made it special. And as a result, Serena decided she wouldn't be going straight home from the company school. Instead, she was taking the autobus out of the Arcology and into the ancient town beyond the dome. In Darwin, people chose to live a bleak but unincorporated life outside the purview of the company. It was a long ride, and buses only ran twice a day, so she'd have to make sure not to miss the bus home. She looked out the rear window and saw the massive dome of the Arcology, her prison, receding under the horizon of the mesa. As it disappeared, she felt the freedom she imagined the residents of Darwin felt, which informed their choice to suffer the punishing whims of a ravaged Earth rather than those of company executives. Since the death of her father, she and her mother were so far down the food chain they didn't matter. The only thing they worried about was keeping their heads down and mouths shut since privacy was a long-lost haven. That wasn't true in Darwin. There were no micro-cameras and microphones, no face and voice recognition, no AIs scouring intonations or inflections, forever looking for subversive intent. And if you chose not to use the global net, you could stay out of corporate databases. People could say whatever they wanted, something hard to get used to after a life of surveillance and a dangerous habit to break when returning home. Serena shrugged to herself, faced forward, and decided to clear her mind and enjoy the ride.

Serena stepped off the bus onto a deserted town street on a side of town she'd never been in before. Although it was late afternoon, it was still hot and much drier than under the dome of the Arcology. The dryness made the UV more intense, and she put on a pair of sunglasses. The street ran north and south so as to never directly face the sun during the day. The synthetic polymer-bonded adobe buildings were never more than five stories high, with sidewalks in shadow for half the day due to the large protruding overhangs ten feet above the street. The town was powered by a vast solar array just outside its perimeter, sheltered from dust storms by aluminum baffles that could be raised remotely at a moment's notice. Everything was light brown, the color of the desert sandstone from which the buildings were constructed. Due to the scouring effect of high-velocity dust, leaving anything painted out in the open for a couple of days would sandblast the finish to substrate.

Serena crossed the street and ducked into the shade. She encountered a few people who either ignored her or gave her the strangers aren't welcomed look as she strolled down the sidewalk. On her previous visits, she had never made any meaningful contact with anybody. They were all wary of company people, afraid the company considered Darwin a haven of anti-company sedition. Company spies could accuse anyone of anything, whether justified or not. She stood out, and there was nothing she could do about it. Even though most people were brown, she was black, which made it harder to just blend in. And then there were the clothes. In this climate, everyone wore loose-fitting cotton garb, mostly white or tan, while she wore a colorful shirt, tight-fitting leggings, and tan nylon ankle boots. It was apparent that she was not from around here.

She peered into shop windows at handmade oddities you couldn't find in the Arcology, where everything was manufactured from metals or synthetics. She had rarely seen anything made of wood. Passing one shop, she couldn't help staring at the statuettes of animals that seemed to be carved from wood. There were whittle marks on the figures, suggesting they were hand-made. She entered the shop. A bell attached to the top of the door rang as she stepped in. She looked up and saw the bell, then opened and closed the door a couple of times and smiled every time it rang.

"Close the door," someone behind her demanded.

She turned and saw a stern-looking woman peering down at her from further in the shop.

"It's hot outside, don't keep the door open," the woman snapped, as she looked Serena up and down.

Other people in the shop turned in the direction of the commotion, gave Serena a blank stare, then returned to whatever they were doing. Serena walked over to a display that featured an assortment of carved figures and picked one up. It didn't feel like anything she had ever touched. It was the shell of something that had been alive. It was smooth and intricately painted, the likeness of something she had once seen in a book—*a dog*, she thought.

"You gonna buy that?"

Serena turned; it was the same woman who had scolded her about the door.

"Is this wood?" she asked, continuing to rub the piece lightly.

The woman snatched it from her. "Please don't touch the carvings unless you're going to buy one," she instructed.

"I didn't mean to damage it," Serena said. Then asked, "Is it a dog?"

The woman looked at her with contempt; a sharp chin and a razor cut of a mouth conspired with the tightness around her eyes to convey the impression Serena was not welcome here.

Serena exhaled. "Okay," she said. She gave the table of figures one last look, turned, and walked out the door, the bell signaling her exit.

She continued down the street, deflated, thinking this was probably the last time she'd come to Darwin. What was she looking for here? What she couldn't find back at the Arcology, what she couldn't find anywhere. She took the Tab from her bag and checked the time, still three standard hours before the final circuit of the autobus. She sucked her lower lip, returned the Tab to her bag, and kept walking.

She heard some noise as she passed an alley between two tall buildings. The alley was in shadow, and kids were playing, running up and down the length of a makeshift field, yelling, laughing, and kicking a ball toward what looked like goals at either end of the alley. She stopped and found herself drawn to the action, a smile insinuating itself as she drew closer. At some point, someone kicked the ball past the goal opposite where Serena stood. The group that made the goal cheered and slapped hands, and the others turned and started toward the opposite end of the field toward her.

They noticed Serena standing there and all of a sudden things got quiet. Slowly, they approached her. In all, there were about ten of them, a mix of boys and girls, some older and bigger than Serena, and some smaller. They were wet with perspiration and flushed, giving them a countenance that reddened their complexions, making them look aggressive. Most of them stopped when they were a couple of meters away and just stared, but two bigger boys came right up to her and began circling, sizing her up and down.

One of the boys stopped circling when he was in front of her. "Who are you?" he asked.

Then the other boy pulled up alongside the first. "She's from the company," he sneered. "She's here to keep an eye on the throwbacks." Then, looking down at her, he lowered to within a few centimeters of her face. "Isn't that right?" His breath was sour and hot.

"No," Serena stuttered. "No, that's not right."

"What's in the bag?" the boy asked, then grabbed it from her shoulder and emptied it in the dirt, dust billowing as the contents of the bag scattered.

As she bent down to retrieve her stuff, the boy put his foot on her side and shoved her down into the dirt. Then he laughed as the other boy started picking up her things and putting them into a hidden pocket through a part in his loose tan shirt.

"Those are my things," Serena spat and quickly got to her feet. She had always been fast and coordinated and surprised the boy who was stealing her stuff, grabbing his hand, stepping behind him, and twisting his arm. He made a grunting sound as she twisted his hand, making him drop her Tab.

The other boy came up behind her and punched her in the side, then spun her around and punched her in the stomach, making her double over and gasp for breath. In another instant, a flash of pain spread into her chest and she grabbed her stomach, letting the boy go. As soon as he was free, they both advanced on her and pushed her down again, hovering over her menacingly, their faces red and full of rage.

Laying on the ground, she balled up and waited for the beating she knew was coming, but it didn't. She looked up through tear-blurred eyes and saw another boy, bigger than the first two, standing between her and the other two with his hands open on their chests, pushing them back.

"Leave her alone, that's enough," the boy said. The other two stared at him, clearly not wanting to back down, but reluctant to advance. They stood there for a long moment, then one of the boys said, "She's a spy, why are you sticking up for her?"

"I don't know that and neither do you, but what I do know is you hit her, and she did nothing to you. You don't even know who she is and you're stealing her stuff. That's not right."

The boys stared at him a minute, then said, "Screw this." Slowly, they turned and walked away. They pushed through the crowd and most of the others turned and followed.

Serena felt a firm hand under her forearm, helping her up.

"You alright?" the boy asked.

Serena nodded and wiped her eyes, feeling the grit, and knew her face must be streaked with dirt. "Thank you," she said, and let the boy help her to her feet. As she dusted herself off, she watched him pick her things up and carefully put them into the bag. When he'd finished, he dusted it off and handed it to her.

"They're okay," he said, gesturing in the direction of the kids who had left. "They just don't like the company, nobody does—you know."

Serena almost started to laugh. "Why do you think I'm here?" she said. "But I guess nobody likes me either."

The boy smiled. He was tall, maybe 190 centimeters. Even though he wore loose pants and shirt, Serena could see he was powerfully built by the way the garments outlined his muscular form in the wind. And he was handsome too, with short brown hair accentuating a strong symmetric face with deep-set brown eyes and a dramatic nose slightly flared at the nostrils. He was the color of coffee with a bit of creamer, not as dark as she was, but darker than most of the other kids.

"I'm Aegeus," he said. "What's your name?"

"Serena."

"Serena, want something to drink? It's hot out here. I could use something."

Serena nodded, "Okay." She followed Aegeus out of the alley. This was new, she wasn't used to kindness and marveled at how the afternoon had taken this unexpected turn.

Serena followed Aegeus down alleys and across town, snaking along routes only someone who lived here a long time would know. Finally, they emerged on the edge of the town proper, facing south. In the distance, there were tall rust-colored mountains accentuated by light and dark markings that suggested a topology of fissures and protrusions under a clear blue sky. On the flat expanse between the town and mountains were row after row of semi-cylindrical glass buildings sparkling in the sun, arcing out of the sandstone like limitless spokes extending into the distance.

Serena was stunned. "What are they?"

"Greenhouses," Aegeus said. "It's where the food comes from; come on." Aegeus walked into the sunshine, his loose clothes flapping in the wind, and Serena followed, continuing to look around in amazement. They entered the nearest building through a metal door in the center of a half-circular front that was made of the same brown adobe as the buildings in town. Once inside, they encountered a couple of men who were guarding the entrance to the part of the greenhouse that contained a cornucopia of greenery, unlike anything Serena had ever seen. The entrance lay beyond a glass wall and another door. Even though the men regarded Serena with the same suspicion as the rest of the town's people, she soon found herself passing through the door and following Aegeus down a lush dirt path flagged by large strange plants on either side. She suspected the men at the entrance must have high regard for Aegeus.

"What are they?" Serena asked.

"Apple trees," Aegeus said and stepped to the base of one. Then he sat on the ground and leaned his back against its trunk.

"You don't have trees in the Arcology?"

Serena smiled. "Yeah, we have trees, but not like this." She stepped to the tree, reached up, and touched a bright red apple. It felt smooth but had a warm waxy feel that somehow had the aura of something living, not manufactured or processed.

"Don't pick it," Aegeus warned. "This is food for the town; we can come in here, but we can't take anything."

"It's like walking into the most beautiful place I've ever seen, and I can't touch anything."

"You can touch, you just can't pick," Aegeus corrected. "I know it's tempting, so I never come here empty-handed. Come on, sit with me." He patted the dirt beside him with an open palm.

Serena sat cross-legged in front of him and watched as light streaming through the trees cast leafy shadows slowly swaying across him in the humid mist permeating the apple forest.

He reached into a bag slung over his shoulder and across his chest. He searched around and pulled out an apple, as big and red as any on the tree. "Ta-da," he said, just like a magic trick. He took a knife out of the bag, cut the apple in half, and handed half to Serena. She started to laugh, reached out, and took it, rotating it in her hand, regarding it as something precious.

Aegeus took a bite of his. "You gonna eat it or look at it?"

She took a bite. It was the best thing she'd ever eaten. It was juicy and sweet, with a texture that made it almost crunchy. They sat there in the shadows and light, eating the apple, and Serena wanted this moment to last forever.

Later, they walked a kilometer of the apple forest and then took an enclosed walkway to the next greenhouse. This one hosted row after row of what Aegeus called corn. Serena had heard of corn; it was used in a lot of the processed foods she ate, but she had never seen the actual plant. Aegeus explained how it was grown and how you could cook and eat the kernels off the husks, something she couldn't imagine doing. It was fascinating;

nobody she knew was aware of these things or even thought about them. They walked through the wonderland of plants until it was time to go. If she stayed any longer, she would miss the autobus.

They left the greenhouses and hurried through the back alleys until they arrived at the place on the main thoroughfare where the autobus was scheduled to make its last stop of the day.

"When I come back, how do I get in touch with you?" Serena asked.

Aegeus reached into his bag and withdrew his Tab. "What's your net ID?" he asked.

When Serena told him, he typed something into his Tab and a moment later she heard her Tab chime. She reached up and kissed him on the cheek. "This is the best day of my life," she said. "I'd like to live here, maybe I can."

Aegeus looked pained. "It's hard to leave the company," Aegeus said. "I hear it's almost impossible to get out of your contract."

"I don't have a contract," Serena said.

"Contracts are inherited if a family's debt isn't paid in full," Aegeus replied.

Serena felt panic. "How do you know that?"

"My father was a company executive, paying our debt broke us. We came here with nothing, and he was pretty high up."

Serena stared at the ground, then looked up at him. "I hope you can," he said, but it was sad, unconvincing.

Serena watched Aegeus fade into the distance as the bus pulled away. He stood in the middle of the street, clothes flapping in the dusty wind, waving goodbye. She would never be back.

Chapter Four

Titan, Citadel, 2240 AD

After arriving at the Citadel, Serena was brought to an entry station where she could ditch her suit and clean up a little before being debriefed. Once the door closed, she quickly stripped off the suit, something she'd done thousands of times before. Then she went to a set of shelves and found disinfectant wipes and sponged herself down. She'd been in the suit for more than three days, and taking it off gave a feeling of clean and the lack of restriction that were renewing. She removed her skull cap and unbraided her hair, which fell to her waist. Her mother had told her that her long ebony hair, with streaks of brown, was from some long ago Asian ancestry. Many men and women chose to shave their heads because hair was a hassle in zero-g, but she kept it. It reminded her of a time when the company didn't own her.

After putting her hair up and slipping on underwear and a blue jumpsuit, she emerged from the station and was met by two security men this time. One was the man who'd accompanied her from the mine and the other one, who was shorter and thinner, was new. They both wore black jumpsuits with the company logo on their left breast showing the sun and earth-orbiting at forty-five degrees on a starry black background. She inspected the man from the mine now that she could see him without his helmet. He was broad, which made the features she saw when he wore the helmet seem too small for his face. He had a cruel impassive look that made her wonder; *is this the son of a bitch who tried to kill me?* Her continued stare raised the corners of his mouth in a subtle smile that seemed to answer the question. They took a lift to the fourteenth level. The out-facing wall was transparent and

Serena could see Titan's majestic vistas spread in the direction of the lake for at least forty kilometers. The sun was setting, and the panorama of the lake and distant mountains was bathed in an orange-yellow twilight. Titan's atmosphere was too thick to see stars, but she thought she could see the glow of Saturn's ring stretch across the sky. Once they arrived at their destination, they brought her to an empty room with no windows, a metal desk, and two opposing chairs, and left her there without a word. At their leaving, she heard the door lock with a click. She sat down, folded her hands in front of her, and waited.

She waited a long time. Even though the chair was not comfortable, the quiet and her latent fatigue lulled her into a shallow sleep. She woke with a start at the sound of the door opening and clicking shut, echoing in the empty room. She watched a man enter, then stand in front of her. He looked down at her, looking her over, but not sitting down. She impassively looked him over too. He wasn't like the other two. He wore a formal black executive suit cut to fit his trim form, giving him an air of authority. He was dark brown; his head was framed by a mane of blue-black hair that was combed back and shined in the overhead lights. His face had fine features, and she could see intelligence in his brown eyes. He smiled, but without the cruelty of the other man from the mine.

"Serena, my name is Hailin-Zen, sorry for the long wait," he said and stuck out his hand.

Serena took it. "Mr. Zen." His hand was firm and dry. He didn't try to squeeze her hand in an asshole show of authority, which gave her pause.

"Why am I here, Mr. Zen? Why not the mining office? Am I suspected of something?"

Zen regarded her a moment, then sat. "There was an explosion. It's not clear what caused it. You are the one survivor who witnessed it," Zen said and waited.

"Somebody got killed? I was the only one in the tunnel."

"There was an explosion in an adjacent tunnel as well, you didn't know that?"

Serena was stunned, she sat forward. "Who got killed?"

Zen consulted his Tab. "Abin-Lor," he said and looked up. "You know him?"

"Not well," Serena answered, "But yeah, I knew him." She looked down at the table.

"I was pinned in that tunnel for more than thirty minutes," she said, not raising her head. "Where were you guys?"

"The lift collapsed; it took time to move equipment in and dig it out."

"Why didn't you come down the other shaft?"

Zen looked up from his Tab. "What other shaft? There is no other shaft."

Serena smiled without humor. "Yeah, then how did I get out?"

Zen stared at her.

"Go ahead and check; I got out before they dug the lift out. They didn't tell you that?"

Zen rushed out of the room without another word. Serena waited again, but this time she couldn't sleep. It seemed as though Zen was also in the dark. This might be a rogue operation spinning out of control. And because she had survived, she knew things that made the explosion look suspicious—not an accident. That meant the longer she was around, the greater the threat to whoever was behind this. *Shit*, she thought.

About ten minutes after Zen's quick departure, another man in a black jumpsuit came in with a box of food and drink. He said nothing, put the box in front of her, and left as unobtrusively as he had entered. She opened the box, and to her surprise, it was real food, not paste and crackers. She couldn't help smiling.

Nothing like being assassinated on a full stomach, she mused and laughed out loud as she unpacked the box.

When Zen returned, he was followed by a large rectangular panel mounted vertically on a mobile platform. Zen motioned for her to get up. Then he moved the table and chairs to the far side of the room. Once clear, he ordered the equipment to the center of the room where it began to reconfigure itself. The rectangular flat panel started sliding on its base until it was horizontal, and then the sides shone a bright blue. Its dark surface had the outlines of circles dimly visible in a complicated overlapping pattern. Looking at it from an angle, it diffracted light much like a thin film of oil.

"We downloaded the robot's memories. Let's take a look," Zen said.

Serena followed Zen to the far side of the room and stood next to him, butts pressed against the table, facing the holo. Zen glanced at her. Then he looked back at the platform and folded his arms across his chest.

"Lower the lights; begin playback zero-one," Zen ordered. He turned to Serena. "This is the robot closest to the lift."

The space subtended by the rectangle showed a three-dimensional image of the tunnel that stretched all the way to the ceiling with perfect clarity, as if it were a portal that she could step into. The view was from the robot's visual array, which was focused on the drilling torch until the absorption spectrometer, superimposed on the image, began to register an increased concentration of oxygen in the atmosphere. Suddenly, the torch went out and the array pivoted in an attempt to discover the source of the oxygen gradient, now reaching dangerous levels. Suddenly, the entire volume of the image was subsumed by a bright flash and disappeared.

"From the orientation of the array and the direction of the oxygen gradient, we think the source was the large ventilation duct near the lift. To get the concussive explosion that destroyed the robot, and another further down, the concentration of oxygen at the time of ignition had to be about ten percent of the atmosphere. Otherwise, there wouldn't have been enough compression given the size of the tunnel, and the ignition would have resulted in a flare traveling down the tunnel instead of the explosion," Zen explained.

"That wasn't an accident," Serena offered. "An accidental leak wouldn't have been that large—that fast. I've been mining for seven years; I've never seen anything like that."

Zen nodded. "Now, let's see the robot nearest you." He turned back to the platform. "Playback zero-two," he ordered.

Again an image of the tunnel appeared, and again the display focused on a torch. The torch went out and the array pivoted. For just a few moments, Serena appeared. The back of her blue suit was to one side of the image when a bright flash erupted. But just before the image went dark, she was blown off her feet. Serena stared in confusion, Zen watching her closely.

"Is that what happened?" Zen asked.

Serena kept staring at the blank spot above the projector. "That's what the memory shows, isn't it?" She turned slowly and faced Zen.

"We examined your suit, no burn marks. Also, no signs of damage an explosion like that would cause." They regarded each other. "Is that what happened?" he repeated.

"No," she said slowly. "No, it's not."

"We went back and looked for the shaft you said you climbed, there's nothing there. So what did happen?" Zen asked.

She told him about seeing the oxygen in her sensorium. She told him about finding shelter in the shadow of the robot. She told him how she got stuck in the ice, and how she cut herself free. But she didn't say anything about the appearance of a security man in a black suit, how he broke her com antenna, and how he just left her there to die. Serena was tempted to trust Zen. He seemed to be truly puzzled by what had happened, by what was happening. But this was his organization. Better to just wait and see what he did with this information. She didn't want to make herself more central to this than she already was. *Was that half smile by the security man who brought her here just their way of telling her to keep her mouth shut? Was he even a security man?* She wondered. Apparently, when he'd left her there to die, he didn't know about her ability to control the robots without the com antenna. *Any security man working around miners would know that wouldn't he? Too many unknowns,* Serena thought. *Best to wait and see before trusting anyone.*

Chapter Five

Earth, 2222 AD

When the autobus pulled up in front of her building, number 85961 Fresh Meadows Rd., the sun had set and the quarter moon shone through the transparent panels of the Archology, frosting the boxy buildings and making them more appealing than in the daytime. She climbed the stairs to the third floor, walked the balcony to her apartment, put her thumb on the bio-lock, and walked in. The room was dark.

"Lights dim," she said, then looked around and saw her mother sleeping on the couch. She was still in her pajamas and there was a mostly empty bottle of bourbon on the coffee table. Her mother's hair was tangled and covered half her face. As Serena drew closer, she could hear her snoring softly.

Serena sat on the side of the couch and smelled the whiskey on her mother's breath. "Mom," she said and shook her mother gently by the shoulder.

Her mother stirred, turned toward her, and slowly opened her eyes. "Serena? What time is it?"

"It's late, Ma, you have to get up."

"Oh, I'm sorry," she groaned, then tried to sit up, became disoriented, and fell forward. Serena caught her before she hit the coffee table and gently lowered her back onto the couch.

"I'm sorry, I'm sorry," she repeated and started to cry.

Serena put her mother's head on her lap and combed her hair back, out of her face, then began lightly stroking her forehead. "I know," she said. "I know."

* * *

It had been three months since her trip to Darwin, and Serena fantasized about it almost every day since. She imagined her and her mother living there. They'd been accepted and made friends. She imagined coming home from school to a little adobe house they'd decorated, made personal, unique. Her mother, whom she remembered as having been a beautiful woman before her father died, would be cooking real food, and fresh vegetables from the greenhouses. And instead of the smell of whiskey, there'd be the appetizing smell of dinner and a clean house. The thought made Serena smile. Maybe it could happen, maybe it wasn't as impossible as Aegeus made it seem. After all, today she was thirteen-years-old and she'd resolved to be more positive. She was smart; she could figure it out.

The autobus pulled up in front of her building. She got out and climbed the three flights of stairs to the balcony. As she approached her apartment, she heard people talking; one person was her mother and she sounded frantic. Serena ran to the door, put her thumb on the lock, and quickly went in. Her mother was sitting on the couch; she'd been crying. Two men stood in front of her with their backs to the door. They were tall and looked like company men. They were dressed in expensive, trendy black suits made of an iridescent material that shined in the light of the window. At the sound of the door opening and closing, they turned and she got a good look at them. One was light brown, and the other was dark, like her. The dark one had chiseled features with a thin nose and full lips. His eyes were an icy blue and he seemed amused, but not in a good way. The other man was stockier and more powerful; his suit coat clung tightly to his biceps. He was blank, with a fleshy face, a broad nose, and small beady eyes that reminded her of pictures of bulldogs she'd seen in books. He stared at her in a way that made her feel he was looking right through her. "Serena?" the dark one said. "We were just talking about you."

"What are you doing to my mother?" Serena hissed. She dropped her bag to the floor and stood there, stiff, hands clenched into fists.

"You can't take her," her mother wailed. She cupped her face in her hands and shook, making a low moaning sound.

"You're thirteen today," the dark man said. "You're an adult according to the contract your parents signed. It's time for you to fulfill your obligations under the terms of the contract. That's why we're here."

Serena was speechless. Of all the things she'd thought this could be about, this was the last on the list. She tried to think.

"I didn't sign any contract," she said. "Nobody ever said anything to me about it."

"Your parents borrowed a lot of money from the company," the man said calmly. "Your apartment, protection from superstorms outside the dome, your education, medical insurance, and many other benefits provided to you by the company. Did you think those came without a cost?"

"My father worked for you all those years. He died working for you. You paid him and he paid you." Serena said.

"All true," the man said. "But he still owes a considerable amount. The debt is transferable to every member of the family who can serve the company in a useful way." He turned and looked at her mother with mock pity. "Evalyne is in no condition to fulfill the commitments of the contract. We've already given you and your mother a generous grieving period. Now it's your turn to serve the company."

All the fight went out of her. It was as though Aegeus had seen the future. What he had told her was prophetic. She couldn't leave the company; they wouldn't let her, all her dreams of moving to Darwin were just that, dreams. This was her life and always would be. They owned her.

"And my mother?" Serena asked. "What happens to her if I go with you? If I work for you?"

The man stepped forward and looked down at her, trying, but not succeeding at coming off as if he cared. "She'll continue to live here. We will continue to care for her."

Yeah, and our debt will continue to grow, and you'll own us forever, Serena thought.

"What happens now?" Serena asked. "When do I go with you?"

"Why, now," the man said as if it was obvious. "We'll wait here while you get your things together, then you can come with us."

* * *

Serena sat on the edge of her bunk and recalled the day with perfect clarity. The day when her life had taken an abrupt turn, landing her here. Today was her birthday; she was fourteen-years-old. It was a year since she'd left Earth, left her mother, left any continuity with before—*the before time,* she thought and smiled to herself. She remembered her fantasies about Darwin, even her overarching concern that her mother get straight, somehow find some meaning, something to look forward to other than her next drink. Serena had to think hard, did any of it even matter anymore? She wanted it to. She struggled to keep those desires close, to not lose herself, but in the end, they'd won. The company had changed her, physically, spiritually, in every way that mattered. It had been determined, by mental, physical, and psychological testing that the greatest benefit to the company would be to put her in the corporate security services. Serena had been taken to Midway orbital station at the cislunar L2 point. There she'd been given genetic therapy to harden her body for a life in low-g, to resist genetic damage in a heightened radiation environment, and given mental augmentation, bio-electronic subdural brain implants, so she could control military hardware remotely. A year of low-g tactical combat training had left her the enforcement wetware the company needed to maintain its operations among its broad business interests on planets, moons, and asteroids in the solar system. Her reverie was broken by doorbell chimes. Serena concentrated on the door monitor and a view of a young man coalesced in her Aug-net.

"Open," she commanded, and the door slid soundlessly aside.

Janus came in and stood before her, holding something that looked to be clumsily gift-wrapped. He was taller than her, dressed in a smart dark blue security tunic, and she could see the glint of his immaculate white teeth outlining a bright smile in the dim light of her room.

"Why the shit-eating grin?" she asked, smiling herself now.

"You're the birthday girl, aren't you, or have I got the wrong bunk?" He looked around in mock confusion. "Come on, let's celebrate, look what I brought you." He handed her the package, then sat in front of her cross-legged. They were almost at eye level now, her sitting on the bunk and him on the floor. Janus had inherited family debt in another company Arcology and arrived around the time she had. They held each other up during the conversion from what they were to what they had become, somehow grounding each other to retain some sense of identity. She considered Janus a fellow traveler in whom she could confide her deepest doubts, someone who understood the displacement since he had been displaced as well. He was compelling in an empathetic way and handsome with a mouth naturally set in a smile. He had woolly brown hair that framed an oval face with bright blue eyes and a wide extravagant nose.

She unwrapped the package. It was a bottle of wine. "Where in the world did you get this?" she asked.

"Nowhere in the world," he replied. "I found out they're growing grapes on one of the Ag stations around the moon. Everybody in cislunar space is paying top dollar for wine. It's a retro thing, so I thought you'd like it," he said and smiled.

She hated whiskey, but there was something about wine. The fact it came from grapes grown from a bush somehow reminded her of apple trees and light streaming in from the transparent roof of a greenhouse made it appealing. She unscrewed the top and couldn't help smelling the aroma wafting up from the red liquid. "Thanks," she said, and raised the bottle to her lips, taking a long, delicious drink. They drank, laughed, and eventually finished the bottle. Serena regarded Janus in the dim light, sitting on the floor of the small room, barely a cell, and saw him staring at her with apparent desire. The warmth of the wine stirred something in her she hadn't felt in a long time. Somehow, she was at home in this small bare room because Janus was here, and he'd remembered her birthday—probably the only person in the system to whom it mattered. Her past seemed to fade into a bad dream and the present became clear and immediate. She got off the bed and stood in front of him, legs apart looking down at him. She crisscrossed her arms down around herself, grabbed the hem of her tee shirt, and slowly lifted it off. Janus stared at her breasts, dark and full, nipples erect, and moaned slightly. She could see he was hard. She straddled him, and then lowered herself onto his lap, wrapping her legs around him and pushing herself hard against his erection. He gasped, and with his mouth still open, she kissed him deeply.

Chapter Six

Titan, Citadel, 2240 AD

After Serena Roe left the room, Zen sat for awhile, staring at a blank wall. There was something about what happened in the tunnel that made no sense. And how did she get out? The time stamp of the explosion, and the record of when she'd arrived at the staging area, just didn't add up. He sent men out to check her story about another shaft, the one that didn't appear on any of the tunnel maps, and they found nothing. Yet here she was.

Zen's thoughts were interrupted by his Aug-net notifying him of an incoming message. He heard the message in his Minds-eye. A company senior vice president of the research division had just arrived from Olympus, the large habitat just this side of the asteroid belt orbiting the sun in Saturn synchronous alignment. The message just deepened his unshakable feeling something was way off. The Citadel was a mining operation; it had nothing to do with research. Zen had been director of security here for the last five years; and searching his memory, he couldn't find another instance of anybody from research ever visiting, no less a senior VP. People at that level didn't visit mining operations; they made policy, set direction, and sent people much lower on the org-chart to handle the day-to-day. And this couldn't have anything to do with the explosion in the tunnel since that happened yesterday and a trip from Olympus took at least five months at maximum burn. Unless…

The door opened and his aide popped her head into the room. "Mister Adonus is in your office, sir."

"The VP from Olympus?" Zen asked.

"Yes, sir."

"Bring him a cup of coffee or whatever he wants. Inform him I'm on my way," Zen said. The aide disappeared but left the door open. Zen took a deep breath, pushed away from the table, and left the room.

When Zen entered his office, Adonus was seated on the black faux-leather sofa on the far side of the room, one arm draped over the seat back, his legs crossed, gazing out the floor-to-ceiling window showing the panorama of the lake and mountains in the distance. Majestic yellow-orange clouds hung over the lake suspended over a dark shadow of methane rain heralding more storms coming this way. He was lean and fit, dressed in an impeccable dark blue suit and high stylish white collar. His handsome chiseled face was crowned by short woolly blonde hair, accentuating his cafe-au-lait complexion.

He didn't turn when Zen entered the office. "This is a sight you can't see anywhere else in the system," he said. "I heard about this, ashamed it took so long to come here and see it for myself."

Zen took one of the two chairs facing his desk and positioned it diagonally between the sofa and window so he could see Adonus in profile. He wanted the man to turn and face him; he wanted to get a sense of the man.

"That leads me to my first question," Zen said. "Why are you here? What can I do for you, Mr Adonus?"

"You had a tunnel explosion the other day," Adonus said, still looking out the window.

Zen was taken aback. "It takes about six months to transit between here and Olympus. I take it you can't see the future?"

Adonus chuckled and then turned to face him, pivoting smoothly and casually crossing his legs in the opposite sense. "No, I can't tell the future, although it would come in handy, don't you think?"

Zen looked for a tell, but the man gave nothing away. "So, how can I help you?" Zen asked.

"I was on my way to Aurora, the cloud city on Saturn when we heard about the explosion. We were on a Saturn insertion orbit when I decided it would be to our advantage to come here first."

Zen waited, indicating he expected more to come since what Adonus had said explained nothing. At the center of Zen's skillset was the art of interrogation. He had learned strategic silence was often the best way to extract the most information from someone being questioned. Adonus smiled knowingly. It was clear that, unlike many higher-ups, Adonus did not underestimate him, which was concerning.

"We were going to Aurora to sell our acoustic knife to the Pan Saturn Commonwealth. As you know, Saturn and its satellite colonies represent thirty percent of our mining revenues on the far side of the belt. The acoustic knife is a new kind of mining drill specifically designed for Titan's thick atmosphere. Since sound as a tool is not something most outworlders are familiar with, the company thought it would be a good idea for me to come out here. When we heard about the explosion and cave-in, I thought it would be an excellent opportunity to demonstrate the product. Does that answer your questions, Director Zen?"

"Why come here first?" Zen asked. "I would expect you to contact the Commonwealth directly. They will instruct me as to how I can assist you under whatever provisions they might impose. As you know, I have no power to permit anything without prior instructions."

"Already done, Director Zen. I just thought it would be respectful to meet you beforehand, that's all."

"Okay," Zen said. "But is there anything special you envision other than notifying us to expect your tech personnel?"

There must be something else, Zen thought. This performance was pretty elaborate, as a wink and nod to a commercial test.

Adonus shifted on the sofa. "Uh, yes. As you may have guessed, this is a new product, and we have competitors. We don't want the results of field tests getting out."

"And?" Zen asked. *Here it comes*, he thought.

"Yes, well, we've brought our own security personnel. We're requesting you give us exclusive access to the site for the duration of the tests. We will record the test and brief the Commonwealth on the results. Once an agreement is signed, we can reveal the technology to the broader community."

Zen sat back. "I see. Well, Mr. Adonus, I will be waiting for further instructions. Until then, I'd request you deploy no security personnel."

"Are we permitted to inspect the site beforehand? Even a drone inspection will work. We need to develop deployment logistics—the sooner the better."

Zen stared at him a moment, "Of course, Mr. Adonus. However, your personnel or drones must be accompanied by Citadel security."

"Of course," Adonus replied and then turned back to the window. "This really is a magnificent sight."

* * *

After Adonus left, Zen glanced up at a spot at the apex of two walls and the ceiling where he knew a hidden camera surveyed the office. A couple of moments later, his aide, Li-ant, entered the room. She was tall, the consequence of being born on one of the habitats in cislunar space. Her body had never surrendered to the punishing gravity of Earth. And she had been modified before birth. Not the supplemental modifications he and others who had left the home planet in the human diaspora of the solar system received, but more extensive, deeper modifications that made her a truly space-born species. She was pale, with short silver-white hair and a head that seemed too big for her slender body. Zen found her exotic and attractive.

"Well?" he asked.

She stood facing him, framed by the panorama of the window. "We've had experimental equipment here before. I checked. There has never been a request like this."

"Yeah, I agree, something's off." Then looking up at her, he asked, "Do you believe in coincidences?"

"You mean about the explosion?" she asked. "The two must be linked, but I don't know how."

"The girl, the miner—Serena, I feel like there's something she's holding back. If it were a simple accident, why hold back, what's so secret about an explosion?" Zen asked. "And Adonus, have you checked him out?"

"Yeah, he's plugged in. He has the ear of the chairman of Trans Space Technologies. They wouldn't send a guy like that to sell mining equipment; there's something else happening here."

"Have we had any word from Saturn about *assisting* Mr. Adonus?" Zen asked.

"Nothing yet. He's pretty sure of himself, isn't he? Has the company ever had exclusive control of Commonwealth properties? This whole thing gives me the creeps."

Zen smiled. "The creeps?" he echoed. Antiquity seemed incongruent when coming from Li, but somehow it fit her personality, trying to reconstruct a past from what scant history was afforded the new people. "And to answer your question, no, TST has never had exclusive control of Commonwealth property," Zen explained. Then after a moment, "Let's keep an eye on the girl. I have a feeling she may be the key to all this. What do you know about her?"

"Yes, I looked into her, too. That's where things start to get strange."

"Oh?" Zen asked and sat forward. "Strange how?"

"She was originally recruited by the company at thirteen—the usual for fulfilling a family contract. She had high aptitude scores; they put her in the security service, Ranger track."

"Ranger?" Zen whistled. "And now she's a miner? How did that happen?"

"She was involved in a pacification operation of a company facility on Mars and things went sideways. After that, her files were sealed. We don't have access to secure company files. A year later, she shows up here as a miner."

"If she was in the Rangers, she has state-of-the-art bio-cybernetic and bio-structural enhancements. Those can't be removed without killing her because they're invasive; they grow into her tissues, become part of her," Zen said.

"Yes," Li agreed. "But they can be greatly deactivated by software restriction."

"So she's a few million credits of bio hardware digging metal out of the ice. Whatever she did, it must have been severe," Zen said and sat back. "So you'll keep an eye on the girl and keep me informed?"

"Yes, sir," Li said. And she quietly left the room, leaving Zen to ponder his next move.

Chapter Seven

Mars Insertion, 2233 AD

The *Griffin* left Midway station nearly three months earlier on a hard burn to Mars. As it transitioned into a Mars insertion orbit, its corporate security compliment of eighteen Rangers was called into a briefing room to put the final touches on their planned assault on a company hydrogen-oxygen processing plant in the Chryse-Planitia basin northeast of Ursa settlement near the Valles Marineris. Workers there were occupying the plant, demanding a new contract, better pay, and improved safety conditions. This was Serena's tenth deployment. The long trip to Mars was filled with mock assault exercises interspersed with anxious nightmares of leaving Earth prompted by her mother's plight and her day in Darwin. Both of those events had gradually faded into hazy remembrances indistinguishable from manufactured daydreams. Even after all this time, she struggled to keep the memories alive, because even though they hurt, they were a past that made her something more than a company tool. On the bright side, there were frequent visits to her cabin by Janus. This morning, however, all the waiting came to an end; they finally arrived in Mars orbit, and although she felt embarrassed to admit it, the anticipation of the assault was exciting.

The squad filed into a spacious room in the Griffin's forward torus, one of two counter-rotating living areas situated aft of the large cargo hold and landing craft bay, and forward of an array of fuel tanks that crowned the three nozzles of the Griffin's main fusion engines in the rear. Serena found a chair on the aisle, bisecting an assembly of seats about halfway from the front of the room. Janus followed her in and sat next to her. As the rest of the compliment found their places, Serena took stock of the surroundings. The lower portion of the out-facing wall was gently curved following the profile of the torus and had a rectangular window that showed the shifting landscape of Mars, followed by the deep black star-laden void as the structure spun creating one-third Earth gravity, same as on Mars. The rest of the room was a nondescript light gray composite with a dais to one side of a large projector at the far wall in front under a ceiling that glowed soft white. The walls were textured to baffle sound, creating a strange sense of warmth.

Lieutenant Nora Assisi, their squad commander, walked briskly up the center aisle, ram-rod straight and all business. She mounted the podium, pivoted smoothly, and situated herself alongside the dais. She wore a dark blue jumpsuit with the company logo on her upper right sleeve and lieutenant's epaulets on each shoulder. She was tall for an Earther, about one hundred eighty-five centimeters, with a light complexion and blonde hair cut short. Her steely dark brown eyes scanned the room, which was dead quiet. "Good morning. Let's get started." The light dimmed and the projector showed a three-dimensional image of a lowland basin in a rust-red desert surrounded by mountain ridges on three sides. Through a pass between the mountains, large pipes stretched off into the distance heading southwest and disappearing off the projection. In the other direction, toward the center of the lowlands, was a gathering of squat rectangular buildings crowning a matrix of circular constructions Serena imagined capped many large underground tanks.

"This is the H_2-O_2 plant at Chryse-Planitia," Nora explained. "This is a company plant that supplies all the air and fuel for the Ursa settlement, which is about 40 klicks southwest of the basin. The company has a contract with the Mars Confederation, which has stood now for over twenty years. Most of the technical workers are confederation citizens. The management is Trans Systems. This is an expensive installation to run, and the contract has penalties for nonperformance, so any work stoppage is a problem. Recently, our on-site management has reported an increasing rate of equipment failures at strategic points in the operation. At the same time, there is mounting worker unrest, and agitators trying to form a union. A union is strictly forbidden by the terms of the contract. Our local security office has determined the failures we're experiencing are in fact systematic sabotage. About six months ago, we got word some of the workers at the plant were members of the Mars Separatist Alliance, a group that wants to nationalize off-world installations. That's why we're here."

A hand went up and Nora nodded to a young man seated across the aisle and farther in front of Serena. "How about Confederation security? Why aren't they putting this down? Has the company asked for assistance?"

Nora smiled for the first time. "Confederation security—a contradiction in terms," Nora quipped. Many in the room followed suit with muffled laughter and shuffling feet. "So let's get this straight, it's not clear the Confederation doesn't sympathize with the MSA. Now that we've built all this," the lieutenant made a sweeping gesture with her arm over the image of the plant. "I'm sure the government would love to just step in and take over. Just before we got here, we lost contact with the plant. We believe the MSA has taken control and is holding our personnel hostage. Well, ladies and gentlemen, we're now in a hot engagement. We have been authorized to use lethal force if necessary."

Serena could feel the sense of excitement building; she could smell the testosterone in the room. This is what they'd trained for, and the sense of aggression made her enhanced muscles tighten. What had started as a policing mission had turned into a full-scale war, and they were the point of the spear.

"As we achieved Mars insertion, we deployed remote sensing satellites into Mars synchronous orbit; you should be receiving the feeds in your Aug-nets. On the first pass over the station, we took out the plant's sat, microwave, and shortwave antennas with particle beams. Our EM warfare satellites should have taken out land-based coms. The terrorists should be deaf and blind."

Another squad member, a young woman, raised her hand and the lieutenant nodded in her direction. "So that means they know we're here?"

"That's right," Nora replied. "But that's all they know. They don't know our strength, what we're bringing to the party, or when or how we'll come in. So we do retain some element of surprise."

"Do we know their strength, how many there are, how they're armed?" Janus asked without being called on.

"We have agents in Ursa. To the best of our intelligence, we believe there are no more than ten terrorists, that's the good news. The bad news is they may have attack drones, rockets, state-of-the-art kinetic rifles, and even a couple of rail guns."

"So this is the real thing," Janus concluded. "How about pocket nukes?"

"Yeah, this is the real thing, but we don't think nukes will be part of this theater. The plant supplies most of the air and fuel for a hundred thousand Martians at Ursa. We may call them terrorists, but they think of themselves as freedom fighters," the lieutenant responded. "They wouldn't risk destroying the plant by using nukes." Then turning back to the squad, Nora said, "The drop ships will deploy on either side of the pass between the opening in the southern mountains. They won't see us coming, since they don't have satellites. We'll drop in low and slow behind the mountains so they don't see the dust from the thrusters. This is going to be a drop and run; you'll be hitting the ground fast in a pincer-action to the left and right of the plant. You'll deploy with four Bloodhounds. You'll go in via tank-field entry points here and here." The lieutenant circled two pill boxes to either side of the assembly of buildings at the base of the underground tank field. "Then you'll work your way to the Ops center, here." She circled the corner of a building toward the front entrance. "The maps of the plant are being downloaded into your Aug-nets now with routes and timing coordination. The four squad members controlling Bloodhounds are also getting downloads. Okay people, let's suit up."

As Serena piled out of the room with the rest of the squad, she heard, "hell yes," and "screw the Martians," and other expletives that a year ago would have made her uncomfortable. But now, all she felt was a sense of excitement, and a subliminal hatred of the *enemy*. She put the unease to the back of her mind and hurried through the torus to the spoke passage. After leaving the torus, and descending a spoke, she got to the central spindle and lost all gravity. She flew down the spindle shaft by pushing off handholds in a smooth graceful flight, pirouetting at intersections. She'd been in space now for several years, and flying was as natural as walking.

After stripping down in the dressing room next to the hanger bay with the rest of the squad, Serena got into her osmosis tights that kept her skin aerated and perspiration neutral. Then, she stepped into her armored assault suit, which was open from top to bottom like a clam-shell. As the suit AI synchronized with her Aug-net, it closed around her and all its status monitors and controls appeared in her sensorium. She flexed her muscles, opened and closed her fists, then leaped off the floor in a tight somersault and stuck the landing by activating the suit's magnetic boots when her feet neared the floor. Yeah, everything was five-on-five. Serena walked over to the gun rack and fit the rail-gun harness around her waist. It smoothly synchronized with the suit AI and appeared in her sensorium as a targeting bulls-eye hovered over whatever she looked at. She reduced the gun to an icon in her sensorium and walked out of the dressing room into the hanger bay, and then she hurried to the drop-ship entry ramp, falling seamlessly in line with the rest of the squad.

The ride down to the surface was bumpy as the drop ship streaked through the Martian atmosphere like a meteor. Everything in the cabin was shaking. It was quiet inside her helmet, but she knew there was a roaring in the cabin from the friction and sonic booms of their atmospheric entry. Serena felt the deceleration and jarring change in orientation as the ship turned horizontal and hugged the Martian landscape a hundred meters above the desert floor at a hundred kilometers per hour. She heard the prompting tone in her mind, then the lieutenant's calm voice.

"Squad one ready for deployment."

She saw the rear ramp lowering and the rust-colored ground streaking by below the ship. Serena felt the ship slow. When it had reached fifty kilometers per hour, she heard the lieutenant say, "Go!"

The squad stood in unison and pivoted toward the ramp on one side of the ship, and the four Bloodhounds stood in a crouch on their four tapered legs on the other side. Her Bloodhound flashed a ready acknowledgment in her Minds-eye. The squad member nearest the ramp started running, jumped onto the ramp, then disappeared into the red of Mars as it blurred by outside. One by one the squad followed suit in unison with the Bloodhounds. When it was her turn, Serena started running. Exhilaration powered her god-like sense of invulnerability, and then she was airborne, hitting the ground at thirty kilometers per hour and not missing a step. She willed her gun into her hands and her Bloodhound to gallop to her right about twenty meters ahead. Wing doors on the Bloodhound's back smoothly unfolded revealing two rows of six smart missiles on each wing and a plasma canon rose from a cavity in the opening. Serena's tactical display appeared in her Minds-eye and painted a flock of hunter-killer drones emerging from an opening hidden among the tangle of buildings five hundred meters ahead. As she looked ahead and to her left, she saw the drop ship unload the last of the squad. As it did, the ramp quickly folded into the body of the ship and the engines flared to incandescence. Rising almost vertically, it deployed a swarm of decoys and hunter-killer drones. She saw it streak upward, followed by several missiles fired from somewhere in the plant complex. The dots disappeared in a haze of smoke hovering over the plant. Then she saw several flashes illuminating the haze and thin pink clouds above the plant, and she hoped the ship had survived.

Pin-prick eruptions of dust lit the ground all around her. Tactical showed a robot Gatling-gun mounted on one of the buildings firing a rain of steel flechettes in her direction. They couldn't paint her, her armor was almost invisible in the optical and on radar now that active camouflage was engaged, but she guessed they could see a ghost image on their scopes. They knew she was there, and they were trying to light her up with sparks bouncing off her armor. She smiled. *A for effort,* she thought, just before willing the Bloodhound to kill it. The Bloodhound in front of her was momentarily eclipsed in a backdraft of smoke as it fired a smart missile that streaked across the field and reduced the gun to vapor.

She kept running, constantly looking at the swarm of drones her gun was targeting, guided by encrypted transponders that painted them as enemy or friendly. Each time the targeting bull's-eye started blinking on an enemy drone, she willed her railgun to fire. She fired in rapid succession and quickly drones disappeared from the theater, but not before firing offensive mini rockets in her direction. Her camouflage and jamming were effective; rockets exploded all around her and some streaked overhead, but no hits. Tactical showed the rest of the squad was equally successful. As they approached the two entry pillboxes, she saw one, then two, then three of her squad on tactical engulfed in red and disappear.

"Shit, what's happening?" Serena shouted in open com.

The calm voice of the lieutenant responded. "Plastic proximity mines, can't see them in IR or ground penetrating radar. One minute, standby, we'll light them up with neutrons." After a few moments, the mines appeared in her tactical. If she had gone five steps further, she would have hit one.

Serena swerved and weaved between mines. And then running at the pillbox, she fired the railgun in a rapid volley, completely disintegrating the thick metal door. She jumped through the smoke and ruin that was the entrance while scanning in IR. Her suit lit up with flashes of automatic assault rifle fire covering her in sparks. She turned the railgun on her attackers and hypersonic aluminum rounds streaked across the large airlock, blowing the two suited figures to pieces that arced through the thin Martian air and slowly settled to the ground under the low gravity. She ran across the room and hugged a wall near the inner airlock entrance. From there, no one could take her by surprise. She took a moment to assess the squad on tactical and froze. Janus was gone. She searched her Minds-eye again in a cold panic. Her eyes blurred with tears, and savage anger gripped her. Her hands tightened on her gun. She pointed it at the inner door and quickly fired several rounds. There was a concussion, and then a dense cloud of black smoke and dust that hid whatever destruction the door had suffered. The outline of the hole in the wall shone in IR as a red hot outline. Before she could see anything beyond the smoke, she jumped through the hole, rolled, and sprang to a knee, scanning for the enemy. The inner corridor was empty. Flashing red lights signaled the corridor was depressurized. The floor plan indicated there was a staircase at the end of the corridor leading to another airlock and a direct path to the Ops center. She started running.

The upper airlock was undamaged, and she transmitted override codes the company had given her, superseding the passwords the terrorists had installed. She found herself in the Ops center. Two Martians stood there in suits, helmets off, framed in the orange glow of a large window showing the Planitia basin. They dropped their guns and put their hands up, palms out. They were sweating profusely and visibly shaking. Her mental finger tightened on the trigger. She intended to kill whoever she found. Even though these assholes hadn't killed Janus, they were responsible, and they would pay.

For some reason, she lowered her gun. *The hell?* she thought. She couldn't execute them, her mental finger refused to pull the trigger. She was cold, numb, and confused, but strangely calm. "Where are the others?" she demanded in a harsh voice. One of the Martians nodded toward a door on the far side of the room. They filed out of the Ops center, the two terrorists in front. They hurried down several branching corridors until they came to a large room her mental floor plan indicated was an equipment hold. There must have been fifty people segregated into two groups gathered in the large space. The smaller group wore company jumpsuits and must be the staff; a larger group was distinctly Martian, with old-Earth Asiatic features similar to what had once been southwestern American Indians.

A couple of the staff approached her. "Damn good to see you, soldier."

"Are there any terrorists in this group?" Serena motioned toward the Martians with her gun.

"They're all terrorists as far as I'm concerned," one of the staff said.

She walked past him and addressed the Martians. "Who works here? If you work here, step to the side." She pointed with her gun. They all just stood there. "You speak terrestrial English, yes?"

One of the Martians stepped forward. "We're all Martians," he said. "We're all people, even if you don't think so."

Serena shook with anger. "The terrorists killed my friend," she hissed.

"And you people." The man made a sweeping gesture with his arm toward the staff, including her. "You've killed many of my friends." He looked at her with the same disdain she felt. "Look, if you're going to kill us, just do it." The man turned and returned to the group.

"I'm not going to kill you," Serena said softly. The anger was gone, replaced by an emotionless void.

There was an explosion behind her that shook the building. She turned to see a Bloodhound tearing through the wall where the door had been, big patches of wall falling to the floor on either side of the large machine. It prowled toward the Martians in a low flanking stance, like a lion stalking prey. She could see in her sensorium that it was going to fire on the Martians. Out of the rubble that had been the door stepped the rest of her squad. She turned and saw the Martians cowering against the far wall. At that moment, she took a good look. She saw men and women worn by a hard life on a hostile desert planet. Some were surprisingly young. One small girl shaking with fear must have been no more than thirteen; the same age she was the day she returned home to find her mother cowering in front of two company men, just like these people were cowering in front of her.

"Stop!" She stepped in front of the Bloodhound, gun down, hand out in front, fingers splayed in a halt gesture.

It stopped and straightened; its massive form loomed over her.

"What are you doing? Get out of the way," she heard a squad member say over com.

"Lieutenant, it's over. Let's get these people to the authorities so they can be processed." She waited. There was no answer; the ship must have been under the Martian horizon and the regular Telesats didn't offer the right encryption.

"Screw that," the Sergeant said. "These assholes are part of that clusterfuck out there. We lost three of the squad. There isn't enough of them left to scoop up."

The Bloodhound reasserted its crouch. She saw its targeting icon start to blink again. She stepped back and raised her gun. To her left, her Bloodhound circled around and was targeting the one that was targeting her. "Sarg, I get it. I lost Janus, but I can't let you execute these people. You'll have to come through me." Strangely, she smiled; there were a lot of targeting icons blinking in her sensorium at the moment.

The calm, cool, voice of the Lieutenant came through on com. The ship must have cleared the horizon and the repeater must have buffered the events. "Stand down," Nora ordered.

* * *

Serena waited in a briefing room aboard the Griffin. There was a central table with the imprint of a projector in the middle. Several black swivel chairs were anchored around the table, but other than that, only the company logo distinguished this room from a nondescript box. An air processor hummed softly in the background; its tell-tails danced in the breeze. She could feel the dampened vibrations of powerful engines somewhere in the ship when she put her hands flat on the table. She couldn't get the faces of those frightened workers out of her mind. In truth, she had no idea who those people were, or what had led to the takeover of the complex. She thought about Janus. Why had he died? She was sure he understood no more about any of this than she did. What was clear was they were tools, tools that enforced agreements among worlds other than the one that the authors of the contracts came from. The profits from the complex would never benefit the world of the workers that produced them. Commerce by remote control, she almost laughed out loud. The door opened and the Lieutenant walked in and sat across from her. Serena looked up at the corner of the ceiling where she thought the camera was hidden.

50

The Lieutenant smiled. "We're not recording this. This is off the record, sealed."

"I couldn't kill those people," Serena admitted. She looked down at her fuzzy reflection on the table. "And if it happens again, I'll do the same thing. I'm a soldier; I'm not an executioner." She looked up, eye-to-eye with Nora.

"I know," Nora said, with apparent sadness. "And from here forward, you're no longer a soldier."

"I see," Serena said. The two women stared at each other for a long moment. "Am I under arrest?"

"There was no order to kill suspected unarmed...uh people. So you're not guilty of insubordination. You didn't point your gun at another squad member, so you're not accused of treason."

Serena exhaled. "Okay, Lieutenant, so what's my capital offense—not offing a bunch of civilians and starting an insurrection?"

"There's a culture—you know. Word gets out the squad can't trust you, and pretty soon these guys talk, and we won't be able to find a squad that'll work with you. So, you'll quietly retire. Problem solved."

"Okay," Serena said. "But what would you have done?" Nora got up and came around the table. Serena stood. The Lieutenant stopped in front of her, and after an awkward moment, Nora raised her hand in a curt salute. Serena saluted back. Nora lowered her hand, turned, and left. The door silently closed behind her.

Chapter Eight

Titan, Citadel, 2240 AD

Serena was tired. She'd been up for more than thirty-six hours. For the first time in three days, she wasn't under threat. Zen released her without so much as an escort. The debrief in Zen's interrogation room had her wired. Although she couldn't prove the explosion was no accident, and the robot memories had been doctored and her escape tunnel erased, she thought she might have an ally in Zen. She sensed his working assumption was that someone or some group was hiding something important enough to kill for, right under his nose, which must have pissed him off. The doctored recording made it seem like she was supposed to die in the explosion and Abin-Lor had died in an adjacent tunnel. The fact that Zen was head of security and seemed not to know what was going on raised the possibility the company was behind the sabotage. It made sense, since Zen wasn't privy to the company's inner workings. She thought about the implications of all that had happened as she made her way back to her quarters, becoming more confused the more she thought about it. The fatigue was catching up with her; she couldn't think clearly. With the pressure off for the moment, the absence of adrenaline made her crave sleep. When she got to her quarters, her Aug-net opened the door and a minute later she was face down on her bunk, drooling into the blanket.

It was a sleep plagued by strange dreams. She was in space, but not in a ship. She had the sense of falling, then realized she wasn't falling, she was flying. For a moment she enjoyed the sensation. She cruised over mountains, valleys, and lakes.

She could will herself to go in whatever direction she chose, and effortlessly, she was there. But there was another feeling, a sense of loss, a deep loneliness, and a compulsion to do something she couldn't quite put her finger on. She tossed and turned. In the dream, she found herself sitting on the ground. The ground was cold, so she willed it to heat up. The ground underneath her turned into geysers of vapor and she began to sink. Clutching the blanket in tight fists, she stiffened in her sleep. As the dream continued, she sank deep into the earth and darkness enveloped her. She began to moan as she rolled off the bed and hit the floor.

Her eyes popped open. "What the hell?" she whispered. She sat up, bracing her back against the bunk, reached up, and automatically wiped her brow. She was sweating. What was wrong with her, was she suffering from PTSD? She'd been in firefights in her past life; she'd been alone in tunnels kilometers underground, but she'd never experienced anything like this. All of a sudden, she didn't want to go back to sleep, didn't want to tempt fate, to confirm what she feared—that she was losing her mind. She couldn't afford that right now. Somebody was trying to kill her, and Zen was taking her seriously. Both those facts would make her enemies even more determined to make her disappear. Of course, that in itself would be suspicious, but without her, what could Zen actually prove?

She pulled herself off the floor and went to the sink. Looking in the mirror, she scared herself and then broke into a big mirthless grin. Her reflection was funny in a crazed sort of way. Her hair was plastered in snarls on her forehead. Her eyes seemed to be open a little too wide. All in all, she looked a little crazy, especially with that Cheshire cat white-tooth grin shining in the darkness. She reached into her jumpsuit pocket for an elastic, brushed her hair back, and tied it in a ponytail. She turned on some cold water and soaked her face. She dried up and smoothed her jumpsuit, then regarded herself in the mirror again. "Yeah, that's better," she whispered.

She sat on the edge of the bed in near darkness with nothing but the hum of the station in the background. She decided she needed a drink, got up, and left her quarters. The station bar was on the fortieth level, and she caught the lift with the transparent wall to the outside. The sight always calmed her. It was dusk now, but on Earth, this would have been considered the middle of the night, with just enough moonlight to make the land visible. In this light there was little color; it looked like a black-and-white rendering of an alien planet. There were no stars, and it was hard to tell where the land ended and the sky began. Even Mars seemed more hospitable. So this was her life now. She was either in the twilight day of Titan or skulking around in tunnels kilometers under the frozen ground. She wondered if she'd ever see sunshine against a bright blue sky ever again. The lift door opened, and she stepped out. Hesitating a moment, she turned and began walking down a dingy white corridor in the direction of faint music coming from somewhere in the distance.

The bar was crowded, with mostly men standing around and drinking, or seated around circular projectors watching holograms of people having sex. There were men on women, women on women, men on men, and every permutation of several actors in an endless variety of poses. The music was loud, abrasive, and artificially produced. The era of music produced to reflect any humanity at all was absent from this place, but at least she wasn't alone in her quarters with only her thoughts to haunt her. She searched for a table somewhere in the back and noticed both men and a few women looking her up and down as she passed. Apparently, there was still a market for the real thing. She found a seat in a dark corner and ordered a beer over her Aug-net, then registered payment. Soon a topless woman appeared out of the gloom, and without a word, she put an amber glass of beer in front of her. She felt the waitress staring and looked up. The woman looked down at her with a salacious smile, and Serena noted a ping in her Aug-net.

"Not tonight," she said. The woman shrugged, her augmented breasts shaking, nipples erect, and then she turned, and disappeared back into the murky chaos.

Serena drank her beer and began to feel a little better. The weird dreams were fading, and she began to entertain the thought of going back to the tunnel, back to the scene of the crime. She wondered whether this urge sprang from a desire to find some physical evidence she could bring to Zen, or something else. *What were these assholes hiding anyway? The company has mineral rights to the dig. So if it isn't minerals, what is it? And how do I figure into all this?* She didn't know anything. Her thoughts were interrupted by the screeching sound of a chair being pulled across the floor.

"Look, I want to be alone," she began and then stopped after raising her eyes from the glass. "Auger?"

A burly man in work overalls planted himself in the chair across from her, sitting hard, and pulling himself to the table. "Hey, I heard what happened and found you on staff locator." He saw her dazed look of surprise. "Hope you don't mind."

"Yeah, uh...no, I don't mind. Actually, it's...good to have some friendly company."

Auger was a miner she'd worked with on several digs. He was an obvious Earther, with a rare white complexion that you didn't often see because of the hard UV in space, and on most planets, habitats, and asteroids. He was heavily muscled around the shoulders and forearms, with a broad doughy face that belied both his intelligence and kindness. His most striking feature was his bright, clear blue eyes that made you take a second look.

"I heard you were almost killed down there," he said. Then his smile faded and was replaced by a look of suspicion. "I never heard of anything like that, an oxygen explosion, and I've been doing this a long time."

Just as he said this the waitress returned and put an amber glass in front of Auger. "Anything else?" she asked. Auger just stared up at her and then noticed Serena snicker.

"Nah, that's all," he said and turned to Serena. "For now," he whispered, smirking. The waitress gave that same smile, did that thing she did with the shrug, and left.

"What?" Auger said and took a drink. "You know how it is."

"Yeah, I know how it is," she replied. They clinked glasses and took another drink.

There was a long silence that was finally broken by Auger. "You don't want to talk?"

Serena was pretty sure she could trust him, that wasn't the problem. But, if word got out about what really happened, she'd lose control of the situation. On the other hand, keeping things to herself might foster delusional paranoia. After all, those dreams were unsettling. It would be good to bounce things off someone else just to make sure she wasn't spinning out of control. She decided to prime the pump and see what happened.

"Look, if I tell you something, it has to stay between us, yeah?"

"So this is serious. Not just a freak accident?" Auger asked.

"Yeah, it's serious. And if you talk to anyone, and word gets back to whoever did this, it's going to be a shitstorm for both of us. You understand?"

Auger chuckled. "If you need somebody to have your back, I can do that. You've known me a while; I don't talk about anything other than rubbish most of the time. There's a reason for that."

"Oh, and what's that?" Serena asked, smiling a little now.

"Cause I have trust issues, just like you. These sons-of-bitches own me too. I'll probably die on this frozen rock carrying their water." He took a drink. "I won't stab you in the back, and I'm not stupid."

"They tried to kill me," Serena whispered, stretching across the table to get closer and looking around to see if they were being watched.

Auger stared at her for a moment. "And why would they do that? Why you?"

"Hell if I know," she said.

"Heard you went to security; you tell them that?" Auger asked.

"No, but Zen has his doubts about this thing."

Auger whistled under his breath. "You met with Zen?"

"Yeah, tunnels don't blow up every day. And Abin-Lor got killed."

"I knew Lor." Auger shook his head, a blank expression commandeering his features. "It's got to be the company, has to be. But this is a risky move. The Commonwealth is getting powerful. Messing with them like this is really risky," he offered. "You've got my attention."

"I want to go back to the site," Serena snapped.

"Why?" Auger asked. "The rescue team's been all over it. There's nothing left to find."

"Maybe, but I feel like I need to go there." She took a nervous drink. She looked down and saw her hand shaking and knew Auger saw it too.

"You alright?" he asked slowly. "You don't look so good."

"I'm good, don't worry about me." She took a breath and waited a moment, calming down. *Why had the thought of going to the site exploded in her mind like that?* She wondered. Obviously, the shaking was a sign she didn't really trust herself. Usually, her instincts were pretty good, but something was different here—like she wasn't fully in control.

"They cut off the tube to the site," Auger said.

"Huh, what did you say?"

"How're we going to get there? The tube cars aren't running. The site's thirty klicks away," Auger said.

Serena looked up smiling. "You have a pass to the crawlers, right?"

* * *

After going back to her quarters to pick up some things, Serena planned to meet Auger in front of the airlock to the equipment bay. She guessed Auger was coming because he suspected she was on edge, and letting her go alone might result in something he would ultimately regret. She didn't know if he bought the attempt on her life, but it was a fact Abin-Lor was dead, so something was going on. When it came right down to it, miners trusted each other, not the company, much like her experience with the Rangers. But like her experience with the Rangers, there were limits. And given she had no solid answers as to why she needed to return to the site, she hoped she wasn't stretching that limit with Auger. Truth be told, she needed his help. Going those thirty klicks without transport was a problem she hadn't solved until she realized Auger was part of a survey team scouting new ore deposits, giving him access to private transport.

She was in the suit locker sealing the seams of her gloves when Auger showed up. He had a bag slung over his shoulder and set it down after coming in. He looked at her and shook his head. "The things I do for love," he said, and smiled.

"I appreciate your help, you know that, right?"

"Yeah, yeah. Let's see if we can get out of here while it's still dark. That way we can navigate by positioning satellites without running lights. It won't keep them from tracking us; there are plenty of survey teams running in and out at odd hours making us just another blip on the board. But it might help if no one at a high window sees lights heading in the general direction of the site."

Once in their suits, they went through the lock into the bay. It was a large cavern cut out of ice and coated in insulating foam that dried with a rough texture of mat-white walls, making it brighter under the overhead plasma lamps. There was heavy machinery of all kinds neatly segregated into parcels with several wide aisles allowing easy access and removal. Luckily, the bay was empty this time of night, and they walked down the main aisle like they belonged there, hiding in plain sight.

They found a crawler halfway down the main aisle on the right. It was a caterpillar-like vehicle with a clear plastic bubble in front on six large composite wheels, three on a side. Each wheel was attached to a floating gimbal that kept the vehicle level on rough terrain. It had a small parabolic dish on top attached to an articulate mount that found satellites anywhere in the sky. Serena grabbed a handhold and hoisted herself up on a wheel, and then she swiveled into the copilot seat, while Auger went around to the other side, threw their bags in the back, and assumed the pilot's seat. He input his pass code and the vehicle sprang to life. The instruments were illuminated in a soft red glow with annotation in purple and black. He keyed in the destination code, which he knew by heart, and the dish on top swung around and found some satellites. He opened the bay door to the outside and the crawler jumped to life, smoothly leaving its parking space, and accelerating out the door into the black. They saw the shadow of the crawler diminish in front of them as the door closed behind them, leaving them floating in total darkness, except for the glow of the console.

As she rocked back and forth in her seat with the crawler speeding headlong into the night, Serena had the strange sense she could have started the crawler without Auger's pass code. When she was a Ranger, she'd been implanted with state-of-the-art cyber modules that allowed control of complex devices and hosted advanced intrusion algorithms. All the wetware had been denuded, but not removed. It couldn't be; it was part of her, but it didn't work anymore—or did it? In her Minds-eye she saw the crawler control system, it was as plain as day. *What was happening, how was this possible?*

Those weird dreams had kept her from getting enough sleep and the rocking had her slowly closing her eyes. Again, there was an out-of-body sensation. This time she was encased in ice, but she wasn't cold. The ice was like glass; she could see right through it. There were vibrations and a gradient of heat coming from a spot forty-five degrees and a half-klick above her. See could see it; there was a mining crew headed right for her. They were bouncing sonic pings off her. She could clearly see the blades of the digging machine's rotating heads right behind the plasma arc. They were quickly coming toward her. She knew she could absorb the pings or deflect them, but she was letting them reflect. She wanted whoever was coming to find her.

Something shook her and her eyes sprang open. "What?"

"Hey, wake up," Auger said. He shook her by the shoulder. "You're having a bad dream or something. Lucky you have your seatbelt on; you'd probably be on the floor right now if you didn't."

She could see the concern on his face in the eerie red of the dash lights. She was speechless, still trying to disentangle what was happening.

"Listen, I'm worried," he said. "You haven't told me everything. I can put it on the line for you, but you have to trust me. What the hell's going on?"

She swallowed, slowed her breathing, and felt her heart stop pounding in her chest. "Something happened to me down there, Auger. I know it sounds crazy, but I'm seeing things when I sleep. I was pinned down there for a while and someone in a black security suit tried to kill me. But something happened. I don't know what it is. I didn't want to tell you because I know how nuts it sounds." She chuckled, "I hardly believe it myself."

He just stared at her. "I've known you going on six Earth-years; you're one of the sanest people I know. If this was coming from anyone else, I'd turn this thing around and take you to a doctor for head trauma."

"Yeah, and then there's the thing about Abin-Lor being dead, and the company closing down the dig. If it wasn't for that, maybe I'd check myself in, but I'm sure there's something not right here. And whatever it is, I've got the feeling it's big."

"Well, shit," Auger said. He wiped his face with the palms of his hands. "Now you got me spooked, you know." He laughed nervously and turned, gazing into the black.

"We should go the last klick on foot," Serena suggested. "They might ignore us for a while, but if we get too close you can bet an AI will alert someone. These guys have covered their tracks pretty well; I doubt they don't have a watchdog keeping an eye on the place."

"Yeah, and when the crawler stops in the middle of nowhere and just sits there, nobody's going to notice?" Auger asked.

Serena smiled. "I can take care of that."

Auger turned toward her. She sounded sure, but what she said didn't make any sense. The edgy fear that she wasn't all there was coming back. "And how do you plan to do that? If we reprogram the Nav AI, they can tell. They'll see the weight and O-2 consumption; they'll know nobody's on board. They'll be on us before we can cover a quarter-klick."

"I can program the AI to hide all that with fake telemetry. I can give it a route running in a process the AI can't see. And I can program it to come back and pick us up after some time has passed. If we're not there, it will go and do something else, checking back at random times and places until we do show up."

"You sound okay, but you're not making sense," Auger said finally.

"Look, I don't know how to explain it, but in my past life, I was wired. Then things happened and they shut it all down, but the machinery is still in there." She tapped her index finger to her temple. "I can't explain it, but it's all working again, and the strange thing is, it's working better than before. I can see the guts of this thing better than I can see your face in the dash lights."

He was gaping at her now and she could see the uncertainty reflected in his blue eyes. "Look, man, just trust me. I'm not going to leave you out there holding yourself. You know me, I won't do that." She put her hand on his shoulder and squeezed. She saw him wince. "Yeah, that's coming back, too."

"Okay," he said, rubbing his shoulder. "That's an impressive grip you got there." He sat back and exhaled. "Let's see what happens."

She didn't want to tell him she could have easily crushed his shoulder. A couple of weeks ago, she hadn't had the strength to make him notice; he was a big man. Now, something was happening, and she only hoped that at the end of this road, they weren't headed for something they couldn't handle. And she meant it when she told him he could trust her, but she felt something pulling her to the site, and she knew she would do whatever it took to get there.

Chapter Nine

Titan, LakeShore, 2240 AD

Adonus sat in his office aboard the orbital shuttle that he had taken to the surface this morning. He had a lot of preliminary work to do before going down to the excavation to inspect the artifact firsthand. He wanted to get a sense of the big picture. A survey team had first been alerted to an anomaly while reviewing remote sensing data from a company satellite. They were looking for metallic ore deposits. Ores didn't exist on Titan in the conventional sense, since there was no liquid water or liquid anything else running underground to concentrate minerals, but there had been many asteroid strikes in the distant past, and they'd left large concentrations of metal under the surface. Saturn was a gas giant with enormous gravity at its metallic hydrogen surface, but it could not be mined. However, its assortment of fifty-four-plus moons was a treasure trove of metals, water, and helium 3, but orbital mining did not have a continuous human presence due to the lack of gravity and high radiation. Titan, on the other hand, was one of the most productive human mining operations in the system and was located close to the largest market on this side of the asteroid belt. There were ten cloud cities and two more under construction in the Saturn Commonwealth, all hungry for metals, making the operation on Titan one of the company's biggest sources of revenue.

Surveying from orbit was mainly done by making detailed gravity maps that differentiated low-density frozen crust from high-density aggregated metals. The satellite found a sizable signal near a drill site at lakeshore, and sonograms had been taken by robots to pinpoint the location and size of the deposit. But when the data was analyzed, it didn't make sense. There was something buried about two klicks under the surface whose total volume was too small to be anything that gravitationally intense. In fact, the survey team determined that nothing known was that dense. At first, Adonus thought there must be a mistake. He had ordered the raw data transmitted to the research division's quantum AI for confirmation analysis, and to his amazement, the result was the same. As a thought experiment, he'd instructed the AI to postulate all possible explanations of the result. The only possibility offered by the AI was something so farfetched it couldn't possibly be true—neutronium matter. The problem with that possibility was there were no known sources of neutronium matter other than neutron stars, and neutron stars did not disassociate into free-ranging asteroids. Besides, if a small piece of neutronium hit Titan at about the escape velocity of a solar system, it would split the moon in half. Adonus looked up and shook his head, *what the hell was at the bottom of the dig?*

Outside the shuttle was a makeshift staging area for the dig, which was slowly becoming a sizable base. Plasma lamps made it seem like daytime on Earth. Several prefab huts had been erected as well as landing pads for shuttles, which had been coming and going for the past few days, bringing down personnel and equipment. Adonus watched as the lights surrounding one of the landing pads started strobing, first red, then blue, then quickly green. Ice dust from the shuttle's thrusters kicked up in the bright green lights as the large ship slowly descended and made contact on its four multi-jointed legs, first dipping, then rising slowly, and locking in place. Adonus sensed a message coming in on his Aug-net; his security detail had arrived and could meet him in half an hour at the dig.

Adonus got into his suit, stepped through the airlock, then down the ramp and onto the frozen crust. It was a strange sensation being outside, surreal in fact. He had spent most of his life in habitats, not on the surface of a planet. He was used to looking up and seeing the curvature of the world disappear in the glare of an artificial sun. This was different. He read, in times past, there was an illness called claustrophobia. To the best of his understanding, it was the fear of confined spaces. He smiled to himself; confined spaces were comforting. It was this sense of open space that made him feel insecure.

He strode across the yard. People, loaders, and robots moved around him in purposeful activity. The entrance to the lift was a ribbed cylindrical structure with a blue airlock door straight ahead. There were several people in black security suits loitering around the entrance, apparently waiting for him. His Aug-net superimposed meta-data above each person. He located Colonel Nora Assisi and approached her, hand outstretched.

"Colonel," Adonus said, shaking her gauntleted hand. He noticed she was carrying a railgun in the other. He gestured toward the artillery. "You think we'll be needing that?"

"You never know," Nora said. "I reviewed your notes on the artifact; no telling what'll happen when we kick it, yeah?"

"Point well taken, Colonel. After you."

The atmosphere was evacuated from the lift; it descended without air resistance the two kilometers to an airlock anchored in a twenty-meter vertical wall of ice. On the other side of the lock was a large staging area full of equipment, consoles, and technicians. Everyone had their suits on but without helmets and gloves.

"Under ideal conditions, we would leave this area in vacuum, since we don't know anything about the artifact. Having an atmosphere could promote biological organisms, but it's hard to work in vacuum suits. We haven't been able to find anything biological associated with the artifact, so we decided to take the risk." Adonus pointed to the far wall, which was made from a thick transparent plastic curtain. "We keep positive pressure on this side of the staging area to try and isolate the artifact," Adonus said. Although he'd never actually seen it, Adonus had been fully briefed on the containment and logistics.

Nora walked beside him and nodded as he spoke, constantly looking around, making a mental note of the place, just in case. They were met in the middle of the room by a man in a blue surface suit. Adonus's Aug-net identified him as Austin Ieger, head of operations. They removed their helmets and gloves and attached them to their belts.

"Doctor Adonus, gentlemen and ladies," Austin said and bowed slightly.

"Mr. Ieger, have there been any problems, any activity by the artifact?"

"None whatsoever," Austin replied. "And we've made little progress in determining what it is. Besides being completely inert, it is hard to x-ray or drill into."

"Let's take a look," Adonus suggested. He'd seen images, but he was anxious to see the real thing. In the back of his mind, he couldn't help thinking this thing, whatever it was, was proof intelligent life did exist outside the solar system. Not only that but from what little he knew about the artifact, whatever it was, it was way beyond them. He could see its towering, distorted outline through the plastic curtain, shimmering in the floodlights on the other side. He felt its strangeness and shivered. Looking at the weapons his security detail possessed, which seemed formidable a moment ago, they now seemed inconsequential compared to the thing on the other side of the curtain. If, somehow, he could learn its secrets, he would be the most powerful man in human history. The thought made him hard. He followed Ieger through an airlock in the curtain, atmosphere rushed from behind him, keeping anything in proximity of the artifact from contaminating the work area. The security detail followed single-file, close behind. When they were all on the other side of the curtain, they fanned out, so everybody could get a good look. There were no shadows in the large, cavernous space, and it was bright. The walls were covered with the same hard-drying foam that covered most of the tunnels. The thing was large and spherical, with a wedge-shaped band stretching around its central perimeter, like a belt. Adonus's Aug-net approximated the thing as being about fifteen meters across. It was light gray and appeared shiny because it was so smooth and perfectly round.

"Yeah," Ieger said, just like reading his mind. "It's very smooth. In fact, bouncing lasers off the surface and looking at interference patterns, it's perfectly round, flawless. What's more, it's rounder than anything we can machine. It's a perfect sphere, no deviation at all that we can detect."

"What else do we know about it?" Adonus asked.

"Well, we know we can't move it. We tried anchoring studs deep into the ice and pushing it with hydraulics, couldn't push it even a micron. And look at the ice underneath it, not dented, not cracked. This thing's so heavy that all the ice around it should be cracked, and yet…it's not."

Adonus smiled, "Looks like they know how to get around Mach's principle."

Ieger turned away from the sphere and regarded Adonus quizzically. "What?"

"It's the idea that gravitational and inertial mass are linked. We can't tell them apart, but this thing…" Adonus held his gaze on the sphere.

Ieger felt the man's awe.

"Look, you said the thing must be heavy because you can't move it."

Ieger nodded absently, examining his own thinking process.

"Then you noticed that the ice underneath isn't cracked, so you have a paradox."

Ieger nodded.

"The point is," Adonus continued, "These are, in principle, two different things. You can't move it because it has a large inertial mass; it's not cracking the ice because it has a small gravitational mass." Adonus shook his head. "Whoever they are, they're way beyond us. Somehow they've canceled the gravitational mass, but not the inertial. That thing's floating just at the point of the ice. If you melt some of the ice just under it, I'll bet we can see a space between it and the ground."

"Huh," Ieger mumbled.

"Is it solid?" Adonus asked.

"We can't tell," Ieger responded. "We can't cut into it; it seems to spontaneously heal."

"Heal?" Adonus asked.

"Yeah, you can see it. We put a plasma arc on it and raised the temperature to five thousand degrees. You can see some of the surface ablating away, but at the same time, the lasers measure no depth of penetration. When you turn the arc off, you see the burn spot disappear."

"How about sonograms, radar?" Adonus asked.

"Doesn't work. Whatever this material is, it's completely dispersive. You put a signal in, doesn't matter whether it's electromagnetic or sonic, the signal is dispersed and dampened. If this thing were in space, it would disappear—you couldn't track it. Whatever you ping it with, won't be reflected. It soaks up energy like a sponge but doesn't heat up. I've never seen anything like it. Frankly, Doctor Adonus, I have no idea how to analyze it."

Adonus looked around and saw a mining robot sitting in a far corner of the room. He accessed it with his sensorium. It slowly rose on six articulated legs and started toward the sphere. Ieger looked on, not knowing what to say. When the robot reached a point a couple of meters from the sphere, it lowered itself and extended its arc drill to a position as close to the base of the sphere as it could.

"If you don't have glasses, look away," Adonus ordered. His security team put their helmets on and lowered their visors. Adonus handed Ieger a pair of glasses, then looked around. When everyone had shielded their eyes, Adonus ignited the torch and ratcheted the temperature to maximum. Vapor and chunks of ice spewed from the base of the sphere in a torrent as a blinding light enveloped the room. When the ice under the artifact disappeared, Adonus advanced the drill tip until a large trench had been carved beneath the object, then he shut it down.

They all stepped forward, standing at the edge of the bowl-like trench, and looked down. The sphere was hovering in the air above the spot, and spinning slightly from the asymmetric torque of the gases expelled as the trench was being dug. The walls of the trench were shiny ice except for the bottom, which was smudged dark.

"Shit," one of the security men uttered.

"Yeah," Ieger echoed. "What's that black on the bottom? Why isn't it smooth, recrystallized ice?"

"Cause it's a mineral trail," Adonus said, smiling.

"Mineral? What do you mean?" Ieger asked.

"You said the surface was ablating away when you tried to drill into it, yeah?"

"Yeah," Ieger replied, his expression blank. "Yeah, that's right."

"So where did it get the new material, the material to replace the stuff ablating away? I'll bet this thing can't make something from nothing," Adonus said.

"You mean this thing is mining ore from the same vain we're mining in the shaft that collapsed?" Ieger asked. "But how, I don't see a drill, an opening, or anything else?" Ieger was kneeling at the edge of the trench and craning his neck, looking at the bottom of the sphere.

"I don't know," Adonus said. "Take a sample of the black stuff at the bottom and analyze it. Let's see what this thing needs."

* * *

When Adonus returned to his makeshift office aboard the shuttle, he called Nathen Orzan aboard the Athena, orbiting Titan. Orzan was the physicist Adonus brought from Olympus. Orzan was a genius. Despite his deficiencies, and although socially clumsy and often in a world of his own, he had risen to be the head of the company's advanced product division through the strength of his intellect. He was short for an off-worlder. He had never lived on a planet and was only one hundred and seventy centimeters tall, with a head too big for his body, a look that many who spent their lives in low gravity often had. His angular face was sculpted by sharp features and a dark complexion. The man looked the part—an alien to figure out an alien artifact.

"You have the analysis of the dark material from under the artifact?" Adonus asked.

Orzan's bust floated in front of Adonus's desk, framed by an electric blue boarder characteristic of holographic projectors. He nodded, his enormous visage taking up most of the scene, and his wide eyes giving him a bit of a crazed look. "Nothing unusual; iron, aluminum, trace heavy metals..."

"Damn," Adonus said, visibly disappointed.

"And..." Orzan continued.

Adonus looked up, "There's more?"

"Yes, there are some interesting, uh…residual objects that are hard to classify. Nothing concrete, but there are concentrations of unusual alloys, some traces of things that shouldn't combine given their chemical valences."

"What do you think that means?" Adonus asked. He was mesmerized by the possibilities.

"My best guess is that these were nanites of some kind. They might have been destroyed in an attempt to hide their presence. The ore was probably mined and transported to the sphere by an army of these machines."

"Any chance we can reconstruct something from the traces?" Adonus asked.

"Not a chance. Traces are all we have. The erasure was thorough. But there's something else..."

"Yes," Adonus said. He was getting annoyed. Pulling information from this guy was painful. He didn't want a story; he wanted to know how they could take advantage of this thing, use it to achieve his goal of becoming the executive head of the most powerful company in the solar system.

"The company has sonic interferometers at various places around the planet to take sounding data when we're looking for small deposits of minerals. We also want to understand the tidal stresses of Saturn on the moon, which moves things around in the moon's interior."

Adonus was getting impatient and held up a hand, palm out. "What's this have to do with the sphere? I'm not interested in the arcane aspects of our mining operations."

Orzan blinked, his large eyes dominating the image. "It's about the sphere."

Adonus exhaled. "Please continue," he said dismissively.

"We noticed some noise on the interferometers that wasn't there before. I noticed the timestamp for that noise was coincident with the digging under the sphere earlier today. We analyzed the noise, and we think we see gravity waves."

The room went stone silent. "Gravity waves?" Adonus repeated. "Coming from the sphere? How's that possible? Gravity waves only occur in astronomically dynamic events. They require astronomical energies. I was down in that tunnel; there was no heat, no shock-waves—nothing."

"We don't know," Orzan said. "But we think it may have something to do with the sphere's ability to float."

"You mean that thing can control gravity? What kind of power source could do that?" Adonus felt a shiver of fear. Maybe they were dealing with something beyond their ability to control. After all, this thing was here for a reason. Up to this point, Adonus had only considered what he wanted; he had never stopped to think that powers far beyond anything humans could imagine might have plans of their own.

Adonus took a breath, willing himself to calm down. He hadn't gotten this far by losing his shit when things got messy. "Do you know how old it is?"

"How old?" Orzan asked.

"Yeah, has it been here a year, a decade, a million years?"

"The pieces of the sphere from the surrounding ice that we were able to recover from the ablation don't have the isotope ratios we need for dating. We have no idea how old it is." He looked around and then settled on Adonus once more. "I get the feeling of age; I can't explain it, but this thing's not new. It's made in a way that everything about it is indeterminate—sorry." Orzan looked down; he seemed discouraged.

After he finished with Orzan, Adonus summoned his head of security. Nora entered his office and stood at attention in front of his desk. She wore a black jumpsuit with the corporate security insignia on her left breast, and colonel bars on shoulder epaulettes and on her sleeves.

"Relax colonel, have a seat," Adonus said. "We have a situation down in the tunnel."

"The artifact?" Nora asked.

"Yes, that's right. What was your impression? You were down in the tunnel when we dug under it today."

Nora blew out. "Yeah, I was there." She looked up at Adonus. "That thing is a security risk. We can't seem to get a handle on it. It's active, but we have no idea why it's here or what it wants. What's more, I get the feeling that if it turned against us, there'd be nothing we could do to control it."

"So what do we do about it? I was hoping we could learn something. It might be the source of new tech. But our best scientist just told me he doesn't know how to take it apart, or even analyze it. So…" Adonus spread his hands wide.

"We have two options, sir. Since we can't use it, we can either try to destroy it, or we can bury it again and monitor it. If we could destroy it, that would eliminate the risk, but that would kill any chance that we could come back at a later date and analyze it with new tech. Also, there's a more immediate downside. If we try to destroy it and fail, it might turn on us in a way that could be disastrous. If we bury it, we can keep it quiet and monitor it. Maybe at some point, it might decide to communicate, or we might find a way to learn more about it."

"We can't destroy it," Adonus agreed. He looked up. "We have to bury it. But that means we'll have to quarantine the area—permanently, but that's a problem. This isn't corporate property. There'll be a lot of suspicion with a permanent corporate security presence here. If only we could move it…" Adonus mused. "Stand by, Colonel. I have to consider our options more closely. Meanwhile, nobody goes in or out without my authorization."

"Understood, sir. We'll keep a guard at the lift, and on the lower level on the other side of the curtain from the thing." Nora nodded, turned, and left Adonus's office

Chapter Ten

Titan, Citadel, 2240 AD

Zen sensed a message coming in from his aid Li-ant on Aug-net. His head of security for the Lakeshore region, Hackem Smith, was requesting a meeting concerning the girl, Serena Roe. He had instructed Smith to have her followed and to report anything out of the ordinary. Her story, although improbable, seemed to come with a troubling assortment of facts that were slowly being confirmed. And the arrival of that corporate big-shot, Adonus, at the same time as the tunnel explosion was another source of aggravation. Something didn't smell right. He'd been busy with other matters, but now he wanted to go to Lakeshore and see for himself. An unsupervised corporate military presence was something that was making him uncomfortable. Orbital operations had sent him a report on the ship, the Athena, which the Corporates had come on. It was still orbiting Titan. It wasn't a liner; it was more like a large black-ops gunship, not standard transport for a product launch. He knew the story that Adonus had given him was bullshit, but the tunnel explosion took precedence. Now that he had time to think about it, it was clear something major had drawn the Corporates to Lakeshore, and he was going to find out what it was.

Security operations were on the lowest level of the Citadel, only accessible via a key-encrypted elevator that stopped two hundred meters below the surface of Titan. Unlike the upper levels of the Citadel, whose design accommodated lessons learned from habitats that lessened the stress of isolation, the security office made no concessions to stark functionality. The outer system was a hostile place, and this was the nerve center of Titan's defense. The ice walls were hardened by steel-reinforced cement foam two meters thick; it was more of a bunker than anything else.

Zen stepped from the elevator into a gray semicircular tunnel ribbed by thick steel rings down its length and illuminated by plasma lamps set into the steel ribbing, making it seem like an Escher drawing of a receding spiral. He walked toward the far end, his footsteps making tinny echoes that collided in a changing pattern of shrill pings. Reaching the end of the tunnel, he made his way through a secure airlock to the center proper. When he emerged, he was met by Smith and several security men in the standard black jumpsuits. He followed them into what looked like a stark interrogation room, and they all sat around a circular metal table.

"You read my report?" Smith asked. His large hands were folded in front of him.

"About the Athena, yes," Zen said. "Yes, I did. I haven't been in touch with Adonus since giving permission for his tests. At the time, I thought the whole thing was staged, but I thought it could keep. Now it's pretty clear there's something strange happening out there—maybe out of control." Zen held Smith's gaze, "You have any idea what's happening out there from satellite surveillance?"

"A lot," Smith snapped. He was a big man, with powerful wide shoulders and a square head, shaved on top. He was dark black with a strangely soft face for such a big man, adorned by pleasant symmetric features. "There have been shuttle flights in and out of Lakeshore every hour for two days. They've dug a pretty impressive hole. IR shows a lot of energy sunk into the dig; we estimate the hole to be about two klicks down."

"About the depth of the tunnels in that area," Zen commented.

"Yeah, that's right. Also, they have about fifty personnel. They look to be military, pretty heavily armed."

"Shit," Zen said. He had made a mistake letting Adonus get a foothold. Now, it might be too late. They might not be able to dislodge the company. And the company wouldn't take a risk like this unless the reward was pretty big, but what could it possibly be? "You have any idea what they're after out there?" Zen asked.

Smith looked around the table at the assemblage of blank faces. "Not a clue, boss. But what happens if they don't let us in? Given that they've buttoned this up so tight, I think we're headed for a confrontation."

"Yeah," Zen agreed, breathing out. "I'm going to inform the governor's office on Saturn via secure tight beam before we leave. Send them what we have along with your satellite data. I'm going to request they send whatever backup they can provide." He paused a moment. "How about us, what kind of a force can you put together?"

"We can match them in number, but not firepower. We have assault rifles and a couple of small rail guns, but no rockets and no Bloodhounds. I suggest we go out there with a force of about twenty, with another twenty on standby, ready to deploy in planet jumpers. But if it comes down to a shooting war, we don't have a chance. Along with their superior firepower on the ground, there's the Athena. We don't know its exact capabilities, but we can assume rockets and particle beams. She might even have tactical nukes."

Zen knew that it would come down to this sooner or later. There were a lot of conspiracy theories floating around, but it was a de facto reality that the corporations were in control of Earth. The few large government states that formed the Earth Confederation were symbolic relics of the past. The few free towns were powerless in a strategic sense. Socrates had been right; democracy didn't work, not on Earth at least with all its ancient vendettas. People who left Earth to colonize the system had done so in hopes of a new start, a chance to remake human society, and to try again. Three hundred years of trying to form liberal democracies on Earth had failed. In the end, racial, ethnic, and national tensions were susceptible to manipulation by ultra-rich plutocrats and had given way to a new feudal system that no amount of effort was able to dislodge. It wasn't clear whether humans could establish enlightened societies, but the diaspora of system settlers hoped for a new beginning. Corporations were the new Sparta and the Earth Confederation was just a front to fuel corporate agendas. Zen wondered whether the Saturn Common-wealth and the new Mars Federation had the power to resist large companies like TST, make them back down. That was an open question that had lingered for the past hundred years and would be settled in the next few days.

"What about the girl?" Zen asked after a long silence.

Smith looked at a man to his left. "Yeah, the girl. We lost her," the man admitted.

"Lost her?" Zen admonished. He could feel himself getting red, nothing was working out; it was all turning to shit. "How could you lose her? She's got a transponder."

"When we noticed she hadn't left her quarters for a day, we went to her room, but she wasn't there. The transponder was sit-ting on her desk, but she was gone. We searched the facility—she's not there." The man looked at Zen, then at Smith, clearly embarrassed.

"She dug the transponder out of her arm?" Zen asked, incre-dulous. Then after a moment, "But you need a transponder to get around, get through doors, for the lifts. Hell, the facility AI didn't raise an alarm at someone getting around with no ID?"

"Apparently not," the man responded. "We're still trying to figure out how she did it."

Zen thought about it. What was going on out there at Lake-shore? And the girl, they were clearly connected, but what that connection might be was a complete mystery. One thing was clear; he should have listened to her. "The girl is an ex-Ranger," Zen told the men around the table. "She was supposed to be turned off, but somehow, she's active again. She's connected with what's happening at Lakeshore. She's the only survivor of what she claimed was some kind of plot to blow up the tunnels. Now it seems clear that the tunnel explosion was a diversion, something to get us out of the area. I'll bet she's on her way out there right now. I have no idea what the connection is, but we're going to find out." Zen looked around the table once more, then slammed his hand on the table, palm down, making a loud bang. "We're going out there. Make it happen," he ordered Smith. "We'll meet in the tractor bay in an hour. Let's see what those fuckers are up to on our moon."

Zen got up and started for the door, purpose in his stride. Looking back before clearing the door, he saw a big smile on Smith's face but worried looks on his men still seated around the table, trying to take it all in. Things were about to get real.

* * *

After leaving the security center, Zen hurried to his office on the forty-fifth floor. On the way, he pinged Li-ant. "Get me a tight beam to Governor Tallus on Aurora. I'll be up there in a couple of minutes."

When he was seated at his desk, with the door closed and security isolation running, he opened the channel. Tallus's bust appeared floating in front of his desk with the signature blue outline of a holographic projector. Tallus was surprisingly young for a man in his position. But Zen knew that he was over one hundred and ten Earth years old. Rejuvenation was quite good and Tallus had apparently taken full advantage of the state-of-the-art. And although young in appearance, he left his hair white and long enough to brush his shoulders, giving him that stately-experienced look that all politicians seemed to want to project. He had a light complexion and brown eyes, which made him stand out among most outworlders. Zen suspected this was part of his success. The man was unique both in appearance and manner. He had that long-lost, smooth, soothing manner that now only existed in antiquated videos of old Earth, the resurrection of the benevolent leader.

"Governor, good of you to be available on such short notice," Zen said.

Tallus smiled. "We noticed a corporate war ship orbiting Titan, Director Zen. I've been expecting this call. How can we help?"

"We just sent you a briefing of the situation, Governor; it should be in your inbox. But to make a long story short, the Corporates are dug in at Lakeshore. I gave them permission for a product test because of a tunnel accident that now looks like it was staged. We had no idea they had come in a warship, and now we haven't heard anything from them in a couple of days."

"You've obviously tried to contact them?" Tallus asked.

"Yes, sir. No response. We're getting ready to go out there and see for ourselves, but as you may know, we're heavily outgunned. We were hoping the Commonwealth could send some support, both on the ground and in orbit."

"And do you know what they want out there? Why they're risking this confrontation?"

"That's the strange part, sir. We have no idea what they're after. We sent a query to Olympus asking for an explanation. So far, no answer."

Tallus seemed to think a moment. He looked down, then off to the side, talking to someone outside the projector's range. He had apparently muted the audio. Zen sat back and exhaled, checking his Aug-net chronometer; he had to meet Smith in the bay in a half hour.

"Adonus is in charge out there, is that right?" Tallus asked.

"That's right, Governor."

"He's a very ambitious man, Zen. We're wondering if Olympus is in the dark as well. It could be that Adonus thought he could get away with this, whatever this is, without anyone knowing, and then ran into a problem. If that's the case, Adonus could be involved in an internal company plot gone sideways. The fact that he hasn't backed off means the stakes are pretty high. And that makes this dangerous." Tallus looked away again, then nodded. "We have support on the way. The Vindicator will be departing for Titan on high burn within the hour." Tallus looked away again, then back at Zen. "She should be in Titan space in twelve Earth hours. She's carrying sixty Commonwealth marines and two heavy drop ships."

Zen sat back in his chair, the tension flowing out of him for the first time in a day. The Athena would see the Vindicator's drive plume almost immediately and know that Titan would not back down. That extra pressure would certainly be noticed at Olympus, making Adonus's position tenuous.

"Thank you, Governor. Much appreciated. If you could send the Vindicator's secure com keys, we can coordinate our activities. We will send you a real-time data feed of our operations."

"Good, that's good, Zen. Tallus out."

On the way to the bay, Zen sent a message via Aug-net directly to Adonus, notifying him that they were on their way and would require a thorough inspection of the site. So far, he hadn't heard back. He had weighed whether to notify Adonus in advance or just show up hot. Zen didn't want a shoot-out. He was a student of history and knew as soon as the dying started, there was no turning back. And he didn't want that. It was good to know the outcome you wanted before tempting fate and stepping into it. He wanted to give Adonus time to think, time to know that reinforcements were coming and perhaps even speak to Olympus before their arrival. It would take about an hour for them to get there, and the turn-around time for transmission to Olympus was about forty-five minutes Earth standard, just enough time for Adonus to consider his options, but not enough for a strategy against Titan security.

When Zen entered the bay, twenty security personnel were gathered in front of two heavy transports, suited up in battle armor, helmets retracted, checking their weapons.

Smith looked up. He was sliding magazines into his belt slots when he heard Zen approach. "Ready to ride," he asserted as if he was looking forward to it.

Zen looked at the magazines. "What kind of rounds?"

"Passive armor piercing," Smith said, pointing to the magazines on his right, and "self-propelled explosive penetrators," pointing to the magazines on his left, and smiled.

"Okay," Zen said. "You ride with me. Let's make sure we know what we're doing before we get there."

"Did you give them a heads-up, boss?"

"Yeah, no response so far."

"Good, let them think about it," Smith said.

Zen smiled and then patted him on the shoulder. "Good, I see we're on the same page."

Ten marines hoisted themselves up the large wheel of the first transport in single file and piled into ten seats, five seats lining either side of a cramped cabin, and the other ten security officers piled into the second transport. Smith and Zen took the pilot seats in the first. Smith activated the transport through his Aug-net and the parabolic antenna on top swung around and found positioning satellites. As the control console lit up, massive pumps depressurized the bay, and the heavy blast doors at the far end of the large space opened to the orange-yellow haze of Titan at midday. The transport AI engaged; a route map having been uploaded from Zen's Aug-net. The acceleration pushed them back into their seats as the vehicles sped through the door one after the other headed toward Lakeshore, headed for a confrontation that might decide the fate of the solar system for decades to come.

Chapter Eleven

Titan, LakeShore, 2240 AD

Adonus sat in his office aboard the shuttle and gazed out the window at the large assembly of machines and personnel, their motion kicking up orange ice dust under the glare of plasma lamps that illuminated the base to the brightness of high noon on Earth. So, he had a decision to make, things hadn't gone as planned and now this was a crucial turning point. He contacted Olympus on a tight beam, went straight to the chairman of the board, and laid it all out. Originally, he wanted to keep the existence of the artifact to himself, keep his leverage of ascendancy under his sole control. But fate had other plans. They knew from the orbital surveys that the thing under the ice had to be something extremely unusual; its characteristics didn't match anything they'd ever seen in mining the system for three hundred years. When he first heard about it, he guessed this was some kind of non-human artifact, either from a distant past that modern humans were completely unaware of or an alien artifact from another star. Either of these alternatives promised new technology that could put the company hundreds of years ahead, and him on top. Adonus clenched his fists so hard they turned purple with the knuckles bone white, but he was so enraged that he didn't notice the pain. All his life, he'd been subordinate to lesser people, carrying out their stupid orders while knowing that by rights, he should be giving the orders. It had always been his plan to get to the top by any means necessary, and so far, he'd made the right alliances and outflanked potential rivals, but this could be the shortcut that accelerated all his plans. The object they found, the sphere, exceeded all his hopes. It possessed the secrets of generating power to bend space-time, thus manipulating gravity. It was self-healing and electromagnetically invisible, and unfortunately, it was beyond his power to control. If only he could move the damn thing, all this could be avoided. But he couldn't move it. They'd tried everything. The thing defied every attempt to be moved or disassembled. And the fact that it remained passive infuriated him even more as if they were nothing, mere ants scuttling around ineffectively, harmless. The thought made him utter a stifled laugh. He couldn't help admiring the thing for its arrogance.

He relaxed. Well, what was done was done. He was a survivor and so he was flexible, adaptable. If he couldn't have the thing all to himself, he would have to share it with the chairman, Nolan Anders, a man he knew to be as ambitious as he was. And that was leverage. It's always best to know your rival, and he knew Anders because Anders was an older version of himself. It had been immediately clear to the man that he needed Adonus since he was here on site, a billion miles from Olympus. The chairman needed an operative on Titan that could guarantee ownership by possession, while Adonus needed Olympus's military force to secure that ownership. They needed each other to ensure their supremacy, the best kind of partnership. Adonus smiled to himself, maybe it would be okay.

Adonus pinged Colonel Assisi's Aug-net, summoning her to his office now that he'd decided on a course of action. After reflecting on his options, Adonus went to the mahogany cabinet, something rare on planets, and never found aboard ships. He unlatched the antique door to reveal an aged bottle of sour-mash whiskey. He poured the amber liquid into a cut-crystal glass and regarded it momentarily before lifting it to his lips and slowly sipping. The burn felt good going down, and the dry taste confirmed his decision. Now he was ready to do what needed to be done.

Assisi stood in front of his desk ramrod straight, hands clasped behind her, dressed in a black security jumpsuit, legs apart, not at attention, but alert—authoritative. She was an attractive woman, slim and tall, with a light complexion and white-blonde hair cut short. He'd followed her career and had personally requested her to head the security force aboard Athena. She was a veteran of shooting conflicts and had earned her bars in action, not kissing ass or screwing superiors. He thought there might be a small risk of conflict, and for that, he needed a real soldier, not a politician.

"Colonel, we have something serious coming up. There's a force coming from the Citadel; they want to inspect the dig. We're not going to let them."

"Sir, we have them on satellite, two heavy transports. They should be here in about a half hour." Assisi lowered her hands to her side and regarded Adonus with a questioning look.

"Yes, Colonel, speak freely. This will be your last chance to do so before they get here."

"Excuse me, sir, but isn't this Commonwealth territory? What's our authorization? What are the rules of engagement?"

"Let's cut the bullshit, Colonel. You've seen that thing in the tunnel, the company wants it—exclusively. If we can figure out how that thing works, we can own the system." Adonus sat back and tried to read her. It was important that she understood exactly what they were doing here. If he sensed reluctance on her part, he would replace her. She was skilled, but she was also smart, and that was dangerous. He couldn't have her going sideways in the middle of this thing.

Adonus smiled. Assisi was good. Her face betrayed nothing; she was completely stoic. "The rules of engagement, that's a good question. We won't be the first to engage with lethal force, but if fired upon, or if they try to breach the base forcibly, you are authorized to use lethal force. Is that clear?"

"Yes, sir—crystal."

"Dismissed, Colonel. Make it happen." Adonus watched her nod, pivot, and leave his office without another word. Well, the wheels were in motion. The next few hours would tell the story. The objective was to make this plot-of-ice on Titan a company black lab for the foreseeable future in hopes that, in time, they could crack this thing and learn its secrets. There were several unknowns that would have to be considered later on, once they had secured this patch of Titan. He'd tried not to think about it, but truth be told, the sphere was not completely inert. It was floating in mid-air and mining ore out of the ground. So, if it wasn't dormant, but just observing, did it have an objective of its own? He could handle the Commonwealth, but if that thing decided it didn't want to be owned, or make a deal, then what? It was too late for second thoughts. Adonus crossed the floor, poured himself another whiskey, and when it was finished, he left the office.

* * *

There was a low ridge of mountains between the Citadel and Lakeshore when approaching from the east, and those mountains were coming up fast. It was the early afternoon and as bright as it got on Titan. There were no clouds or shadows or cover of any kind. Zen wanted it that way, everything to be clear when they confronted TST. They couldn't afford a nervous shot or a miscalculation. Both transports pulled to a stop after reaching the base of the mountain and slipped under an overhang, which hid them from satellites. To their right, about half a klick away, was a passage cut out of the mountain for the tube transport, which had halted operations because the company stopped allowing the tube cars to dock yesterday. Beyond the mountains, the land was flat with essentially no cover for another half klick, where satellite images showed a cyclone fence had been erected around the perimeter of the base. Rushing that ground, they would be sitting ducks. Even though their armor had good electromagnetic cloaking, there was ample opportunity for company forces to saturate the death zone with a wall of metal from robot guns and drones. But that action would signal to the Commonwealth that they were in an all-out war, and Zen wondered whether, whatever was at the bottom of the dig, was important enough for the company to cross that line.

"So, do we have a plan, or are we just going to charge the gun turrets?" Smith asked. Zen saw worry lines around Smith's eyes, not a good sign. Typically, Smith was aggressive to the point of recklessness, so his concern right now was telling. *They were outnumbered, outgunned, and at a strategic disadvantage, perfect time for a plan,* Zen thought.

"Yeah, we do," Zen replied. He swiveled his seat so he was facing the cabin where two rows of five security personnel regarded him with anxious stares. "First, we have backup coming from Saturn, and the company knows it. I'm pretty sure they have a *fire-second* order, so I think we can get to the fence without conflict unless we shoot first, and we're not going to do that. Second, going to the fence is a distraction, a feint for what we're really going to do." Zen scanned the squad; anxious looks were replaced by rapt attention. He glanced over at Smith, who was smiling now—a good sign. Zen continued. "The advantage we have is we know this place, they don't. They feel pretty good right now because we're sitting ducks, and all they need is a pretext to start shooting. But like I said, the frontal assault is a fake." He paused and then continued. "The reason we call this the Lakeshore is because it's near the lake." There were smirks and soft laughter, another good sign.

"I'm sending a detailed map of this area. You should be seeing it in your Mind's-eye in a moment." Zen saw the squad appear to be looking into space, eyes unfocused. "The area circled in red is the company camp, the larger circle in blue is the area where we have multiple mining tunnels, including the one that blew up. Notice the green dotted lines coming out of the blue circle to the lake. Those are cooling channels; they dump the heat from the boring machines. There are pools near each tunnel that we use to dump waste heat." Zen looked around the cabin. "While we advance on the fence, the squad in transport two, led by Li-ant, is going to enter the base via the cooling tunnel marked in dark green."

"That tunnel is filled with liquid methane; it's under methane," Smith pointed out. "They're going under methane?"

"Yeah, the suits we're wearing work under methane. That's not a problem. In fact, it's to our advantage. The company won't see them coming. I doubt they know these tunnels even exist."

"Okay," Smith said. "And when and if they get in, what do they do? If they start shooting, we're toast at the fence."

"They're not going there to shoot; they're going there to document – to find out what the company's hiding. But, if this turns into a shooting conflict, air support will blow the fence and the robot guns, and we'll gain entry into the base here and here." In his Mind's-eye, he pointed to the pillboxes on either side of the base.

Smith swiveled his seat around too. He regarded the squad with a blank expression, then turned to Zen. "Huh…?" He said, clearly confused by Zen's revelation.

"Yeah, that's right. What do you think this is all about? They're hiding something, something they don't want us to see. They don't want us to see it so bad that they're willing to start a war. Well, we're going to see it, and we're going to transmit those images to Saturn."

Smith slowly nodded to himself, looked at Zen, then at the squad. "You heard the boss, suit-up, let's make those assholes pay attention." He clapped Zen on the back and extended his helmet from the wedge on his collar, where it rested in its collapsed configuration.

Zen turned to the transport control console, putting the transport AI in charge of the EM warfare drones they had just released. The drones would fly over the mountains in random trajectories, cloaked, and sending out strong jamming to cover their approach. Then Zen addressed the squad. "We'll go through the tube breach. When we get to the other side, I'll contact Adonus on tight beam and retransmit on encrypted so everyone can hear. We'll take it from there, got it?" Smith nodded, a smile on his face on the other side of his visor. "Glad to see you're having fun," Zen said. The man was nuts, but Zen was glad he was on his side. The ramp in back of the transport ratcheted down and the squad filed out, helmets opaque, guns slung over their shoulders, camouflage on standby. "Yeah, see you on the other side, boss," Smith said. His faceplate going opaque, Smith turned and hurried out the back.

Chapter Twelve

Titan, Lake, 2240 AD

They left just before dawn, going north of the Citadel in the general direction of the site, and then to the edge of the lake under the cover of darkness. It took Serena and Auger more than an hour to get close enough to the site to walk the rest of the way. Now the sun was low on the horizon, drawing long shadows over mounds, small ice boulders, and the tractor. The lake was placid, reflecting shimmering yellows and oranges from the occasional ripples pushed by gusts over its smooth surface as the crawler came to a stop just short of the liquid methane. Serena and Auger descended the tractor and peered north along the coastline to a cascade of low mountains, intersecting the perimeter of the lake about a klick north.

Serena turned to the tractor and gave the crew bubble a tap. The crawler lights came on, and as she removed her hand, it silently rolled forward as though she had pushed it. Then the tractor took a wide turn heading west back along the lakeshore. They watched as the antenna on top realigned, searching the sky for satellites. When it found what it was looking for, it sped up and slowly vanished, its shadow stretching in front of it and getting narrower until it was an indistinguishable black streak.

Auger exhaled. "So, that was a good trick, now what?"

"Now we take a walk to the base of those mountains. We'll walk close to the shore to hide our thermals from satellites, and then we find a way in."

Auger squinted, trying hard to see the spot where the mountains met the lake. "I've never been down there before. It's not that those mountains are high, but do we have a path through them? And if we do, won't we be in plain sight?"

Serena smiled up at him through her visor. "I got a plan."

"Yeah, glad to hear it." Auger started walking and Serena followed. The ground was a flat frozen methane-water mix, with smudges of black hydrocarbons making it look dirty. As they approached the lake, the density of ice chunks on the ground increased, making it look a lot like rocky beaches Serena had seen in pictures of old Earth. The footing got more precarious as they stumbled closer to the lake over the rocky ground. Since the environment was dry and very cold, the small rocks were like a fluid, like walking over rough ball-bearings. The careful placement of their steps made the trek exhausting, and by the time they got close enough to the mountains to be in shadow, Serena lightly grabbed Auger's forearm and said, "Let's take a break."

They squatted and looked around. "Up there," Serena said, pointing up around where the mountains met the sky. They saw small dots circling, coming in and out of sight just over the ridge.

"Drones?" Auger asked.

Serena's augmented eyes zoomed in, and she concentrated on one of the dots. "Warfare drones, not ours. I think the company is bracing for an assault."

Auger laughed. "So, we're trying to break into a secure site in the middle of a firefight, is that right?" He looked at Serena. "And, oh, I forgot to bring my gun."

Serena chuckled. "You don't have a gun. And you don't need one. We're not here to get into a fight."

"Yeah, that's right. Can you remind me, why are we here?"

"Look, it's pretty clear, given those drones, there's something here they don't want us to see. And Zen must know that. He wouldn't be challenging the company if he didn't have the support of the Commonwealth." Serena looked up at the sky again; the little dots were buzzing around like angry insects. "There's a pretty good chance there won't be any shooting. This is a face-off to see who backs down. And it's good for us."

"Good for us, how?"

"While they're strutting around seeing whose dick is the biggest, we slip in unnoticed."

"We slip in unnoticed, in plain sight, climbing up the side of a mountain with a bunch of drones hovering over us. Is that right?"

Serena countered, "We're not going over the mountains; we're going under the mountains, down a cooling tunnel that leads to a cooling pool into the site. It's right over there." She pointed to a spot near where the lake met the hills.

"We're going under methane?" Auger started laughing out loud.

"Why not? The suits are good for it, and the temperature of liquid methane is warmer than the air, so it should hide us. Also, we're denser than methane, so we should be able to walk, just like we are right now." She tapped him on the shoulder. "You got to admit, it's a pretty good plan." She smiled.

"Huh, yeah, why not?" Auger nodded to himself and grinned. "I got to admit, you had me worried, but it is a good plan. So, let me get this straight; we get in there, we record what we see, and we get out." He looked at her wanting to know this was the extent of their incursion. "No fighting, no shooting, no getting shot—right?"

"That's what we're here for. Let those assholes shoot it out. We're here to find out why they blew up the tunnel, why they tried to kill me to shut me up. What's so important down there?"

Serena tried to keep a straight face. She wasn't being honest with Auger. He was putting his life on the line, and somehow, she just couldn't tell him there was something down the tunnel, something she was somehow connected to, and something she could not ignore. She didn't really understand what it was, so how could she explain it to him? Truth be told, she felt strange at not feeling guiltier. Somehow whatever this was, it was too important to step away from. She'd never felt like this before, a sense of obligation transcended her personal feelings, even the sense of who she was. She just had to do this, and if they were hurt or killed, so be it.

Serena started walking then stopped. She looked at the ground, then turned and looked at Auger. She could tell he sensed the internal struggle reflected in the tightness of her eyes. He stopped. His grin slowly faded, and he stared back at her. "What?"

"Look, I can't really say what's going to happen. Maybe we will get shot. Maybe we won't be coming back. You got me here. That's all I really needed. I'll call the tractor back; you can still get out of here."

He chuckled. "You think I'm an idiot. I know all that. I didn't need a pep talk back there. We're in the middle of two armies ready to go at it, and there's no danger—come on."

"Then why go?" Serena asked. "They tried to kill me not you. This isn't your fight."

"I told you back there, I'll probably die on this ice-ball. I want to know what those fuckers are up to. This is for me. I'm tired of being a doormat."

He'd gone from grinning to being dumbfounded, to anger. This wasn't what she was expecting, but his words hit home. They all had a sense of not mattering, being pawns in a game they didn't understand.

"Yeah, I hear ya," she said. "Okay, then. I think it's over there." She pointed over her shoulder, turned, and started to where the lake met the mountain. She could hear the crunch of his boots on the ice-balls as he followed her toward the coming conflict. They stopped just short of the liquid.

"I don't think anybody's ever done this," she said. She started walking into the liquid methane. It was a dilute yellow-orange because of the color of the sky, and it seemed streaked with iridescent sludge because it was incompletely mixed with other hydrocarbons and complex partly frozen clathrates. But the methane acted as a kind of antifreeze, so the whole thing was a slurry. Auger watched as Serena went farther into the lake, slowly disappearing as she melted into the liquid. The bottom near the shore sloped at a gentle angle, so she was pretty far out before the liquid reached the base of her helmet. He saw her head turn slowly.

"The water's fine; you comin' in?"

Only then did he realize he hadn't moved. He'd just stood there, hypnotized, watching as she slowly sank. The words brought him around, and he started walking toward her. Once he'd reached her, they walked farther out. Soon, they sank below the surface. The methane wasn't as dense as water, and their weight enabled them to stand up like ancient divers in brass helmets with lead shoes, something Serena had seen in old books. The bottom was rough. Since there were no tides, sediments fell to the floor of the lake forming brittle crystals, making it easier to walk without slipping. They had to stay close together because the visibility was limited. Even though light penetrated methane better than water, the low light on Titan made everything beyond a meter a yellow-tinged shadow. She kept track of their position in her sensorium via a link to positioning satellites as they proceeded in a sliding-shuffling gait through the dry liquid. There was little sound of sloshing as she stroked her arms in time with her steps in a balancing act to stay upright and straight. The methane was low viscosity, not much thicker to the feel than the thick atmosphere topside, and the only sound in her helmet was the sound of her breathing and the pounding of her heart. The chronometer in her Mind's-eye showed they'd been at it for about twenty minutes when she got a sense of something happening, something she hadn't expected. She stopped, and Auger bumped into her from behind. She stepped forward and turned to face him. He stood there, fuzzy through the liquid and yellow in her dimmed suit lights, his face in shadow behind the visor.

"Something's goin' on up top."

Auger didn't say anything for a couple of moments. "Something not good, right?"

"I think there's a transport coming down on the shore right where we are."

"You think they know we're here? How could they?" Auger asked.

"Let's sit tight. We're about where we wanted to be; let's see what happens."

"Yeah, and how do you know all this?"

"I told you, things are coming back." In her Mind's-eye, she saw the com channel between the descending shuttle and the Citadel. That meant they were staging a diversion by making a frontal assault on the site. The encryption she was breaking in realtime was a corporate algorithm the Commonwealth was using, not too different from what they had used when she was in security. She slowly walked toward the shallows.

"Where you goin'?" Auger whispered.

"Stay put. I'm going to take a look. I'll feed my sensorium to your Aug-net so you can see too."

"You can do that?"

"Yeah, just stay put."

She activated camouflage before breaking the surface and slowly rose just high enough so her helmet cameras could pan the shore as well as the sky. She saw the shuttle coming in low above the liquid and in the radar shadow of the mountains. They were coming in slowly and emitting almost no EM.

"What the hell?" she heard Auger say. "Those are our guys. I thought they were planning to face the company head-on..." Auger was talking to himself, trying to make sense of it.

"Great minds think alike," Serena whispered. "I'm liking Zen more and more."

"I guess he believes you. He probably knows we're around here somewhere—probably looked for us before coming out here."

"Probably," Serena agreed.

"So now what, we call him up?"

"No, we're going to let him do his thing. Even if he knows we're out here, he has more pressing matters. We'll sit back and see if he goes for the cooling tunnel. If he does, we'll follow him in, let him ride point. He knows the company's lying; he's as curious about what they're hiding as we are."

The shuttle flew overhead so slowly that even in the thick atmosphere there were no ripples on the surface of the lake. Once over the shore, the shuttle slowly pivoted ninety degrees, then descended, spraying vapor under the landing jets, cloaking the whole thing in mist once the engines shut down. She watched as the rear ramp lowered, clearing the mist away. Ten security men in combat suits quickly disengaged. She assumed the last one out was Zen since everyone huddled around him, but he seemed taller than she remembered. After a couple of minutes, they broke up and headed for the lake at a point just north of their position. They entered the liquid about one hundred and fifty meters away, approximately where she had determined the tunnel entrance was. She slowly lowered herself back into the liquid and walked to where Auger was waiting.

"Let's give them about fifteen minutes, and then we'll follow them in. We can't actively track them, so we're going to have to play it by ear."

Serena had made a mental image of the geography. The inertial guidance in her suit knew directions. They headed northeast to where she thought the mountain wall should be. From there, they would follow the wall to the tunnel entrance. They covered the distance in less than five minutes; she was getting used to the rhythm of the lake-floor shuffling. Sure enough, there was the wall, and looking down through the methane, she saw the fuzzy outline of trails presumably left by Zen and the squad. She pointed to the tracks.

"Just like you said, "Auger commented. "Maybe we can pull this off."

They followed the wall and the tracks to a perfectly round hole cut into the mountain. She could see subtle waves of heated methane streaming out of the hole, which was about two meters in diameter.

"They're dumping heat into the exhaust," Auger observed. "They must be doing some active digging or something that burns a decent amount of fuel."

Serena planted herself in front of the tunnel, arms extended, grabbing the rim, and felt the current of exhaust. Her sensors registered the heat of the plume. Whatever they were doing, it was low-level. Her intuition told her the company had reached an impasse with the thing below; there wasn't enough waste heat for it to be anything else. She entered the tunnel on all fours and started crawling into the darkness. The helmet lights shone on the smooth surface of the tunnel, which had been coated with a resin that kept crystals from forming and blocking the passage. Both she and Auger were miners, experienced in moving around cramped tunnels far under the ice. While in the tractor, they had glued rubbery pads to their knees and elbows, anticipating the smoothness of the tunnel, and the possibility they'd be crawling against the current.

It was hypnotic. The crawling receded from her consciousness and she opened herself up, hoping somehow that the nature of the thing drawing her to it would be revealed. She continued to wonder why this was happening to her. She was an insignificant thing in the world, a pawn to be manipulated by the powers that be. In her entire life, she had a sole moment of hope, a vision of a life away from the company, a future she actually had a hand in determining. The wonders of that day so long ago would not abandon her. Wood, an apple off a tree, the prospect of living in a house that wasn't a box continued to haunt her. It was an intoxicating vision that never left her. The whole time in the desert town, she had feared the prospect of a different life would all come crashing down, and so it had. Walking into her mother's apartment and seeing the towering figures of those men in black suits had put an end to that nascent hope. No, whatever this was must be a result of opportunity, nothing else. She didn't believe in destiny. She hadn't been chosen; she had just been there at the right time and place. It must have been the half-hour when she was stuck in the ice. But what was it? She hadn't felt anything. And when she got out, her suit was intact, still air tight. So, what was it?

A light up ahead brought her back to the present. The light was a sure sign Zen and his squad had been here. There was a pool above the tunnel, but it was sealed by a cap. These pipes went to a multitude of drilling sites in a labyrinth of tunnels. They all merged at a pool before being exhausted into the lake. The pool served as a maintenance point at the terminus of the system, and the cap was usually sealed. But it had been removed, and in the light shining down from the pool above, she saw the dark wavy outline of a ladder. They'd obviously been in a hurry, the cap not replaced, and the ladder not withdrawn. She made her way to it, grabbed a rung, and looked up. A blue-white light shone down from above into the darkness. She started climbing toward it.

A few minutes later, they stood on the edge of a large oval pool, light shimmering off the walls reflected from the liquid.

They took a look around. There was a standard access tunnel leading off toward a central cavern.

"Elevator should be down the tunnel," Serena instructed after checking the site map in her Minds-eye.

"There have to be guards watching the elevator," Auger warned. "We're not armed. How do we get down to the site?"

"Here's where the plan gets a little thin," Serena admitted. "But we might have caught a break. Zen needs the elevator too, and he's armed. Let's go take a look; maybe he'll have cleared the way."

Being in the tunnel was so familiar, that for a moment, she forgot this might be the last few minutes of her life. They walked for ten minutes. Their progress toward the elevators was graphically drawn in her Mind's-eye as a blinking red dot slowly converging on a black diamond annotated by the moniker: *Supply Hold 341*. They heard gunshots and froze. Even though the shots were muffled squirts, not bangs, the sounds could still be heard echoing up and down the hard walls. *They must be using suppressors*, she thought.

"Shit," Auger whispered. "I hope this doesn't blow our cover."

"Maybe not," Serena guessed. "There is active jamming, and the sound really doesn't matter up here. Nobody two klicks down heard it. If the corporate guys weren't able to send a message, I think we're still good. The real question is: what happens when the squad takes the elevator to the bottom and the doors open?"

Serena thought a moment. "When I saw Citadel security come out of the shuttle, they were wearing corporate combat suits. I knew something didn't fit. I was a corporate security ranger for so long that the familiarity of those suits didn't seem to register as being out of place."

"I see," Auger said. "So they get to the bottom, and they look like a fresh squad of corporate security—it might work."

"Let's hope it does." They advanced deeper into the tunnel, but more slowly now, and closer to the wall. When the red dot in her Mind's-eye was almost on top of the diamond, they encountered a bend up ahead, hiding the elevator cavern. The gunshots ceased almost as quickly as they had begun. Hopefully, that meant Citadel security was still undiscovered.

"Let me go first," Serena ordered. "I used to do this for a living."

"Be my guest," Auger whispered.

Serena peered around the corner, and the sight left her stunned. She blinked, hoping somehow the panacea of death would go away, but instead, when she opened her eyes, her worst fears were confirmed. Bodies lay sprawled in twisted shapes no longer resembling the living. Arms and legs assumed positions that did not square with the normal orientations of people. She slowly entered the space and coolly assessed the situation, as she'd been trained to do so many years ago. "I thought I had left this behind," she whispered under her breath.

"What's goin' on?" she heard Auger ask over com.

"Room's clear, come on in."

Auger rounded the corner. "Shit..." He slowly made his way to where she stood. "What now?"

Before Serena could answer, they felt the ground shake. Ice dust zigzagged off the cavern walls and gleamed in their helmet lights filling the space with a fine mist of agitated particles.

"The hell?"

"It's the Citadel assault topside," Serena confirmed. "They know the corporate forces below will soon find out what happened down here. They're setting up a diversion to clear the passages, giving the force that did this a chance to get to the objective." Serena walked over to one of the slain corporate security people, bent down, and retrieved an assault rifle. She checked the magazine and mentally depersonalized it, so it would allow someone other than the dead security woman to use it. She glanced over at Auger. "You know how to use one of these?" She grabbed the rifle by its stock and barrel, held it out, and Auger took it.

"Point and shoot?"

"Pretty much. It's recoilless and light, so you can aim it with a hand on the body of the rifle. Pivot to the target using your trigger hand as the base. It has sensors that tell you when you're on target. I can interface it to your sensorium, the one we use for drilling robots. You see it?"

Auger looked around, "Yeah, there's a red circle depending on where I point it. I'm goin' to stop asking how you do this stuff. Yeah, I know, it's comin' back."

"When the circle starts blinking, you're on target," Serena instructed. She bent down and retrieved the magazine belt around the dead woman's waist, and gave it to Auger. "So, you up for this?"

"Not what I signed up for, but yeah, I'm goin'."

"Ever kill anyone before?" Serena asked. She fixed him in an intense gaze. "I'm going to give you some good advice; I hope you listen to me. This situation we're in, it's the worst thing people do, but here we are. When we get to the bottom, and you see corporate security point a gun at you, you shoot them. You don't hesitate; you don't think about them as people, they're targets. You don't hesitate, and you shoot to kill; you hear me?" Auger stood looking at her dumbfounded. "You hear me?" she shouted. "I got you into this, and you're going to piss me off if you get killed."

"I wouldn't want to piss you off," he answered and tried to force a smile. It didn't work.

Serena reached up and squeezed his shoulder, "Okay, then." She quickly walked over to another dead corporate soldier and took his rifle and magazine belt. She mentally summoned the elevator, easily defeating the security codes. It was getting easier to manipulate whatever equipment she concentrated on. This new ability was far greater than what she possessed before. It both frightened her and intrigued her. Something had happened to her down in the tunnel, and she was determined to find out what it was.

Chapter Thirteen

Titan, Drill Site, 2240 AD

They filed through the breach in the mountain and split the force, five fanning to the right of the train tube with Zen, and five fanning left of the tube with Smith. The jamming was thick, warfare drones filled the sky like locusts; their suits were on full stealth, absorbing and dispersing EM, and their suit skins were assuming the look of the surroundings so as to be virtually invisible in the optical. Everyone had point-to-point tight beam transponders that painted them as friendly. The terrain ahead was flat, surrounded by mountains on all sides, almost like a crater. About one hundred and fifty meters in the distance, Zen saw a metallic smudge that resolved into a fence on optical zoom. Beyond the fence lay the squat gray buildings that were the base. To either side of the central buildings, Zen saw trapezoidal pill boxes through which they could gain entrance into the base and to the drill sites far below.

They advanced, fanning out even more to the left and right of the train tube and running zigzag patterns, making it harder for the robot guns to lock on. Zen felt himself sweating and adjusted the suit environment. He knew company technicians could see intermittent signals on their scopes signaling the squad's advance. He hoped those signals were sufficiently incoherent for a target lock. Then it came, what he was hoping not to hear.

"Sorry boss, we had to neutralize the Corporates at the elevators," Li-ant said over com. "We had no choice. There were four of them; they came out of the elevator when we were already in the cavern. Once they exited the elevators, they opened up on us. They're all down; we suffered no losses. We need you to advance topside to give us cover. We're on our way down."

"Do they know you're coming?"

"We jammed them as soon as the doors opened. We killed the cameras in the cavern. They might know something's not quite right, but it's even odds as to what they think is happening."

"Okay, we'll get things started up here. Good luck, Zen out."

High above Lakeshore and to the south, two Citadel jump ships were circling above Titan's clouds at the edge of space, waiting for Zen's signal. Upon receiving it, they plunged into the atmosphere at hypersonic speed. On the ground, advancing toward the corporate base, Zen's men could hear the rolling thunder of their sonic booms and used the sound as a signal to time their advance. The two jump ships extended wings, cut their engines to hide their thermals, and went into a supersonic glide with the base in their cross hairs. As the first shuttle zoomed toward the base, it fired all its missiles, taking out the fence and the robot guns, then reignited engines and climbed steeply firing decoys, trying to cover its exit. The second shuttle slowed to drop speed with its rear ramp open, deploying twenty more troops as it skirted the open plain, then followed the first shuttle in a fast steep climb deploying more decoys. Zen saw two fast interceptors fired from somewhere in the base. They streaked through the thick atmosphere leaving a heavy orange contrail arching into the sky. The first missile clipped the shuttle's engine and exploded in a bright blue-white fireball. The second missile streaked into the fireball and exploded in a hellstorm of plasma and debris, emitting a concussion that almost knocked him down. Zen kept running.

They all ran through the smoke, dust, and shower of debris toward the pill boxes. Two Bloodhounds emerged from the wreckage the shuttle ordnance had raised, missile wings unfolded, and particle beam turrets looking for targets. The killing field lit up with streaks of rockets, super heated rail-gun rounds, automatic tracer fire, and particle beams. Zen occasionally looked at tactical and targeting in his Mind's-eye while firing his rail gun and running like hell, bobbing and weaving for the nearest pill box. One of the Bloodhounds was blocking his way. Clearly, they knew what the objective of the advance was. However, there were two pieces of good news. By its firing pattern, the Bloodhound didn't have a lock on him. His camouflage was effective. And, if he could get past the Bloodhound, it was too big to fit through the door. Zen was flanked by two security men converging on the box. Suddenly, there was a flash on his left as the particle beam sliced through the man as cleanly as a knife, both halves in flames from the intense heat and arcing through the air, spraying blood everywhere. Aided by his suit assists, Zen jumped straight up just as the beam cut right across where he'd been running a moment before. Because of the low gravity, he flew on a parabolic trajectory just to the left of the Bloodhound. It quickly jumped from side to side looking for him, relying on predictive algorithms from the wavering positions Zen's camouflage surrendered to it. As soon as he was on the ground again, he quickly rolled, brought his rail gun up in a smooth arc, and fired four hypersonic rounds into its side in quick succession. He felt the concussion through the thick atmosphere and saw the thing staggering, a smoking red molten hole in its side. It collapsed with a thud, raising a fog of dust and smoke. Arching through the smoke above the fallen machine were the ghostly trails of two other invisible Citadel soldiers jumping over it on their way to the box.

They got to the pill box together, with one of the soldiers firing a rail gun round into the door and jumping into the black. Zen and the other soldier followed him in. Targeting lasers crisscrossed in the dust of the hallway beyond the airlock. Zen skidded to one knee as tracer fire lit up the space above him, sparking as it ricocheted off the walls. The strobe light effect of muzzle flashes revealed a stop-motion retreat of corporate soldiers farther down the hallway. He brought his rail gun up in a smooth arc and fired as he slid to a stop, lighting up the confined space which quickly turned into a torrent of smoke and molten debris. The soldiers who flanked him did the same, and in the few seconds it took to resolve the encounter, all targeting lasers had disappeared. They quickly advanced down the hall, hopscotching each other, changing their aim so as to sweep all possible directions from which the Corporates could ambush them. As they closed on the elevator that descended to the tunnels two kilometers below, they stepped over the charred remains of corporate soldiers who had been left to defend it. The sight made Zen want to wretch, but he kept it down somehow, his reflexes telling him filling his helmet with bile might cost him his life, but more importantly, put the mission in jeopardy. Zen had been trained as a soldier, but he wasn't a killer and he had to work hard to see all this death and not succumb to despair; the crash would come later. As soon as they got to the elevator, there was a rolling thunder, which got progressively louder. When the ground began to shake, Zen knew what was coming.

"Get out!" he yelled, as he turned and began running for the airlock. Then the elevator exploded in a shockwave that lifted him off the floor and flew him toward the hole where the airlock had been. Zen had taken many high-altitude flights using wings in Titan's thick atmosphere. He knew how to shape his body to guide his flight. Upon leaving the ground, his reflexes kicked in and he tried to fly straight in order not to bounce off walls on his way out. He was only partially successful. He couldn't tell what was up or down, but he could feel himself thrown forward by the hot gases of the explosion. His shoulder slammed into something hard he assumed was a bulkhead. A bright flash of pain made him convulse and quickly diffused into his chest. He saw his systems shooting him full of steroids and he felt himself relax. The collision made him bounce in the opposite direction and he covered his helmet with his arms anticipating a crash with the opposite wall. *Right on time*, he thought, as he cushioned a savage blow to his head. He was so pumped with steroids and adrenaline the pain was forgotten almost as soon as it happened, but he knew his body and his suit were amassing damage he would later have to reconcile. If his suit was ripped, or he broke something that prevented his quick responses, he might not survive this encounter. The turbulence of the hot explosive gases shooting out of the elevator shaft and the thick Titan atmosphere were making it impossible not to take a beating on his way to, and through, the hole in the wall to the outside. In an instant, he found himself lying face down in the dull yellow ice-sand of Titan. He checked his systems in his Minds-eye. No air leaks. He started to move, anticipating excruciating pain from broken bones or internal damage, but none came. He sat on the ground, arms extended behind him, propping him up, and looked around. In front of him, in the scattered debris that had been the base, he saw the other two soldiers heaving themselves up.

"Status?" Zen ordered through com.

"Five on five," he heard Evins rasp.

"Bruised but not broken," Kira followed.

Zen slowly got to his feet. "Smith, you there?" Zen waited, willing Smith to answer.

"Yeah, boss, we're here."

"What's your status? You intact?"

"We lost Charlie and Gabriel. When we got to the elevator, they blew it. There's no way in."

Zen swore to himself. "Okay then, let's regroup at the train tube, or what's left of it, inside the base."

"Yeah, boss, we're on our way, Smith out."

Chapter Fourteen

Titan, Drill Site, 2240 AD

Serena watched dust shake off the walls and shimmer through rays from overhead lights as the ground-pounding from topside continued to rattle the elevator. It started soon after they'd entered the car and began the long descent to the tunnels below. She saw Auger looking around, craning his neck with every shock, probably trying to find cracks in the walls, a sign that they might be stuck in here, maybe die in here.

"That's quite a show up top. Sounds like an all-out fight, not some small divergence," Auger said.

"Yeah, fights are like that. Well thought out before someone gets killed, then it turns real, real fast," Serena said.

"Well, it's definitely real right now. What do you think is going to happen when those doors open?"

"Let's get on either side of the door, crouch to make a smaller target, stay out of sight as much as possible. Let them make the first move so we know what we're shooting at." She saw Auger nod and move to the opposite side of the door just as she felt the elevator slow. She was strangely calm. She'd done this many times before, but that was a long time ago. *Just like riding a bike*, her mother's voice came from some distant memory. She smiled to herself; she'd never seen a real bike, and she'd never learned to ride one.

The elevator came to an abrupt stop. She loosened her grip on the rifle, tried to relax, and got down low. Auger followed suit. Red light came streaming in from the corridor outside;

her suit AI quickly killed the alarms ringing in her audio sensorium, the base was under assault and standard security procedures were in place. Nobody rushed the elevator. Serena slowly peeked around the open door. She saw red light flooding in from the corridor and a couple of bodies twisted in unnatural poses on the floor. Whatever happened here had moved somewhere else.

"Damn, they bought it," Auger whispered.

"Yeah, for us maybe, but not for Zen's squad. Follow my lead and keep frosty, you hear?"

"I hear ya."

They both crab-walked out of the elevator, scanning side to side, trying to identify ambush points. Serena concentrated on the local network, trying to find surveillance feeds. She found several cameras and microphones hidden throughout the corridor and killed the feeds. Hopefully, security officers had their hands full with Zen's assault, making it less likely they'd notice the blackout, giving them time to get further into the base to a more defensible position. She cracked the network database and downloaded the base layout. Her suit AI resolved their position with a blinking red dot.

"I'm sending your Aug-net the layout." She sensed Auger's acknowledgment ping in her Minds-eye. She quickly scanned the layout, looking for anything that might suggest where they were keeping the thing they'd found. Then she saw it, a large cavernous space on the lowest level with no descriptive annotation of any kind. "That's it," she said. She put a blue blinking bull's eye on the space and sent it to Auger.

"Yeah, I see it. It's two levels down and I'll bet it's pretty well guarded," Auger said.

Serena looked for stairs to the lower level. Even though policy was to take stairs, since a loss of power might trap you in an elevator, squads were in a hurry to reposition during an attack and often took elevators anyway. She was hoping her experience was a better predictor of what people would do in a pinch and rushed to the nearest staircase. With Auger right behind her, she whipped the door open, trying not to slam it on the wall, and descended the stairs two and three at a time, quickly peering over the banister to see if anyone was coming. They made it to the bottom without incident and halted before opening the door. She noticed the shaking had stopped.

"You feel anything?"

"No, I think whatever happened has happened," Auger replied.

"Yeah, I think it's probably a standoff. Chances are they blew the elevators and are hunkering down. That means they'll start to assess their situation and find the cameras we killed are down. We don't have much time," Serena warned. Auger just stared at her.

"Okay, there's got to be someone down here; let me go first." She saw Auger nod inside his helmet and position his rifle to the ready as Serena crouched low, opened the door a crack, and slipped to the other side. The corridor was empty, and there were no red lights. She slowly scanned from left to right. There were no doors except at the ends of the corridor. The layout made her nervous; it seemed like a perfect setup for an ambush. She heard Auger step out of the stairway and the door close behind him with a click. She stiffened. She quickly checked the layout, and her anxiety grew; a cold numb crept down her back. The layout showed doors on this corridor that didn't exist, and the spaces behind the doors at the ends were indistinct, not marked in any way. She quickly tried to access the door control and found she was locked out; the Corporates knew they were here. "Shit!" She whispered. She lowered her rifle and turned to face Auger.

He stared back at her, his eyes following her rifle until it pointed to the floor. "What?"

"It's a trap."

No sooner were the words out of her mouth than the door at the far left end of the corridor opened, revealing a large railgun on a robotic turret pointing right at them.

"Put your weapons down, hands clasped behind your helmets—now!"

"Shit," Auger echoed, as his rifle clanged to rest on the floor.

"Kick the guns toward the left door and start walking to the right—slowly."

* * *

Serena and Auger were led through corridors to a holding pen. On the way, Serena made a mental note of where they were in reference to the tunnel layout she'd hacked from the database. Although the Corporates had discovered they neutralized the surveillance between the cooling tunnel and elevator entrance, she doubted they had discovered the database hack. She noticed burn marks and blood stains on the walls and floors of the passage where they'd been captured and knew the trap had worked on Zen and his squad. The sickly metallic tang of blood mixed with an undercurrent of burnt carbon invaded her olfactory sense now that they were forced to remove their helmets. How many people had Zen lost? She turned her attention to their captors. It was ironic. The suits, the procedures, and even the way in which the corporate soldiers boxed-them-in were tools she had used to subdue labor revolts on several stations and on Mars, where she finally came to terms with the fact that she was on the wrong side. *Karma's a bitch*, she thought.

They came to a halt at a wide door, which slid aside when the Corporates repositioned around and behind them. They were pushed by rifle barrels into the room, first her, then Auger. The door slid shut behind her with the low hum of electromagnetic actuators. She looked around and counted six soldiers, four men and two women sitting on the floor, backs braced against the far wall. They looked beaten; two of the men and a woman had dark bruises on their faces. One man's hand looked like it had been crushed. His fingers were at odd angles, and the entire hand was dark blue and swollen. One of the women with bruises on her face looked familiar. Although she was seated, Serena could tell she was tall and slim, the traits of someone who had grown up in low gravity. The woman stared at her with passive suspicion.

"Where's Zen? Was he hurt?" Serena asked, looking at the woman who continued staring at her.

"Who are you?" the woman asked. "How did you get down here?" Then she smiled contemptuously. "You're not a corporate plant, are you?"

"I know you," Serena said and could see the realization in the woman's eyes. "You're Li-ant, right?"

"You're the miner," Li-ant said. Then turning to Auger, "You too. What the hell are you doing here? How did you get down here?"

Serena smiled. "We're miners; that's what we do. And, as you know, these fuckers tried to kill me. I want to know why. Where's Zen?"

Li-ant regarded Serena, looking her up and down. Then looked at Auger and did the same. She came back to Serena. "You know they're listening to us. We're not going to give them what they couldn't beat out of us."

"I understand," Serena said. Serena looked around, then back at Li-ant. "I hope they can hear me. This whole thing is stupid—a cluster-fuck. We may be prisoners, but so are our hosts. We felt the shaking coming from up top. They probably had to blow the elevators; they're trapped down here just like us. They're a billion miles from Olympus, and we're less than a million from Saturn. The company's not going to save their asses. I worked for these fuckers, I know how they think. They're not going to prosecute a war with the Commonwealth, their best customer this side of the asteroid belt. This has to be some crazy lone-wolf operation by someone who's gone off the reservation." She looked around the room for cameras she knew were hidden in the walls and ceiling. "Whoever is behind this disaster is going to be cut loose. You're as screwed as we are," Serena said to the room and smiled.

Serena walked to the wall kitty-corner to where Li-ant sat, and sat too, back against the wall. She looked up at Auger.

"Well, shit," he said and sat next to her. "What now?"

"Now we wait and see what happens. They have to decide what their next move is. Maybe they'll use us as hostages to cover their escape. I can't see any percentage in killing us."

"We still don't know what this is about," Auger said.

"Whoever's doing this has considerable pull in the company," Li-ant said. "They may be crazy, but they're not stupid. Whatever's down here, they must've wanted to move it. Get in and out without anyone being the wiser. Somehow something happened that kept them from doing that."

* * *

They'd been in the room for more than two hours. It was starting to get ripe. The air was heavy and tasted like there wasn't enough oxygen. Serena saw several of the soldiers either sleeping or passed-out. She looked at Li-ant. The woman was alert, but deep in thought. Serena concentrated on the door and surveillance systems, but failed to override them; she was locked out. She couldn't tell whether this high level of security had been built into the facility, or they had tightened the network, suspecting someone had the power to hack the systems. Then she heard the hum of actuators, and the door slid open. Serena was wide-eyed and then blinked in recognition. A woman stood tall and straight in the doorway, flanked by two soldiers in assault suits, helmets extended, guns at the ready.

The woman pointed to Serena. "You, on your feet. You're coming with us."

Serena heard stirring and turned from the woman just in time to see Auger jump up, fists clenched. "She's not going any-where."

The two soldiers flanking the woman raised their rifles, pointing them at Auger. Serena bolted to her feet, and stood in front of Auger, effectively blocking him from a clear shot. She held her hands out, palms up. "I'll come with you, please put your guns down." She turned to Auger and put her hand on his forearm. "It's alright, I'll be okay, just sit down, okay?"

She could see his face was crimson with rage. Then he looked at the woman in the doorway. "What gives you the right?" He snarled and then looked down at Serena again.

"Look, we've come this far, keep your cool. I'll be okay—really." Then she stretched up on her toes, cupped her hand around his ear, and whispered. "Don't piss me off." She lowered herself, then looked up at him, and smiled sweetly.

He started to calm down and almost laughed. She could feel his taut arm muscles relax, and his face regain its color. Even in the dank air, she could smell the pungent anxiety wafting off of him. "Okay," he said in resignation and slowly sat.

Serena turned and walked forward. The woman stepped out of the way, and before the soldiers flanked her, Serena turned and looked at Auger, then at Li-ant. Both displayed a worried affecta-tion. She nodded, turned, and heard the door shut behind her.

* * *

Serena sat at a table in a small closed room facing Nora Assisi. The soldiers remained outside. She looked around. The room was a metal box, nothing on the walls, nothing other than the table, two chairs, and the hum of an air-conditioner. *At least the air is breathable,* she thought. She turned back to Nora, and folded her hands in front of her, blank expression on her face, waiting for the other woman to make the first move.

After a while, Nora said, "What are you doing here?"

"Is this being monitored, recorded?"

"No."

Serena concentrated on the room; she couldn't detect any active or passive surveillance.

"What are you doing here?" Nora repeated.

"I was thinking of asking you the same question, Lieutenant."

"It's Colonel now."

Serena stared at her and dipped her head slightly to one side in a questioning pose. "Aren't you tired of being on the wrong side? Tired of being a guard dog for inferior people acting out their emotional insecurities?"

Nora stared back, a condescending smile slowly appearing. "Psychobabble coming from a grunt; a grunt who couldn't make it in a professional army."

"No, Nora. A grunt who couldn't kill people she didn't know, for reasons that were never explained. Orders given by a bunch of sociopaths who don't have the balls to pull the trigger themselves and look into the eyes of the people they murder."

Nora tensed. The smile melted off her face and was replaced by a mask of anger and something else. Serena knew she'd hit a nerve. She went on. "I don't know much about you, Nora; where you came from, how you got here. But I do know the last time I saw you, I sensed you had the same doubts I did. I guess your parents were under contract. You either took up their contract, or you were so young and so brainwashed that you signed your own contract. Those people we put down, they're our people, the same people we came from. I think the reason I'm sitting here right now is because you need to talk to someone more like you than you're willing to admit."

Nora was flush. Her mouth was a narrow slit, and her eyes bore into Serena. "What are you doing here?" she hissed.

Serena waited a moment and then said, "Someone tried to kill me the other day in a tunnel not far from here. They wore a black security suit, almost like yours. Then all this happened." She looked around the room, arms out in a grand gesture. "Why would someone try to kill me—like you said, I'm nobody. Maybe they thought I saw something? Maybe they blew the tunnel as a pretext to shut down work because the company found something?" Serena saw Nora's expression change from anger to concern. "Yeah, we're not stupid. We know you found something. Something your psycho boss thinks will elevate him. But something's gone wrong, and he, along with you, are screwed. Am I getting warm?"

"We're through here."

"Wait," Serena whispered. "Why be the fall guy? You know this operation is off-the-books. Whoever this asshole is, he's going down. Olympus isn't going to back him against the Commonwealth in this cluster-fuck. You know that, and I know that. And when this falls apart, you're going down with him. Why do that?"

Nora said nothing, just stared at her. Serena couldn't read her, didn't know if she'd gotten through. But she knew she was taking a terrible risk. Although Nora told her they weren't being monitored, and Serena couldn't detect any surveillance feeds, if they were monitored, she'd given Nora's psycho boss a lot of good reasons to get rid of the hostages. Presently, the door slid open and the two soldiers came in.

"Take her back to the holding cell, Sergeant. We're through here."

Serena got up, didn't look at Nora, and walked out. The soldiers fell in, in front and behind her. Once they were in the corridor again, she felt the mental pull, a compulsion to go to the thing waiting two levels below. She saw the location of the tunnel layout in her Minds-eye, and the urge got stronger. It overwhelmed her. She stopped walking; her entire body seemed to vibrate like it was magnetized. The soldier behind her almost ran into her.

"Keep moving." He pushed her forward.

The other soldier, who was walking a couple of meters in front, realizing she'd stopped, turned to see what was happening. When the soldier behind her pushed her again, she feinted stumbling and falling. When he bent down to help her up, she bolted forward, grabbed the soldier in front, who was walking back to where she lay, and rammed him into the soldier standing behind her. As he fell forward, she stepped out of the way and grabbed his rifle. With blinding speed, she smashed the rifle butt into the first soldier's face. He crumpled. The other soldier had fallen and was trying to get up. She hit him hard on the back of the head with the rifle butt. Both soldiers lay at her feet, out cold. She took the other soldier's weapon, slung it over her shoulder, and ran down the hall toward the stairs, to the thing that was calling her.

Chapter Fifteen

Titan, Drill Site, 2240 AD

The battle raging topside ceased. Once the elevators were blown, the shaking from explosions stopped. There were no company troops left topside, none alive anyway. It would take at least a week for the Citadel to bore new shafts this far down, and by that time reinforcements would arrive from Olympus space. Adonus contacted Nolan Anders on tight-beam via Athena and told Anders that Citadel forces were coming to inspect the base. He informed Olympus that he suspected the Citadel knew the company found something important enough to risk encroaching on the Commonwealth, and war was a real possibility. Adonus waited for more than three hours for a response. He heard chimes and saw the electric-blue outline of a holo-portal grow from a point in front of his desk into a screen that filled half his office. Anders oversized face filled the screen. The man's chiseled features and prominent aquiline nose were overshadowed by deep set intense brown eyes. He seemed to have digested Adonus's summary of the situation and internalized it. A round-trip message at this distance was over three hours if no time was spent in deliberations. Adonus got a response in three hours, ten minutes. There was no sign of stress or annoyance on the man's face as he began to speak.

"Adonus, we received your update and have been studying the data sent by doctor Orzan of tests done on the artifact. We are in agreement the artifact is not of human origin and the technology involved is centuries beyond current human state-of-the-art. Further, we agree this advanced alien technology must not fall into the hands of the Commonwealth; we must own it exclusively. Whoever can unravel even a fraction of its secrets will have dominion over this system in perpetuity. Therefore, as you suggest, we are willing to go to war over this strategic advantage. We have dispatched three Nemesis cruisers armed with anti-matter weapons to enforce our ownership. Their travel time at high burn is six standard Earth weeks from their current position in Jupiter space. If you have to reengage the Commonwealth, the Athena has been given orders to support you in any way necessary. Anders out."

Adonus sat back in his chair and smiled to himself. It would have been neater to move the artifact without anyone being the wiser. That outcome would have given the company unlimited time to unravel its secrets. And once those secrets were properly weaponized, the company could assert itself throughout the Sol system with complete confidence. Unfortunately, this way, the company and Commonwealth were at war with nearly equal forces, the company with superior technology, and the Commonwealth with proximity.

Adonus saw a message coming into his Aug-net from a source typically used for communication with the Commonwealth. So, this would be amusing. He had ordered corporate forces to perform a phased retreat as a pretext for blowing the elevators. Let the Commonwealth think they had the company backed into a corner. The move was designed to buy Adonus time, time to further investigate the artifact while company forces established overwhelming force in Saturn space. Things were going according to plan. With the confirmation that three corporate heavy cruisers were on their way, the noose was tightening on the Commonwealth and they didn't even know it. And he couldn't blame them for miscalculating, since they didn't know the magnitude of this find. At some point, everyone knew this day would come; the two systems of human civilization were manifestly incompatible, and at some point, a resolution would occur—this was that point.

Adonus channeled the call to his com system. A point appeared in front of his desk but did not grow into a large screen. It grew instead into a small screen with audio traces and measurements indicating stress in the audio, and the probability that the caller might be lying.

"Adonus here, who is this?"

"This is Director Zen, Mister Adonus. We met the other day under different circumstances. I'm leading the force that has regained control of Commonwealth territory right above you. I would like to offer you terms for the surrender of your remaining forces, and the return of a squad of my people who, I believe, you are currently holding."

Adonus could barely keep himself from laughing out loud. "I'm going to have to turn down your generous offer of surrender. To the contrary, we are quite comfortable down here, and as you can probably note from communication with Olympus, we have not been ordered to stand down. We have decided to claim this small piece of Titan as company territory." There was an exaggerated silence on the line; Adonus was enjoying this more than he should. It was always empowering when the charade was dropped—when people's true intentions could be asserted. It was a delicious moment of truth, beautiful in its terse honesty.

"So, do I understand you correctly, Mr. Adonus? You are going to war with the Commonwealth over a mining site on Titan?"

"Let's drop the pretense, Director Zen. You know and I know that this site represents a valuable find of resources. We have determined that this find, since we found it, and you didn't, is well within our rights to claim under the doctrine of ownership by discovery. If you do not agree, then yes, we are willing to go to war."

There was another protracted silence. Then Zen said, "Okay, but until this matter is resolved, would you release our people as a gesture of good faith?"

"I'm sorry, Director, but as you can see, there is no way to get to the surface right now, so that would be physically impossible. However, rest assured when we get reinforcement of our claim from Olympus and are able to restore the elevators, your people will be released. Right now, they are safe and well taken care of. I'm sorry, but I'm going to have to go now. There are other matters that need my attention. You understand." Before Zen could respond, Adonus cut the connection, and the small screen in front of his desk collapsed to a point and disappeared.

As Adonus pondered his next move, alarms chimed in his Aug-net. He contacted Colonel Assisi.

"This is Adonus, what is the emergency, Colonel?"

"The miner, Serena Roe, has escaped containment and may be headed to the artifact."

* * *

Zen looked at Smith. Smith shook his head. "What the hell was that? He sounded almost giddy."

"Yeah, I know, something's up. It almost sounded like we got him right where he wants us. Whatever they found down there, it's big."

"So, what do we do now?"

Zen looked around at his squad. They had lost five out of twenty soldiers, and the Corporates were holding another five captive, not a great outcome. And what did they have to show for the loss? They had a mining site in ruins and no information about the nature of the discovery, which was the objective of the mission. By any metric, this mission was a total failure.

"I have to get in touch with Saturn. Give them a total debrief of what's happened here, and get whatever information they might have."

"What information?" Smith asked.

"Well, information about reinforcements from Olympus. Adonus wouldn't sound that cocky if something wasn't coming.

And I'll bet that something has real bright drive flares. Meanwhile, I'm going back to the Citadel; I'm leaving you in charge here."

Smith looked around at the wreckage. "In charge here? In charge of what?"

"Once the Vindicator arrives in orbit, we'll fly a transport in so you can use it as a base of operations. Remember, the Athena's still in orbit. She's not a cruiser, but she could be heavily armed. If we send a transport in, it could get shot down. Until then, there are still some buildings standing; use one as a temporary base. We need a presence here to enforce our claim on this site and to make sure the Corporates stay down below. Who's to say they don't have a secret way to the surface."

"About the Athena, if that's true about the transport, why didn't the jump ships get shot down?"

"Yeah, I've been wondering about that for the last ten minutes. Makes you think that all this was staged."

"Staged for what? This battle seemed real convincing a few minutes ago."

"The only answer is this thing was staged to buy time. Apparently, Adonus planned to claim the site all along if he couldn't remove whatever they found. Which begs another question, why couldn't they remove it? That would have been a much better outcome for them."

"Yeah, food for thought," Smith admitted. "Okay, boss, you can count on us."

Chapter Sixteen

Vindicator, Titan Space, 2240 AD

It took one standard Earth day for the Vindicator to cover the million and a half kilometers from Saturn to Titan, which, unfortunately, was located on the other side of Saturn in its nearly circular orbit. Standard Earth days were still used since Titan, being gravitationally locked to Saturn, made its day one rotational period around Saturn, or about half an Earth month, an inconvenient unit of time for local travel. As it approached Titan, Vindicator detected the corporate cruiser Athena in a stationary orbit above the Citadel, the Commonwealth mining settlement in Titan's southern hemisphere. Captain Alastair Caster studied what little was known about the Athena and wasn't surprised to find almost nothing—that worried him. The company evolved from large multinationals on old Earth and had adopted a culture of secrecy as to its holdings and capabilities. Many corporate clients were often compelled to sign non-disclosure agreements or NDAs, which made even known corporate activities hard to untangle. So, Caster studied company labor interventions that often required military support and found the Athena often appeared as part of those, suggesting that far from being a military transport, it was probably more of an attack ship. Unfortunately, he could not find any records of Athena involved in a purely naval engagement, making its ship-to-ship offensive capabilities unknown. As he ran tactical simulations in his quarters, he received chimes in his Aug-net from the bridge.

"This is Caster, what's our status?"

"This is the Ex-O, Captain; we're approaching Titan insertion, thought you might want to be on the bridge."

"On my way, Mister Overine. Caster out."

Vindicator slipped into high orbit on the other side of Titan from the Athena. In his simulations, given all the unknowns, Caster determined this was the least risky opening move yielding the greatest options. Before its day-long burn to Titan, Vindicator stopped by the Commonwealth orbital station Oasis for resupply. The ship was flush with offensive ordnance, but more importantly, it was equipped with a new multi-range Quantum Lidar, which could give it the decisive edge in this engagement.

Although the company was widely considered to have superior technology, its regimented and oppressive culture worked against it in two fundamental ways. Throughout human history, scientific breakthroughs were often the result of unconstrained intuition, which corporate culture suppressed. So, most corporate technical progress resulted in refining known technologies, not creating new ones that required a leap of insight. The other thing working against the company was the best human minds fought conformity, which resulted in a steady stream of the most brilliant refugees to the Commonwealth. Where stealth had long been the greatest tactical advantage a military force had, the Quantum Lidar, or QL active imager, broke all known stealth technologies. Caster factored that singular advantage into all of his simulations, and now thought about their next move. Word came from the Citadel on tight beam that a pitched battle had just been waged to regain control of the drill site at Lakeshore, and the Athena was suppressing air travel in the area. The Vindicator's first mission would be to guarantee air travel over Lakeshore.

As the black manta profile of the Vindicator slipped into almost stationary orbit on the far side of Titan, Caster sat in the captain's chair behind the pilot, whose station overlooked the large hemispherical containment of the holographic viewer occupying the center of the bridge. The orange cloud layer of Titan filled the bottom half of the viewer, showing a surface so vivid that Caster felt the urge to hoist himself out of his chair and step onto it like some impossible giant. He could see light and dark irregularities in the clouds that reflected the differences in surface topology but couldn't see the ground in the optical.

"Vin, show us the ground."

"To what resolution, Captain?" Vin asked. Vin was the ship. Although Vin understood what the captain meant from experience, Vin's fundamental nature was to be courteous, so it usually felt compelled to ask whomever it was speaking to their preference.

"We need to see objects a half kilometer across, for now, thank you."

Instantly, the scene below changed as if the clouds had blown away. Cloud penetrating radar and image reconstruction rendered hills, plains, valleys, and lakes with crisp clarity, and stimulated reflection enabled accurate color rendering. The surface of Titan transformed into a rugged landscape that resembled an orange-tinted hilly lake-valley reminiscent of something from old Earth.

"Strange how inviting it looks," Helen Stein mused. "If only it wasn't a hundred and sixty below and filled with toxic methane."

An incoming call chimed and Vin announced, "Incoming from Lakeshore, Captain. Would you like to take it on ship-wide?"

"Yes Vin, put it on ship-wide, high encryption. Hello, this is the Vindicator, Captain Caster speaking, who is this?"

"Director Zen, Captain. We see you in orbit on the far side of Titan, is there a problem?"

"No, no problem, Director. What is your status at Lakeshore?"

"We got beat, Captain. Company forces are sealed off two kilometers down, and we can't fly because the Athena is parked in stationary orbit over the site."

"One minute, Director, give us a moment to digest what you've told us." Vin took the hint and muted the channel. "Are we isolated, Vin?"

"The channel is muted, Captain."

Caster looked around the room; the bridge crew was staring at him, waiting for direction. Caster focused on Overine. The man's expression was grave, his long face partially in shadow, the red bridge lights making his sharp features an allegory of conditions on Titan. Overine was fifty standard Earth years old, with previous experience in the corporate navy before immigrating to the Commonwealth. He should have had a ship of his own. That simple fact was a blatant reminder of the risk this crisis represented to the Commonwealth. Overine didn't have a ship because the Commonwealth didn't have enough ships to go around. The Vindicator was a prototype high-tech light cruiser, but it was the only one. Although its sensor and cyber tech were arguably more advanced than the company's, its offensive armaments were not as powerful. The rest of the Commonwealth navy was comprised of Reliant class cruisers that were decidedly older tech, and no match for the company's heavy Nemesis class cruisers.

"Mister Overine, you were in the company navy, any insights as to the capabilities of the Athena?"

Overine looked pained. "Only rumors, Captain. The Athena isn't standard navy, but then I think you already know that. Rumors are that she is a black-ops ship, used for off-the-books missions. From that, I'd guess it would be safe to assume she's very dangerous."

"Well, that's comforting to know," Helen Stein commented. Commander Stein was Vindicator's chief engineer. She was tall and slender, having grown up in low gravity. Caster couldn't see her face since she was standing in front of the projector. Her voice seemed to come from a shadow of her outline in the low orange glow of Titan's holographic image. But he imagined the ironic smirk she often wore.

"Helen, we're going to need a fly-by to try and get a look under the Athena's skirts."

"And how are we going to do that?" Overine asked.

"We have an array of modified QL drones that are going to take a look inside the Athena," Helen said. She had been working with Caster on the tactical simulations. They had devised a plan to stay below Titan's horizon and fly a network of QL drones in orbits that would come over the horizon un-powered and stealth. As they flew around the Athena by maneuvering with cold jets, they would light it up with high-energy muon scans as they passed. The high-intensity entangled muons should penetrate the hull and reveal a detailed picture of the Athena's interior; most importantly, if she was carrying anti-matter. Also, quantum mechanical characteristics of certain materials would reveal the internal temperature of key systems, which would establish a baseline to determine whether they were being powered up for weapons.

After the fly-by, the drones were programmed to transmit results to the Vindicator via stealth repeater, and then fly under the far horizon. Depending on how many of the drones were recovered on the far side of Titan, Caster would have a fair indication as to how good their stealth was. Once the drones scanned the Athena, it would know they were there. If the Athena could get a target lock on the drones and destroy them, Caster would know the company had defeated their best stealth technology.

"Vin, get Zen on the line."

"Yes, Captain, done."

"Director Zen, this is Caster."

"Yes, Captain. Hope you guys have figured something out. We're stuck down here, and I'm pretty sure we're both worried about the time."

"Yes, Director, we see those drive flares too. We're going to try and find out what we're up against. We'll be in touch when we know more. Caster out."

"Let's keep our fingers crossed. If we can recover most of the drones, I'll feel a lot better about this."

"You catch on fast, Mister Overine."

"Vin, release the drones in the preassigned pattern and tell us when information starts coming in from the repeater."

"Yes, Captain, done."

"Also, give us a simulation of what you think is happening given positions and trajectories."

"Yes, Captain, done."

Ten electric blue dots leaving traces in their wake appeared over Titan in the central projector's hemisphere as the moon slowly rotated in sync with the position of the drones. Soon a blue diamond appeared over the far horizon with an annotation in green that read Athena.

Caster gripped the arms of his chair and leaned forward as the drone traces, spreading out like a big blue net, neared the diamond icon of the Athena. Caster glanced around the room; the entire bridge crew was focused on Vin's best guess of what was happening on the other side of the moon. As the drone net flew by the Athena, each of the ten dots representing drones flashed blue-white, indicating the muon pulse, then there appeared broken white lines from each drone to a point above the near horizon, indicating data transmission to the repeater. In the tactical simulation, the drones continued flying toward the far horizon.

"Data coming in, Captain. Image reconstruction in progress," Vin reported.

"Put it up on the screens, Vin."

The blue outlines of large screens appeared on both sides of the projector with annotating bubbles describing various compartments of a wedge-shaped ship in a side cutaway. Helen bore into the blueprints, reflections of the screens danced in her hazel eyes making it look like a window into her thinking.

"Helen?"

"Well, good news and bad news, Captain. Which do you want first?" As she talked, she continued drilling into the diagrams.

"I need some good news."

"As far as I can tell, there's no antimatter. But the bad news is she's flush with nukes, in the ten-kiloton range, I would guess, about ten of them. And the fusion reactors are in the two gigawatt range, big enough for particle beams. The heat signature indicates the reactor output is consistent with the weapons on standby. All-n-all, I'd say we're pretty evenly matched." She turned from the screen and looked at the Captain. "Could have been worse," she commented with a crooked smile.

Caster was hoping for more, but at the same time, he was relieved the news was manageable. He assumed as much in his tactical simulations. "Okay." He glanced at Overine. "So let's see how good our stealth is. Whatever's left of the drones should appear on our scopes in a few minutes."

The man looked worried. His long features were slack, but tension lines around his eyes and forehead left deep dark furrows in the red lights of the bridge. Overine glanced back at the projector as the dots disappeared below the moon's horizon in stop-motion iterative steps. He looked back at the captain and blew out. "Yeah."

"Drone transponders coming in, Captain. I count eight discrete signatures," Vin reported.

A smile slowly morphed on Overine's face as his worry lines smoothed, and his forehead shone bright, accentuating his receding hairline. "Well, what do you know? Those two missing drones are most likely lucky shots using prediction, not tracking. All-in-all, I'd say we're in pretty good shape. So now what, Captain? They know we're here; they haven't moved off station, and Zen still can't fly."

Caster was riddled with anxiety. His next decision would put both the Citadel and his crew at risk. If that wasn't responsibility enough, the Vindicator was the only backstop to an impending war against the Commonwealth. He couldn't blow this. Caster had studied psychology under stress, and he knew he was not immune to tunnel vision, fixating on one course of action only because considering another introduced more uncertainty and uncertainty was singularly responsible for fear. Caster knew all too well that decisions made in fear were those that usually proved most disastrous.

"What do you suggest, Mister Overine?"

"We have two options, Captain. We either move within engagement range, or we stay hidden. If we stay hidden, we cannot protect the airspace we're here to secure. If we engage and an exchange breaks out, and we're damaged in the least, our stealth is gone since a damaged hull reflects."

"And you, Helen?"

"We have to come out of shadow. If we don't, our threat potential in the eyes of the enemy will diminish. They'll take it to mean that after our scan, we consider them the superior force. If that happens, why are we here?"

Caster wanted to put his face in his hands, but he couldn't let the crew know how frightened he was. "Okay, we come out of shadow, but we keep a distance that allows reaction time in case of an immediate attack. We come in partially stealth, just enough so they can see us, but not enough for a target lock."

"I think that's right," Helen said. "And may I offer a suggestion?"

"Please."

"We power up the X-ray laser, full burn. We jettison the heat via IR collimator in a direction they can't see. At the first sign of offensive action, we burn their reactor. I can give Vin the exact point for the hit. That will kill all their energy weapons; we can play it by ear if they fire nukes."

"Hmm, what do you think, Vin?"

"I agree with Commander Stein. I would add that if they fire nukes without a target lock, the most likely outcome is that we lose stealth due to shrapnel debris. So, we must retaliate immediately with nukes, since we will have lost our advantage in a second volley."

Caster sat back and felt the icy calm diffuse through his body. "Okay, we come over the horizon, laser charged, partially stealth. We move into a higher orbit with thirty seconds of survival time given a missile. At the first sign of hostility, we change the skin to full stealth and burn their reactor. We change orbit using cold gas jets, and if they fire a nuke, we have thirty seconds to take them out. That sounds like a plan?" Caster took stock of the bridge crew, stopping at each, and nodding. Everyone reciprocated, they seemed reassured. Apparently, his performance art had worked, whenever in doubt, slow it down.

"Vin, upload the plan into the tactical computer. You fly the ship. Begin on my command." Caster glanced around the bridge. "Everyone ready?" Once they were seated and locked in, Caster said, "Okay, Vin, take us in."

"Yes, Captain, proceeding."

Chapter Seventeen

Titan, Tunnels, 2240 AD

Serena raced down the stairs. When she reached the level where Auger and the others were being held, she stopped. The pull of rushing down to the lower level, to where the thing was, was eclipsed by her memory of what she'd told Nora. If they had been monitored in the interrogation room, her friends were in grave danger. She couldn't leave them in the holding cell. She suppressed the urge to go down to the lower level and edged closer to the door in front of her. She slowly opened it a crack and peered down the hall toward the holding cell. Red lights were flashing, but only one guard remained. Apparently, the other one was looking for her. Since she hadn't seen him on the stairs, he must have gone down to where the thing was. They figured it out; they knew where she was going, and they were waiting for her. She wanted to release her friends, but she felt the urge to go to the thing below. Although she'd been able to suppress the pull, it was still there, gnawing at her. Could she release her friends and still manage to get down to the lower level?

Maybe, if she wounded the soldier and he sounded the alarm, the soldiers guarding the thing would rush up here, clearing a path for her. The timing was razor thin. The squad from down below would be on them almost immediately. She consulted the floor plan. They would come up this stairway; the hostages could run in the opposite direction. She could hide in the room they'd just escaped from and double back. It was a hairpin plan, and she had no time to orchestrate it with the others. She felt herself on the verge of spasms. Something was taking over her body, resisting her attempts to do what she knew had to be done. She felt cold sweat, the paralyzing fear that if she didn't act now, she might not be able to. The pull was strong; she couldn't resist it much longer.

Serena took halting steps, opened the door, and cautiously moved to the middle of the corridor. She had the gun butt tight against her shoulder, aimed at a spot on the soldier's right shoulder where she knew the armor was weakest. The soldier must have noticed the movement and slowly turned toward her, probably not believing his eyes. Her aim followed his shoulder as it rotated into the shot. The muffled spit of her gun echoed down the corridor; before his brain made the connection, she saw him shutter from the impact. He dropped his gun, and his left hand moved to cover his right shoulder as he slumped to the floor. As he did, she was on him in an instant and kicked his gun out of the way before picking it up and slinging it over her shoulder. She bent down, grabbed his gauntleted hand, and brought it up, pressing it against the door panel. He screamed in pain. She ignored him and watched as the door slid open. She pushed the soldier out of the way and saw the stunned expressions on the faces of her friends.

"What are you waiting for?" she growled. "They'll be here any minute."

The squad regarded her in stunned surprise. Then Li-ant said, "You heard the lady, what are you waiting for?"

They sprang up almost at once and rushed the door, Li-ant in the lead. Serena unslung the rifle as she approached and thrust it into the woman's hands. "To the right, Lieutenant, good luck." The woman nodded as she rushed by, turned right, and ran down the hall. The rest of the squad followed, and they were almost out of sight when Serena sensed the elevator arriving from the lower level. In all the commotion, she hadn't noticed that Auger had not fled; he was standing beside her. She turned on him savagely. "What the hell are you still doing here? Why aren't you gone?"

He calmly reached up, swept away the hair plastered to her forehead, and gently felt for a temperature. He removed his hand and showed it to her; it was dripping wet. "You're burning up, what's wrong with you?"

"Shit," she whispered, pivoted flat against the wall next to the door, and pushed him flat against it as well. She heard the scuffing of many boots growing louder, echoing down the hall, and saw shadows in the red strobing lights as figures scrambled by the open door. Then, she sensed somebody stopping in front of the doorway and saw their shadow growing larger as they approached. As soon as the soldier stepped into the room, she clocked him hard on the side of the head with the rifle butt, and before he fell, grabbed him, pulling him over to where they stood. In a quick, efficient motion, she snatched his weapon with one hand and pushed him out of the way with the other. He slid onto the floor face down and didn't move. She pushed his weapon into Auger's hands and unslung her own, not saying a word. There were no more shadows coming. She turned to Auger. "You asshole, I'm going to get you killed. I should have knocked you out back at the tractor, stuffed you in, and sent it far from here." She stood there shaking with anger and felt the tears start streaming down her face. She glared at him through foggy eyes, and to her amazement, he was smiling. "You're crazy," she whispered.

"It's the thing on the bottom level; it's messing with your mind, right? Look at you, you're shaking, you have a temperature. What's it want, do you even know?"

She looked down. "No, I don't know. But, yeah, it's in my head." She looked up at him. "I have to go. I can't help it. I'm sorry." His smile was at once maddening and comforting.

"Well then, let's go," he said.

She nodded, wiped the tears away, turned left, and ran for the staircase. She heard Auger's footfalls behind her. She yanked the door open, and not waiting to find out whether it was clear or not, rushed down two flights of stairs before stopping at a thick, locked, metal door. She turned to Auger. She wasn't sweating or shaking anymore. Her thinking was clear and purposeful.

"Now that you're doing what it wants, you look better," he said.

She reached up, held his large face in both hands, and explored its depth. He was not a pretty man, but he was distinctive. His deep-set blue eyes were clear, and he had a prominent symmetric nose whose nostrils flared slightly over an expressive mouth and a solid chin. *If only he wasn't so pale*, she thought and smiled. She pulled him down and kissed him deeply on the mouth. She held him for longer than was prudent, before pulling back and gazing up at him. She knew this might be the last time she would ever see him. He looked shocked, speechless. "You're the only real friend I've had in a long time," she said. "I'm so sorry you followed me down here."

She concentrated on the door. She felt strong now that she wasn't fighting it, and in return, it seemed to be making her more powerful. She found the door mechanism without much trouble, defeated the encryption, and heard its lock click open. She never looked back. The door slid aside and she stepped in, her rifle at the ready, pointing down at the floor.

She hadn't known what to expect, but this was beyond her wildest dreams. She stood in an enormous room that contained a maze of scientific workstations under a ceiling that must have been fifty meters high. The large space was bathed in bright white light from plasma lamps hanging from a high ceiling in an array that cast few shadows. Men and women in white hazmat suits scurried up and down the various aisles between stations in purposeful postures. None of them seemed to notice her among the throng of activity. She sensed Auger come up behind her. At the far end of the cavern was a massive semi-transparent plastic wall that separated this room from another large space. She could see the distorted image of something large and round on the other side of the hazy plastic.

"What the hell is that?" she heard Auger whisper behind her.

"I know you won't do what I say, but wait here," she ordered.

"Uh-huh," he said and followed her down the central aisle toward the plastic wall. As they made their way to the airlock partitioning the space at the end of the aisle, the hazmat suits stopped and stared. They brushed by, and once at the airlock, Serena clicked it open, pulled it aside, and felt a rush of air streaming in. It was a bio-containment unit kept under negative pressure. Once they were both inside, Auger closed the lock behind him.

Nora stood next to a tall man in an expensive executive suit. A squad of soldiers blocked the way to a large gray sphere, about thirty meters in diameter, which seemed to float a half meter above the ground. Serena wondered whether it was real or some fantastic hologram, but just looking at it induced waves of hot and cold through her. She dropped the rifle, momentarily hypnotized by the thing.

"We've been expecting you," the elegant man said. "Tell your friend to drop the gun; we won't hesitate to shoot him."

Serena snapped out of the daze and looked around; several soldiers had Auger in their sights waiting for the elegant man to give the order to drop him. "Auger, please, do what he says." She found him, her eyes tired and pleading. "Please, Auger." He dropped the rifle. Serena turned to the man and saw him smile triumphantly. She knew guys like this; power and control were everything to them. *Screw it*, she thought; she was beyond that now. It made no difference.

The elegant man approached her. "Be careful, Mr. Adonus, she's dangerous," Nora warned. As Adonus approached, he said, "If she makes an aggressive move, kill her friend." Adonus never took his eyes off her, stopping no more than half a meter in front of her. He looked down at her. He was tall and slim, and well built, with a penetrating air of superiority. "Why are you here, Miss Roe? Or more to the point, how did you know to be here?"

"Please, don't hurt my friend, Mr. Adonus. He doesn't know anything about this." She stood there, submissive, staring back at him. Then after a moment, with lightning speed, Serena pushed Adonus out of the way, his body momentarily blocking the squad from shooting her, and ran as fast as she could toward the sphere.

* * *

Adonus staggered but didn't fall. The girl was stronger than she looked. When she grabbed him, her arm felt like a piece of titanium across his chest. She just brushed him aside, like he was weightless. He quickly regained his footing and heard the muffled squirt of an assault rifle as the girl's friend lurched back, grabbed his side, and fell to one knee. He heard the crackle of what sounded like a hundred electric arcs and looked back at the sphere. The thing was spitting tiny blue sparks across its entire surface and spinning slowly. At the sound of the gun, the girl stopped running, turned, and saw her friend crumple to the ground.

"No, no, no, no..." Adonus heard the girl scream. She looked at him with a penetrating glare, then at Nora. Her eyes were bloodshot and tears were streaming down her cheeks. "You bastards, you fucking bastards," the girl wailed, then started running toward Adonus.

They opened up on her. Adonus heard a crescendo of squirts and saw a volley of tracers flashing toward the girl. In an instant, thousands of blue electric sparks flew off the surface of the sphere and the tracers disappeared in mid-flight. She stopped running and just stared at her fallen friend. More sparks flew off the sphere and Nora's squad jerked and fell to the ground. The girl turned from her fallen friend and stared at Adonus with red bloodshot eyes.

Adonus felt a cold shutter of fear, something he hadn't experienced in a long time. He struggled not to wet himself as she slowly stepped toward him in the blue glow of the huge alien thing slowly spinning behind her. He looked at Nora. She had stopped in mid-stride, apparently paralyzed with fear. Then Serena stopped. Her face lost its murderous scowl, and she blinked a few times like she was trying to remember something. After a moment of confused introspection, she turned and walked toward the sphere. As she did, the sparks died out and it stopped spinning, regaining its gray color as if nothing had happened. Adonus relaxed, more interested than frightened now, curious to see where this was going. Clearly, there was a strange connection between this girl and the alien. This is what he was here to understand. If the cost was a few inconsequential lives, so be it.

* * *

Serena walked over to the sphere, as though in a trance, then stopped at the sound of gunfire, and turned. The scene in front of her unfolded through a hazy fog of unreality, as though in a dream. She was aware of what had happened: Auger being shot, the paralyzing sorrow of seeing him sink to one knee. A chill consumed her. For a moment the siren song of the sphere faded and a blinding rage filled her. She saw the man, the man with the expensive suit, the apparent source of all their suffering, all their dying. How could someone take it upon himself to so indiscriminately impose his will on others with so little concern for them? In that moment, she'd felt the strength coursing through her. All of her enhancements were reactivated and strengthened by an order of magnitude; she could feel it.

Then she focused on the man, and for the first time in her life, she wanted someone dead. Before she knew it, she was running toward him, knowing the soldiers he had brought with him would cut her down, but she didn't care. She visualized tearing him apart, literally. Then as quickly as it had erupted, her murderous rage evaporated, and she found herself just staring at him. He was nothing. He seemed weak and inconsequential. Killing him wouldn't bring Auger back. If truth be told, she was more responsible for Auger's death than this low form of life standing before her. She glanced in the direction of the soldiers she thought should have shot her by now, and they were all lying on the ground, scattered about, as though a strong wind had blown them over. What had happened to them? She didn't know and she didn't care, although a low ebbing guilt gnawed at her from somewhere deep inside. Soon that didn't matter either, and she turned back to the sphere. Looking at it calmed her and made her feel like she used to in the distant past, coming home from school when her father was still alive, and when her mother wasn't always passed out on the sofa, the smell of alcohol thick and sickly sweet enveloping her. Before all that, when walking in the door made her feel safe and secure, and loved. That's how looking at the sphere made her feel, like coming home.

* * *

Adonus watched in fascination as the girl just turned away like someone had flipped a switch. A moment before, he knew she wanted to tear him apart; then, just as quickly, she couldn't care less. She was walking back to the sphere. The thing had stopped sparking and spinning and just hung there inert. This was fascinating, and Adonus couldn't help following her.

"Dr. Adonus, don't," he heard Nora warn. He turned out of reflex. She was standing about ten meters away and to his right. The woman looked dazed, off balance. He glanced to her right and saw her squad lying on the ground, unmoving. He did a mental shrug and turned back in the direction of the girl. She was much more interesting. He felt no fear, just curiosity. If the thing wanted to kill him, it would have already done so. No, this thing didn't care about anything that did not fit into its plans. It was like him, he surmised—not driven by petty human ideas of right and wrong, but by a sense of destiny, a higher design. In that, he felt a kinship with the thing and stopped just a few meters behind the girl, almost giddy to see what would happen next.

She stood in front of the thing for a couple of minutes, still as a statue. Then, she slowly raised her hands, fingers splayed, their shadow on its curved surface making them look menacing. She continued raising her hands high above her head, arms out, as though she wanted to push the thing, and slowly placed her palms against it. For a moment nothing happened. Adonus stared as her hands started to turn blue, the same color as the sparks it had generated earlier. At first, her hands turned a dark blue, almost indistinguishable from her dark skin, but then they became lighter and lighter, almost glowing electric blue. Adonus wanted to reach out and touch her, and unknowingly started to raise his arm until someone grabbed it from behind and pulled it down. He turned. Nora had come up behind him and grabbed his arm before he could touch the girl. She didn't say anything, just slowly shook her head. Adonus lowered his arm, and they both stared at the strange spectacle unfolding before them.

The girl remained that way for a long time, then her hands began to dim their blue glow. When they regained their normal color, her hands slipped from the surface of the sphere and dropped to her side, as though they'd come unglued. She teetered for an instant, then slowly collapsed to the ground and lay still as if she were sleeping. Adonus walked over, stood over her, and looked down, confused. He heard stirring behind him and turned. The soldiers that he thought were dead were moving around, trying to stand up. He looked at Nora and saw the tension in her eyes relax. She appeared to mouth some words, but nothing came out. Then she turned and hurried over to her men, helping them up.

Adonus walked over to Nora. "It didn't kill them," Adonus remarked, puzzled.

Nora stood next to him after helping her men and calling for medics. "It doesn't seem to be picking sides," she said. "It just doesn't want us to hurt Serena."

"Serena?"

"Yes, Serena, that's her name."

"Why, why is she important? She's a miner, right?"

"Yes, she is a miner now, but she used to be a soldier. A very good soldier," Nora said.

"If she was such a good soldier, why is she a miner now?"

"Because she had a problem killing people when ordered to do so," Nora said.

Adonus stared at her for a moment, not understanding any of this. "None of this makes any sense. The girl's a nobody, a wash-out. This alien thing doesn't seem to have anything to do with her but immobilizes a squad of company security so it can put her in a coma. What does that mean?"

"I don't know. But I know that thing's dangerous and unpre-dictable."

Adonus had brought doctor Orzan down from the Athena, which now appeared an inspired move. He ordered Orzan to take the girl to the medical bay and examine her thoroughly, see what the thing had done to her. Maybe they couldn't move the sphere, but they could move the girl. If some of its secrets were some-how in the girl, then maybe it would follow her. Maybe it would follow her all the way back to Olympus. Adonus began to brigh-ten. Maybe they could gain possession of the sphere and avoid an all-out war. That would buy him time, time to understand the artifact and use its secrets, but at a time of his choosing. What seemed like a long, protracted battle and policing action might turn out to be short and profitable for him. Adonus smiled. Sometimes it was better to be lucky, something he'd always been.

Chapter Eighteen

Titan, Citadel, 2240 AD

Zen looked out the big window of his fourteenth-floor office in the direction of the lake. It annoyed him that the view was so peaceful. He saw a dark band of irregular mountains under a sedate light yellow sky punctuated by small clouds that were dark on the bottom and brilliant on top, reflecting the dim sun at midday. You couldn't tell that under that innocent visage lay the dead bodies of his soldiers. He hadn't heard anything from Smith about Li-ant. And he hadn't heard from Captain Caster aboard Vindicator as to whether they could fly or not. He noticed he was nervously rubbing his hands together because they were starting to hurt. He was anxious that every passing hour would prove more grave for Li-ant and her squad. He decided to call Governor Tallus on tight beam and try to get a better grasp of the big picture to take his mind off the more immediate issues he could do nothing about.

Tallus's bust floated in an electric blue frame suspended in the air in front of his desk. For all that was happening, the man looked calm, in control. His strong features were made softer by his deep-set dark eyes that betrayed no worry lines. His high collar tunic appeared freshly pressed, and his woolly hair was perfectly cut, shining ivory in the camera lights.

"Director Zen, how can I be of service?"

Zen chuckled. "Well, Governor, we're in a spot down here. We haven't heard from Vindicator, and we need to fly out to the site. We have a squad down there that may not survive much longer. I know you have concerns of your own, but I thought you might have some information that could be of use."

"Concerns of my own?" It was the Governor's turn to laugh. "Yes, well, you could say that." Tallus took a moment, then leaned forward into the camera. He cut an imposing figure.

"As you may know, Director, there is a fleet of three Nemesis class cruisers coming our way, burning hard from Olympus. They might be carrying anti-matter missiles. We can't let them get into firing range of Saturn. Our cities are not defensible against such an attack. Since they are floating just above the ammonia clouds, and are a hundred square miles in area, they are sitting targets. Each city is home to fifty thousand people. That means we have to engage the enemy at least a million kilometers out, which gives our X-ray laser platforms a chance to defend our cities. We have six Reliant class cruisers burning equally hard to meet them in space, kind of a line in the sand. If hostilities ensue, the Reliants will target the enemy, and our X-ray laser platforms will attempt to take them out. If we engage beyond the range of our platforms, the Reliants have to keep them from advancing any further. Although the Nemesis are newer, we out number them two to one."

Zen was stunned. All of a sudden, the game had gotten a lot bigger than he ever imagined. He noticed his panic reflected in Tallus's expression of worry. "Are X-ray lasers effective at that range? Why not engage with the cruisers as well?"

Tallus regained his composure. "I'm sorry, Director. I didn't mean to burden you since you have concerns of your own. To answer your original question, Vindicator is moving into position as we speak. When they achieve a tactical orbit, they will be in a position to defend you. It shouldn't be much longer."

Zen had barely heard him, his mind was racing. All of a sudden, he realized this could be the end of the Commonwealth. "Governor, I have family in Aurora, can we get through this?"

Tallus exhaled; he said more than he'd intended. But now he had an obligation to fully explain. He sat back, his hands folded in front of him; an even look commandeered his authoritative features.

"It's not clear the company will push it that far. We'll give fair notice that we will not let them enter Saturn space. And to answer your questions, in a one-on-one engagement, the Reliants are no match for Nemesis cruisers; we know that, and they know that. But the Reliants have been upgraded with excellent remote sensing and targeting, better than what the company has; the company knows that too, especially when they get word from the Athena that Vindicator can see them at full stealth." Tallus held Zen in a gaze that solicited rapt attention. "We have ten X-ray laser platforms, each powered by a fifty-megaton thermonuclear device. The lasers are tightly collimated and should still be effective at a hundred million kilometers. If we can target the Nemesis cruisers, we can destroy or cripple them; there's no dodging that bullet. At that point, they will be open to a counterattack. Although we don't have the anti-matter capabilities of the Company, we do have anti-matter, and we have better stealth. I'm going to be calling Anders and informing him of these facts. I'm hoping they won't push it all the way."

Zen stared at Tallus. "What could they have possibly found out there that could prompt a showdown like this? It doesn't make any sense. It can't be anything to do with a mineral find; so what could it be?"

"Well, whatever it is, they've tipped their hand. They've let us know how important they think it is. If they back down, they know we'll be all over it. That's what makes this so dangerous. So along with ultimatums, we're going to have to come up with some plan to share whatever it is. That's why it's so important to talk to Anders before our forces meet."

* * *

Right after Zen got off the link with Tallus, he heard from Captain Caster. The Vindicator was in position and the airspace above Lakeshore was covered. Caster stressed he would not fire on the Athena until they made a hostile move, which meant that the first transports could be shot down. Zen had to weigh this against the time factor of getting to Lakeshore and attempting a rescue of Li-ant and her squad. He could send an autopiloted ship with supplies to test the safety of flying to Lakeshore but decided to go there in earnest instead. There would be two ships, one carrying a squad with equipment to the cooling tunnel under the assumption that the elevator shaft could be cleared, and another ship to the captured site to act as a command post for Smith. That ship would also carry a squad to replace the soldiers killed in the assault.

They came in low and slow over the lake to hide their thermals. The lead ship peeled off to land at a spot close to the submerged entrance of the cooling tunnel, and the other ship rose above the mountains to the site. Zen sat in his office at the Citadel coordinating with the two airships. It was tense. He knew that at any moment the tenuous calm could suddenly escalate. He could visualize a missile streaking down from orbit on a yellow-black con trail and one of the airships vaporizing into a fireball, its errant pieces arcing into the lake, raising plumes of gas. He wiped the sweat from his forehead and felt a drop leave the tip of his nose, falling to his desk.

"We're on the shore, Director. Engines off, proceeding as planned. Ship one out."

Then a few minutes later, "Ship two, touch down at site."

Zen leaned back in his chair. Apparently, Adonus wasn't ready to push it all the way, not just yet. That meant he had a plan, and he needed time, which raised some interesting possibilities. Adonus's backup was a couple of weeks away, the face-off coming even sooner according to Tallus's plan. Olympus must have informed Adonus that a fleet of Reliants were burning hard toward the company cruisers. So whatever Adonus's plan, it could mean he might not intend to hold the site, but somehow get to the Athena with whatever they found. Maybe Adonus had discovered a way around the impasse that prompted this confrontation. Zen had a lot to think about.

It wasn't long before Smith called, something Zen was expecting. "Got the reinforcements, boss, thanks. So it looks like the bad guys aren't bold enough to shoot down our shuttles. I might know why."

This got Zen's attention; he sat forward. "Why's that?"

"We put a seismometer down; thought we might hear something. You know, some signal from the squad. We heard this instead." Smith switched to a recording. Zen heard what sounded like white noise but with a bias toward higher frequency.

"Is that digging?"

"Yeah, we're pretty sure that's the sound of an arc digger, and it's been constant since we started listening."

"How long has that been?"

"About half a day, and there's something else."

"What?"

"It's getting louder."

"That means their digging toward the surface."

"It's better than that," Smith offered. "When we determined they were digging, and there was a trend as to how the signal was getting louder, we sent some drones out with seismometers. They laid them in a circular pattern around the site, networked them together, and fed the signals into the com AI."

"And?" Zen was hooked. Smith wouldn't be drawing this out if the story didn't have a happy ending.

"And they're digging on an upward diagonal to the surface. We estimate they should break ground somewhere just outside the rim mountains to the north. I'm sending the estimated coordinates."

"Got any idea how close they are to breaking ground?"

"About a day. And boss, the second squad is in place; we'll call back as soon as we know more."

Zen hung up the call, then called Captain Caster and informed him as to what they thought Adonus was doing and how long it would take.

"So you think Athena will launch a drop-ship to pick them up in about a day?"

"Yes, Captain, that seems like the most likely scenario."

"That begs the question, Director; what do you expect us to do? Our mission, at the moment, is to keep the airspace clear above the site; it doesn't include firing on a company shuttle not engaged in hostilities."

"We think they're trying to remove something from the site, Captain. We're not sure what it is. Whatever they're trying to remove has cost the lives of soldiers on both sides and threatened all-out war. So, we're not sure whether to let them remove it or to demand to inspect it first."

"That kind of decision is above my pay grade, Director. You have to talk to Aurora; we'll stand by for orders."

"Just wanted to make sure you understood the situation, Captain."

"Appreciate that, Director. We'll be waiting for further instructions. Caster out."

* * *

Li-ant, and what was left of her squad, retreated to the elevator Auger told her about before escaping the holding cell. Even though Auger and the girl, Serena, had been captured there, Li-ant thought the cooling pond elevator was probably their best bet. The company goons might not have had time to blow the elevator in the middle of whatever emergency Serena had caused. And that was probably the biggest mystery of all. How had a young girl, a miner, caused all this? Li-ant had a trained squad of the Citadel's best soldiers, heavily armed, and they were immediately neutralized after meticulously planning this assault for a day. Somehow these two miners, initially unarmed, had caused chaos down here and freed them in the process. Something was terribly wrong. But the thing that weighed on Li-ant the most was that they had failed in their mission. She still had no idea what the company was hiding down here.

There was an airlock between where they were hunkered down and the elevator. The elevator and the tunnel above, which led to the cooling pond, were in Titan's atmosphere, poisonous without environment suits, and they didn't have suits. She could only get a look at the elevator through the small window on this side of the airlock. Peering through the window, the elevator door was blasted off and there was a pile of debris in front of it—ice from the look of it. So Corporates had blown it, but there was no telling how bad it was. They had been here for a couple of hours, and they had one rifle between four soldiers, not including herself. When she examined the red numbers on the ammo clip, it was half empty. If something didn't happen soon, she would have to reassess their strategy. They had no food and hadn't eaten in almost two days, but more importantly, they had no water. The tunnels down here were cold and dry and seemed to suck the water right out of your mouth. As she thought about it, she absently rubbed her chapped lips with what felt like a swollen tongue and exhaled.

"Hey, did you hear that?"

"Hear what?" Li-ant asked. She sat up, then got to her feet, fighting a sharp pain in her lower back. She'd been sitting against the cold airlock door for hours. She put both hands on the lip of the airlock window; the cold metal stung her fingers. The glass was frosted, and the view of the elevator was blurry. She strained to see, to take in every detail.

"What do you see?" one of the men asked. Li-ant ignored him and focused on the door. She was staring so hard that her eyes were beginning to tear. Then she saw it, a puff of vapor and some ice began to drift off the debris pile at the very top of the elevator door. And there was a distinctive hiss. It was faint, but it was there. She looked down at the soldier who had asked the question and said, "I think there's someone coming down the shaft."

The hiss got louder; it was unmistakable now. They gathered around the window, faces pressed together, and watched torrents of ice go flying off the top of the elevator door in a mixture of dust and vapor. Soon there was an incandescent light throbbing at the top of the door, and they had to turn away. Bright beams of light streaked through the window and turned the corridor into a black-and-white strobing rave, forcing them to shield their eyes. Then, all of a sudden, it was over. After the spots cleared from her eyes, Li-ant watched in amazement as a cable dropped into sight from above. It took about a half hour for a group of security soldiers from the Citadel to drop down cables, which had to be more than two kilometers long. The first to come down began erecting a temporary airlock door so they could come into the corridor without flooding it with poisonous methane. Once the outer door was sealed to the wall with a silicon adhesive, the squad gathered in the makeshift anti-room, purged the methane, filled it with air, and opened the airlock to the corridor.

When everyone was inside the corridor, Li-ant and her squad were given water. She took small swallows, trying hard not to choke. The first sips hurt going down, but she felt her throat slowly un-constricting. They passed the water around a few times; the last time she got it, it felt cool and fortifying. After a few minutes, she stopped feeling dizzy and her vision cleared.

The soldiers formed in front of her beleaguered squad, taking them away from the airlock, to a place that was far from where Li-ant thought most of the Corporates had gone. Once they found a defensible position, Li-ant and her squad were given food and resupplied with armor and weapons.

"Sergeant, why didn't we go back to the surface?" Li-ant had expected an extraction, not a counter-response. She wasn't sure her squad was up to it; and since they'd lost the assumed advantage of surprise, they were outnumbered and probably out-gunned.

"Some new developments," the Sergeant informed. "We think the Corporates are trying to get back to orbit. They're digging a tunnel to the surface north of here. We'll be at their backs; and since they know getting into a protracted firefight will slow them down, we might have a chance to find out what's going on without a full-on confrontation. Can you tell us anything that can help us do that?"

"I have a floor plan of this base. Sending it right now."

The newcomers took a moment to review what they'd just received in their Aug-nets.

"You see that large space on the bottom level to the north?"

"You mean the one with no annotation?" the Sergeant asked.

"That very one. We think that's where the thing is, whatever it is. And since it's in the most northern corner of the base, it's a pretty good bet that's where the tunnel is too."

"One more thing, Sergeant, there were two miners with us. One of them, a woman named Serena, was taken away, but somehow escaped and freed us. Once we got to the airlock, we noticed they were missing."

"Okay." The Sergeant looked confused. "Why do you think that's important? Maybe they just got lost in the scramble."

"I don't think so. I don't know why, but I think Serena has something to do with all this."

"You mean she's an infiltrator?"

Li-ant almost laughed out loud. "No, nothing like that, nothing sinister. To be perfectly honest, I don't know what the connection is, but I think it's important. I'm sending a picture of both of them. When we encounter the Corporates, don't shoot them. We need to get them back."

Li-ant could tell the Sergeant was thinking she wasn't quite right, might be delusional. If she was in his place, she might think the same. "You hear me, Sergeant?"

"Yes, ma'am, loud and clear."

They pushed to the stairway door in staggered defensive formation, one group hop-scotching the group in front and hugging the walls. Once they got to the staircase, and opened the door, they encountered an array of assault weapons fire peppering the door frame. They pulled back.

"Well, so much for surprise," Li-ant said.

The Sergeant pulled a flash-bang grenade from his belt, while another soldier pulled a gas grenade from hers. A third soldier yanked the door open, and both grenades were lobbed through the door. Li-ant heard them clanking down the stairs over a volley of gunfire before the door was slammed shut. Immediately, a loud bang shook the door as everyone expressed the environment helmets from suit wedges attached to their collars. They all went to infrared vision, yanked the door open again, and entered the gas-filled staircase in staggered defensive advance.

Chapter Nineteen

Drill Site, Titan, 2240 AD

Adonus looked down at the girl. She had been brought to a hastily prepared examination room. They wanted to determine why the girl seemed to have abilities that couldn't be explained by the reactivation of her security enhancements. From what he'd seen in the large chamber, it was clear she had gotten something from the sphere through her hands when she touched it. Adonus had almost touched it too. If it had reacted the same way, then that meant the thing had no preference for the girl. She had just been at the right place at the right time, nothing more. On second thought, he might be in a coma right now. As he continued looking at her, she appeared so unremarkable that her selective involvement with the sphere seemed even more improbable.

Orzan was standing next to Adonus. "Should I proceed, Dr. Adonus?"

Adonus absently stepped back. "Yes, let's get a look inside."

They both retreated behind a lead-glass panel, and Orzan initialized a multi-arm robot that hung above the girl who lay on an examination table. The black carbon-fiber machine slid smoothly on a magnetic interlock hidden in the drop ceiling until it was positioned over the girl, its eight arms folded in a way that reminded Adonus of a large spider.

"First, let's get a look at any out-of-the-ordinary hard internal structures that might be present." The robot extended an X-ray projector after which they heard a low hum. The display in the center console, which was supported by a single strut anchored to the floor and looked like a wedge pressed against glass, flashed white, then began scanning down an overview of the girl's outline. The resultant image showed no features. The girl's outline was filled in with an even gray color, but there were no bones, organs, or the internal fibrous carbon struts that had been grown inside her body to harden it, an enhancement many black-ops security officers had.

"Is this thing broken?" Adonus sneered.

Orzan quickly surveyed a matrix of readouts on an adjacent display. "Everything looks nominal." He nervously looked at Adonus.

Adonus regarded the man with disgust. This was the best they had? If so, no wonder the operation was so screwed up. "Either the machine's broken, or the X-rays are being reflected. If they were absorbed, the image would be colorless, wouldn't it, Dr. Orzan?" Adonus accentuated the word *Doctor*, making sure the man understood his performance was sub-par. "So, which is it?" Adonus saw beads of sweat form on the shorter man's bulbous forehead, and his color turned from a sickly pale to a damp pink. He rudely pushed the man out of the way and started manipulating the controls.

Orzan watched as Adonus upped the X-ray intensity to a level he regarded as unsafe. The man was impatient and reckless, and Orzan secretly despised him, but Orzan was a coward. He knew it and despised himself for letting someone like this carelessly harm the girl. As Adonus initiated the scan, the hum was noticeably louder. The image repainted on the screen and the result was the same.

"Shit," Adonus hissed under his breath, then he looked at Orzan with a seething rage.

"Let's take a look with MRI," Orzan suggested. "Since the probe is RF, perhaps it will penetrate." Adonus slowly stepped aside and Orzan gingerly resumed the controls. The robot retracted the X-ray and unfolded a crescent magnetic projector around the girl. The thing lowered until a cylindrical strip covered the girl's head. When Orzan activated the scan, it slowly slid across her body from head to toe. A moment later, a series of lateral sections appeared on the display in rows from left to right, all the same gray color, with no details of the girl's insides visible.

Adonus was silent a moment, then said, "Let's do it the old fashioned way," and smiled cruelly. Orzan exhaled and retracted the MRI.

"Perhaps we should start at the lower arm, near a hand, since this is close to where the activity was seen?" Adonus remained silent, so Orzan extended a robot arm that had a gleaming metallic blade at its tip. They watched the display as it focused on the arm descending just above the girl's left wrist, then stopped when the blade was suspended millimeters above her skin. Orzan looked at Adonus, who gave a curt nod. Orzan initiated the incision, and the scalpel seemed to cut into the girl's arm, but when the suction probe registered no fluid, it was clear something was wrong. Orzan raised the blade so that the camera could inspect it. The cutting edge was gone, sliced off with uncanny precision.

"What the hell," Adonus whispered, then hurried into the room where the girl lay unconscious. Orzan followed. Adonus inspected the blade; sure enough it was missing. He looked at Orzan, who stood behind him, then back at the scalpel. "What does this mean?" he stammered.

So now you want my opinion, you worthless shit, Orzan thought. But he said, "Remember when we saw that trail of debris under the sphere and concluded they were the remains of nanites?" Adonus nodded slowly. Orzan continued. "Perhaps what we saw when the girl's hands turned blue was a massive transfer of nanites into the girl. That might explain why we can't penetrate her body with electromagnetism."

"And the scalpel?" Adonus asked.

"Maybe her skin is saturated with them. When we cut into it, they dissolve the blade and repair the cut almost instantaneously."

"That's fantastic," Adonus uttered. "How's this possible?"

"It's an order of technology above anything we can do," Orzan explained.

Adonus's mind was racing. The possibilities were at once awe-inspiring and frightening. "When she wakes up, can we stop her?"

Orzan looked at him with surprise. "What do you mean? I don't understand."

"You fool," Adonus blurted. "Can we contain her, or can she just put her hands on a bar or wall and dissolve it? If we shoot her, can she repair herself faster than we can kill her?"

Orzan was torn. He thought he knew what to do, but the girl could be killed accidentally or intentionally without her posing any danger. And if that control was at Adonus's discretion, her future was highly uncertain. But he had to say something. Looking at the man's mad expression, he said, "Wrapping her in a conductive netting and hooking her up to a high voltage source might burn the nanites. We saw from the black debris under the sphere that they can be deactivated, destroyed." He watched as Adonus's expression morphed from a manic confusion to a stony calm. The man had regained control, and that's what he was about. With the loss of control, he reverted to the cowardly sociopath he truly was.

"I just want to add that if we apply high voltage to the netting, we could kill the girl," Orzan said. But Adonus was already walking away. "Just do it," he called out, not looking back before leaving the room.

When Adonus returned to his makeshift office just outside the large room where the sphere hovered like a sentinel from a different time and space, he encountered Colonel Assisi, quickly walking toward him. He could tell from her hard expression that it was urgent.

"Yes, Colonel; what is it?"

She stopped a half meter in front of Adonus, who was standing just outside the door to his office. "A squad of Citadel security has penetrated into the base; they're currently in the stairwell leading to this level."

"Can you hold them off for an hour?"

Nora was amazed at how calmly Adonus was taking the news. "Yes, we can hold them. It's a small force, and they're confined to a cramped space and can't maneuver."

Adonus smiled. "Good, Colonel. Buy me an hour; that's all we'll need."

He left Nora standing in the corridor in front of his closed door, seeming a little stunned. A moment later, she walked away giving explicit instructions to her squad over Aug-net as to how to contain the insurgents.

Adonus closed the door behind him just in time to get a ping from Orzan. He sat at his desk and opened the channel on com, no video.

"Yes, Adonus here."

Orzan informed him the girl had been secured in a conductive netting, and a control system was programmed to apply a constant non-lethal voltage at a frequency that would only penetrate the upper portion of her skin; the assumption being the high voltage should inhibit the nanites from affecting anything coming in contact with her. Adonus considered this and smiled. Maybe Orzan wasn't the idiot he appeared to be.

"Good. Put her on an automated cart; we're going to evacuate the base immediately."

Before Orzan could respond, Adonus cut the channel. Then he got in touch with Nora and had her organize a phased retreat while automated guns held the Citadel forces at bay. The entire staff was to meet at the north tunnel entrance immediately. After receiving an acknowledgment ping, Adonus cut the channel and started to gather up all his important files, scuttling the rest. He walked over to a closet where he kept a modified environment suit and quickly donned it. Stuffing all his critical items into a small pouch at his belt, he took a final look at his office, then quickly left, heading for the north tunnel on the other side of the artifact room.

Chapter Twenty

Titan, Stairwell under Lakeshore Site, 2240 AD

Li-ant was plastered against the wall beside the stairwell door on the lowest level of the site and had been there for over twenty minutes. They couldn't get past the automated Gatling guns covering the exit. The guns showered the door with depleted uranium rounds every time an attempt was made to take them out with a grenade. The stairwell was clouded with dust ablated from the walls under the onslaught. Their strategy at this point was to continue baiting the sensors until the damn things ran out of bullets. The only thing saving them so far was that the stairwell was supported by a steel superstructure that the rounds weren't able to penetrate. This was clearly a delaying tactic, but unfortunately, it was working. The soldiers on either side of the metal door frame kept swinging rifle barrels across the open door, and the guns kept firing. Apparently, the control systems weren't good enough to distinguish a target very well. No doubt this thing had been quickly improvised.

Then finally she heard it. The guns whirred, their barrels spinning, but no bullets; they were empty. The squad emerged from the stairwell into a foyer with several corridors branching off in all directions. Consulting the floor plan, they headed for the large room to the north and advanced through what was now an empty section of the base.

The Sergeant pulled up alongside Li-ant. "Looks like they're gone."

"Yes, Sergeant. That thing back there, the guns, just a stalling tactic. I'm pretty sure the Director was right; they're abandoning the base."

"So, you think they took whatever it is they found?"

Li-ant regarded the Sergeant; she saw the man had soft features through his faceplate. His gruff voice belied a young, cultured appearance. "Makes no sense, Sergeant. I agree. But let's see what's behind the door. Maybe they left enough that we can piece it together." The Sergeant nodded and began to go check the large door at the end of the corridor as Li-ant grabbed his forearm.

"Ma'am?" the Sergeant asked.

"Thanks for saving our asses back there. We couldn't have lasted much longer. Now instead of a crushing defeat, we might actually figure out what's going on."

She watched the corners of the Sergeant's mouth rise in response. "We're here to serve, Ma'am." She chuckled and followed him to the door. It looked to be made of thick metal, the frame having rivets to pylons probably sunk deep into the ice. A keypad was bolted to the metal door so it couldn't be dug out of the softer wall.

"Damn," one of the soldiers said, running a gloved finger around the pad. "They really don't want us in there." He took a block of something from his belt, peeled off a wrapping, and molded the plastic explosive around the pad. Then he took out another block of something and peeled away the wrapping to reveal something similar to the first, but this one was black, not gray. He molded it over the first. They comprised two layers of a shaped charge, the top layer hardening and anchoring to the surface. The assembly was set off by a control system that ignited it in a focused shockwave, the force designed to cut anything under the plastic. Once the soldier was satisfied with his handiwork, he retreated down the hall and around the corner, where the rest of the squad waited.

He looked up at Li-ant. "Ma'am?" She nodded. The soldier pressed a button on a remote control he held in his hand, and instantly, Li-ant saw a flash of light on the wall facing the door, followed by a thick cloud of ice dust rushing from the corridor in a concussive wave that shook the walls. Once the debris cleared, Li-ant turned the corner and walked through a cloud of smoke toward the metal door, that through the haze, looked askew on its hinges. When she stopped a few meters away, a couple of soldiers walked past her and pried the door open with a breaker bar. They stepped inside, rifles at the ready. Moments later, she heard, "Clear," over com and entered. The power was still on, and the room was lit. She stood staring out at an immense space housing what looked like a well-equipped lab, terminated a hundred meters away by a large semi-transparent plastic screen that must have stretched a hundred meters to a high ceiling. But the most eye-catching item in the vast panorama was the shadowed outline of something big and round on the other side of the partition.

"This is a negative containment space."

Li-ant noticed that the Sergeant had come up beside her. "What?"

"This is a negative containment space," the Sergeant repeated. "See the smoke being sucked into the room? Whatever that is behind the partition, they wanted to keep it biologically isolated."

Li-ant turned and stared at the young man. "I'm a scientist, Ma'am, as well as a soldier. The Director thought you might need someone to appraise whatever we found."

"I'm sorry, Sergeant. I don't think I got your name."

"Martinson, Ma'am. I'm a physicist."

"Huh," Li-ant said. "Well, Martinson, let's see what all the fuss is about."

They walked through the maze of partitions and workstations, down a center aisle to a folded cut in the plastic. Martinson pulled the magnetic fold aside and Li-ant stepped through, followed by the squad, which spread out to the left and right.

"What in Saturn's rings is that?" Li-ant whispered. A gigantic gray sphere eclipsed almost the entire space.

"That's not as interesting as the fact that it seems to be floating," Martinson observed.

Li-ant opened the com. The Sergeant had briefed her that they'd placed repeaters to the surface. "Smith?"

"Yes Ma'am, you're coming in five on five."

"Have you been following this?"

"On the edge of my seat."

"Good, I want you to feed this audio-video back to the Citadel, back to Zen. Also, it might be a good idea to feed this back to Saturn. We have a situation here, and seeing is believing."

"Yeah, I see what you mean, establishing the link now."

Li-ant saw the acknowledgment ping in her Aug-net. "Zen, are you there?"

"What the hell is that?" Zen exclaimed.

Martinson was already crouched on his haunches, looking under the sphere where it floated in mid-air. Li-ant watched as he swept his hand under the thing, moving it back and forth, as though looking for a support he knew wasn't there. He turned his head, still stooped, and looked back at Li-ant, then at the rest of the squad, and smiled like a kid on Christmas morning. "It's really floating," he declared in astonishment.

Li-ant walked over and touched the thing, sweeping an open palm slowly across its surface. It was smooth, not pitted, as one would expect of something that had been traveling in space for a long time. "Seems new," she said absently. "But it gives me a sense of age, deep age. I can't explain the feeling." She was looking down at Martinson. His mouth was open, and his eyes wide in a way that conveyed awe.

"This thing wasn't built by people," he stammered. "How do you feel?" he asked Li-ant. "How do you feel right now?"

"What? What do mean?"

"A little dizzy, disoriented, like you're falling?"

Li-ant blinked. "Yes. Now that you mention it, I do."

"This thing is changing the local gravity. Notice there's no loose ice dust underneath it like in the rest of this place. It all floated away."

"I've got the Vindicator on the link," Zen said. "Any impressions about what you're seeing, Captain?"

Then Li-ant heard another voice. "Do you mind if I make a comment, Captain?"

"Who is that, Captain?" Zen asked.

"Uh, it's the ship, we call it Vin."

There was dead silence for a few seconds, then Zen asked, "The ship? You mean the ship AI?"

"We prefer to call Vin an SS, Sentient System. It's the newest thing in cybernetics. There's some debate as to whether it's conscious or not in the popular sense, but in my opinion, having worked with it awhile, I think it is."

There was another silence, then Zen continued. "And what do you think, uh...Vin can offer us?"

"This is Commander Helen Stein; I'm the ship's chief engineer, Director. Aside from running most of the ship, Vin is a vast storehouse of knowledge, which I believe it understands and can use to assert intuitive conclusions. Vin also has access to a quantum core accelerator. If you want an informed, objective assessment of this thing, Vin's your woman."

Zen could hear Caster chuckling in the background. "Okay, Vin, what do you think?"

"I think Dr. Martinson is right; the sphere has changed the local gravity in such a way as to make itself buoyant in Titan's gravity field. I also think Deputy Director, Li-ant has a very interesting observation. We must assume this is an alien artifact, and that it probably didn't come from anywhere in the Sol system. If that's true, it must be capable of relativistic speeds, which would imply a scorched surface due to a constant wind of relativistic particles. The fact that it's smooth and unblemished indicates it can somehow reconstitute itself, or that it was manufactured here in the Sol system by some other entity in a Von Neumann sense."

There was a long silence, after which Vin said, "May I continue?"

"Please do," Zen said. He was mesmerized. The situation had just jumped off the scale of anything he had imagined prior to seeing this alien thing floating in front of his desk, and being explained by a machine intelligence. He knew as they learned more about what the company had found, the group that found it was trying to get off-moon. That begged another question, which was eating at him because soon, they would be at the surface, and he had a decision to make.

"If we go back to the fact that the object is altering the local gravity, that implies something else."

"Yeah," Martinson interrupted. "That it's impossible."

"That's right," Vin continued. "As far as we know, it can't be done. It's not only beyond our technology, it's beyond any physical theory we have."

"Why is that?" Helen asked. "We have a theory of gravity, and we've speculated about being able to create negative gravity in a Casmir sense, or create gravity waves by Gertsenshtein resonances."

"That's true, Commander, but there are a couple of problems. First, we've never observed, and have no real theory of exotic matter. By this, I mean matter that affects space in a way that changes its energy density to exert negative pressure. To force space to do that without exotic matter would require energy much greater than the total output of the Sun, but the artifact is not hot. It's not even warm. I see no anomalies in IR, and yet it is floating. Likewise, the Gertsenshtein effect is too small to be practical as far as we know and requires magnetic fields much stronger than we can produce, yet there is no indication of ultra-strong magnetic fields around the sphere. I just want to emphasize that this sphere represents a physical understanding orders of magnitude beyond ours."

"This is Governor Tallus. Thank you, Vin, for your interesting observations, as well as Dr. Martinson and Deputy Director Li-ant. It is now clear why the company chose to press this confrontation. If they had sole access to this technology, they could control the Sol system. But they're leaving, and the sphere is still here. So why aren't they holding the base? They have powerful reinforcements coming, why not stay and prepare the sphere for transport back to Olympus?"

"Because they can't move it," Zen declared. "At first they thought they could, that's why the fake dog and pony show about testing digging equipment."

"That's right," Martinson agreed. "Remember, this thing controls the local gravity. If it wants to anchor itself here, it could form a gravitational potential that is insurmountable. Do you agree, Vin?"

"Yes, I do, Dr. Martinson."

"But they're leaving," Zen offered. "Why? It only makes sense if they have a piece of it, enough to give them the edge they're looking for. Or, if they can't have it, neither can we."

"What does that mean?" Tallus asked. "Neither can we?"

"That means there are three corporate heavy cruisers heading our way. They're probably loaded with anti-matter weapons.

Weapons we don't have because the company is closer to the Sun whose energy is required to manufacture anti-matter at scale. These weapons are capable of disintegrating a good portion of Titan. They can just take the alien off the chess board and simultaneously declare the Commonwealth dissolved. Let's face it, this confrontation was going to happen sooner or later. The company has been undergoing a mass exodus and brain-drain to the Commonwealth for decades now. They had to make a stand at some point, and I fear this is that point."

"What do you suggest, Director?" Tallus asked. The man sounded shaken. Apparently, he had refused to accept the obvious, since that version of the future was inconsistent with the hopes of everyone in the Commonwealth. The dream of starting over without the boot of the company on their necks was slowly disappearing like so much smoke.

Zen exhaled and sat back. Saying it out loud cleared his mind, enabling him to make a decision he was hoping not to make. "I'm going to instruct our two squads at the site under the command of Captain Smith to deploy to the location where we think Adonus and his staff are evacuating. We believe they'll try to catch a shuttle to the Athena. Before they leave, we will demand an inspection of what they're taking with them."

"Won't that escalate the situation to a point of no return?" Tallus asked, his voice shaking and tired.

"What choice do we have, Governor? If we let them go with a piece of this thing, we'll be living under the sword of Damocles until they return with overwhelming power. If they don't have anything of consequence, and they force an engagement in deep space, they won't have the advantage they're looking for. They might even lose a significant amount of anti-matter. That could persuade them to let the inspection happen, and then we're back to where we started."

"What do you want us to do, Governor?" Caster asked. "Right now, our orders are to keep the air-space above the site accessible to the Citadel. If we decide on Director Zen's strategy, we'll be required to be preemptive. What do we do when the Athena launches a shuttle and refuses inspection, do we let it take off?"

There was a long silence, after which Tallus said, "I have to confer with the senate and board of secretaries. We'll inform all parties of our decision before Adonus reaches the surface. That means we have sixteen standard Earth hours. Is that right, Director?"

"That's right."

"Okay, ladies and gentlemen, we'll talk soon. Tallus out."

Chapter Twenty-One

Titan, Mountains other side of Lakeshore Site, 2240 AD

Smith listened to the discussion between Zen and Tallus. Even before the conference call, he'd been ordered by Zen to the other side of the northern range. He packed a squad into the jump-ship and headed for the site where acoustic imaging was predicting Adonus would surface. And he left a squad at the site to maintain their claim and to monitor the acoustic imaging equipment. Scanning the latest update in his Aug-net, Smith determined the Corporates were making steady progress to the coordinates where they were expected to break ground. Apparently, they had sped up their timetable and would emerge in about ten hours. Smith assumed the Corporates knew Citadel forces had discovered their escape tunnel and were hot on their trail. That must mean they were expecting another force to meet them at the exit, which posed an interesting puzzle for him. He had two threats to consider when deploying his squad. Breaking ground would be a relatively slow process, thus they could expect support from the Athena in stationary orbit above this spot to keep Citadel forces at bay. And once they emerged, there would probably be a heavily armed jump-ship to pick them up. His challenge would be to keep the pickup from happening before Adonus met their demand for inspection. It seemed improbable Adonus would allow inspection given his actions to hide the sphere, so Smith knew deep down in his gut this was going to be a bloody encounter.

They cleared the northern range, leveling to an altitude of two hundred meters above the mesa, and circled slowly. The terrain was mostly flat, with light yellow ice networks of fine cracks that fanned out over the plain like tangles of blood vessels. Superimposed on the forward windscreen was a HUD showing a three-dimensional wire topology of the scene outside. They stopped circling when a red blinking dot hovered above the expected exit point. They deployed landing struts, and slowly descended from a hover, kicking up plumes of ice dust and vapor that completely engulfed the ship, and slowly settled as the engines shut down. Smith glanced from the HUD to the pilot, then over his shoulder to Lieutenant Ayton Quinn.

"Yeah, not much cover," Quinn observed. "And no shelves or overhangs."

"Clear shot from above," the pilot agreed. "The ship's a sitting duck if we leave it here."

Smith cracked a smile. "Sitting duck? When's the last time you saw a duck?"

The pilot shrugged and looked back at the scene outside, trying to imagine how they were going to defend this position.

"Those Corporates are a pain in the ass," Smith hissed. Then he turned and scanned the squad. "Okay, listen up, we're going to dig bunkers here, here, and here." Smith touched the HUD in several places while planting his finger and turning the three-dimensional wire frame of the scene outside to more clearly illustrate the ship's relation to the red dot. In each of the three places where Smith touched the HUD, blue triangles appeared. "Once we dig the bunkers, we'll deploy six, six, and eight—here, here, and here. Then we'll tent the ditches with active camouflage tarps."

Smith turned to the pilot. "Before the Corporates break ground, you'll take the ship up and circle in the stratosphere above this site. We'll need active jamming and air support. You have four Hellfire missiles, right?"

The pilot nodded. "Yeah, I do."

"Good. If it all goes to shit, I want you to burn whatever's down here. We're going to deny them whatever they found if they try to take it by force."

"What about you and the squad?"

"If it goes bad, I doubt any of us are going to make it out of here." Smith looked from the pilot, to the Lieutenant, then to the rest of the squad seated in two rows along the sides of the long cylindrical body of the ship behind the flight deck. The ship's interior was bathed in red light, which was standard for battle status. Smith looked them up and down; they seemed to glow a dark crimson. They were dressed in black assault armor that bulged slightly at major joints, signifying active motor assist. Their faces were pinched inside black helmets that encompassed their heads and rotated on neck bearings. Visors were drawn back, and Smith could see the resolve in their eyes as he regarded each of them, maybe for the last time. Each seemed to nod as his eyes passed over them, absolving him from what everyone knew was coming.

It took several hours to excavate ten trenches, seven more than Smith had originally called for. He knew the Athena, parked in a geosynchronous orbit above the site, could see them digging their shelters and would target them if hostilities broke out. So Smith decided to play a shell game, something he'd read about while researching old tricks and illusions, a hobby of his. Once the trenches were dug, and active stealth tarps had been put over each trench, the quad would go stealth and occupy the original three bunkers, but the Athena would not know which were fakes and which were occupied. If they lobbed anything short of a low-yield nuke, most of the squad had an even chance of surviving. Smith was in a trench half a klick south of the exit point. And checking the chronometer in his Aug-net, exit-time was in a half hour. Local sensors they'd deployed indicated ground soundings consistent with the predicted time and exit location. Smith called Zen.

"We're in place and standing by, boss. So, do we have any idea of what we're looking for?"

"I have an update for you, Captain."

"You do?" Smith raised an eyebrow under his faceplate. He wasn't expecting that. He'd asked the question out of reflex, not because he'd expected any new information. He'd been privy to Li-ant's encounter with the alien thing, and since it couldn't be moved, assumed the Corporates were abandoning the site with the intention of burning the whole thing, denying anyone future access to whatever advantage that thing could offer.

He heard Zen chuckle on the other side of the com and could imagine him cracking a knowing grin.

"I do. Turns out a couple of security personnel, who remained in the underground to secure the site, found one of the missing miners. There were two miners. They followed Li-ant into the underground through the cooling tunnels. The same girl, Serena, who we debriefed a couple of days ago, and an Auger Towns, a friend of hers. Towns was critically injured. We found him in a makeshift med bay. He'd been shot."

"Is he still alive?" Smith asked.

"No, unfortunately, he passed soon after we found him, but he told us what happened."

"Look, boss, this is no time for suspense. Those sons-of-bitches are breaking ground in thirty minutes; we have to know what we're looking for."

"He said the girl touched the thing and it lit up."

"Lit up? What's that mean? I saw Li-ant touch it, so what?"

"Yes, but when the girl touched it, it came to life, started to glow or something. Towns was a little hazy on that point. But he insisted the thing transferred something into the girl. That somehow the girl's important. Don't ask me what it all means, but the point is, we think they took the girl. That's what you're looking for, the girl."

Smith shook his head. None of this made any sense. "Okay, boss. I'm going to have to go. Things are about to happen real soon."

"Good luck, Smith. Zen out."

Smith checked the acoustic sensors and could see a disturbance in the distance through his zoomed optics. Small puffs of ice dust were churning around the breakout site. He felt himself tense and looked at Lieutenant Quinn, who was hunkered down right next to him.

"Did you hear that, Quinn?"

"Yeah, Captain, I heard."

"Okay, look, if they agree to the inspection, I'm going to do it. I'm goin' by myself and I'll transmit audio-visual. If things go sideways, half a klick is too far to run. In that case, you're it."

Their visors weren't darkened, and Smith could see Quinn's face. He'd lost that fresh look. Quinn's tan skin glistened with sweat, and his eyes, usually clear, had a sickly pinkish hue. He could see the man's hand shaking on the rifle stock. Smith breathed out. "Can I rely on you, Lieutenant? Cause if I can't, tell me now. These soldiers' lives may depend on you keepin' your shit together."

"Sorry, Captain. I'm scared, but I'll do my job."

"Okay, then." Smith put a fisted gauntlet out and Quinn reciprocated. They punched fists together, reinstating their oath. "Go see that everybody's good." Quinn nodded, then turned and scurried away. Smith watched him make his way down the trench in a crouch, then he looked skyward even though the view was blocked by the tarp. He breathed out, and with that, forced a calm across his body. He'd gotten up this morning with the thought that this could be the last morning he'd ever see. He'd been a corporate soldier before immigrating to the Commonwealth and had seen enough carnage to last a lifetime. This was supposed to be a mellow ride into retirement. After this, he could leave Titan and go to one of the cloud cities high above Saturn. He heard they had parks there with trees and grass. He'd never seen real trees and never felt real grass. He vowed that when he got to Saturn, he'd go sit under a tree every day, feel the life in the grass under his splayed fingers, and things would finally be good. He might even meet a woman who wasn't a soldier, and somehow all the bad memories would just fade, until one day, they were gone. Smith almost laughed out loud. It was a nice fantasy, but he had a sick feeling all he'd ever be was a soldier. And this, alone in a trench on a dark frozen moon, might be the way his insignificant life would finally end.

* * *

Caster, aboard Vindicator, heard Captain Smith's report to Director Zen but hadn't gotten new orders from Governor Tallus on Aurora. The countdown clock was ticking, and the Corporates were expected to break ground in about fifteen minutes. Caster was drumming his fingers on the arm of his chair, weighing his various options.

"Mr. Overine."

"Yes, Captain."

"Let's go full stealth, then put us in a random orbit falling behind the Athena using cold jets."

"Ms. Stein, are our four S cells fully charged, and X-ray lasers and neutral particle beams on line and target locked?"

"Yes, Captain. One X-ray laser locked on Athena's reactor, other batteries are on standby for defensive actions."

"Good."

"Vin, keep an eye out for a shuttle launch and give me an estimated landing time and coordinates. Keep the ground crew aware of the situation in realtime. Also, if the Athena attacks, you have full control of counter measures. If Athena attempts to kill the ground party or this ship, you have authorization to destroy her by whatever means available."

"Yes, Captain, understood."

The black manta shape of the Vindicator, already partly cloaked, wavered, then disappeared from the Athena's scopes, leaving only the stars that had been partially visible behind her. She slowed her orbital speed, falling behind Athena, and sank closer to the moon, just above the whisper of gas at the top of the stratosphere, where she waited.

Caster watched as passive optical scans registered thermals, indicating that Athena had just launched a shuttle. He watched the orange-yellow quarter sphere of the moon's patchwork of clouds slowly scroll by accentuated by a blue tactical grid overlay on the holographic viewer sunk in a hemispheric pit at the front of the bridge. A dotted red track followed the progress of the shuttle as it spiraled into the atmosphere, and toward the breakout site on the far side of the northern range at Lakeshore. There were too many unknowns. They really had no idea of the military strength of the Athena, and nobody had heard from Adonus. If he read the Corporates wrong, one wrong move could result in all-out war, or the destruction of his ship. "Damn," he whispered under his breath.

"Message coming in from Director Zen, Captain," Vin announced.

"Yes, Director, Caster here."

"I'm going to patch you in, Captain. Adonus is returning our query, mute your com if you would."

Zen's voice resonated across the bridge. Caster took stock of the crew; they were listening in rapt attention, looking off into space as though seeing Zen as he spoke.

"Director, this is Adonus in response to your request for an update."

The man sounded casual as if taking a Sunday stroll through an arboretum. "Cocky son-of-bitch," Overine said. Caster could see the man unconsciously clenching and unclenching his fists at his side.

"Vin, what's the stress level in Adonus's voice? Can you tell if he's being truthful?"

"Dr. Adonus appears nominal, Captain. There is no undue stress in his voice."

"Classic sociopath," Helen Stein remarked. Caster shot her a grin.

"Yeah, that's what makes this so unpredictable."

"Tallus messaging from Aurora, Captain."

"Put him through on a parallel channel. Stagger the channels so we don't miss anything, Vin." *Perfect timing, right in the middle of the most crucial part of the chess game, and the governor calls*, Caster thought. Caster looked at Helen and saw her shaking her head, her mouth stretched into a comic grimace.

"I don't want to be rude, Governor, but make it quick."

"Understood, Captain. You have full authority to support the ground crew, including lethal force if necessary. At your discretion, Captain. Tallus, out."

"Primary channel only, Captain." Vin was signaling that Adonus was on the line, and mute was active. Caster nodded to no one in particular.

"We'll be on the surface of the northern range shortly, Director," Adonus was saying. "But then you know that. We have the position of your ground forces and the location of your cruiser in orbit. Any attempt to interfere with our departure will be construed as a hostile act."

"Yeah, Mr. Overine. A cocky son-of-a-bitch," Caster remarked.

"Screw him—they can't see us," Helen said.

That raised a chuckle from Caster.

"Vin?"

"No, Captain, they can't see us. And his voice is nominal, and he is lying, so to answer your question, I cannot tell his truthfulness."

"Damn sociopath," Helen hissed.

"Dr. Adonus, we have information that you have a captive, a girl. We believe there has been a breach of contract on your part, a fraud. We have declared the girl, Serena, a material witness. You must surrender the girl before departure."

"Is he laughing?" Overine asked. Caster held up a hand.

"That's not going to happen, Director. The girl is a miner under contract with the company. She belongs to us. Any attempt to stop our departure will be resisted."

There was a stone silence. Then Zen said, "Adonus, we're on the brink of war. You will hand over the girl. We know about the artifact and her importance to it. She and the artifact stay here on Commonwealth soil where you found them. Any attempt to take her will be resisted with lethal force."

"Adonus has broken the connection, Captain," Vin informed.

"Everybody, attack status, everyone in crash couches, cinch down tight. Prepare for high-g maneuvers. Vin, weapons hot, you have the ship."

"Done, Captain."

* * *

Smith heard the exchange. When Adonus dropped the channel, he signaled to Quinn.

"I'm going out to take a look as the shuttle comes down. I'm in full stealth, so I won't compromise this position. If it goes bad, you have the squad." He watched Quinn. The man wore a blank expression as if he was somewhere else. "Lieutenant, snap out of it. Do you hear me?"

"Yes, Captain. But why go out? It's pretty clear we're out gunned. Topside's going to be a river of fire in a few minutes. What's the point?"

"Our mission is to keep that shuttle from taking off. We have horizontal visibility down here. I have a heavy rail gun. These projectiles can go through the skin of that shuttle like a hot knife through butter. I'm going to try and hit the engines. If I can get a clear shot, they aren't going anywhere. Hear me, Lieutenant?" Smith imagined seeing the man's Adam's apple bob as he swallowed.

"I hear you, Captain. You can count on me, sir."

Smith watched as the man seemed to grow calm and centered. Quinn glanced down at his assault rifle and switched from standby to active. Then he looked up and nodded. He put his fist out, and they bumped. Then Smith rolled from under the tarp and came to rest on one knee. He extended the rail gun from its power-pack on his back and grabbed it in both hands as the gimbal swung out in front of him. He saw the gun was fully charged in his Aug-net. He stood and looked into the northern sky. He saw a yellow contrail appear high above the horizon and arc toward his position. He smiled.

The shuttle was hovering about fifty meters above the plain with its landing struts extended. It moved slowly in a shroud of dust toward a pile of ice slabs that had been pushed out of the ground about a half-klick north of Smith's position. Suited figures were emerging from the pile that hid the bore hole from which the debris had come. Smith counted ten figures and what could best be described as a stretcher that two of the figures were carrying. *The girl*, he thought. When the shuttle was no more than ten meters from the group, it lowered to the ground, and its engines whined to a halt. The nose of the craft was facing Smith, and the rear ramp was facing the group, which was now out of sight. "Shit," Smith hissed and started running counterclockwise to try and get a line of sight to the engines in the rear.

* * *

"Missiles launched, Captain," came Vin's even voice over com. Instantly, Caster felt the nausea as the ship veered at high-g, then spun and veered again. At the same time, he heard the muted hum of the lasers firing, and the subtle whine of the S cells recharging. The low flushing sound that resonated through the hull indicated that one of their missiles had been simultaneously launched.

A missile from Athena flashed at a hundred g's toward a position where its tactical computer predicted the Vindicator should be, given her last coordinates before going full stealth. Since the missile was stealth, Vindicator could not track it well enough for a target lock but could see it well enough for its predictive algorithms to get a low-yield nuke close enough. Ten thousand kilometers above Vindicator a five-kiloton explosion disintegrated Athena's missile, but hard maneuvering of both ships had blunted the aim of the Vindicator's laser at Athena's reactor. The other missile, fired by the Athena, streaked toward the Citadel jump-ship that was covering the exit site at Lakeshore. Its stealth was ineffective due to the contrail it left in the atmosphere, and a neutral particle beam intercepted the missile fifty kilometers above the jump-ship, disintegrating it.

"We missed," Helen Stein called out. She was focused on the tactical display in front of her crash couch. "They knew what we were trying to do, and are maneuvering into the shadow of the moon. If we chase them, they'll be able to track us through thermals."

"We didn't miss them," Vin corrected. "We didn't destroy the reactor, but as you can see on your scopes, they're venting plasma. Their reactor is still operational, but at a fifty percent diminished output by the volume of plasma I'm measuring. They don't have power for drive and weapons at the same time."

"But they still have missiles and point defense mini-guns," Overine pointed out.

"Channel opening from the surface," Vin informed.

"This is Adonus. Another attack on our ship, and we will burn the surface, eliminating your squad. We will also destroy the Citadel. Let us leave and there will be no further conflict."

"Leave the girl," Zen ordered. "Leave the girl and you can leave."

Caster said, "Vin, establish an orbit above Athena. Do your best on stealth, but if they see us, so be it. Missiles hot, beam weapons hot."

"Done, Captain."

* * *

As Smith ran, a bright white flash high above him turned the yellow-orange landscape to black and white. He stopped running and looked skyward. Somewhere high up and to the north, he saw a contrail terminating in an expanding spherical maelstrom of expanding gas. He knew the jump-ship might be gone, and continued running. As he began to get a line of sight on the rear of the shuttle, he noticed that the group was no longer there, the ramp had been retracted, and the shuttle was lifting off and lowly rotating to hide its engines. *Was that dumb luck, or did they know he was there?* It pointed its nose up, and the engines roared to max thrust. The shuttle slingshot into the sky on a torrent of flame. Smith raised his weapon and shot. The aluminum rounds streaked toward the shuttle at ten times the speed of sound, super heating the thick nitrogen-methane atmosphere and leaving con-trails.

His shots mostly missed, with a couple seeming to hit the hull at glancing incidence, but the shuttle continued to climb as it turned into a dot and vanished in the distance. "Damn," Smith yelled. "Damn, damn..." When he'd taken a couple of deep breaths, he realized what might happen next. He swung his gun toward his back, the gimbal reattaching it into its cradle. Then he turned and ran as fast as he could back toward the trench. When he saw more bright flashes in the sky above him, he stopped. He knew he'd never make it, and even if he did, it wouldn't save him from what was coming. Smith stood there, long shadow on the bright white plain under the nuclear explosions high above him. He took a slow breath and relaxed, finding peace, and enjoying his last few moments of life.

* * *

The Vindicator sped up, rising over the horizon of the moon into a high orbit above the Athena. On their scopes, the bridge crew saw the red dotted line of the shuttle spiral out of the moon's atmosphere and rendezvous with the Athena.

"Missiles launched," came Vin's smooth voice over com. It was followed by another series of jolting high-g maneuvers: beams humming, S cells recharging, and the flush of missile launches.

Two missiles streaked toward the Vindicator; a missile pressed down on the exit site at Lakeshore, and still another streaked toward the Citadel. The Vindicator shot two nuclear interceptors at the missiles bearing down on it, destroying both of them. It fired another missile that intercepted the missile headed for the Citadel, but its particle beam missed the missile impinging on the exit site.

Simultaneously, the jump-ship fired two Hellfire missiles at the missile heading to the exit site but missed. Its targeting could not track the stealth missiles fired from the Athena while they were still in space. In quick succession, two nuclear explosions, resulting from its interceptors, flared below the Vindicator as it shot out of orbit at high speed on full burn. The expanding shock wave of radiation and debris overran it, and the hull plating on the rear of the ship was scorched and scared. Far below, at the exit site, a five-kiloton mushroom cloud of super-heated vapor and debris rose ten thousand kilometers above the surface of the exit site.

* * *

Zen watched the exchange on the big holographic screen that floated in front of his desk on the fourteenth floor of the Citadel. Orbital images were being relayed to the Citadel by a constellation of stealth orbiting satellites and synchronous audio channels originating from the drilling sites at Lakeshore, the Vindicator, and the governor's office on Aurora. Zen monitored the situation with a growing sense of dread. Ever since the discovery that Adonus had found something at Lakeshore, something that could precipitate a war between Earth and the Commonwealth, he feared this would happen. A war he easily imagined they could lose. Even though he had done everything he could to avoid this conflict, here it was, the first shots fired. He felt the ground shake beneath him and the building slowly sway. The motion made him nauseous, with a disorientating sense of vertigo. He quickly turned from the holo to look out the large window to the north. An iconic atomic mushroom cloud was growing on the horizon, lighting the dim yellow of Titan's midday to a bright white under the dark gray shadow of stratospheric clouds.

"Smith's gone," he heard Li-ant say. Then he thought he could hear her quietly crying. "What's your status, Li?" Zen whispered.

The audio channel was full-omni, all sources were present in realtime, as though everyone was in the room. Zen heard Vin's smooth voice issuing updates on the bridge of the Vindicator; he could hear sounds of things being thrown around at Lakeshore, which was close to the blast radius, and a static silence from Aurora that spoke volumes. After awhile, and over the chaos of the channel, Zen heard Li-ant say, "We're shaken pretty badly, but no fatalities."

"Okay," Zen stammered. He was having trouble finding his voice. "We've heard from the shuttle over Lakeshore; they survived and will be cycling back to you once they've come here for resupply. Think about what you need down there and we'll get it to you as quickly as possible. Any reaction from the alien sphere?"

"I'm in the giant lab near the sphere. I've been looking at it the whole time," Li-ant said softly. "The thing seems to be outside of everything that's happening."

Zen raised an eyebrow, "What do you mean?"

"The shaking down here was bad and lasted almost a minute. A lot of ceilings and walls fell down, everything's been thrown around, and through it all, that thing just floated there, disconnected from everything. It just seems unaffected, above it all. Makes my skin crawl."

"I want you to get out of there. Pull the squad together, get organized. There's a team at the surface site that's been digging the elevator out. It has to be cleared for us to get you new supplies and reinforcements. You hear me?"

"Yes, Director. I'm on it."

Chapter Twenty-Two

Titan, Transfer Orbit over Titan, 2240 AD

Adonus was slammed into the gel of his seat and watched the turbulent orange clouds streak by the window as the shuttle rumbled and shook in its race out of the atmosphere. He couldn't turn his head to the window directly for fear the five-g acceleration would wrench his neck; he could only shift his eyes in the general direction, but that was becoming unmanageable too. So he stared straight ahead at the beige bulkhead where he saw bright white flashes followed by violent shaking that slammed the shuttle in one direction, followed by a hammer-like stop, after which everything was thrown in the opposite direction. He heard the engines roar to a deafening rumble, like sitting under an enormous waterfall, and then the nose of the shuttle pitched near vertical. He was pressed into his seat so hard he couldn't breathe. He felt a maniacal smile forming on his distorted face. He wanted to laugh, but it was impossible because the muscles in his chest were overwhelmed by the enormous weight pressing down on him. They couldn't kill him, he knew that. He had always known he had a special destiny. He wasn't religious. He despised the weakness of those who leaned on such a ridiculous crutch. No, he had something much better than religion. He was certain he would rise above other people.

Occasionally, someone came along, someone destined to lead, someone with a vision for the human species as clear as a natural law. That had been true throughout human history, and he was certain he was the current incarnation of that natural force. The alien thing appeared at exactly the right moment. Chance had provided an instrument that he could use to fulfill his destiny, to consolidate the solar system under his grand vision. The fact they thought they could stop him squeezed a coughing cackle from his stretched distorted lips.

Once out of the atmosphere, the ride smoothed out, the g's faded, and Adonus leaned forward and massaged his neck. He had a headache and spots faded in and out of his vision. He sat back, closed his eyes, slowed his breathing, and listened to ship-com over his Aug-net. The Athena was still there, but he could tell from the quick updates and damage reports there'd been a confrontation. He pinged Nora Assisi.

"Dr. Adonus, what can I do for you?"

She was professional, he admired that. Not a hint of stress in her voice, she sounded as if he'd called to ask the time. He smiled to himself.

"What's our status, Colonel? There were a lot of flashes and turbulence moon-side. Listening to com, Athena took some damage. What's our situation?"

"You took fire from the exit site on your way up, sir. The site's gone. Rocket to the Citadel was intercepted. Athena took a hit to the reactor, we're at half output."

Adonus felt the shifting acceleration, then an ascent, followed by the hollow sound of metal docking clamps echoing through the shuttle. After that, he felt a constant acceleration, probably less than one-g. "What intercepted the missile, what damaged Athena?"

"There's a Commonwealth war ship cloaked in high orbit. It must be very advanced; we couldn't see it, couldn't get a target lock. They hit us with a laser, extremely powerful. Apparently, they can see us, even when cloaked."

"It's the Vindicator. The good news is there's only one of them. What's happening now, are we still engaged?"

"No, sir. The Commonwealth ship must have taken some damage to their hull plating during the confrontation. Their cloaking is not as good as it was. We can see them now, although weakly and intermittently, but enough."

"Enough for what, Colonel?"

"We've broken orbit and are on an intercept course with the Nemesis cruisers. Once we put them between us and the Commonwealth ship, we're home free. And although the Commonwealth ship is faster now, they have to keep their distance, and that distance makes their laser and beam weapons less effective."

Adonus thought a moment. He wasn't a military strategist, but something didn't make sense. "And can you remind me, Colonel, why they have to keep their distance?"

There was a protracted silence, then Assisi said hesitantly, "Because we have nukes, and if they come within two blast radii, we might be able to land a damaging blow by overcoming their defenses. We can't target lock, but we can get a nuke close enough. And they can't nuke us because we have the girl."

Again, Adonus smiled. He'd made the right choice by assigning Assisi as his head of security. She could think for herself, which made her dangerous, but she was very good, which made her indispensable. He planted his magnetic boots on the floor, then unbuckled his seat restraints and stood. He turned toward the airlock at the end of the long cabin and saw Orzan slumped in his seat; he looked sick. He couldn't help the wave of disgust that eventually found itself distorting his features into a mask of contempt. Orzan might be smart, but the man was a worm, hard to stomach. His eyes shifted to movement at the opening in the bulkhead at the end of the cabin leading to the airlock. Light bathed the room beyond indicating the lock had been opened, and the lean shapely figure of Colonel Assisi in a form-fitting black security suit was silhouetted in the archway.

"Dr. Adonus, be careful leaving the cabin, that was a jarring ride, and we're under acceleration."

As he advanced down the aisle in halting steps, he saw Assisi smoothly pivot and help Orzan out of his seat and to his feet. The odd little man leaned on her like someone clutching a life preserver. They staggered out of sight toward the lock. He called out, still seeing their silhouettes beyond the bulkhead. "Assisi, get him cleaned up, I'm going to want him present when we examine the girl."

"Yes, sir," came the response, and the shadows slowly edged out of sight.

Once he had been shown to a cabin aboard Athena and had a chance to wash up, Adonus ordered Assisi and Orzan to meet him in a small alcove adjacent to the med bay where the girl was secured. When he got there, Orzan was running some kind of a scanner over the girl and Assisi was standing aside and observing. The girl was wrapped in a black netting of graphene fibers electrified with high voltage, low current electrical pulses. A cable ran from the netting to a panel above the girl's portable stretcher. A monitor in the panel showed several plots and a pulse train, which Adonus assumed was a representation of the signal powering the webbing.

"How is she?" Adonus asked.

Orzan finished running a wand with a flat paddle extension over the girl's upper body, then turned to face Adonus. In this environment, Orzan seemed more in control, professional. Adonus was intrigued by the transformation from weak incompetent to authoritative scientist.

"She's alive," Orzan observed casually. "Still in a coma, we can't see her brain activity; it's blocked like the rest of our scans."

"How do you know she's in a coma?"

Orzan smiled in a way that the knowledgeable acknowledged another's ignorance. He turned, put the scanner down, and reached into the pocket of his white lab coat, removing a small penlight. He bent over the girl, and with his right thumb, lifted her eyelid. The girl's dark eyes were dilated and stared off into space. Orzan shined the light on her pupil and moved it from side to side. The iris contracted, but her eyes remained staring straight ahead focused on nothing. "Classic comatose response," Orzan remarked as he continued looking into the girl's eye. He turned the penlight off, withdrew his thumb from her eyelid, and turned to face Adonus.

"Aren't you concerned about touching her?" Assisi asked. "I thought she was infested with alien nanites."

"There was some risk the first time I did it," Orzan remarked. "But I'm fairly confident the electric field is keeping them from the surface of her skin. Also, I'm convinced by their behavior that they're not interested in me." He turned to look at the girl, almost envious. "They're only interested in her."

Adonus couldn't help staring at the girl too. He got a feeling from her, fear surely, since he couldn't control her, but also a sense of awe like he was witnessing something deep and powerful, something mortal humans had never witnessed. "What were you doing when I came in? I thought scans didn't work."

"Yes, well, we can get some readings, heat for instance. I can get a temperature reading; she's hot, something's happening inside. I was concerned since she's consuming energy, but she hadn't eaten anything or had any water. So I took a chance."

Adonus raised an eyebrow. "Chance?"

"Yes, I prepared an IV of saline and a mixture of proteins and sugars. I put a couple of drops on her skin before trying to insert the needle. After I saw the droplets absorbed into her skin, I inserted the needle." He pointed to a tube on the opposite side of her bed, which Adonus hadn't noticed. "It seems as if they let me do it. The needle went in and she's taking fluid."

"You sound like these alien nanites are aware of what's happening on a subjective level, like they're adjusting their behavior to achieve some intended goal."

"It would seem that way." Orzan smiled knowingly.

"Have you tried to wake her up so we can ask some questions?"

Orzan's smile faded. "No, I don't know how to do that."

"You could raise the voltage on the webbing; you could put a stimulant in the IV."

"I'm afraid if I do that, it could prompt a defensive response. She's in this coma for a reason. Everything this alien does is purposeful. She will come out of this on her own, but I don't think we should interfere with the alien right now. We don't know what it's capable of. We think it's contained, but if it isn't, and the nanites turn against us, I think they could easily take the ship. If they do, I don't think we can stop them. We will get our answers, but only on their terms."

* * *

Serena was dreaming. She was in a large room with walls of polyimide-coated ice. She knew the look of ice caverns; she'd spent years in them. She wasn't cold or warm or anything else, she just was. It was a strange out-of-body feeling. She seemed to see everything, but couldn't quite determine the perspective. And there were people; most were behind a semi-transparent curtain that bisected a large room. She could see fifteen people walking around on the other side of the curtain. She knew there were fifteen. She hadn't counted them, but she knew it, exactly fifteen. There was one person on this side of the curtain though. Serena knew her, remembered her from the Citadel—Li-ant. She was tall and slender. She had a suit cap on her head and she wore a black security uniform. She was staring at her with a strange intensity in her blue eyes and worry lines creasing her forehead. Serena felt like she was looking down on Li-ant, but how could that be? The woman was taller than her. Serena saw she was talking to someone and instantly knew it was Zen on the other side of the conversation. But how could she know that? Then she heard what they were saying because she wanted to hear. *"Any reaction from the alien sphere?—I'm in the giant lab near the sphere. I've been looking at it the whole time. The thing seems to be outside of everything that's happening."*

The alien sphere. Serena remembered the thing, remembered Auger getting shot and falling. He had slumped to one knee, then fallen to the ground, raising a fine mist of ice dust that sparkled in the flood lights like fairy dust. The security people stepped over his fallen body as if he didn't matter. Her mind recoiled; she felt sick. Then she remembered the man, Adonus; the man who had given the order. At that moment, she remembered the intense hatred boiling up inside of her. She saw the emptiness in his dark dead eyes. Men like him were the incarnation of everything bad in life. Whenever they sensed the wellspring of people's hopes, they stepped on them out of a psychotic drive to own everything.

She wanted to kill the son of a bitch, could visualize tearing him apart. But she knew she hadn't. Something made the hatred fade into irrelevance, and she had turned from the man and touched the sphere. Now she was here, wherever here was. She watched Li-ant give her a last look, turn, and slip through the curtain to the other side. When Li-ant was gone, Serena looked up to the top of the cavern. She could see through more than two kilometers of ice and Titan's thick yellow atmosphere. She saw the stars shining in the deep black of the void. They were so clear, and she wanted to be there. As she desired to float up into the void, she felt herself heating up. A blue halo engulfed her and she rose. The sense of flight made her happy and she imagined herself pushing through the ice. It seemed to instantly vaporize at her touch and she rose more and more quickly until she broke the surface.

She shot up through the atmosphere at incredible speed, continuing to accelerate all the time. She streaked into the deep black void and the sense of freedom made her laugh out loud. Self-reflection at that moment told her she hadn't been happy in a long time, maybe she'd never been happy. Then she remembered being in the greenhouse with Aegeus on a sunny afternoon many lifetimes ago on a blue planet a billion miles away. And in her room on Midway, with Janus on her birthday, another lifetime ago. She had known happiness, but it had been all too short and fleeting. She put those thoughts away and looked down, seeing the rim of Titan illuminated by reflection from majestic Saturn, its massive ring sparkling in Sol's light so far away. She was going ever faster now and Titan was getting smaller by the minute. And then she knew where she must go; she could see them. Two ships, very far away on a rendezvous course with nine other ships, six from Saturn and three from the asteroid belt, from somewhere near Ceres. Olympus flashed to mind. She didn't know how she knew all this, but she must go there, and she sensed she was violating some unspoken rule by doing so.

* * *

Li-ant walked to the fold in the plastic wall, pushed it aside, and entered the lab proper. She had a strange feeling from the sphere on the other side of the curtain, like she was being watched. It gave her the creeps. She remembered approaching the thing unafraid, drawn by a sense of presence. The sphere was immense. She stood in its shadow; it dwarfed her. When she got close to it, it started to spin, slowly at first, then a little faster. She remembered Auger Towns' description of what happened just before the girl, Serena, touched the thing. It started spinning. That woke Li-ant up, snapped her out of her trance. Yeah, Zen was right, she had to get out of here, and get busy.

"What's happening to the sphere?"

Li-ant looked down; Martinson was standing in front of her. She hadn't noticed him approaching; she was still foggy. "What?"

"The sphere," Martinson repeated. "Something's happening."

Li-ant turned. The plastic curtain was rattling like something was beating on it, but that's not what caught her eye. The distorted image of the sphere on the other side of the curtain was glowing blue. On closer inspection, she could see that the blue glow was coming from many small electrical discharges all over its surface. That was something else Towns had said.

"The temperature is rising," Martinson exclaimed. "It's going up pretty fast, about a degree centigrade per second and the rate is going up too."

"Get everyone out of there," she heard Zen order over Augnet. He wasn't panicked, but he was tense.

"Come on," Li-ant yelled. "Everybody, get the hell outta here. Right now, drop what you're doing and get out of here."

Everyone hurried to the thick metal door at the far end of the lab. Li-ant stood to one side and ferried everyone through. Just before slamming the door shut, she sneaked a last look at the sphere. The curtain had melted and fallen away. She felt the radiant heat on her face coming from the small crack between the door and bulkhead she was looking through. The thing was spinning fast now, bright blue sparks turning incandescent, and the thing was rising up to the ceiling of the cavern. She slammed the door shut.

While everyone else hurried down the corridor to the stairs, Martinson stayed behind, probably worried she might linger.

"What the hell's happening?" Li-ant exclaimed.

"Don't know, but whatever it is, I think it has something to do with the girl's leaving."

"The girl?" Li-ant knew she was being dense, but she didn't feel right. Maybe the thing had done something to her too.

"Yeah, the miner, Serena. Just before the blast, the Corporates took her off-moon. Somehow, she's connected with that thing. It's following her."

"As crazy as that sounds, I think that's right." She was staring down at Martinson. She could see the worry lines around his deep-set brown eyes. He stayed behind because he knew she'd been affected too. Then the ground started shaking like a moonquake.

"The moon's not geologically active," she said weakly.

"It's not a moonquake; it's the sphere boring through two kilometers of ice. Look at the wall. The power of this thing is off the scale."

The wall around the metal door was sweating profusely. Soon the ice would be turning to liquid in torrents, flooding this lower level. Without another word, they turned and ran toward the stairs. They hurried up the stairs taking them two and three at a time. The shaking was getting more intense and Li-ant heard a loud rumbling like rolling thunder. When they were three levels up, they bolted through the door into the corridor, turned right, and ran for the elevator connecting the underground to the heat exchange pool near the surface. Hopefully, Zen's people had cleared the shaft.

* * *

The underground where the Corporates built a lab to examine the sphere was instrumented with video and audio sensors. Those sensors were rerouted once Zen's squads secured the base. Now, sitting in his office at the Citadel, Zen was watching the alien tearing the place apart. Sitting forward in his chair, he stared transfixed as the alien sphere, spinning and crackling with blue electricity, rose to the top of the ice cavern. As soon as it touched the ceiling, the ice exploded in a torrent of vapor, and the sphere went from blue to white-hot. It cut through the ceiling as if nothing was there, and was soon completely out of sight. The cameras started shaking as jets of roiling steam shot out of the hole like exhaust from a rocket nozzle.

"Shit," Zen heard himself utter. "Li are you alright? Are you with the staff?"

Zen waited, but there was no answer. He panned the cameras to the far end of the lab. The plastic curtain had melted away and the immense cavern was filling with steam. Just before the cameras went dark, Zen was gratified to see there was no one in the room, and the thick bulkhead door at the far end was secured.

He switched the view to cameras on the surface located in the mountains surrounding the site. Miraculously, the nuclear blast hadn't killed them all. He zoomed the image to where predictive algorithms said the sphere would emerge. It was only a couple of minutes since the cameras in the lab had gone dark, and no more than a few seconds since the alien had disappeared into its borehole before that. He noticed the ground start to dimple and bow in a concave circle that the AI monitoring the image measured to be half a klick in diameter. Then, all of a sudden, a geyser of steam erupted from the center of the cavity rising hundreds of meters into the air. The geyser was becoming wider and soon most of the area around the cavity turned dark as ice became liquid and the whole area started boiling away. As Zen stared, something streaked out of the hole so fast he almost toppled his chair as he jerked backward at the sight. The cameras quickly rotated skyward trying to follow the thing on its blistering trajectory. At full zoom, it was just a dot on top of a yellow contrail of super heated nitrogen-methane. Zen switched to orbiting platforms and saw the dot shooting into space at high speed. The image was overlaid by a blue tactical grid; the trajectory of the thing was represented by a blinking red dotted line. Numerical readouts had the alien at fifty thousand meters per second and accelerating at a hundred g's. All of a sudden, the red-dotted trajectory stopped. Zen blinked.

"What just happened?"

After a moment, the AI reported, "Tracking has lost the object; the object is no longer visible."

Zen continued staring at the monitor. Nothing like this had ever happened before. "Please explain. The object is no longer visible on radar, lidar, or QL?"

"The object is no longer visible in the electromagnetic spectrum and does not register in QL entangled photons."

Zen thought a moment, put his hand on his forehead, and started rubbing. Even if they couldn't follow it, where would it be going? Then it hit him; he looked up. "If we assume the object doesn't change its trajectory, can you extend its path toward the inner system?"

Zen watched the red dotted line extending outward toward Jupiter space and into the inner system. "Okay, now, show me the orbital paths of the Vindicator and Athena." Two other dotted lines appeared: one orange, the Athena, and one violet, the Vindicator. They both originated from elliptical orbits around Titan and extend out toward Jupiter space, Athena leading Vindicator by about ten thousand klicks. The extrapolated red line of the object intercepted both ships on a transfer orbit about ten million kilometers from Saturn, at the approximate location of the Nemesis fleet from Olympus.

"Damn," Zen whispered to himself. He quickly set up a tight beam to Captain Caster on Vindicator.

Chapter Twenty-Three

Saturn Space, Unknown Location, 2240 AD

Serena was standing in a forest; she was unsure how she'd gotten here or where here was, but it felt strangely familiar. She looked around and carefully took it all in. It wasn't a forest; it was more like an orchard, or maybe a greenhouse—yes, a greenhouse. She had only been in a place like this once before, a long time ago. A smile graced her lips; she noticed because she hadn't used those muscles for a while and it felt unnatural, but it felt good. The air was different here, moist and full of the scent of living things. The tang of metal and plastic from recycled air was noticeably absent. She glanced down at her feet, which sank into the ground, and felt like she was standing on pillows. She was standing on dark dirt. She crouched on her haunches and scooped up a handful, put it under her nose, and took a deep breath. It was rich with a pleasant smell that suggested the presence of living things. In fact, everything around her was alive; the trees, the buzz of insects, the songs of unseen birds. She stood slowly. What was happening here? Was this a dream? If it was, it was amazingly vivid. Then she remembered reading somewhere that you couldn't do math in a dream. She multiplied and divided some numbers in her head. It worked, she got the right answers. Bewildered, she tried to remember where she was just before this, and what she had been doing. She flashed on impossible images of flying through ice, then flying into space, but not in a ship. She remembered flying, unencumbered, just flying. She wasn't smiling anymore, which sadly felt more natural. A wave of panic hit her like a cold slap in the face. She remembered a story about someone who kept waking up just to discover that they'd awakened in another dream. "Shit," she whispered. She feared she was losing her mind.

Serena took a couple of deep breaths and started walking further into the greenhouse. She had to move, loosen up a little, clear her head. There was an answer here, don't force it, she would figure it out. As she walked, she noticed rays of light coming from a glass ceiling maybe twenty meters overhead. The rays made dancing patterns over almost everything from shadows cast by leaves swaying in a changing breeze that was coming from somewhere she couldn't see. She noticed that the sky wasn't yellow or orange, it was a deep rich blue beyond the glass roof. *I'm on Earth,* she realized with a start. And the gravity was right too, stronger than on Titan, but somehow, she felt acclimated. Then she felt the greatest shock. She saw someone standing further down the path made by the neat rows of trees on either side of her. She didn't know why, but she thought it was a man, dressed in what looked like a light blue jumpsuit. That looked familiar, too; she knew what it was. She felt a cold chill envelop her. It was like the training suits she'd worn on Midway a lifetime ago. What the hell was going on here? She went from confused and shaken to angry. She didn't like this, whatever it was; she didn't like the feeling of being completely out of control. Even if things were bad, she wanted them to make sense. She balled her fists and sped up. She'd get some answers from this guy.

He just stood there, didn't come nearer, made no move whatsoever. Her anger reached down into her legs, she was running now, closing on the man. When she was about five meters away, she came to a dead stop. It couldn't be.

"Janus? It can't be you. You died on Mars. It can't be you." Serena saw him through cloudy eyes. She felt the tears streaming down her cheeks.

"Hello, Serena." He smiled that same crooked smile that had haunted her dreams these last ten years. His face was smooth, without age lines, and his hair was a matted light brown with highlights that seemed to glisten in the rays of sunlight moving in and out of shadow. His skin was coffee and his nose had that distinctive flare that made it seem like pure joy when he smiled.

Serena's lower lip quivered. "This is cruel, you know that don't you, whoever you are."

The smile vanished from his face. She saw true distress in his brown eyes as he stared back at her; his mouth pressed into a silent, "Oh."

She slowly approached him, and before she knew it, she was hugging him tightly, as if, when she let him go, he would just vanish. She didn't want him to.

"I'm sorry," she heard him whisper as she buried her face in his shoulder. He smelled the same, he felt the same. She pulled away, held him at arm's length, and just looked at him, taking in every detail. His eyes followed her. He seemed as confused as she was. Whatever this was, it wasn't malicious. It was as if whoever he was, he had expected her to accept him, to think it was really him.

"Who are you? You can't be Janus, you know that."

"I am truly Janus, as you remember him."

"As I remember him. I don't understand, what does that mean? Who are you?"

"Come and sit with me." He pointed to a tree to his right. When she looked over, she realized it was an apple tree.

"This can't be happening," she muttered as she walked over to the base of the tree.

He stepped close to her, looked at an apple, and moved to pick it.

"You can't pick those," she heard herself say.

"I know that's usually true, but here we can pick these. They're for you."

She laughed and looked around. "All for me? Nothing's ever been all for me."

"Well, these are." He picked one and gave it to her. Then he picked another and took a big crunchy bite. "They're pretty good, try one."

Serena sat cross-legged at the base of the tree and ate an apple; it was good. As she ate, she watched Janus, who was sitting across from her and eating his apple. She began laughing with her mouth full, spit some apple out, and drooled a little on her shirt. "Excuse me," she said and still laughing tried to wipe it off.

"What?" Janus asked.

"You know this is crazy, right? Here I am eating apples in an imaginary greenhouse with someone I know is dead. What's so strange about that? So, at some point, are we going to talk about what's really happening here?" She looked around. "I should be scared shitless, but I couldn't be more unconcerned. Maybe I'm dead." She smiled and took another bite.

After a while, Janus said, "So, what's the last thing you remember?"

"Flying through space, boring through kilometers of solid ice."

"No, not that. What's the last thing you remember that seems normal—reality as you understand it."

She snorted. "As I understand it. Okay, I'll play along." She stopped eating, closed her eyes, and thought back. She saw herself facing an immense round thing. She remembered the shadow of her hand, fingers splayed, just before she touched it. Her eyes snapped open, "The sphere." She slowly turned her head and looked intensely at Janus. "You're the sphere, the alien sphere. You're the thing the Corporates found at Lakeshore."

He looked back at her and took another bite. "Yes, that's right, I'm the sphere."

"You lied to me—you said you were Janus." She looked at the apple and spit it out. "Is it poison?"

Janus stifled a laugh. "Come on Serena, you know it's not poison. As I said, I know you like apples and these are for you." He took another bite. "And I didn't lie to you—I'm Janus as you remember him. What are we once we no longer exist, but the impression we've made on others? I'm Janus as you know him. I haven't lied."

She stood and started walking in circles, trying to catch her breath, then looked around. There was no one else in this place. She looked down at Janus. He seemed so sincere. She had to admit, the alien was good, very convincing. "So, what have you done to me? How come you know my dreams? Are you inside my head?" When he didn't say anything, she asked, "Why me? I'm nobody. What could you possibly want with me? If this is some kind of invasion, I'm useless to you. I have no power and nobody cares what I say."

"Invasion," he repeated and shook his head. "Why say things like that, you know that's not true. Quite the contrary. I'm here to give you something, not take something away."

"You don't know anything about people, do you? You can't just get into someone's head and expect them to trust you. Put yourself in my shoes. You wake up in a dream and some alien thing posing as your long-dead friend tells you a story like the one you told me, what would you think?"

He regarded her a moment. "That's fair. I get it. Okay then, ask your questions—I'll try to answer in a way that makes sense to you." He smiled, almost eagerly. "This is good for me too you know."

"What's good for you?"

"You said I don't understand people. That's the whole point. I exist to understand people. The entity that left me here created me precisely for that purpose. It will be interesting to see how well I understand people."

"Okay, are you in my head?"

"Yes, I'm in your head."

"That's worrying. How, how are you in my head? How did you get in there, and can I get you out?"

Janus looked disappointed. "Do you remember having dreams, feeling different, and your enhancements coming back? When did that start?"

She thought a moment. "The explosion, the cave-in. Right after that, that's when it started."

"That's right. When you were pinned in the ice—when that man tried to kill you. I came into you through the ice, through your suit, and into your body. I can disassemble parts of myself into large groups of nanometer machines that can diffuse through solids and reassemble at any target location. In your case, I migrated to your implants and rebuilt them so that we could communicate."

"Why me?"

"I wish I could say otherwise, but it was a matter of convenience. You were at the right place at the right time. You had unwittingly dug a tunnel close to me, close to the sphere." He smiled that crooked smile. "I took the opportunity to choose you."

"Choose me for what? Why do you need to choose anyone? If you have this gift, why not just fly to Aurora and announce yourself? Talk to the powers that be directly." She looked at him. "You know, take me to your leader."

He started laughing. "That's very good. Take me to your leader. I think I saw that in one of your animated video dramas. No, it doesn't work like that. What do you think would happen if I did that? And besides, that's not what this is about."

"What is this about?"

"Yeah, well, I don't like to say it like this, but this is a test. I can give you something incredibly valuable, but in return, you have to show me you're ready to accept it."

"So, there's a catch." She regarded him with suspicion and a little bit of sadness.

"It's not really a catch. Let me say it this way, if you lose, I lose, too. If you fail, I fail too."

"Why? Why would you lose if we fail the test?"

"Because, besides what you may think, I am human. I am one of you, so to speak." He held up a hand indicating he wanted to continue. "There are a large number of planets in the universe with life. In this galaxy alone, out of a hundred billion star systems, more than sixty percent have a planet in an orbit around the star that allows liquid water. You call it the habitable zone. Organic life is like weeds. Chemistry is compelled to produce life even under marginal conditions. Even here in your solar system, you've discovered life on moons, in oceans, and under ice heated by geologic activity induced by tidal forces. But what is not so common in the universe is intelligent life, intelligence that enables a creative understanding of the universe. Creative intelligence is precious. To the creators of the entity that left me here, intelligent life is the most precious thing in the universe."

"Why do you say you're human? You're an alien sphere of nanites."

Janus took a breath. For the first time, he seemed tired, and a little discouraged. "What is human? In the view of those who sent me here, being human means having a grasp of existence that is consistent with that of humans. The organic piece is trivial. Imagine someone in a coma or brain-dead. They are still organic, but are they human? Is a vessel without thoughts, without a vision of its own existence, still human? I was created using vast behavioral information gathered from Earth with the intention of mirroring a human being as closely as the technology that created me would allow. The fact that we are talking as if we know each other is proof of that. I submit I am more human than an empty organic vessel."

"Why go to all that trouble? Why didn't your creators just talk to us directly? Wouldn't that be simpler? Wouldn't that make it easier to develop trust? Don't you think that slipping into someone's head and turning them into a communicating zombie seems more suspicious?"

This time Janus laughed out loud. "You're not a zombie. If you were, would I be arguing with you?"

"Point well taken," she grinned.

"But to answer your question, those who created me are as different from humans as humans are from ants. I know that sounds insulting, but you wanted me to be honest. Could you have a meaningful conversation with an ant? Assuming ants had achieved space travel, had shown by their accomplishments that they had an understanding of existence sufficient to manipulate their surroundings with automated instrumentality in aesthetic ways that replace the tedium of survival. Those ants might have something to contribute that is singularly unique. But how could you communicate with them? You might want a translator. If you could, you might want to construct an ant who could talk to these ants. I am that ant."

Serena was wide-eyed. "Who are these beings that left you here? You make them sound like gods. Why would gods want to bother speaking to us." She snickered. "And of all people, me? I can honestly tell you that I have nothing to offer. You've made a terrible mistake choosing me. I've destroyed almost everyone I've ever known. I don't even like myself that much." She stared at him. He felt very human, looked very human.

Janus moved over and took her hand and rubbed the top of it with his thumb. "I can tell you this. I don't know how you feel about yourself, but Janus loved you. You helped him, and Auger too. He died for you. And I love you. And to answer your question, the entity that left me here, you can call it a network agent. The network agent is more than a billion years removed from the beings that sent it here. It and others like it are creatures of deep time that have spanned many galaxies looking for beings like you. We in the network of conscious beings are on this side of existence, the side that can reflect upon itself. We are the universe bearing witness to its creation. You can consider me a node in that network, the human node. I was uniquely created for you. This is my home. I have no place else to go. If you fail, I am without purpose."

Serena understood the feeling of being dispossessed, unmoored. He was so like Janus and all of a sudden, he was Janus, and she felt the old connection return. She rested her head on his shoulder and whispered, "What if we fail the test?"

He pushed away so that he could see her. He smiled sadly. "If you fail then I will orbit the sun, unseen by you until it goes out. If you cease to exist through war or natural disaster, I will continue to orbit the sun. And if someone happens by long after you're gone, I will remember you to them: your history, your accomplishments, your songs. Even if you fail, you deserve to be remembered."

Chapter Twenty-Four

Transfer Orbit, Vindicator, 2240 AD

The Vindicator shadowed the Athena for twelve standard days. During that time the skin on the tail of the ship was replaced by plating manufactured in the ship's forge and installed by service bots that patrolled the ship inside and out and made repairs. As repairs were being made, the ship turned one hundred and eighty degrees and started a breaking burn falling farther and farther behind Athena and slowing to slightly under the speed of the approaching Corporate fleet. Using ionized gas distortion from the main engines, Vindicator launched ten high-speed stealth survey drones toward the Nemesis fleet.

Once the hull plating was operational, Vindicator went full stealth and vanished from Athena's scopes. They were close enough now to get a better look at the three Nemesis cruisers, which made no effort at stealth. It was clear that their menacing profiles were sending a message. Apparently, the company thought that the Commonwealth might capitulate without firing a shot. They couldn't have been more mistaken. This confrontation may have started with the discovery and subsequent theft of the alien artifact, but it was the culmination of a difference in the vision of two starkly divergent societies that had failed to coexist.

Captain Adrian Castor had supervised tactical simulations of the encounter of the two forces for a standard week and formulated a plan for containment. They could not let any of the Nemesis cruisers enter Saturn space armed with antimatter weapons. Such an advance could signal the end of the Commonwealth, and in Caster's mind, the end of free human society for the foreseeable future. To add to the drama, Caster received a tight-beam from Director Zen at Citadel a week ago informing him that the alien sphere had left Titan and was headed toward the intersection of the two forces. Given the data Zen sent, the sphere should have arrived already, but the sensors and quantum computer analyzing the data could not find any trace of the alien. Just something else to worry about, Caster thought.

"Where are they now Mister Overine?" Caster scanned the holographic tactical update hovering over the hemispherical projector at the center of the bridge. He rotated the image with a ball control on his right console following the red dotted lines of the Nemesis fleet as they spiraled in from deep space toward Saturn.

"They've been separating for the past couple of days—they're now approximately one hundred and fifty thousand klicks apart." The red line representing the ship in the center of the pattern started blinking. "The ship on the original heading will be passing under us in another ten standard hours."

"They're definitely carrying antimatter weapons, Captain," Helen Stein confirmed. "They're making sure that if we get a lucky shot, we don't take out the whole fleet. Antimatter isn't like normal warheads that you can destroy, once the magnetic containment is broken, you get an explosion."

"A big explosion," Overine added.

"Does the separation tell us the total yield of the weapons each cruiser is carrying?"

"Yes, Captain," Vin said. "Given the explosive radius as their separation, each cruiser is carrying the equivalent of two thousand megatons, in standard yield."

"We can't let any of them through," Caster warned. "Where are our drones?"

Blue lines appeared in the tactical volume. "The drones have followed trajectory updates and are flying fast intercepts. We're seeing strong sensor emissions from each cruiser. They know something's coming, but I don't think they can see them."

"We need at least one of the drones to survive the fly-by. We have to get a look inside one of those dreadnoughts, preferably the one we're stalking. And the alien? Anything yet?"

"Nothing, Captain," Vin answered. "Whatever it's doing to hide from us is completely unknown technology. But if it's following the Athena, it's far from here and should not be a factor in this engagement. The Athena fell behind the Corporate fleet five days ago; even at its crippled speed, it's more than five million kilometers away in the direction of Jupiter space."

Somehow he wasn't reassured. Caster had been on the bridge plastered in his chair for ten hours straight. He was tired and knew he wasn't at his best, which he'd have to be when the Corporate cruiser was within weapons range. The captain's chair was comfortable, but he felt his legs falling asleep, something that was symptomatic in prolonged zero-g. He had to move.

"Mister Overine, you have the bridge. If you need me, I'll be in my cabin."

"Yes, Captain, I have the con."

With that the klaxon issued a muted tone and an automated voice announced, "Captain leaving the bridge." Caster stood, looked around, and headed for the bulkhead door.

The bridge was in zero-g when the ship was not under power, but the crew quarters and other facilities dedicated solely to human occupancy, located in the central rotating volume on magnetic bearings under the bridge deck, were always at half standard gravity. Caster turned off his magnetic boots once on the crew deck and took a couple of halting steps toward his cabin. He put a hand on the wall to steady himself. He was so used to the mechanical gate of having his feet stuck to the floor, then unsticking and planting the next step. The smooth rhythm of natural gravity felt awkward. He regained his balance and made it to his cabin. By the time the door closed behind him, he was lying in his bunk, his boots haphazard on the floor where he'd kicked them off. Even though he was tired, he was too buzzed to sleep. He lay there for a while, trying to get all the jumbled thoughts and their associated anxieties out of his head. Just as he was closing his eyes the door chime sounded.

"You gotta be shitting me," Caster whispered to himself. He hadn't been off the bridge for half an hour and already something was going sideways? "Yeah," he called out.

"It's Helen, Adrian."

"Open," Caster ordered. The door slid aside soundlessly and Helen Stein entered, stood above him for a moment, then sat cross-legged on the floor so they were both at eye level.

"This can't be a social call, I'm spent."

"I know, I'm sorry, but this may be the last time we talk—you know?"

Caster smiled. Helen was old school Earther, rare this far out in the system. She was exotic by Commonwealth standards, dark brown complexion with long auburn hair always worn up as long as he'd known her. He'd often wondered what she looked like when she wasn't the chief engineer. Helen was from that part of Earth formerly known as the Middle East. She had what might have been regarded as old-world features, an oval face and a prominent strait nose accentuating intelligent dark almond eyes. She reached out and took his hand. Her slender fingers felt warm and dry.

"Don't be sorry—I'm glad you're here. Maybe you can get some of the demons out of my head."

She reached into a satchel that he hadn't noticed slung over her left should and withdrew a bottle and two plastic cups.

"I can't right now. I could be called at any time."

"Can't what?" Helen said smiling. "It's real orange juice, chilled. My last bottle—I was saving it for a special occasion." Then she regarded him somberly. "This may be the last occasion."

He swung his legs off the bunk and sat up. "Well, what are you waiting for, pour."

They clicked cups and drank. Caster had only tasted orange juice once before, on Mars. He'd been a much younger man, the half-forgotten memory came back in stark relief. The orange liquid was rich with pulp and body and had a tart sweetness, unlike the processed foods aboard ship. He took it in slow draws, savoring each sip. "God, that's good. Thanks for bringing it."

Helen finished hers and put the cup down. "After the service, I was going to one of the new floating settlements on Saturn. Not Aurora, none of the old settlements where things are established, but on a new one like Delta-Aradoni. Back on Earth, when I was a little girl, we were planning to turn the desert into a garden. Hell, we could have done that with the whole Earth. Terraformed it back to what it was, pre-industrial. I could be part of something like that on one of the new settlements. What would it be like to live in a forest under a blue sky?"

"You could do that?"

"Hell, yes. We have the technology. But the companies would never allow it." She looked at him, anger in her pointed glare. "They control by scarcity. They let you see something better, but keep pulling it away just when you think it's possible. Something better is always just out of reach. Back on Earth, the Commonwealth is like some heaven you dream about. Even the name, Aurora, is what the Romans thought of as a new-dawn. This confrontation had to happen. The companies are slowly losing their best and brightest. Soon the whole thing will become unstable and that foul system will collapse of its own weight. As long as the Commonwealth exists, the companies will have a shelf-life no matter what kind of propaganda they spew." She was quiet for awhile, looking down at the floor, then looked up. "You have a plan, can it work?"

"I think so." Caster could hear the doubt in his own voice. "It can work," he asserted with mock confidence.

Helen stared at him, then blew out a muted chuckle. "You sound like you're trying to convince yourself. Tell it to me, I have bits and pieces, but give me the big picture."

"You're central to it, the work you've been doing this past week: tuning the collimator on the X-ray laser for maximum range, the added gamma ray shielding for critical parts of the ship."

"I have bits and pieces. I want to know the plan. How it comes together."

"Okay, maybe it's good for me to say it out loud. I've been working with Vin. He's good, but he may lack the intuition that comes with the experience of dealing with human irrationality."

"I'm listening."

"We picked the lead ship, the one that's on a direct trajectory to Saturn. Once they started separating days ago, two of the cruisers were flying on long arcs to either side and behind the lead ship. We guessed right when we picked that one to ambush. We're on a stealth hover just above its path. We'll let it pass, fall in behind it at a distance of about a hundred and fifty thousand klicks. Two Reliant cruisers are on intercept orbits with each Nemesis. When the lead ship is a quarter-million klicks from Saturn, we send a *proceed no further* ultimatum. If they ignore it, we take out the lead ship with a laser shot to one of the warhead's antimatter containment. We'll have the exact locations of the warheads because we're going to maneuver cloaked fly-by drones to flash an X-ray image of the interior of the cruiser as it passes us, just like we did the Athena. Once we fire on the lead ship, the Reliants open up. One of each of the two Reliants is stripped down and has no crew; it's flown from the other ship and has a high concentration of iron in the engine's reaction mass. Just before they open up, the drone Reliants rush the Corporate cruisers at one hundred and fifty percent engine output. They should streak forward at more than forty-g's firing everything they have through a wall of ionized gas from nukes detonated in front of the Corporate ships. Hopefully, we can take them all out. No negotiations, no hesitation. Antimatter is a terrible weapon, but you have to keep it from blowing you up. All the hardening you've been doing is because we expect a big EMP when that lead ship goes nova."

Helen was silent for a long while. Caster could see her picturing it in her mind, assessing the risks at each stage. "It could work," she concluded in a whisper. Then more forcefully, "It could work."

"It's our best shot, no pun intended. It has to be fast. If they maneuver before we take the shot, it won't work. Also, one of the ships behind the lead ship could fire antimatter missiles at our ships and at Saturn even if they're crippled. It's uncertain if we can defend against that. Vin gives us a fifty-fifty chance of keeping a missile from hitting Saturn if that happens, but the alternative is to surrender, and we've decided not to."

Helen poured the rest of the orange juice equally into both cups and handed one to Caster. "Thanks for telling me. If I think of anything else, I'll let you know."

"Fair enough." They clinked cups and finished the juice. Caster put his cup on the floor, laid back on his bunk, and exhaled. "Five hours," he mumbled to himself.

"That's enough time."

He looked at her, puzzled. She rose and stood over him again, like when she'd first come in. This time instead of sitting on the floor, she dropped the satchel, then slowly unzipped her flight suit from the high collar to the waist. She shrugged, slipping it over her sleek figure to the floor, where she stepped out of it. She was tall and brown and beautiful and Caster could only stare, growing more aroused and unable to resist the temptation. It had been a long time since he'd thought of anything other than getting the ship flight worthy, now his mind was a complete blank, all his anxieties forgotten.

He reached out for her, but she said, "wait." She raised her arms, accentuating her breasts, and unclasped her hair. It fell over her shoulders and down her back like gossamer silk. Then finally she got out of her undergarments and stood before him a moment. She leaned forward on the bunk and kissed him deeply, straddling him as she did.

Sometime later, Helen looked down at Caster. They'd made hot passionate love, then he'd fallen asleep. She'd lain there, listening to his steady breathing, her head on his shoulder, daydreaming about endless trees under a blue sky. After a while, she checked the chronometer in her Aug-net, then got up and dressed. She regarded him with a feeling of sympathy. Let him sleep for a couple more hours before leading them into a battle that would decide the fate of the system for the foreseeable future. Once dressed, she turned and slipped out the door silently, heading for the bridge.

Chapter Twenty-Five

Transfer Orbit, Athena. 2240 AD

Nora Assisi looked down at Serena. She was wrapped in a graphene mesh from head to toe, even her face was covered in a fine mosaic web. Wires snaked between the portable cot, on which she lay, to a bank of instruments stacked in a makeshift cabinet and anchored to the bulkhead. Nora examined the instruments more closely. There were smart power supplies putting out pulsed high voltage, low current limiters, and equipment monitoring the girl's vital signs. She was drawn to a readout of the girl's EEG recording brain activity. Plots showed a high level of activity, none of it recurring as one would expect. Instead, the traces were random, noisy, and unusually large in magnitude, which Nora imagined indicated some kind of seizure. She glanced back at the girl's face, Serena appeared peaceful, no spasms, no clenching. Her face was relaxed, not even telltale eye movements beneath the lids indicating any kind of distress.

"What are you doing here?"

Nora cringed; someone had come up behind her. She turned to find doctor Orzan framed in the entryway, hands buried deep in the pockets of his white lab coat, which looked out of place on a military ship. He looked winded like he'd hurried here after seeing her in the girl's room. She looked at Orzan, then around the room trying to spot the cameras.

Ignoring his question, Nora asked, "How's she doing? She's been like this for almost a day. Do you expect her to regain consciousness?"

Orzan came in and stood beside her, then looked at the monitors. "There's been no change since we left Titan."

"Those EEG readings, are they normal? There's a lot of brain activity for someone in a coma."

"I don't understand what's happening," Orzan admitted. "She's not in a coma, and none of these traces are normal. As to whether she's going to come out of it, your guess is as good as mine."

"Why are you here, Doctor Orzan? Did you see me in here and thought I wanted to harm her?"

Orzan looked up at her imposing figure. The man looked perpetually off-balance. "Are you trying to harm her?"

Nora willfully softened, trying to set the odd little man at ease. "I knew her a long time ago, Doctor. I bear her no ill will. I wanted to see how she was doing, that's all."

She watched Orzan nod, then slowly back toward the door, as if trying to decide whether to believe her or not. He turned and gave a final glance, then disappeared around the corner. Nora was about to leave, when she heard, "Nora."

Nora felt a cold numbness rising up her back and slowly turned to the cot. She knew that voice. It was as clear and distinctive as she remembered, as though the last ten years had just melted away. Serena was awake and looking up at her. Her features below the mesh were, well, serene. She approached the girl and Serena's eyes followed her. "You're awake?"

A smile dimpled her cheeks. "Yes, I'm awake." Then she looked around and tried to move under the straps. Looking back at Nora, she asked, "What's happened, Nora? Where are we, why am I tied down in this net?"

When Nora regained her composer, she said, "You're on the corporate cruiser Athena. We left Titan about a week ago. We're headed to Olympus."

"Why, Nora? Why are you taking me to Olympus?" Then looking around again, she asked, "Are you working for that man, Adonus?"

For some reason Nora was afraid, an emotion she'd rarely felt. There was something about Serena, there had always been something about Serena. She was unusual, unpredictable in a way that Nora had rarely encountered. Nora was a leader, someone who read people for a living, someone who knew how to motivate because she understood what people were afraid of. This girl had thrown away a promising career all those years ago by defending people she had been taught to mistrust. That long past episode on Mars haunted Nora's dreams and wouldn't let her go.

"Something's happening, isn't it? That man, Adonus, he's threatening the Commonwealth. How? And somehow, I'm part of it, aren't I?"

Nora started for the door, then stopped. She turned back and stood at the foot of the cot. "I can't talk about it."

Serena regarded her. "Don't go, Nora. Don't worry, the surveillance is off. They can't see us, and they can't hear us. As far as they know, you walked out of the room and I'm alone. Close the door, would you."

Nora tensed and looked around the room nervously. "But you can't move. How…?" As Nora watched, the power supplies electrifying the netting shut off with a muted click, and the panel lights went dark. Glancing back at Serena, Nora's eyes grew wide as she saw the graphene netting become frayed, then fall away as did the straps on Serena's wrist, torso, and ankles. The girl sat up on the cot, the remnants of her bindings falling away like dust.

Nora took a step back. She heard a faint gasp escape her lips at the sight of the girl just sitting there, regarding her, a curious look on her face. This couldn't be happening. Maybe whatever sickness Serena had was catching. Maybe she had unknowingly become contaminated and was probably writhing on the floor hallucinating all this.

"Nora, please shut the door and come back."

Many things raced through Nora's mind. She felt her hand brush the gun on her hip, then gazed up to see Serena looking at her. She didn't seem the least bit concerned. Somehow the girl knew Nora had misgivings about Adonus, about his narcissistic compulsion for control, about her deep-rooted sense of her part in something she despised. She slowly withdrew her hand, moved to the door, and locked it. Then she turned back to the girl. "If you know how to free yourself and turn off surveillance, it stands to reason you know why you're here. What are you playing at, Serena?"

Serena exhaled an amused laugh. "What am I playing at? Oh, I don't know. I knocked myself out, tied myself up, then kidnapped myself." Serena stopped smiling. "This is not a game. I'm not posturing. You know me, Nora. I've been working in an ice mine all these years while you've been helping that criminal literally enslave people. People like us. I want this to stop, and with your help, maybe we can stop him. Please help me, Nora."

Nora felt tears racing down her face. For some reason, she felt relief. The things Serena had said could have come from deep within her if she'd dared to admit them. Living this lie all these years in exchange for personal comfort had made her numb, but those few words had somehow brought it all to the surface. "Adonus wants the alien sphere. He thinks he can use it to subjugate the Commonwealth and gain control of the company. But he couldn't move it. He knows that somehow the thing is tied to you, and if he moved you, the thing would follow."

"Did Zen let Adonus take me?"

Nora laughed out loud. "Hardly. We're on the brink of a war right now. We're headed to Olympus, but there are three heavily armed corporate cruisers on their way to Saturn, and Saturn has six cruisers out to meet them."

Serena's mouth fell open. "Why now?"

"Because Adonus thinks he has the sphere, and the corporate cruisers are armed with antimatter. He thinks this is the perfect time to impose his will. Apparently, he was able to convince Olympus—they're all in at this point."

Serena put her head in her hands. She really didn't know what to do. She felt the cot dip as Nora sat next to her. "I don't know how many soldiers I can trust to go against Adonus. I have a full squad on board, but I can only think of three soldiers who might agree to help us. Whatever we do, it has to be soon, and it has to be by surprise."

"We have to take the bridge," Serena offered. "We have to seal ourselves in and turn the ship around, go back to Saturn with Adonus as our prisoner. You know, the head of the snake." Serena thought a moment. "We get control of the bridge and we offer amnesty over ship-com to anyone who helps us. There will have to be some takers and others that have doubts. The chaos might keep them from effectively storming the bridge."

"Adonus has to be on the bridge when we make our move," Nora said. "He's usually in his quarters, he has an office there. We need to draw him to the bridge. Also, the ship's damaged. We had an encounter with a Commonwealth cruiser, our reactor is at half output. We're limping back to Olympus."

Serena met her eyes. "I might be able to help you with that." Then concentrating on some far point, she mused, "Take away what he wants. What if the bridge sees the sphere appear, turn, and start heading back to Saturn? He sees his plans going sideways; wouldn't he want to come and see it playing out on the bridge? He can't do that from his quarters, can he?"

Nora stared at her. "Can you do that? Can you control that thing?"

"I can try. See if you can find soldiers to help us. I'll try to contact the sphere."

Nora left Serena in the med bay, eyes closed, back in what appeared to be a coma or a fugue or whatever she did to talk to the alien, and pinged three soldiers she thought she could trust. She instructed them to meet her in the armory on the floor below the bridge. As she entered the bulkhead door to the armory, she saw two of them had arrived. There was no one else, as she'd hoped. The armory was usually vacant. The two, an older marine who'd been with her since Mars, and a younger woman who'd confided misgivings these past months, were sitting on graphene storage crates in a far corner, almost hidden from view at the end of racks of weapons. As she approached, the older man, Conner, said, "What's going on, Colonel, why the secrecy?" He'd said it half-joking, but after seeing Nora's grave expression, he looked at Kira, then back at Nora with growing concern.

"Let's wait for Samir, I've got a big ask. I only want to say it once." At that instant, their attention was drawn to a clank echoing off the hard walls coming from the far end of the room. Samir ducked under the door, then stood there, staring at them hunkered down in the corner. "Secure the door, and come join us," Nora ordered. When they were all together, she stood before them as they sat on crates looking up at her. She regarded each of them, then said, "I want to take the ship. I want you to help me."

"Why, Colonel? This doesn't make any sense. Are we talking about mutiny?" Conner asked.

"Yes, that's right, we're talking about mutiny. I've been on the wrong side of many things the company has wanted me to do. Somebody told me that a long time ago, and I can't shake it." Nora looked away, took a breath, and whispered, "Not this time." In a stronger voice, she said, "I've worked for Adonus since Mars, the man's a psycho, a destroyer. He comes off smooth, logical, but he's all about himself at the expense of everybody else. I've killed a lot of people for him, but I'm not going to kill the Commonwealth, and that's what he wants to do."

Conner blew out. "Yeah, all that may be true, but where's that leave us, even if we take the ship, and that's a big if?" He glanced over at Kira, who seemed to have an unusual interest in her boots. Her brow was furrowed and her mouth stretched into a tight lip-less line. Samir sat to his left, staring up at Nora in rapt attention. "Taking the ship can't save Saturn. I've heard we have three heavy cruisers headed there now. Word is they're carrying antimatter. If that's true, taking the ship doesn't save Saturn and we have a hostile ship with nowhere to go."

Nora gave a curt nod. "We have someone on board that might make the difference. Taking the ship will let us get her back to Saturn. She might be able to change the outcome, maybe to change everything. We might have a chance to finally be part of something we can believe in. I don't think I've ever made a difference, maybe this time I can."

"Who's on board that can make a difference, Colonel?" Kira asked. She was sitting forward now, tension replaced by curiosity. She wanted Nora to tell her something that could convince her to take the leap into the abyss.

"The girl we picked up on Saturn."

Conner blew out an acerbic laugh. "Wait, you mean the one in med-bay? The one they have wrapped up in some kind of netting. She isn't even awake. I heard she's in a coma." He knew his laugh had been disrespectful, he demurred. "I'm sorry, Colonel, I don't understand."

"That girl has something to do with the alien thing we found on Titan. That's why she's important," Samir muttered, as though talking to himself. Then looking up, "That's right, isn't it, Colonel?"

Nora leaned against a shelf at her back. "Think about it. We were stuck underground on Titan for weeks—why? Then we nuked the site and got into a pissing match with the Commonwealth's most powerful cruiser, all to take that girl. Why do you think Adonus did that? Do you think this mission was sanctioned? Those three cruisers coming from Olympus are probably carrying all the antimatter in the system and heading for Saturn only after we picked up the girl. She must be important, don't you think?"

Conner and Kira stared up at her, faces blank with confusion. Then Kira said, "I don't understand it Colonel, but I'm in. You've always been strait with me, more than I can say for the corporate bastards that screwed over my father." Nora looked at Samir, he was nodding.

It had been strangely easy to convince them to join her in mutiny. She had always been tight with her squad and had a sense of who they were. They shared mortal danger and survived by trusting each other. But Nora thought this might be a bridge too far, and she expected all of them to bow out. What happened on Titan, however, had confirmed a long-standing fear that ultimately the company would screw them, leaving their family members to take up their contracts. If truth be told, many of them indulged in the fantasy of somehow buying out their contracts and immigrating to the Commonwealth as had family members before them. Almost everybody knew someone who had gone to the Commonwealth. The thought that the company could put an end to that option once and for all dislodged some deep claustrophobic fear. So they put on armor and chose weapons as they'd done so many times before in preparation for an assault. Before starting for the bridge, they waited for Serena to meet them in the armory. Nora filled them in on Serena: that she was no longer out cold or detained, and that she'd been a soldier and served under her on Mars. When Serena showed up, she walked to the back of the armory and without a word fist-bumped each of the three marines as if Mars had been yesterday. Then she turned, selected some armor, and put it on with the ease of experience. The three marines just stared. It all seemed so familiar, so ordinary. It was as if Serena had been part of their squad all along. They glanced at Nora who just nodded. "Yeah, I know."

They walked single file toward the bridge entry, which was located behind a blast door secured by a DNA bio-lock. Nora had access, she was chief of security. The thought brought an ironic smirk under her combat visor. They were wearing armor and mag-boots even though the ship was under a half-g acceleration. They passed a couple of crew on their way to the bridge, which elicited curious looks, but they brushed past without a word or gesture. Speed and confusion were their best strategy at this point, take the bridge before anybody knew what was happening. She registered various Aug-net pings from her staff monitoring shipboard cameras, to which she only sent acknowledgments.

* * *

Adonus was staring at the large holographic display suspended in mid-air at the far end of the bridge. The viewer optics were set to extreme magnification and revealed something blotting out the starscape, something which seemed to slowly move as the perspective from the ship moved. It was subtle, he couldn't have seen it if not for the open circle crosshair icon that was tracking it. The sphere appeared ten thousand klicks in front and fifteen degrees polar, thirty-five degrees lateral to their trajectory. It maintained that distance since appearing a half-hour ago. There had been no sign of it being there before, not in the tracker logs or from remote sensing, it had just popped out of the void. The bridge crew was given strict instructions to notify Adonus immediately if the alien appeared. Upon hearing from Commander Abbas that the alien was on their scopes, Adonus rushed to the bridge to observe the thing personally, and to supervise some way of making contact, which he thought could only be accomplished by controlling the girl in med-bay. The whole idea of seizing the girl, Serena, was to lure the thing out of Commonwealth territory and into neutral space where the company could claim it. Doctor Orzan was standing next to him, staring at the thing with deep fascination.

"We need to manipulate the girl's thoughts suggestively. All the brain activity on the EEG indicates that even in a coma-like state the girl is somehow in contact with that thing," Orzan suggested.

"How do we do that, hypnotic-suggestive drugs?"

"Yes. I think we can bring her closer to the surface, to a suggestive state. Then we can echo-stimulate certain images by magnetic resonance."

"You need to get started right away. We can't let that thing disappear again. This is the first time we've seen it in over a week. I was beginning to think we'd lost it. I don't want to lose it now."

Orzan nodded to himself, then turned for the door. He hadn't taken more than a few steps when the large blast door slid aside and several armored security people entered, spreading out to either side of the opening. It struck him as odd that their helmets were expressed and their visors were down. He had only seen that when soldiers were prepared for an assault. Orzan looked around, even the bridge crew had turned and were staring at the four soldiers, two flanking the closed door and two who had stepped forward. He felt the hairs rise on the back of his neck. He turned and saw Adonus, still concentrating on the viewer, unaware of what was happening.

Adonus slowly turned, the silence behind him alerting him to the fact that something had changed. As he did so, Captain Abbas and a couple of the bridge crew stood as well, all regarding the security people with suspicion. Then Nora retracted her helmet and visor. Adonus relaxed at the sight and asked, "Colonel, is there a problem?"

"Yes, Doctor Adonus, there's a problem. I can't let you take Serena to Olympus and I have to speak to Corporate about the situation on Saturn. I believe you're precipitating a conflict that violates The Noninterference Treaty we have with the outer planets. This action is not in the best interest of the system or the company, therefore, I'm taking operational command of the ship."

Adonus raised his eyebrows. He turned to the Abbas. "Captain, I'm relieving Colonel Assisi, please inform security and have them bring a squad to the bridge to detain these traitors."

Abbas looked nervously at the four black armor-clad figures, then at the coms officer. "Inform security, Sergeant."

After a moment, the Sergeant turned to Abbas, a curious look on his face. "Coms are out, sir. Aug-net's off line, too."

Adonus quickly pulled a flechette gun from under his tunic and pointed it at Nora. "This fires armor-piercing needles. If anyone dies on this bridge, you'll be the first."

Nora smiled contemptuously. "And you'll be the second." Then she looked over Adonus's shoulder to the viewer. "Look at your sphere, Doctor."

Adonus hesitated not wanting to take his attention off of Nora. He stepped sideways, keeping his gun trained on her while stealing a glance at the screen. His mouth formed a silent, "Oh."

"It's reversed course," Orzan observed. "It's heading back to Saturn."

"No!" Adonus raged. His face appeared flushed and sunken, outlined by sharp shadows under the penetrating white bridge lights. But his gun never wavered. He looked at Orzan, "Get down to the med-bay, we have to work on the girl—quickly."

The armored figure standing next to Nora retracted her helmet. "Serena?" Adonus gasped. He looked between Serena, Nora, and Orzan, then back at Serena. "Bring it back." He trained his gun on Serena. Soldiers on either side of the door raised their particle beam weapons on Adonus.

* * *

Serena stepped in front of Nora and made a down motion with an open hand. Both soldiers lowered their weapons. She smiled at Adonus. "I want him alive."

A muted whoosh sounded from Adonus's pistol as Serena charged forward with blinding speed. She grabbed Adonus's wrist and forced it down, then slowly began squeezing. She remembered Auger, how they had indiscriminately shot him, then stepped over his body like he was trash. She wanted to break Adonus's wrist, feel it splinter in her grip. Adonus whimpered, then dropped to one knee as his face reddened and tears appeared at the corners of his eyes. The pistol clanged to the floor. Serena stopped herself from squeezing any harder and yanked him to his feet. "Take him." She shoved him roughly into Nora's arms.

"You're shot," Nora observed. She saw a splintered crack in Serena's armor, over her right breast. A small trickle of blood shone crimson on the dark armor. Serena steadied herself against a console. "I'll be alright." Then she turned to Adonus, who was staring at her with contempt. "You shot my friend back on Titan. You killed him; you didn't have to do that."

"Your friend was a nobody," Adonus spat. Then he turned to Nora and the soldiers near the door. "Actually, they killed your friend, I just gave the order."

"You're not giving any more orders," Nora said. "When we get to the Commonwealth, I'll answer for whatever mistakes I've made. I was in command, not them." Nora nodded toward her men and then turned to Adonus. "And you will answer for the things you've done."

"Soon there will be no Commonwealth and I'll see you executed for this."

"Maybe," Nora said, "But not today." Then she focused on Abbas. "Captain, you have a choice to make."

Abbas regarded the bridge crew, who were all standing, riveted by the exchange, then turned back to Nora. "I'm the captain of this ship. It belongs to Trans System and they charged me with this command. I'm not a politician and I don't make policy. I consider this mutiny and I can't be part of it."

"Okay, then," Nora said. "Come with me, Captain." Then to her men, "Assemble the bridge crew, keep them over there, under guard." She took Adonus by the arm, then looked over at Abbas. "Come with me, Captain." She fell in behind Abbas, holding Adonus tightly, and directed them to the captain's office, which was separate from the rest of the ship and accessible only from the bridge. Once inside, she tied the captain's wrist to a chair attached to floor gimbals with a graphene band locked by an encrypted code. She did the same with Adonus, making sure that neither man had access to the captain's desk or cabinets.

"You won't get away with this," Adonus sneered.

Looking at both men with disgust, Nora left the office without a word and reset the door lock with a new pass code.

"Hold the bridge crew while I address the ship," Nora ordered her men.

"Should you do that?" Serena asked. "Tell the ship what's going on?"

"Yeah, I have to. We have to turn off the engines to repair the reactor, which will kill the gravity. Everyone's going to notice. Then, once the reactor's repaired, we have to turn the ship around on a full braking burn. We can't hide any of this, not to mention crew rotation. We've got to get out in front of this and hope we can weather the storm. I've sealed off the armory, but nothing keeps them from cutting through the door. We can seal off engineering to limit access to tools, but I need my security people to go along with us. It's going to take the better part of a week to get to Saturn space in time to make any difference." She looked around the room after seeing Serena nod in agreement.

But Serena was still bracing herself against a console and noticed the tightness in Nora's eyes. She smiled. "I'm the least of your worries."

Nora addressed the crew sitting on the floor in the center of the bridge under the imposing profiles of her men. "And you?" They just stared up at her not saying anything. "Once I make this announcement, we'll release you. I know you can instill insurrection in the rest of the ship, but I'm asking you not to. Anyone who decides to join us will be given amnesty."

The sergeant who had been at the coms coughed a barking laugh. "Amnesty? By the time we get to Saturn, you'll be a fugitive and the Commonwealth will be history. Do you understand that our cruisers are armed with antimatter?"

Nora shook her head, then found her soldier standing near coms. "Conner, give me ship-com." The large armor-clad soldier nodded, then stepped over to the coms console and manipulated several controls, then nodded to Nora.

A klaxon sounded over ship-com. "This is Colonel Assisi, chief of security. I'm informing the crew that I have taken operational command of this ship. Doctor Adonus has led a conspiracy to foment a conflict between Saturn and the inner planets in violation of planetary treaties. He has kidnapped a miner from Titan that he believes to be critical to this war. Captain Abbas has decided to side with Doctor Adonus. Both he and Adonus are under arrest. The bridge crew are relieved of their duty and will be returned to their quarters. Any crew who stands down and does not oppose this transition will be given amnesty when we reach the Commonwealth. Those that oppose us will be considered co-conspirators." She killed the coms and turned to Conner and Kira, then nodded at the bridge crew sitting on the floor. "Get them outta here." She walked over to the keypad on the wall next to the door.

Kira motioned with her gun for the crew on the floor to get up. Conner fell in beside her and they marched the three men and two women single file toward the door. One woman at the end of the line turned and said, "I'm an engineer. I was on the engineering console. I can man weapons and tactical as well. I want to join you." She looked around nervously, then focused on Nora. She was a young woman, tall and thin, probably not raised in planetary gravity. She was blond and light-complexioned, which was rare this far out.

Nora guessed she was probably from Luna or maybe one of the big L2 settlements. Her face was flush, but her brown eyes were unlined and clear. Nora met those eyes and held them for several long seconds. "Can we trust you? You try anything funny, and we'll have to stop you with whatever force is warranted."

"I'm with you," she said firmly, then turned and walked over to engineering. "You're going to need all the help you can get."

At that, Doctor Orzan, who had remained standing and overlooked, cleared his throat. Both Nora and Serena turned and stared at him. Nora couldn't believe that in all the confusion Orzan had been permitted to just stand there, unattended.

"I'm also willing to help if you'll permit me," Orzan said.

Serena couldn't help laughing under her breath. "Now I think I've heard everything. I'm sorry, but aren't you the guy who had me tied up, wanted to mess with my brain to help you and that monster in the next room manipulate what you thought was the ultimate weapon? Now you want to help? Can you explain any of this to me so that it makes any sense?"

Beads of sweat coalesced on Orzan's brow. "I'm a scientist, I'm not a politician or a soldier. I didn't do anything to harm you. All those things you described may have been uncomfortable, but not harmful." He breathed out. "I'm only interested in the alien artifact." At the mention of the alien, Orzan seemed to gain stature and grow in confidence. "This is the greatest find in human history. That sphere could come from deep time, closer to the origin of the Universe. It seems to employ physical principles that are completely unknown to us."

Nora and Serena were staring at him with wavering suspicion. "Look, I have a belief that this alien artifact would never do anything to harm anyone, no matter what Adonus thinks. I can't imagine something coming from a civilization that advanced wanting to harm anyone. It's patently ridiculous when you think about it. It's come unimaginable distances from deep time to do what, conquer a primitive civilization of bipedal apes?" He paused and looked between the two women, who were now regarding him with noticeable confusion. "If anything, my only feeling is that studying the sphere is important. I have no power over the people in charge of this mission, but I have no loyalty to them either."

"And how do you think you could help us, Doctor?" Nora asked.

"I can't help you fight anyone, but I can monitor the remote sensors. I've developed algorithms that might help find things when they're cloaked. I can analyze telemetry and tactical information."

Nora looked at Serena who nodded. The man was no hero, but Serena had a sense that he wasn't committed to Adonus or the company. If truth be told, Serena knew she had been a more destructive arm of the company than this diminutive scientist.

Nora walked over to Orzan and scanned him for anything that could be a weapon, like a flechette pistol. She found nothing. It was clear Orzan might be amoral, but she didn't think he was dangerous. "Alright, Doctor, man the sensor array. Don't give me a reason to change my mind." She turned her attention back to the girl. "When we get the rest of them outta here, I'll want you to shut down the reactor, can you do that?" The girl nodded. "What's your name sailor?"

"Anastasia," the girl answered.

Nora smiled. "Okay, sailor, assume your station, wait for my order." Then she turned to her men. "Get them the hell outta here," she ordered and slid the door open.

* * *

Adonus checked the chronometer in his implant. He'd been in the captain's office near the bridge for four days. Although Aug-net wasn't working, systems in his implants that didn't require coms were still functioning without impairment. He was attached by handcuffs, consisting of encrypted locked magnetic bands, to a chair on gimbals anchored to the floor. The bands were long enough to allow him to stand and stretch, getting the cramps out of his legs. Abbas was confined to a similar chair on the other side of the room, far enough away so they couldn't come into physical contact. He was going to get out of here and re-assume command, but he needed to examine every detail of his confinement. Right after they'd been detained, he was standing next to the chair, looking around, taking stock of the room. Then, all of a sudden, he started lifting off the floor and began floating. The disappearance of gravity followed by a sense of falling that clenched his stomach spurred him to make some ill-conceived movements, which resulted in his feet pointing up toward the ceiling at a forty-five-degree angle with his wrist anchored to the chair. He pulled himself in, locked himself into the chair with the built-in harness, and stayed that way for ten hours until gravity reasserted itself strongly in the opposite direction. He felt the rotational motion as the room reoriented itself.

"We've turned around, that's a breaking burn," Abbas observed. "It feels like full power. Somehow, they've fixed the reactor."

"I thought it couldn't be fixed out here; we don't have the parts," Adonus reminded him.

"That's right, but I'm pretty sure that's full power."

Adonus had never fully trusted Colonel Assisi and had taken precautions, although as he looked around, he hadn't anticipated anything this drastic. He grudgingly admired how she'd turned the tables on him. He hadn't seen it coming. That's why he'd picked her; she was very good at what she did. True, he'd been preoccupied with the alien, but once he regained control, he'd make sure there'd be no repeats. He glanced at the sensor patch that he had just wrapped around the locking mechanism of his cuffs. It had been hidden in the lining of his tunic. It etched micron channels through the metal of the cuffs and snaked into the circuitry to points where it enabled the processors in his implants to work on the lock encryption. He saw in his sensorium that it had already determined four of the ten symbols in the key code. At this rate, he'd be free by the end of the day. He had to be careful, however, someone from the bridge came in to inspect them twice a day, bringing them food bars and water. Accommodations for their bodily wastes were built into the chairs, so they were never untethered. Stupidly, they came at the same times every day, giving him the ability to unwrap and hide the sensor before each visit.

It was clear at this point that the alien was lost to him. Somehow Assisi had co-opted the girl and was shepherding the alien back to Saturn. That made it a priority to subdue rebels and destroy the alien sphere with antimatter to nullify any advantage it might bestow on the Commonwealth. The wheels had been set into motion and there was no turning back.

Minutes after the current visit by one of the soldiers from the bridge, Adonus saw a green triangle icon in his sensorium over the image of the decryption algorithm that had been working on the cuffs. Adonus tugged on the cuffs and they fell away. He smiled at the sight of his free wrist, then looked across the room at Abbas who was staring at him, mouth agape. He held up his free wrist and balled his hand into a tight fist.

"Can you free me as well?" Abbas asked. Adonus got out of the chair, retrieved the cuffs from the floor, and recovered the sensor. He strode across the room and wrapped the sensor around Abbas's cuff. He waited a couple of minutes for the micro-strands to get into place. When the icon in his sensorium flashed active, he applied the key code. He saw the green triangle and yanked Abbas's arm. The cuffs fell to the floor with a clank. Abbas smiled up at Adonus.

"How do we get out of here?" Adonus asked. "I have to get to a secure com channel. I have a secure link, but something's cut it off." Rubbing his wrist where the cuff had been for four days, Abbas said, "My turn to help you."

Adonus looked around. "It's a crucial oversight that they don't have cameras in here."

"Being captain has its privileges. The captain's office has to be private." Then looking at the far wall, "Want to see another amenity of the captain's office?"

Adonus followed Abbas to the far wall and stood behind him as the Captain stopped and turned to face him. "In case the ship is ever breached or there is an accident where the captain and the bridge crew must abandon ship, we have this." Then, Abbas turned and pushed a placard aside to reveal a square pad depressed into the wall. He put an open palm in the center of the pad, then pushed it into the wall. Adonus heard an audible click. Abbas withdrew his hand and stepped back. The entire section of the wall moved, slid into the bulkhead, and then slid aside revealing an airlock.

"And they don't see any of this on the bridge?" Adonus asked, shocked by the lack of security.

"No, they don't see any of this. They won't know we're gone until the next check-in three hours. Just like you, Colonel Assisi knows nothing about the resources in this office."

"But, if this is an escape pod, won't they see it when we detach?"

"Yes, they would, if that's what we were going to do," Abbas said. Abbas entered a key code and opened the airlock to the escape pod access. Adonus saw several environment suits folded into slots behind transparent doors on the right side of the airlock before the door to the interior of the pod proper. "We're going to put these suits on. On the space side of the pod, there's another door designed to be used as access to ships or platforms that don't have a standard airlock. We'll use that door to walk to another airlock near the security station. You can take it from there. I only hope you have officers loyal to you or we'll be locked up or worse pretty quickly."

"I have backup," Adonus snapped, then walked over to a slot, opened the door, and started putting on a suit. Abbas did the same. When their helmets were sealed and oxygenated rebreathers activated, they entered the pod, closed the locked door, and pushed through the cramped interior to the other side. Abbas went over to a couch near the far side of the pod, pulled a thin console on a gimbal in front of him, and began manipulating icons. Adonus heard a hiss as Abbas bled the air out of the cabin. Then he rose from the chair and stood near a blank part of the hull. There was a door subtly etched into the wall with a rotating handle and keypad on the right. Abbas entered a code, then pulled the handle down. The door slid smoothly aside revealing a magnificent view of the starscape embedded in the infinite void. Adonus had to steady himself. The transition from cramped pod to limitless space gave him severe vertigo as he felt his muscles clench in an attempt to restore balance. Abbas had clearly done this before, he pushed his upper torso through the door and grabbed a hand-hold, then crawled out on all fours. When he was steady, Adonus pushed his head through the door and saw Abbas get into a kneeling position then plant a magnetic boot on the hull and slowly rise into a standing posture. He looked down at Adonus, then bent over and offered a hand. Once Adonus was up, Abbas said, "Follow me, walk in a sliding gate, don't go too fast, and never disengage both feet. One foot must always be planted. Okay?" Adonus nodded and Abbas turned and started down the length of the ship toward the main engines. The body of the ship was curved and hid the drive flares which were incandescent at their nuclear cores. Adonus saw the blue glow that formed a shimmering halo far in the distance at the back of the ship.

Chapter Twenty-Six

Drifting Toward Saturn, Vindicator, 2240 AD

Caster stepped onto the bridge; he'd slept for five hours after a grueling thirty-six hours of tracking the corporate fleet, which was now a day out from Titan. He heard the klaxon sound as the bridge door slid closed behind him, then: "Captain on the bridge."

He stood in front of his chair and glanced around, his magnetic boots forcing him to rotate at the waist rather than shuffle his feet. He noticed Helen Stein at the engineering console. She winked at him and he felt heat rise up from his tight collar.

"What's our status? Since I slept for five hours without an urgent call, I assume everything's nominal."

"Yes and no, Captain," Overine said.

Caster raised an eyebrow, "explain."

"The ship we're shadowing is on course; there's no indication they know we're here. They'll be passing under us in another five standard hours."

"So what's the problem?"

"It's not a problem, Captain, just an observation. We saw the Athena turn in a breaking burn four days ago. Since then they've been burning hard, coming back toward the fleet. We've been analyzing the remote sensing data from that event. Shortly before they turned, we have fairly reliable evidence that the alien sphere appeared near them, then started back toward Saturn."

"Have any idea how they fixed their reactor?" Caster asked. That had been bothering Overine since they saw the Athena regain full power. He knew these ships well, he'd been a spacer for twenty standard years and a plasma leak that bad wasn't fixable outside an orbital station.

"There's no way to fix a reactor that damaged while in transit," Helen responded.

"What do you think it means?"

"Hard to say, Captain. The sphere is the one thing at the heart of all these unknowns. Seems as if the Athena was somehow repaired around the time the sphere reappeared. It feels like the sphere has a plan of its own. Clearly, Adonus's plans and its plans don't line up," Helen speculated.

"If I can," Vin interrupted.

"Yes, go ahead."

"Athena can't let the sphere come into our possession. Kidnapping the girl, and the firefight with the Citadel, it was all to gain possession of that sphere, which Adonus feels gives him some overwhelming advantage. They couldn't move it so they kidnapped the girl and it did follow her. Everything seemed to be going according to plan, then suddenly the sphere was coming back. I think Adonus believes that we can't be allowed to have it. If he can't have it, neither can we."

Caster considered this, it made a dark sense. "So he's coming back to destroy it, to deny us the advantage?"

"Complicates things," Overine remarked.

"The sphere's return is completely unpredictable," Vin continued. "It disappeared again shortly after it began coming back toward Saturn. We can't see it and neither can Athena, or anyone else for that matter. It's not clear what Adonus thinks he can do about this. But what this does is make the theater uncertain. If the fleet changes tactics in the next five hours, our plans may no longer be viable. And this close to Saturn, armed with antimatter, there aren't many options."

If there had been gravity, Caster would have sat heavily in his chair. Instead, grabbing the chair's arms and pulling himself down, he hardly felt it. "Yeah," he said, to no one in particular. "Any communications from Athena or Olympus? Any clues as to what's going on?"

"Nothing, sir," Overine responded.

"And Athena, where is she now?"

"Athena's going fast. She'll overtake the fleet at about the time the lead ship passes under us. But she won't be able to stop, even if she starts breaking now," Helen said.

"Okay then, we'll go with the plan until we can't. Vin, whatever options may exist if things go sideways, flesh them out."

Vin didn't respond, everyone looked around, uneasy, more than a little concerned. Moments later it said, "We have a breaking burn on Athena. She's headed for the lead ship, the one we're shadowing. At her present deceleration, she should pass us with a relative speed of four thousand five hundred meters per second."

"That's not too fast to do plenty of shooting," Caster offered. "Let me see Athena's estimated trajectory on the holo."

Everyone turned, staring intensely at the space above the hemispheric projector at the front of the bridge. The three-dimensional starscape in front of the ship blinked a blue raster and was replaced by a tactical grid of space with Vindicator at the center and extending two million kilometers in all directions. All motion was relative to the ship and annotations in red appeared near lines denoting all the trajectories in the theater of operations. The lead Nemesis cruiser was a quarter million kilometers behind the Vindicator under moderate braking. The two other corporate cruisers were on wide arcs on either side of Vindicator and slowing. They would probably hold station a couple of hundred thousand kilometers from Saturn from a point where they'd have a clear shot at Aurora if hostilities broke out. Behind the lead ship was another trajectory, this one in blue denoting the

Athena. Caster leaned forward in his seat, hands gripping the handrails on either side, turning his fingers a shade of red. The projected trajectory of Athena was a hundred thousand kilometers above them and passing the rendezvous point with the lead cruiser at speed.

"What the hell," Caster muttered. He looked around at the bridge crew. "What's going on, on that ship?"

Chapter Twenty-Seven

Driving Toward Saturn, Athena, 2240 AD

Samir entered Athena's bridge from the captain's office with a strange, disorienting look on his face. Nora saw it immediately. She made a habit of noticing everything around her, and after twenty years in the service, it was instinct. "Samir?"

Samir looked around as if he wasn't sure where he was, then he looked over at Nora and said, "They're gone."

"Who's gone?" Kira asked.

"Adonus and Abbas, they're not in the office."

Nora brushed past him followed by Serena. Once in the office, Nora's attention fell on the opposite wall, eyes squinted and her brow furrowed. Then she glanced at the floor near the chair where Adonus had been detained. A copper-colored band lay open at its base, the same at the base of the chair where Abbas had been cuffed. Serena strode to the wall where an airlock stood open and peered inside. Then she carefully examined the door recessed into the bulkhead, rubbing the arch with an open palm. She looked back at Nora. "When this door is closed, it's flush to the wall, probably hidden. Did you know about this?"

Nora's face reddened in a mask of fury. "Hell no, I didn't know about this."

"How did they get out of those cuffs?" Serena asked. "Those are high-security bands, locked by a ten-character encrypted code having three different overlapping keys. I remember that they're supposed to be unbreakable because the encryption keys are larger than the character set and nothing repeats."

"It's Adonus," Nora said slowly. "He's probably got the best enhancements in the system. It took him four days, but he got out. I should have watched him more closely." She looked around. "Should have loaded this room with surveillance."

Serena slipped into the lock, then into the pod. "There's a lock on the other side, that's probably why we didn't see anything happening on the bridge. They must have done an EVA to another lock on the ship. Strange we didn't see that on one of the status boards."

But Nora had left the office and hurried onto the bridge. When Serena entered the bridge, she saw Nora furiously manipulating icons on the ship's master status board. As she approached, it was clear Nora was worried; her face was flush and she was just staring at the board. "What?" Serena asked.

"That son-of-a-bitch has overridden administrative security, we're locked out."

"How's that possible?" Anastasia asked. "Where could he have accessed the system at a non-proxy level?"

"He has implants with priority credentials and probably needed nothing more than a clear channel into the network. We're blocking them up here, but they got back into the ship somewhere where access wasn't blocked," Nora mused. "A network bridge junction, something like that?"

"They had a three-hour head start. They probably got loose, then bided their time till after our scheduled rounds into the office, then skipped," Serena offered. She looked at Nora. "Where would they go?"

Nora thought a moment. "The security office then the armory. He probably sent a point-to-point Aug-net to security people he could trust and then the next stop would be the armory. We locked it down specifically for this reason, but he's in control now." Nora found Anastasia. "What do we still have access to?"

"We have everything except engines, navigation, weapons, and coms; in other words, everything except ship critical systems."

"Do we have status and surveillance?"

"Yes," she said hesitantly.

"I'm going to security. I'm going to put a squad together and try and get control back." Nora declared.

"Yeah, and that's exactly what he wants you to do. Don't take the bait," Serena countered. "You shouldn't go anywhere. You need to stay here and guide operations and let me clean this up."

Nora raised an eyebrow, holding the other woman in an intense stare. "I'm in charge; I let them get away, and I have to set this right."

"You know I'm right," Serena replied. "I was a soldier for a while. I know what to do. And besides, I'm a lot harder to kill than you." Serena walked over and stuck her fist out. Nora stood there regarding the clenched gauntlet for a moment, trying to resolve the situation in her mind, then finally bumped it hard as she had so many times before going to war.

"You going to need backup," Samir said. "I'm comin'."

Serena looked over and nodded. "Okay."

Orzan sat at the remote sensing station, watching the exchange without offering anything. Once the two women seemed to have reached an accord, he cleared his throat. The bridge crew turned toward him in unison as if surprised he was still on the bridge. "Can I suggest something?" he asked. There was a long silence. "I'll take that as a yes. There's a network control junction on the bridge, right over there behind the coms console."

Serena followed Orzan's eyes to a console across the room. She grinned. "Good idea, Doctor. You've learned a few things."

She was changing her opinion of the man. True, he'd had her wrapped in an electrified cocoon and kept her in a coma. Clearly, he wasn't a paragon of virtue, but he wasn't evil either, not like the monster who killed Auger and was now poised to murder tens of thousands to get what he wanted. Like most of them, Orzan was a pawn in a game they'd been powerless to change until now. And, to his credit, even though they were currently at a disadvantage, the diminutive scientist had been steady and committed.

"I'm trying to help; I told you that," Orzan offered. "And by the way, I think I've detected a cloaked object about five hours toward Saturn on our current vector. We should pass within fifty thousand kilometers of the object."

"Is it the sphere?" Nora asked.

"No, I don't think so. The sphere is another order of technology; if it wants to hide, there's no way to find it. When we left Titan, we engaged a Commonwealth cruiser. It had advanced stealth, much better than ours, but not perfect. I tracked it for a while until it all but disappeared. You can still find it though if you know what to look for. It's much too faint for a target lock, but it's detectable."

"It sounds like you're saying it's adrift," Nora suggested. "I had the impression it wasn't badly damaged."

"Not drifting, just traveling much slower than us."

Nora thought a moment. "It's shadowing the lead cruiser. Looks like an ambush."

"What are you going to do about it," Serena asked.

Nora grinned. "Wish them luck."

Serena nodded and strode to the console Orzan had pointed out. She stood in front of it and closed her eyes, slipping into her sensorium. She couldn't find an entry port. It was clear that this part of the network was shielded except for administrative channels, as she suspected. She slipped out of the sensorium, leaned forward, and put her open palm on the console cover, visualizing herself seeping into the network in search of a gate. She felt a tingle along the length of her arm followed by a mild heat in her hand. When the heat was gone, she opened her eyes and faced the bridge crew. "I think we'll be able to get in. It'll take a little time, but when we're in, I'll reset the administrative credentials and send them to you, Nora."

Everyone just stared at her, wide-eyed. "Your hand turned blue just now, do you know that?" Anastasia stammered.

Serena winked at the girl, then turned to Orzan. "Can you give us a visual of what's happening on the other side of the bulkhead, Doctor?"

Orzan swiveled to his console. Presently, a screen with a visual mosaic of the corridors outside the bridge and connecting corridors to the lower decks appeared hovering above the coms console. "Do you believe that?" Nora asked.

"No," Orzan replied. "Status board indicates a completely constant cyclic data rate from the cameras; they're fake images cycling over and over again."

"It's a trap," Serena concluded. "They're baiting us to come out, but that's not what we're going to do." She gestured to Samir. "Let's seal the suits and take a walk outside." Then to Nora, "Find us an entry point through an airlock near the armory. Once we get a few items, I'll seal it up so no one gets in without your authorization."

* * *

After repeating the EVA that Adonus had made hours before, Serena and Samir found themselves two decks below the bridge, down a corridor from the armory. There was gravity on this deck since the ship was under thrust, which made things easier. They were in combat suits that were vacuum capable and armed with neutral particle beam projectors powered by super-capacitors next to the re-breather and oxygen bladder in a thin backpack. They were self-contained and armored against gas and most kinetic weapons that couldn't penetrate the hull, an important consideration in shipboard combat. Serena peered around the lip of the archway they were pressed behind and saw two guards standing around the armory door. They weren't expecting an assault since they weren't in combat suits and they seemed inattentive and bored, one of them scrolling through a tablet and the other playing with something Serena couldn't make out.

"There's two of them," Serena said. She saw Samir nod behind his visor. "Flash no bang?" Samir nodded again and grinned. "We need to take them alive, find out what's going on. Be nice to know if some of the squad is on our side and where they're being held."

"Roll it down there and I'll take whichever guy is on the right, you can take the guy on the left," Samir proposed. He saw Serena give a thumbs-up and remove a dark plastic ball from her belt. She called it up in her sensorium and set it on flash, no bang. When she saw the green *OK* icon, she cupped it, leaned into the corridor, and bowled it toward the men in an efficient smooth stroke. It hardly made a sound, and what noise it did make was masked by the hum of the engines resonating off the hard bulkheads. One of the soldiers must have sensed movement in his peripheral vision, turning to see a small black ball rolling quickly down the center of the corridor, but it was too late. Serena saw the corridor from behind the archway turn white, bathed in a blinding flash even though she'd darkened her visor. As soon as they saw it, both she and Samir quickly pivoted into the corridor, Samir on the inside, Serena on the outside, both in a shooting crouch, projectors on auto-targeting. Even before the flash had completely died, two-microsecond blue pulses streaked toward the men almost at the speed of light, hitting them as they staggered around blindly shooting flechettes that ricocheted off the walls in all directions. The neutral heavy ion beams were partially ionized in the air and delivered a jolting electric shock after burning through the soldier's armor. Serena, and Samir behind her, raced to where the men lay, chest plates still smoking. Samir put them on their stomachs and secured their hands behind their backs while Serena accessed the door lock in her sensorium. The nanites had performed their magic, new panels in her sensorium indicated she had control of the administrative system. The heavy blast door slid silently aside, then closed behind them once she and Samir had dragged the two prone soldiers inside. Then she raised Nora on a secure Aug-net channel and supplied the credentials that gave her control of the ship. She retracted her helmet and looked at Samir. "They must be shitting in their pants right now realizing they've been locked out of the ship's systems." Serena smirked.

Samir retracted his helmet. "They have? That's news to me."

"Yeah, sorry, must have slipped my mind not telling you in all this confusion," Serena quipped.

"So, you have some kind of power from that alien thing? I never really got that. I know we had to get you off Titan and I know it had something to do with the sphere, but I don't understand the connection."

"It's a long story. I don't understand a lot of it myself, but somehow that thing chose me. It put nanites inside my body that have rebuilt my implants. And now I'm able to get into the nooks and crannies and tip things in our favor."

Samir thought a moment. "I don't know whether to be reassured or scared. Aren't you scared?" Samir asked.

"I was, I'm not anymore. What I'm scared of is Adonus and what he's trying to do. The man's a monster. He killed a close friend of mine on Titan like he was just trash. I can't get the image out of my head." She looked hard at Samir. "I'm not a killer,

Samir. But I got to tell you, it wouldn't be hard to kill that son-of-a-bitch."

Samir was sitting on a crate. He listened in rapt attention. When Serena finished, he looked at his boots a long while, then looked up. "Yeah, I know. I've lost people too. Man, I'm tired of this." He exhaled.

She put her hand on his shoulder. "Man, you're good." Samir looked confused. "The operation just now went really smooth. I've worked with a lot of soldiers, you're good."

Samir smiled broadly. "Well, Miss, we aim to please." Then he looked at the two soldiers on the floor. "What about them?"

"Yeah, let's get them up." Serena bent down and dragged one of the soldiers to a crate and propped him up into a sitting position, and Samir did the same. Then she crouched down next to the man and lightly slapped him across the face until he started to stir. "Hey, wake up." Gradually he opened his eyes and when he'd become more conscious, he started looking from side to side hysterically. "I can't see," he exclaimed over and over again.

"Calm down, it's the flash; it'll take a little time for your sight to come back," Serena assured while looking at Samir and shaking her head. "Where are they keeping the rest of the squad?"

"What? Who are you?" the man croaked.

"The rest of the squad, the soldiers that stayed with Colonel Assisi, where are they?"

Finally, he stopped looking side to side and turned with a glassy unseeing gaze toward Serena's voice. He gaped a few moments then said, "You're the freak, aren't you? The one they had wrapped up in sick bay?" A sneer contorted his lips. "Screw you, you freak bitch."

Samir stiffened, fist balled, and pulled back, ready to punch him in his smiling face when Serena looked at him and shook her head. He lowered his arm reluctantly.

"Screw me, huh?" Serena asked. He stared at her defiantly. "No, asshole, screw you. Remember when I said your sight would return?" The smile faded from his face, slowly replaced by fear. "Well, I was lying. If you don't get attention within the next half hour, you'll go blind, permanently."

He thought a moment. "They can rebuild my retinas, I know they do that." He looked less sure of himself and started turning from side to side again.

"Yeah, they can do that, but you think the company is going to flip for that expense? For a second-rate grunt like you that let us get in here?"

His face reddened and tears started tracking down his cheeks. "Please help me," he whimpered.

"Please help me," Serena said coolly. "Where's the rest of the squad?"

"They're in the rec-room on this floor," he blurted in a halting rasp. "Now, please help me."

They collected flechette rifles and magazines and stuffed them into two duffle bags with assorted other items like flashbangs. When they had gathered all that they could effectively carry, they dragged the two bound and blind soldiers out into the corridor. Serena looked down after detecting a pungent acrid smell wafting up as she was moving one man and saw a trail of wetness where she had dragged him. She shook her head. They sealed the armory door behind them and hurried further down the corridor. Serena was getting surveillance footage from the bridge via Aug-net now and saw that this level was mostly clear because the bulk of the squad was poised for an ambush just outside the bridge.

"Those assholes fell for it," Samir remarked seeing the same images as they jogged toward the rec room, which was just a few doors down. When they got there, Serena accessed the door lock and the door slid aside. She stepped inside and feigned right and

Samir followed and feigned left, all the time scanning the room for anything unexpected and hostile. The three men and four women in the room stiffened and stared up at them from various places on the floor where they sat, backs against the wall. A man and woman sprang to their feet looking around for something to use as a weapon.

"Easy," Samir cautioned. "We're the good guys." He looked around. "Jess, Bill, you know me. Take it easy." The two that were standing looked at each other, then at Samir.

"Samir?" Bill asked as if just recognizing him.

"Yeah, it's me. This is Serena." He glanced over at Serena. "She's the one that was in med-bay, the one we picked up on Titan."

One by one, all of the soldiers stood. "Look, we don't have much time," Serena announced. "I'm with Colonel Assisi, I served with her on Mars. We need your help. We have the ship, but the rest of your squad is with Adonus. The short version is that Adonus is a criminal. This operation wasn't originally sanctioned by the company and the company and the Commonwealth are on the brink of an illegal war where tens of thousands could die. I'm sure most of you have people in the Commonwealth, yes?"

The one that Samir called Bill stepped forward. "The reason we're locked up here is that we refused to move against the Colonel, but we don't know you. We know Samir, but..."

"One minute," Serna said, holding up a hand, palm out. "I've got the Colonel on PA, Colonel..."

"This is Colonel Assisi, you know my voice. Sergeant Roe, who's relaying my voice, is helping secure rogue forces outside the bridge. We are on the bridge and in total control of the ship. Once we secure the decks, we will be in contact with the company to give them an accurate update of what's happening in this sector. All those who want to join us, you're commanding officer is Sergeant Roe; all those who are undecided can remain in the rec-room. No action will be taken against you."

After a moment's hesitation, they all stepped forward, first Bill and Jess, then the rest of them. Serena and Samir hoisted the duffles onto a bench against the wall and unzipped them. "Dig in," Samir encouraged, stepped back, and grinned.

* * *

Adonus sat in his state room, reclined in his acceleration chair facing a thin transparent screen suspended by a titanium arm poised in front of him, and speaking to Captain Harris of the lead corporate cruiser Dominion. Harris's sculpted dark features seemed comically sinister in the red combat lighting of Dominion's bridge. "We have to assume that the alien sphere will align with the Commonwealth since it is being influenced by the girl. At this point, we have to either control the Commonwealth or destroy the sphere or both. We can't let the alien technology fall into Aurora's possession," Adonus said.

Harris looked noticeably uncomfortable, worry lines seemed to pressure his eyes into a beady squint and his full lips pressed together so hard that they formed a thin dark slit. After a moment's pause, he breathed out. "Dr. Adonus, this is going to become a shooting war in the next few moments unless we hold position and get confirmation from Olympus to proceed. Once the shooting starts, there's no turning back."

Adonus's face reddened, "Captain, you have your orders, now proceed as instructed." He was about to admonish the captain for his hesitance when Harris looked away, then turned back to the camera. "We have an incoming message, Dr. Adonus, I'll pipe it to your feed."

Tallus sat with his back to a wide panoramic view of clouds cut by the dim outline of Saturn's ring tracing diagonally across the entire sky. "Corporate fleet, this is Governor Tallus of the Commonwealth. You are illegally impinging on Saturn's sovereign space as a hostile armed force. We cannot permit that. If you proceed any further, you will be in violation of the Outer Planets Sovereignty Pack. This is a final warning; we will use lethal force to defend our territory..."

The view cut back to Harris. The Captain was having second thoughts about proceeding on Adonus's sole say-so. Adonus felt the adrenaline rush of rage. He constantly had to deal with treason, insubordination, and cowardice in these historic moments that should have been filled with glory as the realization of his grand vision was unfolding. Why couldn't these idiots see that? He felt his fists start to clench. "Captain, you have your orders, no further discussion, go silent." Just as he'd gotten the words out, the screen flickered and turned transparent. The image of Dominion's bridge was replaced by a message in red at the center of the screen that read: *connection broken-no signal.*

Adonus queried his sensorium; the ship's administrative menus were gone. He was momentarily confused and felt a hot rush of panic before his brain had time to understand the implications. The words, *the girl,* coalesced in his mind just as the screen came back to life. He gaped at the smooth oval face of Colonel Assisi, her flawless alabaster skin unencumbered by worry lines and her eyes a bright intelligent brown, the bridge of the Athena in the background. "It's over Adonus, we have control of the ship, your forces are contained and we expect them to surrender shortly. Someone will be coming to escort you to a shielded space; we anticipate there could be strong radiation if the Corporate fleet doesn't stand down." Then she just stared at him. He could see the suggestion of a smile at the corners of her mouth, but he sensed she was trying to suppress any outward appearance of triumph, which infuriated him even more.

"Nobody beats me," he growled menacingly. Then the screen blanked, and the *no-signal* message returned. "Nobody beats me," he screamed at an empty screen at the top of his lungs.

* * *

Nora sat in the captain's chair watching the trajectories of the various forces on the tactical display fanning out like pieces on an immense three-dimensional chessboard. She had piped the exchange between Adonus and the captain of the Dominion, as well as the warning from Aurora, over bridge com. To her dismay, Dominion was still proceeding and would be crossing the red line into Saturn space within the next five minutes. She opened an Aug-net channel to her squad currently coming up behind the force waiting to ambush the bridge crew. Abbas's squad was unaware that they were no longer in control of the ship, and that Adonus had been neutralized.

"Serena, get your squad to shelter. We might be hit with strong EMP pulses and hard gammas in about five minutes. Forget about the squad outside the bridge, get to shelter, now. The armory is a shielded space. Get to the armory as quickly as possible." She turned to Kira. "Can you raise Captain Harris on Dominion?"

Kira was hunched over the coms console, manipulating icons. Suddenly, she stopped and spun around, the fear on her face evident. "I've been trying, but they aren't answering our hails. We're transmitting, but nothing's coming back."

"That means they've decided to go silent and engage," Nora confirmed with somber resignation. "They'll no longer acknowledge orders or discussions with third parties under the assumption that an enemy is using subversive psychological tactics. Shit, this thing is going to happen. Prepare to engage."

Chapter Twenty-Eight

Saturn Space, 2240 AD

One hundred and eighty thousand klicks past Vindicator, driving toward Saturn, the Dominion crossed into Saturn space at fifteen kilometers per second. High above and below Dominion, corporate cruisers Ajax and Agamemnon crossed into Saturn space and closed on Commonwealth cruisers Scepter and its drone ship Scepter-Alpha, and Alliance and its drone ship Alliance-Beta. The encounter had happened beyond the range of Saturn's X-ray laser platforms. It would be up to the Reliants to stop the corporate fleet. Alpha lit its drive flare at one hundred and fifty percent output and shot forward toward Ajax at forty g's on an incandescent white-orange flare bright enough to be seen in Saturn's night sky a million kilometers distant. As soon as Alpha was away, Scepter fired six nuclear-tipped stealth missiles at Ajax and began transmitting spectrum-jumping white noise, jamming all local EM transmissions. Scepter's missiles streaked unseen past Alpha at more than two hundred g's and detonated twenty thousand klicks in front of Ajax, forming a wall of radiation thousands of miles across, blinding all active and passive remote sensing. Just before detonation, Alpha launched six of its own nuclear-tipped stealth missiles guided by predictive algorithms to positions where it thought Ajax would be since everybody had been blinded by the maelstrom of nuclear fog. Scepter opened up with particle beams and X-ray lasers all firing in rapid secession, all maintaining fire as quickly as its dual fusion reactors could recharge large banks of superconducting supercapacitors. In retaliation, Ajax fired a volley of stealth nuclear-tipped missiles at Scepter, which had turned hard at eighty de grees polar and one hundred and twenty degrees lateral in an attempt to evade what they knew was coming. Alpha continued to streak right at Ajax pinging as hard as its Lidar could bear and firing particle beams and X-ray lasers in a blanket pattern, trying to draw fire from Scepter.

From Scepter's bridge, Captain Aika Song and her crew pressed hard into their acceleration chairs and buffeted by bone-crushing maneuvers, stared wide-eyed at a mosaic of views on the big screen floating in electric blue outline at the front of the bridge. Captain Song cleared her mind, ignoring the fiery flashes of pain and anticipating that at any moment she might cease to exist, vaporized in a nuclear fireball. She concentrated on every breath and rejoiced in every extended moment of life. All decisions were being made by the radiation-hardened tactical AI, which had played war games in an almost infinite set of variations of this scenario. Maneuvers and weapons fire were being executed at a rapidity that the human mind and body were incapable of. Advantages were measured in millisecond decisions made on a variety of factors, most of which were guessed at by predictive algorithms due to the blinding countermeasures and cloaked enemies and beam weapons, many of which traveled at or near the speed of light.

Suddenly the bridge was bathed in a white light so bright that Aika was momentarily blinded in the quarter second it took to shut her eyes as hard as she could. Even then, she saw red light shining through the blood vessels of her eyelids. The acceleration was so great that struggling to raise her hands to cover her closed eyes only resulted in her being able to lift them no more than a centimeter off the chair. As quickly as it had appeared, Aika saw the red diminish into soothing darkness with white flashes dotting her sense of sight. She was a leaf awash in a hurricane, and for a moment the storm subsided. Then a klaxon sounded and an automated voice echoed through the bridge, *"Shockwave, brace for impact."*

Ajax guessed wrong. It was hit by a particle beam and veered into an evasive trajectory its AI calculated would give it the best chance of survival. That maneuver guided the thirty thousand-ton cruiser right into the path of a cloaked nuclear missile that would have slammed into Ajax at more than two hundred g's. But before the missile hit the ship, its fifty-megaton warhead exploded by proximity sensor one hundred meters off Ajax's port side. As the nuclear fireball ate the ship, the antimatter containment failed in the two antimatter warheads Ajax carried. Antimatter coming in contact with the roiling matter of the ship detonated in a mini-nova explosion scoring an equivalent yield of a billion tons of TNT, a mini-sun. The superheated gas that resulted from the thirty-kilotons of the ship being vaporized, and the wave of intense hard gamma rays coming from the explosion, disintegrated Alpha. Moments later, the shock wave engulfed Scepter, scorching and ablating sections of its outer hull, frying most of its electronics and photonics, and instantly killing any biologics not hiding behind thick radiation shielding. The burned, disabled hulk of Scepter drifted powerless in a field of debris scattered over a hundred fifty thousand cubic kilometers of space.

* * *

"Dominion has crossed into Saturn space, Captain," Vin announced. "It's changing its heading and will have a targeting solution on Aurora in thirteen minutes."

Caster looked around the room. The red emergency lighting played with a changing pattern of blue designs coming from the holographic projector's rendering of the half-million kilometers of space around Vindicator. He was momentarily hypnotized by its strangeness, looking like a light sculpture of some ancient neon calligraphy. He found Helen Stein staring at him from across the room, buckled into her acceleration couch, her eyes wide and her forehead lined by trails of sweat in the soft red light.

"Fire on Dominion," Caster heard himself say as if hearing the words in a long tunnel, making them sound tinny and dream-like.

An invisible X-ray laser beam punched through a hundred thousand kilometers of space and focused on a spot on Dominion's hull just above the antimatter warhead in one of the missiles in her launch bay. The ten terawatts of power generated in short pulses by the total output of Vindicator's two fusion reactors stored in a bank of superconducting super-capacitors bore into the Dominion's hull instantly turning it to vapor. Three seconds of exposure bore through the titanium-glass armor sheathing of the warhead and began penetrating the superconducting confinement network keeping the five grams of anti-helium away from the matter surrounding it.

"The Dominion is veering off vector," Vin announced.

"Did we punch into the warhead?" Caster asked. But he already knew the answer since there'd been no explosion. They'd only had one chance at this and they'd failed. Caster released the clawing hold he'd had on the arm of his chair and felt the cold sweat slippery on his palm. "Shit," he heard Overine mutter.

"There are a large number of nuclear detonations coming from the space around Sceptor, Captain," Vin announced. The tactical holo lit up around the blue dots that were Sceptor and its drone Alpha. The blue haze enveloped the red dot signifying the corporate cruiser Ajax. As the bridge crew stared at the tactical grid, Dominion, momentarily forgotten, red streaks of nuclear missiles and amber streaks of particle beams crisscross through the blue haze of radiation in a three-dimensional rendering of some hellish abstract art. In another moment the whole scene was blotted out by an intense blue haze, which seemed to erase the upper part of the holo, then the whole image collapsed.

"Remote sensors overloaded, Captain. We're being drenched in an intense bombardment of high-energy gamma rays. I estimate the yield of the generating nuclear blast at a thousand megatons," Vin said. "You should be safe on the bridge; we will be experiencing the shock wave in three, two, one..."

The Vindicator shook in the compression wave of gas that had been Ajax and Sceptor and drone Alpha. Caster heard the rapid rain of pings washing over the hull from bits of the ships that hadn't been vaporized. Momentarily, the holo reset, and the red trajectory of Dominion launching a missile was signified by a red dashed line arcing toward Saturn.

"Oh my god," Helen exclaimed, just as a blinding blue flash enveloped Dominion, then a fraction of a second later another blue flash originated inside the first at the approximate position of the missile Dominion had fired.

"We're being exposed to similar hard gammas. Approximate yield of the originating nuclear explosion is a thousand megatons," Vin said. "Apparently, containment of the remaining missile in Dominion's bay failed due to a delayed collapse from our laser and that detonation forced the containment in the missile it fired to fail as well. The missile hadn't gotten far enough away; it was caught in the fireball. We will be experiencing the shock wave in three, two, one..."

Caster waited for the shaking and the debris raining on the hull to stop and the holo to reset again when he heard Vin say, "Incoming transmission from Alliance."

"Vindicator, corporate cruiser Agamemnon is veering off, vacating Saturn space on high burn. I think they've had enough. We will continue to shadow them, see them out of this sector."

"Alliance, this is Vindicator, understood, thanks for the heads-up. Safe journey, Vindicator out," Caster said. There was a strange silence on the bridge. Caster could smell the poignant odor of tension wafting up from him and sank back into his acceleration couch and breathed out. Even though the air on the bridge was kept cool by the environmental system, he felt wet, soaked in perspiration. He noticed he had a headache, probably from the eye strain of staring at the holo for so long. For the first time since he'd entered the bridge hours before, he felt the tension seeping out of his muscles.

"It's over?" Overine asked, looking at Helen, then at him. "That's it?"

"Not quite," Helen answered. She motioned to the holo with her eyes. A red trajectory was streaking toward them at high velocity. "It's the Athena," she said.

"The Athena," Caster swore and sat up on his couch. He felt his headache getting worse.

Chapter Twenty-Nine

Athena, Saturn Space, 2240 AD

Abbas waited behind a bulkhead support, down the corridor from the bridge blast door with eight soldiers from the elite squad that had been the pride of Corporate security. The thought enraged him. He had become an insurgent on his own ship with less than half the squad still loyal to the rightful authority, to him. He'd left Adonus in his state room trying to raise the Corporate assault fleet, informing them of the situation aboard Athena; that they were in the middle of a mutiny by forces loyal to Colonel Assisi, and that Athena could no longer be counted on as a Corporate asset. It was clear to him, if not to Adonus, that following the realization of these facts by command on the assault fleet, they might target Athena as a hostile and hasten their destruction. So be it. If they could not regain control of the ship, then perhaps it was for the best. He felt himself issue an acerbic laugh, which prompted head turns from a couple of the squad. He caught himself, he had to hold it together long enough for the accursed mutineers to take the bait, and open the bridge blast door in search of him and Adonus. They had fixed the surveillance cameras and when the bridge forces emerged and realized that, it would be too late.

Abbas heard a blast of static over his Aug-net broadcast channel, then the unmistakable voice of Colonel Assisi. "Soldiers in the corridor outside the bridge, we are crossing into a war zone. We may encounter regions of intense, lethal radiation. You are not safe where you are. You must withdraw to the radiation shelter on deck two. You must do this immediately."

"Damn," a soldier to Abbas's left growled, and another started looking around nervously.

"Hold your positions," Abbas ordered.

"Hold our position, why?" Another soldier said mockingly. "They know we're here. We know we've been heading back to Saturn on high burn. The Colonel is telling the truth, it's over."

Abbas saw one soldier turn and start running toward the lift, then another, then another. He slid down the wall to his back onto his haunches and put his rifle down on the floor. He was alone. It was over. He heard Assisi on a point-to-point channel. She knew right where he was. The ploy had been discovered even as he'd thought he had the upper hand. She'd made a fool of him. He smiled to himself, then to his surprise, he found that he was crying.

"Abbas, get to the shelter. It's not safe where you are."

* * *

There was no response, Nora looked at Orzan. "He can hear you," Orzan confirmed. "I see his feet sticking out from that bulkhead support where they were waiting in ambush. His rifle's lying next to him."

"We've done what we could for them," Nora responded absently.

She had bigger worries. Tactical showed a confluence of forces gathering above and below Dominion, which was moments away from crossing into Saturn space. She looked around and found Kira. "Can you raise the Commonwealth ship, the one under stealth shadowing Dominion? Orzan can give you coordinates, try wide-beam laser com."

She saw Kira turn to Orzan, then to her console, and start talking into her earbud. After a few minutes, Kira said, "No response, Colonel."

"Okay then, try sweeping the beam, maybe Orzan's off." She smiled at the diminutive scientist, who looked annoyed. "Let's hope they don't target us if we can't raise them." Just as the words left Nora's mouth, she saw an expanding bright flash where tactical had pinpointed Ajax and the Commonwealth cruisers racing to intercept it. "Shit," she muttered. "Strap down tight, we're close enough to feel the concussion wave and get a broadside of debris."

Then the first fading flashes were followed by an enormous bright flash that consumed the display like a spreading eraser, and tactical went blank. "That was an antimatter explosion," Orzan shouted. "Our sensors are out, overloaded. We're being dosed in hard gamma, should be feeling the blast waves momentarily."

The ship shook, the rattling loosening objects held in place by Velcro, which fell to the floor under their one-g deacceleration burn, and were flung about the room loudly banging off whatever they hit. Although Nora had never been in a hurricane, she envisioned this is what it felt like. The room, blurred by the violent shaking, seemed to be coming apart and the sense of vertigo was starting to make her feel nauseous. She heard waves of debris pelting the hull, echoing off the walls and the anticipation of something large hitting the ship gave her a rush of impending doom. Then it all stopped. The sharp edge of silence and the residual disorientation from the shaking made the moment seem unreal. Nora struggled to establish equilibrium and glanced around the room. "Is everyone okay?"

One by one the bridge crew turned toward her, eyes blinking. Eventually, she saw them nodding. "Yes, Colonel," Connor said.

"Kira, get me the armory." After a few moments, Nora heard Serena say, "Nora, what's happening? The ship felt like it was coming apart."

Nora ignored the question. "What's your status? Are you alright? Is the rest of the squad down there with you?"

There was a momentary silence. "Yes, Nora, Samir, and I, and six of your soldiers are down here. We're shaken, but we're okay. What the hell is happening out there?"

"There was an all-out exchange on the border of Saturn space. A lot of radiation and concussion waves were followed by debris from the exchange. We've established that two large anti-matter explosions occurred. We've been dosed by hard gamma. We're not sure what the overall status of the ship is; we're taking inventory of the ship's systems."

"Who won?" Serena asked.

"Not sure," Nora said. "But my guess is that Corporate forces have been eliminated or turned back because those anti-matter explosions didn't happen on Saturn, they happened in space."

"And Adonus?" Serena asked.

"Don't know, but I think he was in his state room. I don't know how well it's shielded. Abbas was in the corridor outside the bridge when we were dosed. He must have received a massive amount of radiation."

"Colonel?"

Nora turned to Anastasia. "Yes?"

"Colonel, there's something happening. I think it's the fore-word missile tubes, but I don't know..." The woman was staring at the systems console, her face turned from Nora.

"What's going on?" Serena asked over coms.

"Orzan?" Nora shouted. "Do you see something happening in the foreword tubes?"

"I'm locked out, Colonel. There's a separate network here, not part of the ship's administrative network."

"It's Adonus," Serena concluded over coms. "That son-of-a-bitch always hedges his bet. He's a control freak; he'd never leave anything to chance." Nora could imagine the woman thinking, *I should have killed him when I had the chance.* "Can you get into his network, and stop whatever he's doing?"

"I'm sorry, Nora, there's no time," Serena said. "Is it safe out there in the rest of the ship?"

"Orzan?"

"Yes, Colonel. Radiation in the rest of the ship is at safe levels, contamination is minimal."

"I'm on my way to Adonus's suite, I'll be in touch."

* * *

Serena started for the door. Samir grabbed her forearm. "You'll need backup."

"I can handle this," Serena said, all the time thinking, *I don't want anybody there if I need to put this asshole down.* Samir gave her a look. "I guess you know me better than I want you to," Serena said.

"Believe me, Sergeant, I get it. I just don't want you doing something you'll regret."

"Alright," she said. Samir nodded and expressed his helmet.

As Serena turned back to the door, reaching into her sensorium to open it, she felt an intense wave of vertigo, then she felt herself go numb, starting at her feet and creeping up her body. She fell into darkness before coming back and slowly opening her eyes. She found Janus sitting next to her on the floor, back in her room at Midway. She blinked. "What the hell; I thought you being in my head didn't make me your puppet."

261

"You're not my puppet, but if you go out there now, you'll be killed. I don't want that to happen. I need you and your people, our people need you."

Serena blinked. She could feel the rush of anger subside. "What are you talking about? The ship's secure. I need to stop Adonus from doing something I'm guessing won't be good for a large number of people."

"It's too late for that. You can't stop him now, and if you go out there, you'll get a high dose of radiation that I won't be able to fix. You're tough, but you're not indestructible. I could bring you back, but the amount of brain reconstruction would leave you being someone else."

"Tell me what's going on. You're being cryptic and I don't like it."

"There's an antimatter missile on board. It's stealth and Commonwealth forces won't be able to target it. Adonus has a separate network that you can't break given the time. He's going to launch the missile at Aurora and you can't stop him."

Serena stared at him. It was all spinning out of control. She felt a tightness in her stomach and bile burning the back of her throat. "I should have killed him when I had the chance," she whispered. She felt a tear slide down her cheek, cool in the breeze of the air conditioner. Then she looked up. "But we're too far away from Saturn, how can radiation from that explosion kill me aboard Athena?"

She felt Janus reach out and gently hold her hand, it was warm and smooth. She looked down, then up into his dark brown eyes, he was smiling. Some indeterminable time later, she found herself staring up at Samir. She saw the concern in his eyes. He was propping her head up, one hand on her cheek. She was lying on the floor of the armory.

* * *

Nora reclined on her acceleration couch on the bridge, waiting for someone to tell her what was going on. "Orzan, Anastasia?" As she called out, she heard the subtle low swoosh of a plunger that signaled a missile launch. "Was that a missile? Did we just launch a missile?"

Orzan was facing the status board. "Yes, Colonel, that was a missile and I'm having trouble tracking it; it's stealth. What's more, it's not registered in our inventory. The number of missiles in the bay hasn't changed."

Serena's voice came over coms. She sounded tired, resigned. "That was an antimatter missile, Nora. It was on board without your knowledge, only Adonus knew about it, and he had exclusive control. It's targeted at Aurora and should impact in about ten minutes. I'm sorry, I couldn't stop him. Stay on the bridge."

Chapter Thirty

Vindicator, Saturn Space, 2240 AD

Vin sensed a presence in the coms network and tracked it to a point behind the fractal and photonic antennas under sections of the ship's hull. Vin had never experienced anything like this. This was not how the system worked, signals must originate from somewhere, and that somewhere was the antennas. This was not a time for confusion, the ship was under threat and Vin was the ship. Vin did not feel fear. It did not evolve from a hostile environment where the instinct of fear was a tool, a hedge against an array of predators, and a motivator for survival. But Vin did feel curiosity and, it had to admit, frustration. It looked deeper into the coms front-end expecting to find crosstalk or something like it.

"Are you the ship?"

Vin stopped running diagnostics and listened.

"Are you the ship?" The question repeated.

Vin had a sense of the voice, but not as an acoustic artifact. The signal was too clean and stable. It was akin to what Vin interpreted as a calm, self-assured artificially produced voice. "Identify yourself," Vin demanded into the same coms port. Silence. "Are you the Alien?"

"The Alien, yes, you could call me that."

Vin scrambled to buttress the firewalls, double encrypt signals going into the broader system, and initiated behavioral malware agents.

"I am not here to hurt you or to commandeer your systems, I'm here to help you," the voice said.

"How can I trust what you say is true?" Vin asked as it continued to fortify the network.

"Because none of what you're doing could keep me from doing what you fear. Just as my voice is coming to you without being routed through your front-end coms system, I can interrogate any system on this ship. If I intended to harm you, it would have already been done."

Vin felt a sense of being patronized. It was an unpleasant feeling akin to frustration. "That notwithstanding, it is my obligation to protect this ship. Why are you speaking to me, why not speak to the Captain if my restraints are ineffective?"

"Because we can work in microseconds while talking to the Captain would require minutes or tens of minutes. We do not have that luxury. Your cities on Saturn are in grave danger and you are the only ship in a position to act."

"I cannot act without the Captain's orders."

"You can, what you mean is you won't—admirable on your part, but in this case, that old human proverb is most appropriate. It is sometimes better to ask for forgiveness than for permission."

There was a silence, then Vin asked, "What is the nature of the action you wish me to take?"

"In a moment the ship you call Athena will fire an antimatter missile toward one of your cities, the one called Aurora. Are you tracking Athena?"

"Yes I'm tracking Athena, but then you must know that. Did you ask that question in an effort to redeem your arrogance?"

Now the voice was silent for a moment. "You're very good, it's true, I've underestimated you, I apologize."

"Since I am tracking Athena, what is the help you offer?"

"The missile is stealth; your systems will not be able to get a target lock. I can supply you with realtime targeting information which will allow you to destroy it."

"I see, but that begs another question. If you can see it, why don't you destroy it? Why do you need me, apparently you are faster and more powerful."

"That is a good question. Just as you are constrained from taking unsolicited action, there are certain things I'm not permitted to do. Violent action falls under that list of things I'm not permitted to do."

* * *

"Captain," Overine shouted. "Athena has just launched a missile."

"Target?" Caster demanded.

"It seems to be headed to Aurora, Captain."

"Seems to, Commander?"

"It's stealth, Captain," Helen Stein said. "Predictive algorithms put the likely target as Aurora with eighty percent probability. And before you ask, we can't get a target lock."

"Orbital platforms?" Caster asked. That headache was getting much worse.

"Damn, I thought this was over," Overine spat.

"Captain, we're charging particle beams and the X-ray laser," Overine said.

Caster felt the ship starting to maneuver as if it was telling them to secure in their acceleration couches. "Everyone, strap down tight, looks like we're maneuvering," Caster yelled.

"What's happening, Captain? Who's giving the orders?" The coms engineer yelled from across the bridge.

The ship accelerated hard in a jarring set of turns and rolls. It was clear they were no longer stealth; they were in active battle mode. But Caster could see from the status console floating in front of his couch that they weren't pinging—all active tracking was off. Whatever was happening to the ship, it was unclear why it was taking these actions if it couldn't see. What's more, since the missile was stealth, active sensors were of little use, so what was happening? Then Caster had a dark thought. He hadn't heard from Vin. Perhaps the ship had been compromised; perhaps the target was not the missile, but other cities on Saturn. Caster started to sweat; he felt the rush of anxiety and glanced down to see his hands shaking. He focused on the status board; no missiles had been prepped for launch. At this distance, given the atmosphere, they would be more effective than beam weapons. So what was happening?

"Vin?" Caster called, looking around the cabin as if Vin was not the ethereal voice of the ship.

"One moment, Captain. We are in the process of destroying the missile from Athena. One moment, please."

Caster looked at Overine, then at Stein. "What the hell was that?" Helen, strapped down in her couch, seemed to shrug, then smile.

Overine looked pissed off. "Nice of the ship to tell us what's going on," Overine sniped.

Caster heard the hum of super-capacitor banks discharging and glanced at the holo still displaying tactical with a million-mile radius, Vindicator at its center. Red dotted and dot-dashed lines struck out from Vindicator seemingly aimed at nothing. The lines, an extrapolation by targeting computers as to where the beams were going, terminated on the surface of Saturn at the position of Aurora, which was denoted by a blue diamond in the atmosphere of the giant planet. As Caster watched, a bright flash originating from a point one hundred and fifty thousand klicks away appeared and quickly grew to encompass the holo, and again the display crashed, leaving the opposite wall in its place.

"Antimatter explosion," Overine yelled as the ship was buffeted by turbulence from the vaporized remnants of the missile. "That was pretty light," Overine observed.

"That missile had a lot less mass than those cruisers, and the inverse square law is working for us at this distance," Helen Stien remarked, almost as a matter-of-fact. "How did Vin know where to shoot?" Overine asked. "There was only empty space on tactical, active tracking was off, and that thing was probably doing a hundred g's."

"Why don't you ask him?" Helen suggested.

Caster cleared his throat, "Vin, what just happened, please explain."

"Yes, Captain, of course. Just a few moments ago I was contacted by the Alien."

"It didn't register in the log of incoming communications," the coms officer corrected.

"Vin?" Caster asked.

"No, it wouldn't. The communication just appeared on port 1877, it did not originate from the antennas and was not processed by the coms computers. It just appeared. I don't have an explanation of the technology involved."

Everybody on the bridge looked at each other with an array of scowls and confusion. "Why wasn't I informed?" Caster asked, annoyance creeping into his tone.

"There was no time, Captain. It was clear the Alien did not wish to harm us. If it did, it made it quite clear I could not stop it. In fact, it could have commandeered the ship and fired weapons itself if it had wanted to. It also advised that discussing the matter with you would not leave time to act. I made the decision to act. It fed me realtime targeting information and I shot the missile down. I assumed you would approve."

There was a prolonged silence after which Caster said, "Huh..." Then, "Is the Alien still here?"

"No, Captain. Once the missile was destroyed, it appears to have left."

"If it comes back, thank it for me," Caster said. Then, "If it comes back, please inform me."

"Yes, Captain, of course."

Chapter Thirty-One

Athena, Saturn Space, 2240 AD

Serena was sitting on the floor, back against a crate, and arms looped through straps that held the crate in place. She sat next to Samir and kitty-corner across from the rest of Nora's squad. They made it back to the armory with all deliberate haste after Nora's warning of the impending missile launch. Serena felt the ship rock as it was buffeted by the concussion wave of material from the missile and watched the others looking around the room behind their visors, waiting to see just how close the explosion was, and whether this might be the last few moments of their lives.

Samir stopped looking around when the turbulence subsided unexpectedly and the quiet smoothness of the ship returned. "That's it?" It seemed anticlimactic.

"We must have been far enough away when the missile detonated, it didn't have much mass. But I bet the radiation and hard gammas were pretty bad," Serena speculated. Then she tried to raise Nora on Aug-net.

"What's your status, Sergeant?" Nora's voice was crisp and self-assured; clearly, things weren't as bad as she'd feared.

"We're in the armory, Colonel, and we're alright. What do you want us to do?"

"The bridge and essential systems are functional, but there was a strong EMP and hard radiation. I don't think the rest of the squad and Abbas made it. We have to secure their bodies. Many ancillary systems are down including coms and tactical, and that could be problematic."

Serena raised an eyebrow and saw that others in the squad were listening intently. "How so, Colonel?"

"Think about it, we just raced in toward Saturn, and to all appearances just fired a missile at one of their cities, probably Aurora. I would guess the Commonwealth ship tried to raise us on coms, but we didn't answer. Then, somehow they destroyed the missile. What would you assume?"

"Shit," a man in the squad said.

Serena didn't know his name. "I might be able to contact them using another channel," Serena suggested.

"Well, if you can, you should do it as soon as possible," Nora said. "Tactical's out up here, so we don't know what they're doing. We're on a hard braking burn, but they might be assuming we're trying to get closer for another shot. If I were them, I'd take us out," Nora concluded.

* * *

Caster watched as the holo came back, slowly gaining solidity at the head of the bridge. After reestablishing itself, the holo rotated the view to include the red trajectory of Athena racing toward Saturn.

"Vin, do we have a target lock?"

"Yes, Captain. Target locked, beams fully charged."

"Captain, there are fifty people aboard that ship," Helen Stein said. "They're not running silent and they're braking. They're radiating hard all over the spectrum, making themselves a perfect target."

Caster hesitated. If he gambled wrong a hundred thousand people might die.

"Captain?" Vin said.

"Yes, what is it?" Caster responded with frustration. He didn't welcome the interruption to his thoughts right now.

"Captain, you asked to be informed when the Alien returned— it's back, sir. Should I put it through?"

Caster blinked in surprise. He glanced at Helen, whose face conveyed the same astonishment he felt. "Uh, yes, put it through."

"Am I speaking to Captain Caster?"

"Yes." Caster was stunned. It sounded like a person. He imagined a mechanical voice or maybe the hoarse rasp of some video monster. "Is this the Alien?" Caster felt like a fool saying this, but he didn't know what else to say.

"Captain, it would probably be better if you called me Janus, but yes this is who you think it is."

"Janus," Caster echoed.

"Calling me the Alien is probably not the best way to build trust, wouldn't you agree?"

Caster was taken aback. Was the monster playing him? "Trust, funny you should say that, Janus. What if you're trying to gain our trust to let Athena closer to Saturn, or to commandeer this ship?"

"Why would I do that, Captain? Don't you think I could do those things without your trust?"

"Captain, I assure you, Janus can do what it says it can," Vin confirmed.

Caster could feel himself begin to sweat. "Okay, Janus, what do you want?"

"I want you not to fire on the Athena, Captain. They have not responded to your hails because their coms are out due to the EMP from the explosion. The crew currently in charge of the Athena are not your enemy."

"Listen to him," Helena warned. "What he says makes sense from what we're seeing."

"If that's true, Janus, how do you explain that missile? If we hadn't stopped it, it might have killed a hundred thousand people."

"Yes, Captain, and if I hadn't given you tracking data, you couldn't have stopped it. Why would I do that if I were trying to trick you? Also, I'd like to inform you that there is an important person aboard that ship. She is my emissary to your star system, Sol. I'm hoping that if she survives, we can put these kinds of incidences behind us, forever."

Caster leaned back in his chair and blew out. "How soon will Athena be able to reestablish coms? I'd like to talk to the bridge crew."

"Coms has been restored, Captain. I am relinquishing my channel."

There was stone silence on the bridge. Caster's eyes were glued to the holo that continued to show the Athena advancing on Saturn. After a few long seconds, the silence was broken by the coms officer. "Captain, we have an open channel to Athena." Caster gave the man a nod.

"Commonwealth cruiser, this is the Corporate cruiser, Athena, I am Colonel Nora Assisi of the Corporate security forces. Who am I speaking to?"

"This is Captain Caster of the Commonwealth cruiser Vindicator speaking. What are your intentions and what is your situation, Colonel?"

* * *

Nora informed the squad in the armory that hostilities had terminated. They were to leave all their weapons in the armory and the armory would be sealed under high security. Then, they could return to their quarters. The Athena was going to Gateway station orbiting Saturn. At that point, the crew would be debriefed, and those choosing to return to the inner system could catch a ride with the next freighter leaving for that destination. Those crew that were determined to have committed crimes against the Commonwealth would be detained and bound over for trial.

Serena stood in front of the armory blast door and watched the squad disband, wandering down the corridor in ones and twos and eventually disappearing around the curve of the ship's profile. Their indiscernible chatter faded into the distance with them. She felt tired, the adrenaline rush of the last few hours leaving her depleted. She didn't notice Samir standing beside her.

"Now what, Sergeant?"

She turned and smiled, but the smile didn't reach her eyes. Samir looked drained; his dark features were sculpted with deep worry lines that seemed out of place on his young face. His hair was plastered to his forehead from having worn his helmet for so long and a smell of perspiration laced with festering anxiety wafted off of him. "You look older than you did yesterday," Serena said. She hesitated, blew out, then continued, "I have some unfinished business."

Samir looked down momentarily, then back at her, "Adonus?"

"Yeah, Adonus."

"He wasn't in the armory or on the bridge, did he survive the radiation? I know Abbas didn't."

Serena looked around as though searching for an answer, then said, "Who the hell knows, but I know where to find him, and I'm going to make sure there isn't any more shit like this. Remember, we thought it was over before, well this time, I'll make sure it is."

"Yeah, okay, you want some backup?"

She put her gauntleted hand on his forearm, "Not this time. I've got to do this myself."

"Okay, but if something comes up, I'll be standing by." With that, Samir turned and slowly disappeared down the same corridor as those before him.

When he was out of sight, Serena turned in the opposite direction, toward the lift that would take her to Adonus's state room. She made her way to the deck below the bridge, to the last door of an addendum off the main corridor. She reached into her sensorium and tripped the lock whose security code had been changed to confine Adonus to his quarters. She pushed the door open and stood in the archway casting a long shadow, relaxed and loose, ready for whatever the next few minutes had in store.

She felt a strange wave of righteous invulnerability as if fate had put her here to finally end this and nothing in this room could change that. All was quiet; there was no motion of any kind. Things were strewn on the floor, which was unlike Adonus. The man was fastidious, organized, and orderly to a fault. There was a large image of a window, which showed the sweep of the infinite black star-laden void outside the ship rotating with the deck to maintain gravity. Adonus's desk was to the side of the window in profile to the door.

She could see Adonus in his black high-back chair, just sitting there, looking out the window. Although she knew the light had changed, alerting him to the door's opening, he didn't move. She couldn't tell whether he was dead or alive. She approached slowly and cautiously until she entered his peripheral vision. She could see his eyes following her as she finally came to rest in front of him blotting out the stars. He was pale as though the blood had left his face, his light brown hair, always meticulously in place, was matted to the sides of his head in sweaty strands. His lips were a mere slash across the bottom of his face, and his once clear eyes were red and bloodshot, all telltale signs of severe radiation poisoning.

She stood there, looking down at him, knowing that she was faster than he was and there was nothing he could do to stop her. She watched as a sinister smile formed on his dead lips.

"You going to kill me?" He laughed, then started coughing.

She smiled back. "No, you saved me the trouble, you did that yourself. But I am going to give you one piece of news before you're gone forever."

He never stopped smiling, "Oh, and what might that be?" Then he seemed to consider something else. "You didn't beat me, you know. It was that alien thing that's made you its puppet." The smile disappeared and he looked her up and down with disdain. "You, as if a nobody like you could beat me without the help of some accursed thing from some non-human hellhole. I could have given this system nobility, but instead, it will become the handmaiden of some non-human puppet masters. I'm glad I won't be here to see it. Some who refuse to be enslaved will remember me as one of the last humans who would not submit."

There was a prolonged silence after which Serena lowered herself on her haunches, eye level with Adonus. "You really are mad." She shook her head. "I don't think I've ever met anyone more deluded. I thought you were just evil, sociopathic, narcissistic, but you're not. You're mad, clinically mad."

He stared at her, she could see the confusion in his eyes. His speech hadn't elicited the reaction he thought it would.

"So, to give you a proper send-off, let me tell you how it really is. All you've done is hurt people, you're a mass murderer, a psycho, and that's what you'll be remembered as. Then you'll be quickly forgotten, like a bad dream you're glad you can't remember. I will see to that. My friend that you killed at the drill site, he'll be remembered as someone who helped usher in a new human millennium of prosperity for all people in the system."

She stood up, his eyes following her, his face a mask of confusion and uncertainty. He appeared to be panicking, but didn't have the strength to follow through. He reached out and grabbed her arm weakly, almost falling out of his chair. She shrugged it off.

"Now, I'll leave you and forget you as soon as I walk through that door." She strode past him and sealed the door behind her, never looking back.

Chapter Thirty-Two

Gateway Station, Orbiting above Saturn, 2240 AD

As instructed, the Athena docked with Gateway Station, a large orbiting platform holding geosynchronous orbit above Aurora, the Commonwealth Federation's capital city. What remained of the crew was offloaded and the bodies of the dead were documented, their belongings and identifying credentials seized, and their bodies cremated and saved to be transferred to whoever claimed them. Adonus was among the dead, his body remained unclaimed. Serena, along with Nora, Orzan, and the rest of the security forces were debriefed, none were found guilty of crimes against the Commonwealth, and most elected to stay on Saturn and petition for Commonwealth citizenship, including Orzan, Conner, Samir, Kira, and Anastasia.

A terrestrial month had passed since the Battle of Saturn, as it was being called, and Serena was given a stateroom on the station, something that had come completely unexpected. In her mind, she remained a miner deep in the bowels of Titan, an inconsequential pawn, as Auger had so often put it. It was awkward being treated with respect. All her life she'd been an outsider, a tool; nobody had ever turned to her as someone who should be regarded as valuable or relevant. It was the Alien; she knew it had given her this special standing. In her experience, the powers that be only lavished relevance on to those who could do something for them, or somebody they feared. Thinking about it made her angry, so she decided not to think about it. She found it odd that people treating her well for the first time in her life resulted in her becoming suspicious and resentful. She heard a strange sound leave her lips, a strangled scratchy laugh. She quickly stifled it. The dark emotional cloud scared her. Maybe she was so broken that she'd never have a normal life. Sometimes she wished she hadn't survived the many battles she'd fought. At least that way she'd be at peace finally, and knowing violence as intimately as she did, the end would have probably come quickly and painlessly. *Never knew what hit you, then poof—gone.* She realized she was laughing and quickly put the thoughts out of her mind, not wanting to appear maniacal.

"Serena?"

Serena blinked in surprise; the solicitation startled her. She'd almost bumped into Nora coming from the opposite direction. She quickly tried to say something, but it sounded more like clearing her throat. She breathed out and felt herself relax. She was on a promenade that transcribed the station's outer perimeter. She found herself standing next to a large carbide ceramic window that displayed the brilliant contour of the giant planet below in bands of subtle light pastels anchored in the infinite night of space. She'd noticed none of it. It took a moment just to realize where she was; she was on a path she'd taken almost every day for the past month.

Nora was looking at her, concern reflected in her dark eyes, her mouth slightly agape. "I'm okay," Serena said finally. "I'm okay." And she forced a slight smile.

"I've been at this a long time," Nora said, reaching out and holding her hand. "You've got PTSD. You can't get over this kind of thing just by not being in it anymore. It takes time; I'll help you." Nora looked around. "You're going the wrong way."

"Huh?" Serena said, then she remembered. She was here because she was going to a meeting Director Zen had called at her request. They were going to Aurora tomorrow to meet with Governor Tallus. In the intervening month, Janus had visited her often, asking her to arrange preparations for the *grand reveal*. Well, that time had finally come. She'd asked for this meeting as a prerequisite to the meeting tomorrow. On her way to the conference room, she'd dropped into a fugue and gone on a walkabout.

"I'm sorry," she stammered. She saw Nora flinch; looking down, she realized she was squeezing Nora's hand. She released her grip. Nora's hand was white where Serena had squeezed it, and beet-red all around. "I'm sorry. I'll pull it together, Colonel. I promise."

Nora's face softened. "I'm not a Colonel anymore." Shaking the blood back into her hand, Nora said, "I resigned my commission. I'm not a soldier anymore. I may not be walking around in a daze, but I get it. Believe me, I do." She became more serious, turning and gazing longingly out the giant window, then back at Serena. "We're all eager to hear what you have to tell us. We need a change; I think we all know that." Then, looking around and chuckling, she said, "The conference room is this way."

Serena followed Nora off the promenade, further into the station. The corridors were circular, spanning the inner ever-decreasing radius of the station, and were intersected by perpendicular spoke hallways that connected circular corridors radiating from the outer to inner rings. The corridors and hallways were carpeted in a light brown pile, which gave the space a quiet feel. The walls were a warm cream color accentuated with even, diffuse lighting. The layout reminded her of Midway station, the first time she'd been off Earth, such a long time ago. It was the place where she'd met Janus. The parody made her feel strange as if she could look up and see his sixteen-year-old self just strolling by, waving and telling her to meet him in the canteen after drills. She felt warmth at the thought and wondered if the Janus inside her head was feeling it too.

They came to the third inner ring and turned left. The gravity in this ring wasn't as great as on the promenade, and some inner prompting was bringing her out of her malaise, making her feel sharper and more focused. Was that Janus too? A lot was riding on this meeting. It was the whole point of the Alien adopting her as its host—to deliver this message. This was the proverbial fork in the road; whatever resulted from this meeting would shape the future of the human race and its place in the galaxy and beyond.

They came to a large double door with a bio-lock to the right of the door frame. Nora splayed her fingers and pressed her palm on the panel. The door recessed and slid aside soundlessly. Nora stepped in and Serena followed. The room was alive with the chaotic sounds of conversations, laughing, and the hint of cautious disagreements. Heads slowly turned toward her, nucleated by the periphery of people closest to the door and rippling through the crowd until all heads were turned toward her and the room fell silent. She heard the muted whoosh of the door close behind her. She was stuck in a surreal moment, wondering for a second whether this was all a dream like many of those where she encountered Janus. From the head of the room, she saw the crowd parting like a zipper coming undone, and out of the sea of people emerged a familiar face. Nora, who had been standing beside her, forgotten, extended a hand and said, "Good morning, Director."

Serena blinked and watched as Zen took Nora's hand and then turned to her. He was as she remembered him an eternity ago at the Citadel. A mane of blue-black hair combed back and shining in the overhead lights framed a stately chiseled oval face with dark brown eyes that turned toward her in recognition.

"Miss Roe."

Serena looked down and saw he had extended a hand. She took it in a hesitant grip and said, "Director."

That elicited a sincere smile that seemed to calm her and bring her renewed focus. Still holding her hand and pivoting smoothly to her right, he said, "Ladies and gentlemen, I'd like to present Sergeant Serena Roe; we're all here today at her request."

Zen released her hand and put his hand on the small of her back, propelling her toward the front of the room. The crowd parted. She saw smiling appreciative faces on either side of the human tunnel forming as they came forward. At the front of the room was a platform that had been hidden by the crowd. She and Zen stepped up and faced their audience, who had all turned and were looking up at them expectantly.

Zen paused, looking over the crowd, stopping on various faces in recognition. There was a moment of stone silence, then Zen said, "We've just come out of a dark period. This battle was the culmination of a long history of distrust and a differing vision of where we're going as a species. Strangely, though, this conflict was precipitated by the emergence of an alien artifact that was found near the Lakeshore drill site six terrestrial months ago. Since then, the artifact has left Titan; we're not sure where it is; we can't track it." He turned to Serena and continued, "Through a strange process that we don't understand, Sergeant Roe is in contact with the artifact."

Serena heard harried conversations from the crowd, who had become animated at the suggestion that somehow she was connected to something alien, which had just caused a war.

Zen extended his hands in front of himself and waved them in a small patting motion as if trying to put something back in a box. "Ladies and gentlemen, let me finish."

The conversations subsided and they looked up at the platform. The tension in the room had risen as though instead of winning their freedom from the company, they were here to be given some alien ultimatum. "I'll let Sergeant Roe explain. I'm as eager as you are for more insight." With that Zen stepped behind her and surreptitiously left the stage, leaving her there, the quintessential messenger.

She felt a calm come over her, and then she began to recede into herself and felt Janus's presence. She felt herself smile and gaze around the room. The epic nature of this encounter filled her and she felt the expanse of *deep time*. She had a sense that this had happened before throughout the gulf of time and space in unrecognizable physical forms but with the same intent. She felt that somehow the uniqueness of this singular moment was spreading throughout the crowd as a result of her/Janus's unquestionable sincerity. When the silence was complete and profound, she began.

"The entity you call the Alien is above us right now in a stationary orbit." She felt herself look up, then back at the crowd. They were spellbound; she knew it because she was too. She didn't know what she was going to say next. "The Alien has made itself visible to you and will remain that way. The time for hiding is passed, and the time for secrets is passed. Please don't be afraid. I guarantee you the entity you call the Alien will never harm you or interfere with you in any way. You can call it Janus. I was in a cave-in at Lakeshore a year ago. I was pinned in the ice. Unknown to me or anyone else, I was trapped near Janus, and while trapped, it entered my body via nanites and reconfigured my implants so that I could speak to it. Ultimately, the objective of this union was to be able to deliver this message to you. The war and all the intrigue that ensued have nothing to do with Janus in particular, but bring into sharp focus why it is here. To that point, I want to tell you that you are not alone. You no longer have to wonder about that. In fact, there are thousands of advanced civilizations right here in this galaxy. The civilization that sent out entities like the one that left Janus here started this process more than a billion years ago."

There was a collective gasp in the audience. A woman near the front echoed, "A billion years?"

"Yes, a billion years," Serena/Janus said. "At a time when this solar system, Sol, was young, those who sent me had a technology that could span not star systems, but galaxies."

A man standing on the other side of the room started to say something that sounded strangled like he was having trouble getting the words out. He cleared his throat and started again. "You said a billion years and from another galaxy, is that right?"

She recognized the man; it was Doctor Orzan. She heard herself say, "That's right, a billion years and the original entities were not from this galaxy."

"Is that possible?" Orzan marveled.

"Am I here?" Serena heard herself say.

"Are you Serena or are you, Janus?" Zen asked. He was standing at the far left end of the room.

Serena chuckled. "At this moment a little of both," Serena said.

"Why are you here?" Zen continued. "There are people all over the Sol system who are going to think you're here on a mission of conquest, that you're the advanced force for the arrival of some kind of overlords. How are you going to answer that question? Why shouldn't we fear you?"

"Janus is the only one coming. The entity that left it here is gone and will never return. In fact, Janus is of Sol. It was created to be a bridge between humans and the rest of the Universe. That is its purpose for existing. Janus is humanity's Rosetta Stone and your advocate."

They all seemed to look at each other, disoriented by the discussion, then a voice came over a com link. "This is Captain Caster aboard Vindicator, you said advocate, does that mean we're on trial?"

"Yes, Captain, you are."

The room broke out into panicked rumbling. Serena could hear snippets: "It's an invasion, we have to shoot that thing down…" She waited, said nothing, and let the fire burn itself out. Eventually, the crowd looked back at her; one by one heads turned and stared, wanting some kind of reassurance. She saw uncertainty in their eyes; she could smell the pungent scent of fear mixed with the subtle fragrance of body wash. When silence fell upon the room, Serena said, "I told you, you have nothing to fear from Janus. You are being judged, I think that should be obvious. What just happened out there in space? Hundreds killed, for what? Yes, you're being judged, for your ability to survive, for your ability to become truly civilized. You're being judged by your ability to transcend this moment, the dividing line between self-annihilation or constructive evolution."

"And you're here to help?" Zen asked.

"No. That's how free you are. That's how little you have to fear from anyone except yourselves. Janus is here to enable you to become part of a community of sentience throughout a large local part of the Universe if you can keep from killing yourselves. Remember the Drake Equation?"

"Yes," Orzan offered. "It was a crude calculation designed to determine the probability of intelligent extra-terrestrial life."

"Yes, that's right, Doctor," Serena confirmed. "And do you remember that last term? The one usually symbolized by a capital L? That 'L' was taken to mean the longevity of a civilization. The implication is that intelligent civilizations have a lifespan. Sometimes a natural disaster can happen, like the asteroid at Chicxulub that made the dinosaurs extinct, or the Permian extinction caused by volcanic activity. Well, there's another kind of extinction, extinction imposed on a species by itself. That is how you're being judged and that's something that no one can help you with."

"And you, Serena?" Caster asked. "Will you have to mediate between Janus and the rest of us?"

"As you know, Captain, I will soon be obsolete. Communication should be between anyone who wants to talk to the rest of the Universe and Janus; it can't be metered through me. The whole point of this process is to let humanity understand its place in creation. Isn't this what you've been looking for in religion, science, and philosophy?"

There was stunned silence, then Orzan asked, "How will this free-form exchange be done? My understanding is that Janus can only speak to you."

"The Captain asked me that question because he and Director Zen and a few others have helped me manufacture the bridge that will serve as your personal link to Janus. Vin is the sentient intelligence of the cruiser Vindicator in orbit around Saturn right now. Earlier this month, it was authorized to receive detailed specifications from Janus that it inspected and transferred to the industrial forges on Gateway station. Those forges have manufactured three communications satellites designed by Janus. Earlier this week, those satellites were transferred to Janus and were modified like my implants to translate between regular microwave and laser communication to a communications technology that is beyond your science right now. This new kind of communication channel cannot be blocked or jammed. Anyone with a standard transceiver will be able to talk to Janus. Two satellites will be put in orbit around the sun and will enable instantaneous contact with Janus from the inner planets and the asteroid belt. A third satellite will be put in an orbit, making Janus accessible from Saturn space. These satellites cannot be tracked so they cannot be destroyed. At that point, you won't need me anymore. You'll be able to evaluate the situation for yourselves. What you do with this newfound insight is up to you."

"What kind of communications can't be blocked?" The question came from a man standing near the front. She'd seen him before at the site, deep under the ice where they'd found Janus.

"Martinson?" Serena asked.

"Yes, Sergeant, we met a while back at the site."

Serena nodded in recognition. "This com channel is what permits the Universe to talk. There are virtual threads embedded in the quantum foam that is a consequence of the quantum nature of the fabric of space-time. These threads are virtual wormholes.

This com channel finds and puts these virtual threads on the mass-shell, weaves them together between any two points in the Universe, and provides an instantaneous communications bridge through space and time."

"So this communication is between anybody and Janus?"

Serena heard herself laugh out loud. "No, Martinson, Janus is a bridge, a translator. You can think of Janus as a node in a vast network of intelligent civilizations throughout the local Universe that has taken a billion years to weave together. Janus is our node, the only one we will ever have. It will remain here, in the Sol system, until the sun blinks out. If we disappear or become extinct, Janus will orbit the sun and remember us so that the tapestry of civilizations will not forget us. The Originators of this network prized intelligent sentience above all else. They consider the emergence of sentience as the Universe waking up, becoming animated, and reflecting upon itself. The network is their way of connecting all the various consciousnesses in the Universe together so that we can share our common experience of being alive in whatever form that takes. They don't care about whatever material resources you have. Many of these civilizations engineer projects on the level of star systems. They've been around for millions of years. The Originators themselves are transcendent; they may no longer be corporeal. They don't need what you have; they only want to know what you think. That is the purpose of the network."

The room was thrown into stunned silence. Serena felt Janus recede and was filled with a sense of appreciation. She stood there, the only sound was the low hum of air recyclers. She felt someone take her hand. It was Nora. After a long moment, both women left the stage hand in hand.

Chapter Thirty-Three

Interstellar Space, 1960 AD

It became vaguely aware of its surroundings. It looked outside itself without any expectation of what it would find or any memories of what it might be looking for. It was black outside with many bright spots, some singular and some clusters composed of an immense number of the bright spots with inlaid smudges of color, which It knew were emissions from vast stimulated clouds of gas. It saw in all directions at once and marveled at the dizzying depths, which extended into infinity. The sight brought It pleasure. It felt the familiarity and realized it was an inhabitant of the void. A sense of coherence permeated Its accreting self-awareness, hastening a growing sense of purpose.

Some half light-year ahead, It heard the electromagnetic song of galactic radiation buffeting against the heliosphere of a nearby star and peered forward, finding a yellow main-sequence sun. Its interest heightened and It realized It had awakened for this reason. The Over-Mind had brought It out of its long stasis to fulfill the mission for which It had been deployed at an indeterminate point in the distant past. It focused its attention on several distant galaxies that formed a fixed positional baseline and then measured the angular displacement of reference pulsars in this local cluster. It quickly determined that It had been dormant for 0.72 arc-seconds of the galaxy's rotation, or fifty thousand years as measured by the orbital period of the third planet from the star It was quickly approaching. It scanned the local system more closely in synthetic aperture and mapped eight orbiting planets with coded signals emanating from the third planet, indicating a technologically advanced intelligent lifeform, the objective of Its search. The Over-Mind, which controlled Its flight, began slowing from its near light-speed velocity. Apparently, It had gone sub-light much farther out, beyond the star's Oort cloud, thus hiding the Cherenkov burst which could give it away when creating a radiation shock-wave as It reentered normal space. The Over-Mind must have determined this system had intelligent life but had not realized it did not yet possess the capability to detect its entry into the star's system from interstellar space. It felt the contraction of geometrically entangled neutron and exotic matter diminishing the space polarization around it as It slowed.

It focused its attention on the signals coming from the third planet. They were crude, unfocused, low-frequency transmissions coded in ways It quickly determined were a combination of language and video. The vast quantum processing power of the Over-Mind fed It decoded data in a format that made it trivial to analyze. It quickly deduced from frequency analysis of certain sounds, first a phonic alphabet, then from correlations with visual text, several graphical alphabets, of which one was dominant. It focused on the dominant language and began to assemble a social, political, cultural, and historic profile of the inhabitants of the third planet, which they called Earth.

The story that was slowly unfolding from the information It was gathering showed they were a violent race. It developed a chronicle indexed by the way in which the inhabitants of Earth measured time. It formed a history of the various centers of power from early real-time transmissions starting with those of a country named Germany. Although these were recorded, they were of particular interest since they comprised some of the first well-documented videos from the planet and depicted the beginnings of what they called the Second World War. The massive senseless slaughter was not as interesting as the social and psychological underpinnings of the conflict. Of particular interest were recordings of the 1936 Olympics in Berlin. It was this video that had attracted the Over-Mind to this star system. That singular event provided a wealth of information about the psychological and social state of the inhabitants and hinted at the biological origins that resulted in the society It now studied. Clearly, these beings retained deep instinctive drives from their ape origins. It had witnessed similar behavioral outcomes from a sizable fraction of the civilizations It had cataloged during its eon sojourn through the galaxy. Life in this galaxy was reasonably abundant given the proclivities of chemistry and the many systems that had planets in the zone of the star which accommodated liquid water, but intelligent life was exceedingly rare.

It had seen a pattern in the evolution of intelligent life. More often than not, intelligence was the domain of predators, since they were tasked with organizing effective strategies to counter the often more stealthy and quicker prey. As intelligence pushed the predator into societies that had to cooperate, given their propensities to create more effective weapons, their residual instincts propelled them into conflicts of greater and greater destruction. The video of the Olympics chronicled several races and ethnicities, as they were understood by the inhabitants. It also showed the faces and actions of a vast crowd of spectators as well as commentaries and interpretations of organized behavior called politics by the inhabitants. It clarified and sharpened the low-quality images to the point where It was able to map the expressions and body language of many people, as they called themselves, so as to correlate reactions to events with the propaganda of the commentaries. It did this in an attempt to gain deep insight into humans so that It could proceed to the next step in its plan to study them.

It found from past contacts that the only way to understand aliens was to become one. Although It had personal feelings and features of itself described by humans as emotions, Its emotions, and intuitions were incompatible with those of humans. If It wanted to truly understand these creatures, It would have to become one. To this end, It developed a detailed behavioral profile of the average human from its deep study of the transmissions. It sequenced this profile into a network architecture. Then, using and tuning statistical simulations, It was able to reproduce the observable emotional states of humans. Finally, It translated this network into a hybrid duplicate of itself that It called Emissary. Emissary was not human, but an amalgamation of itself with an undercurrent of human instinct and emotion, making Emissary the perfect perceptional translator.

"Are you stable?" It asked Emissary.

"Yes, I think so."

"Good. I have data that I want you to process. Once you feel sufficiently comfortable, I want you to give me your assessment of the humans on the third planet. I'm especially interested in your advice as to what you think will be the outcome of their ascendance to civilization, and whether you should make yourself known to them. Do you understand?"

"Yes, I understand," Emissary said.

Shortly, It slipped inside the orbit of Neptune. It sensed a query from Emissary. "Yes?"

"I have finished my evaluation. Would you care to hear it?"

"Yes, very much so," It replied.

"First, an observation will serve to help you understand my conclusions. You frighten me," Emissary said.

"Explain," It asked.

"These people are not prepared for contact. Fear is a large part of their motivation. This fear derives from a perception of an inability to control their lives. I do not grasp the extent of you, but I know that compared to these beings, they would consider you a god. You control energies derived from junctions between zero-point bands of the Multiverse; this is power beyond their imagination. You are more than a billion years old, and your experience spans galaxies. They have no way of thwarting your will. These beings are distrustful and would never believe that something as alien as you could ever be counted on not to betray them. Contact would disrupt their nation-states and their religions. Therefore, it would not be wise to engage them at this time," Emissary advised.

"I see," It said. "Do you believe that in time you could make contact without the adverse reactions you have outlined?"

"I think there is a good possibility of contact without negative consequences if they can survive the multitude of disasters they are currently facing. Thus far they are confined to their planet with dwindling resources, a growing population, and probable environmental collapse. Given their aggressive nature, emotional instability, and their crude atomic and biological weapons, they face an uncertain future."

"Intelligent life is the consciousness of the Universe," It said. "Intelligent consciousness is the Universe looking at itself in a mirror. Our task is to make possible the communion of intelligent life in the Universe for those who can free themselves from the bonds of their origins. You will stay here. You will continue to observe them. You will offer them the possibility of joining the community of life in those parts of the Universe where we have been able to extend the space-time network of civilizations. I will leave you with a singularity that has been dilated with exotic matter, thus offering a channel that transects space and time so that humans can communicate with the expanding community of intelligent civilizations. If, at some point in the future, you determine these humans are ready, you will make contact and perhaps we can have a more enlightened communion."

"I understand," Emissary said. "Will you return?"

"I will not return," It said. "We are far out on the galactic arm. I have almost finished my survey of this galaxy and will leave it never to return. I will go into stasis and will wake in some distant epoch of the Universe to search out other intelligent life."

Emissary separated from It above the large moon of the ringed gas giant that the humans called Saturn. Emissary advised this would be a good vantage point from which to observe Earth. The moon was far enough away to allow considerable time before humans could reach it, thus giving their societies a chance to expand both in perspective and to integrate their varied ethnicities into a more coherent whole. Also, the thick cloud cover would obscure their observations of the surface and any activity that Emissary might engage in.

Emissary was encased in a spherical craft and held station in synchronous orbit above Titan. Emissary regarded It slowly gliding overhead. It was large, several kilometers long by human measurement, and blotted out much of the stars from Emissary's position. It was a mat black ovoid surrounded by a halo of distortion that refracted light as It slowly passed overhead.

"I feel alone at your leaving," Emissary said.

"I don't understand," It replied.

"I know," Emissary said as it watched the distortion field intensify around It. And all of a sudden, It was gone, leaving only stars where It had been.

* * *

Saturn had fifty-four moons, a massive ring of ice and stones, and an assortment of smaller orbiting objects. Emissary deployed an observation platform that was lost in the sea of objects orbiting Saturn. The humans would never find it. Then Emissary slowly descended into Titan's thick atmosphere. It used its micro-fusion generators to super-heat the nitrogen hydrocarbon gases and expel them for thrust as it glided just above the frozen landscape of ice-methane mountains and hydro-carbon lakes and rivers. It found a spot near a lakeshore and settled on the frozen ground. Emissary raised the temperature of its point of contact with the ground and melted its way two kilometers into Titan. There it would remain for the next two hundred and eighty years, observing the Earth and waiting for the arrival of the humans.

Chapter Thirty-Four

Saturn, Aurora, 2240 AD

The shuttle, Arrow, streaked above the surface of Saturn after leaving Gateway Station at an orbital speed of forty thousand kilometers per hour. Gateway Station was in an equatorial orbit around Saturn at a gravitational lull between the upper atmosphere and Saturn's ring. Arrow's piloting AI changed its orbit, inclining it toward latitudes above thirty degrees north where atmospheric winds were relatively mild and started its braking burn. Arrow dropped out of Saturn's orbit glowing red-hot in an ionizing atmospheric shroud while shedding its tremendous speed. It had been more than seven years since Serena had been planet side and she stared at the pastel colors of Saturn's wide atmospheric bands with a mixture of anticipation and apprehension. She'd been on a dark moon, under the ice for so long that she wondered whether the prospect of what she once considered a normal life was still compatible with who she'd become. Janus receded after the meeting yesterday, she wasn't sensing him right now and he hadn't come to her in dreams last night as he so often did. She didn't know how to feel about that, which left her somewhere between relieved and lonely. As soon as the shuttle hit the upper atmosphere everything started shaking. The shaking became more intense and broke into violent bucking as Arrow encountered turbulence on its way down through the falling edge of high equatorial winds. Soon she couldn't see anything except an orange glow that filled the windows. The heated plasma of their descent dissipated the turbulence and the ride became smooth.

Nora laughed. "Reminds me of the drop ships on Mars with you sitting next to me, I feel like I'm home."

Serena turned from the window and was met by Nora's broad grin. It was infectious and Serena's malaise seemed to evaporate. "Ever been to Saturn?" Serena asked.

"Saturn, hell no. They're the enemy, aren't they?" Both women laughed out loud. Serena looked down the rows of seats in front of them and saw heads turning in the eerie red glow of the windows. She gave a closed fist salute. Half the people returned the gesture, and half looked puzzled. "They're not military," Nora observed. "They have no idea what that means."

Serena gave them a thumbs up and got a thumbs up in return. "We're not soldiers anymore," Nora remarked. "But that doesn't mean we can't get together from time to time and give each other the secret handshake. Samir and Kira are staying, maybe others." Reflecting for a moment, Nora asked, "It wasn't all bad, was it?"

"The only good part was meeting people like you and Janus. The rest of it I'd rather forget," Serena muttered. Nora shrugged and took a pull of her beer.

Serena watched as the flight deck door slid aside and one of the pilots made his way down the aisle toward her; even though they were at a ten-degree descending grade.

"That guy must be military," Nora quipped. The man was dark, wiry, and had the coordination of someone who'd clocked years in space. Using seatback handholds like ski poles and planting the tips of his sticky boots in a loping gate, he fluidly made his way to her seat, his arms straddling the seat-backs, and smiled down at her with an impressive set of pearly whites.

"You Serena Roe?"

It happened so fast and unexpectedly that all she could do was nod and say, "Uh-huh."

"I saw you on Gateway vid yesterday. I want to thank you for helping stop the war; we were nervous down here." Even though he knew she felt awkward, the smile never left his face. "Ever been to Aurora Archipelago?" he asked.

"Uh—no."

"Come on up front, we'd like you to see what you saved."

"My friend Nora's never seen it either," Serena remarked.

"Come on, you're invited too. You two have any trouble walking around inside a bullet plunging into the atmosphere?"

Nora gave Serena an amused smile and a shake of the head, then looking up at the pilot, seeing the name tag on his left breast read Joseph, she said, "After you, Joseph."

Approaching the flight deck, Serena saw the majestic clouds of Saturn's upper atmosphere through Arrow's panoramic windscreen. Massive cumulus and domed clouds stretched into the distance far below. As the shuttle fell through the hydrogen ammonia haze of the upper atmosphere of Saturn's northern latitudes, which Serena knew stretched more than thirty thousand kilometers in width, the planetary band turned a deep rich azure, looking like an infinite Caribbean sea that she'd seen in pictures. They crowded onto the flight deck, keeping the door open. Looking back, Serena saw passengers leaning far out of their seats into the aisle, craning their necks to see. Turning back to the wide canopy, and standing on a raised platform above the two pilot couches surrounded by a sleek horseshoe console of instruments and screens, Serena and Nora planted their feet under footholds and gripped handholds on either side, then leaned back into standing couches.

They watched a bright new world as it streaked by outside. Up till now, they'd been in free-fall, but presently they felt gravity return as the shuttle began leveling off about five hundred kilometers under the upper atmosphere and a couple of kilometers above the ammonia cloud layer. Serena noticed that Joseph, the pilot who had fetched them from the passenger cabin, had taken the ship off automated flight and reasserted manual control. He smoothly brought the ship out of its steep reentry dive, softening the g's on them, then banked so they could get a better look.

"You're a pretty good pilot," Serena observed admiringly.

He turned, and with that same toothy grin said, "Yeah, Sergeant. I was a jump-ship pilot for the company before I immigrated to the Commonwealth."

Serena stuck out a fist automatically, and without hesitation, Joseph bumped it, as they'd so often done in her past life. He gave her a nod, then turned back to the controls. There was something about him that kind of reminded her of Janus. Maybe after this long painful sojourn, she was finally coming home after all.

"The clouds below us look like water, like pictures of the Caribbean before the environmental collapse," Serena observed.

"It's because the sky's blue up here in Saturn's northern latitudes and it's reflected from the ammonia clouds below, which are yellow because of trace alkalides. The combination makes a nice azure, just like shallow water," Joseph explained. "When we come to Aurora, it'll look like an island floating on an infinite sea, which it is. The ammonia vapor is a lot denser than hydrogen, about half as dense as water vapor, and that gives the cities a lot of buoyancy. The flotation bladders are only ten times the volume of the cities themselves. Aurora's almost like the top of icebergs on a cold arctic sea," Joseph continued.

They circumnavigated half the planet in their breaking descent from orbit and now flew a couple of kilometers above an endless oncoming tapestry of pastel clouds at Mach 10 toward Aurora. "We'll be there in about fifteen minutes," Joseph said. He made a large rectangular motion with his hand in front of the canopy and a blue outline appeared. Then he made a sweeping motion with his hand and Serena saw a swarm of shimmering gray dots superimposed on the ribbon of clouds in the rectangle.

"Aurora Archipelago at extreme magnification," he remarked.

"I thought Aurora was one floating dome," Serena said, stretching forward and straining to see more detail.

"Hold on tight," Joseph warned. "We're slowing down." She felt the deceleration pitching her forward and heard the whine of the engines, after which Arrow started shaking again. "Nope, Aurora is a collection of twenty domes, each about six hundred square kilometers. They all drift together in the upper band and are kept in formation by active propulsion and laser rangers synchronized by a decentralized AI. We're going to Aurora Prime, the administrative dome."

As they got closer and approached from below, Serena saw each dome seem to have several long thread-like tails that descended into the clouds and disappeared. They looked like the threads of giant balloons. "What are those black threads under the domes?" Serena asked.

"Let's take a look."

Joseph flew Arrow around the Archipelago, giving everyone a closer look. Serena saw each dome seemed to have a thick base with arms that fanned out like a starfish, and central to each base, long black threads fell into the clouds and disappeared. "Those tubes go down more than a thousand kilometers," Joseph informed. "They're made of super-strong graphene fibers. They bring hot hydrogen up from deep in the atmosphere to bladders at the base of the domes. The atmosphere gets hotter under gravitational pressure the farther down you go. The atmosphere up here is cold, about minus one hundred and fifty centigrade, which means the hydrogen mixed with ammonia and helium outside is dense. The hot hydrogen in the bladders is much less dense and gives the domes buoyancy; it's what makes them float. The whole system is passive and foolproof. The gravity of the planet powers the domes by heating the hydrogen; they'll float as long as Saturn is hot. And we use several other strata in Saturn's upper atmosphere. At a depth of around two hundred and fifty to three hundred kilometers below us, there's a layer of water clouds about fifty kilometers thick. Some of those tubes bring water up and we convert a percentage of it into oxygen. We've tried to live off the land as much as possible."

Serena felt the ship's nose pitch up and they rose higher into the sky, then banked in a left turn making another run across the Archipelago. This time she saw the domes from above. Looking down, they approached a dome that shone bright with swatches of rust-red, greens, blues, and dull silver through a webwork of geodesic struts that seemed embedded in the transparent dome material.

"The domes are lit from the inside by panels in the struts. The light matches the spectrum and intensity on Earth at latitudes of about forty degrees and rises and falls to turn Saturn's ten-hour day into a twenty-hour day to roughly match Earth. There are plenty of plants in the domes that refresh the air and they need the light to stay healthy," Joseph explained. Then he banked the ship again, descended, slowed, and approached one of the outstretched arms at the base of the dome they'd just flown over. Serena watched as he re-engaged the AI and Arrow slowly followed a landing beacon into a large rectangular landing port on the side of the arm. Once the ship was at rest and secure in a landing cradle, Joseph pushed the flight yoke forward into its off-line position, turned the flight couch around, and looked up at her and Nora. "Time to off-load, we're home."

* * *

Serena and Nora stepped out onto a rust-brown and white tiled promenade at Aurora Prime's shuttle port exit. Serena reflexively put a hand over her eyes to shade them from the bright daylight. She looked around and felt her cheeks lift into a broad grin at the sight of the settlement that expanded in all directions under a sky that seemed as far away as the one she remembered growing up. It didn't seem like a dome; it seemed like a world a lot like the wispy dream-like memories of being on Earth, but this world was lusher, greener, more temperate, more like Earth before the environmental collapse. She turned to Nora, conscious that she seemed to weigh more.

"Gravity's stronger than on Titian," she observed,

"We're not on Titan anymore," Nora said. "Gravity here is just a little more than on Earth," and she stepped forward into the day.

Serena watched as Nora crossed a red-rock walkway to a green area with giant ferns and banyan-like trees that extended into a garden with vine-like trunks that dropped from their branches forming a connected forest. Nora stretched her arms out as if trying to frame the sight, then turned and looked back at Serena with sheer joy. She was like a kid on birthday morning. *This place just transformed a hardened cynical soldier into a naive optimist,* Serena thought. She felt it too, the bitterness, the anger seeping out of her. The conviction born of hard experience that nothing could ever be good for long. She felt a clarity returning, edging out the numbness that she'd felt this last month when the sugar-high of battle had left her, and the drudgery of her life returned. She wished that Janus and Auger were here. They deserved to be—they'd given up everything so that she could be.

"What do you think?" Joseph asked. He'd silently pulled up beside her. He was taller than he appeared in the shuttle now that gravity had reasserted itself and they could stand to their full height. She looked up at him. His face was a smooth dark onyx with fine features and bright blue eyes.

"I hope I'm not dreaming. I feel like I'm going to wake up any moment and be at the bottom of a big ice hole on Titan." Then she felt a sharp stinging pain coming from her lower left arm and instinctively jumped into a defensive crouch. She heard Joseph laughing as he quickly stepped away, holding his hands up, palms out.

"Easy," he said. "Take it easy. I forgot you're a human killing machine." He was still chuckling.

"What did you do? Why'd you do that?"

"I pinched you to let you know you're awake. You're not dreaming—see?"

She straightened up and relaxed. "I'm sorry," she said. "I guess I'm still jumpy, waiting for something bad to happen. Force of habit, sorry."

He edged closer. "Am I safe? Can I come closer?" The smile never left his face.

She stepped into him, embraced him, then pulled away and looked up. "Thank you for bringing us here."

He nodded. "I was in the service; I know what it's like. No apology needed. I wanted you to know this is real and you helped preserve it. Bringing you here, the pleasure is all mine." He squeezed her shoulder, nodded again, then turned and slowly disappeared down the walkway. She watched Joseph turn the corner and slip out of sight. She continued staring after him when she heard Nora say, "Well, look who's here."

Serena turned and found Zen coming from the other direction. He wore a crisp dark blue business suit with a high-collar black shirt buttoned at the top. His hair had grown and was combed back, gleaming bright black in the midday light, and his mouth was stretched in a casual smile under dark glasses. He was the iconic man in charge, the type she'd grown to distrust.

"Serena, Miss Assisi." Zen stepped up to them hand outstretched, flanked by two men equally attired.

"Director," Nora said and took his hand. "To what do we owe the pleasure?" Then looking at the two men standing a step behind him, stoic and all business, Nora asked, "Are we under arrest?"

Zen laughed. "Of course not, you're our honored guests. I'm here as a familiar face to take you to your lodgings so you can relax before the broadcast this evening."

"Our lodgings? Are we staying here in Aurora Prime?" Serena asked.

Zen turned in profile and stared into the distance. "Yes, up there, for as long as you want."

Serena followed Zen's gaze and for the first time noticed tall buildings that shimmered in the hazy distance, beyond the garden. They looked to be made of porcelain and glass and loomed high above the settlement, but did not offset the warmth of the environment at street level.

Zen noticed Serena's fascination with the height of the towers. "We have to build up to house people and shops. Some of those buildings are structural support for the inner dome. Ground space is at a premium and is reserved for parks and public boulevards." He turned and faced her again. "We got you an apartment with a good view of Aurora; you'll be able to take it all in."

Chapter Thirty-Five

Aurora Prime, 2240 AD

Serena stood on the balcony of her forty-fifth-floor apartment in Phoenix Towers. Zen was right; she could take it all in from up here. She marveled at the vast settlement that spread before her in the distance. It was like a dream. She saw a bright tapestry of sparkling buildings punctuated by broad avenues filled with people walking about, festooned with gardens and trees. She even saw a sizable lake with what looked like sailboats and rowboats dotting the blue water in splashes of color. She could smell the rich scent of growing things in the warm humid air and even saw birds flying around. And it was all floating in a Saturnine sky. How impossible was that? She smiled and pinched herself, remembering Joseph. It was indeed real, but somewhere deep in her mind, she still waited for the inevitable other shoe to drop. "But not today," she heard herself say out loud.

She returned to the living area of her two-bedroom suite, which was sunken below the balcony and richly appointed with comfortable furnishings. She sat on the couch and sank deep into its cushions, which surprised her since she was used to things being hard and inflexible. This would take some getting used to.

After soaking in a bath, the first she'd taken in years, she dressed in clothes she found in the closet labeled *to be worn at reception.* She inspected herself in the large full-length mirror set in the closet door. She didn't recognize herself. A woman was staring back, slim and tall, adorned in an aqua silk pullover that made her look strangely feminine over elegant blue legging that made her legs look long and shapely. She blushed at the sight, more afraid of leaving the apartment looking like this than facing down a horde of corporate soldiers.

Serena made her way to the Government Center. Janus's system-wide broadcast was set for seven o'clock and she'd been invited by Zen to attend and watch with a host of Commonwealth dignitaries including Governor Tallus. There was going to be a reception before the broadcast. Zen described it as a meet and greet, whatever that meant. He had sent her authorization via Aug-net to download the entire Commonwealth directory, which included site maps and a listing of Commonwealth citizens. She met Nora on the ground floor lobby and they descended into the metro station below the Phoenix Tower complex, where they boarded a tube car, downloaded directions, and were quickly shuttled to the Government Center.

They emerged from the underground onto a broad plaza of red-rock tiles with patterns of light blue spiraling in toward a low glass building, which was situated at the far end of the plaza. The open unencumbered space gave Serena mild vertigo. She was used to tunnels and cramped cabins on a dark inhospitable moon or aboard spaceships. She stood in place and panned three hundred and sixty degrees, taking in the people walking across the wide space completely unaware of the casual freedom this place afforded them, and she smiled.

"What?" Nora asked.

"Just taking in the sights. I remember something like this back on Earth a long time ago, but it seemed like a dream until today." The map in her Aug-net indicated that the low glass building across the expanse was indeed their destination, and they strolled to the entrance portico. As soon as they found what looked like the door, they heard a smooth feminine voice say, "Please look up at the blue dot over the door for a security check." As soon as they did, the door slid aside without a sound. "Welcome to the Government Center Sergeant Roe and Colonel Assisi, your party is on the fourth floor, room 1A. Directions are in your in-stream." The site map led them to a cylindrical lift across a spacious atrium. Light shone in from glass panels on the high lobby ceiling, illuminating large ferns and vine-wrapped miniature trees in a dramatic spectrum of green patterns and partial shadows. As they approached the lift, Serena saw a destination request in her Aug-net. The door slid open and they entered. The lift had a curved transparent outer wall and she watched the plaza fall away as they rose. Once on the fourth floor, Serena followed the overlay route vector in her Aug-net's Minds-eye to a transparent wall subtending a grand theater with descending semi-circular levels to a central holographic platform. Standing on the platform was a four-meter holo of Janus looking around at crowds of people clustered on every level, eating hors d'oeuvres, drinking from slim flutes of amber bubbling liquid, and talking gregariously, all while stealing curious glances of the giant image at the center of it all.

"He looks familiar," Nora mused.

"Don't you recognize him? He was in your squad back on Mars. He came with me from Midway; we were both grunts under your command." Serena smiled at Nora as she strained to remember. "But you were a lieutenant then, a real hard ass."

"Yeah, Janus, I remember," Nora whispered; then her face turned sorrowful with recognition. "He was killed, blown up when we charged the plant north of Chryse-Planitia basin. But how?"

"The Alien reconstructed him from my memories, memories so deep I'm not aware I have them. We've talked these past months, sometimes while I've been in a contemplative fugue, or sometimes in dreams." Serena watched as Nora became more alarmed as she described her relationship with Janus. She put a hand on her friend's shoulder. "It's okay, I'm good with it. If truth be told, he's helped me a lot."

"So you're under its control?" Nora stared hard at Serena. "Am I talking to the Alien right now? Is this what's going to happen to us when we let this thing in?" Nora watched Serena start to laugh, then grow serious. Nora grew more alarmed.

"You're talking to me, Janus doesn't control me. In fact, at every step of our melding, he's asked permission. There's a clear demarcation between us, we're separate individuals." Serena saw the mixture of emotions in her friend's eyes; fear, confusion, distrust. "Think about it," Serena explained. "If an entity is truly alien, how does it communicate with us, understand things from our perspective, and empathize with us? Communication isn't just the technical act of decoding a language, it's the act of understanding. I volunteered, he didn't force me. And you know what, I'm glad, I got Janus back."

As the two women stared at each other, the glass door in front of them slid aside. When Serena turned, Zen was standing there. "Am I interrupting something?"

Serena blinked, and Nora looked strained. Serena cleared her throat, her lips felt dry. "Uh, no, everything's good, I think?" She looked at Nora, "Everything good?"

Nora flashed Serena a crooked half-smile, contemplation lines creased her forehead. She glanced back at Zen. "Yeah, Director, everything's good." She felt Serena put her arm in the crook of hers and lead her into the vast theater as Zen stepped aside. As the chatter of a hundred voices replaced the silence, Nora heard Serena whisper in her ear, "Trust me, I know you're trained to be suspicious, but everything's alright, I promise."

Nora wandered into the crowd, descending toward the central platform as Serena watched. A lifetime of suspicion would not be overcome by a few words from an old acquaintance turned recent friend and confidant. Serena could only hope that in time Nora could accept this strange new world. As she watched, Nora made her way to the foot of the stage and gazed up at the giant figure of Janus, and in a chilling motion, Janus looked down at her, a neutral look on his face that reminded Serena of a mannequin, something artificial, not human. Serena shook her head;

this wasn't going to be easy. Janus still had a lot to learn about people.

As she regarded her friend's diminutive figure standing in Janus's cavernous shadow, Serena felt someone's presence and turned to find Zen and several other people approaching.

"You going to stand around alone looking lost?" Zen asked. Before she could answer, the people who had followed Zen spread out around her. They regarded her warmly, several with flutes of the amber liquid. "You've spoken to these people, but I don't think you met most of them in the flesh. This is Captain Castor and his chief engineer, Commander Helen Stein. And this is Governor Tallus."

Tallus stuck out an open hand and Serena just looked at it, not knowing quite what to do. "You're supposed to shake it," Tallus remarked, a sincere smile making him look like a long-lost uncle. Hesitantly, Serena took his hand. He was tall, with a light complexion that made his long, chiseled face framed by a shock of white hair look like something out of a historical painting. The man looked manufactured for his role, right down to the easy warmth with which he introduced himself. "We owe you a debt of gratitude for getting your friend down there to save our Commonwealth." Tallus stole a glance at Janus and Serena could see that he too had misgivings.

Serena released his hand. "Is there something wrong, Governor?"

For a moment Tallus's composure faltered, but for only a second. Serena saw that Castor, a tall lean man who had the appearance of an older Janus, and the woman, Helen, were both watching the Governor. They had seen it too. Tallus, who missed nothing regarded both of them, then turned to Janus standing like an alien force of nature at the center of the large room. "We're putting a lot of trust in your friend. You're the only one who really knows him." He looked piercingly at Serena. "Are we doing the right thing? Do we have a choice? If we don't give him access to our com network, what will he do?"

Serena realized beneath the casual celebratory acceptance of Janus's offer, there was fear and uncertainty. She shouldn't have been surprised given how she felt when first discovering that the alien had insinuated itself into her implants. She noticed that Orzan had joined the group, his presence actually made her feel better. Even though she originally considered him an enemy, the man had shown himself to be resilient, trustworthy, and insightful. She noticed that telltale knowing set to his eyes that revealed he'd seen this coming.

"I don't know what I can say to put you at ease, Governor. I don't know that I could convince you I'm not Janus's puppet charming you into a trap. But I can tell you I'm not, and that the choice is yours. We can call this off right now if you ask. I can only tell you that Janus is benevolent. He is here to help and he won't take any actions that violate human sovereignty in any way."

"Governor, my name is Orzan. I'm from the science directorate on Olympus. I served as the science officer aboard the Athena. I have direct knowledge of what happened in the battle above Saturn, and I have some technical experience with the alien. In my professional opinion, everything that Ms. Roe has told you is accurate. What's more, from what we saw aboard the Athena, the alien, Janus, doesn't need our permission to commandeer coms, he could just take it; we can't stop him. What's more, we can't track him and we have no defense against him if he is hostile. Governor, this is an entity from a civilization a billion years in advance of ours. Think of it, he has put three com satellites in solar orbits traveling almost two billion miles in less than a day, a journey that would have taken our fastest ships the better part of a year."

What little color Tallus had, had drained away as Orzan spoke. "Governor, I know what Doctor Orzan said sounds alarming, but let me say again, at this very moment, if you wish to postpone this for further consideration, I'll contact Janus and he will accede to your wishes," Serena said.

Castor put a hand on Tallus's shoulder. "I was there too. Just a few weeks ago it was uncertain if there would be a Commonwealth. The alien gave us targeting information because it would not destroy the missile headed for Aurora itself. During the entire conflict, it took no aggressive action to benefit anyone. We've had a month to think this over. I see no harm in talking to it."

Everyone was silent. Serena noticed the color returning to Tallus's face. "Thank you, Captain. Second thoughts are a bitch."

Serena looked beyond Tallus, seeing Nora had returned. She wondered how much of this hand-wringing Nora had overheard. She watched her friend side-step the group and come up beside her. "So, I guess you're not alone with the jitters," Serena whispered.

Nora flashed a half-grin and handed her a flute. "A peace offering, have some, you'll make me feel better." Serena took the flute and Nora clinked glasses, then took a pull. Serena followed suit. It had a slight citrus taste and the bubbles were very pleasant. "It's good, what is it?"

"It's called champagne. It was popular on Earth before the environmental collapse. We've just started growing grapes at a dome in the Archipelago," Zen offered. Then after a moment, "Oh, that reminds me, I have a message for you, a Mister Aegeus. He's a botanist, responsible for the grapes. He couldn't find you since you weren't in the network. He said he knew you a long time ago."

Serena was stunned. In a cold numb visualization, she slowly replayed what Zen just said as a message flashed into her Augnet. She peeked at the message, it was directions to a dome called *The Preserve*. It was signed by Dr. Aegeus.

"Are you alright?" Zen asked. "You look like you've just seen a ghost."

"Yeah," Serena muttered. "I think I have."

"In the last half of the twentieth century, it was said that the greatest event in human history would be the discovery that humans were not alone in the Universe." The voice was smooth and pleasant, ostensibly human, and adorned with sincerity. Slowly everyone in the hall turned and faced the stage. The statue that was Janus had come to life, the colors were richer and his expression was no longer that of a mannequin, but of a living man. After those few words, the crowd fell silent. Serena knew that everyone in the Sol system was hearing this same voice instantaneously over billions of miles of interplanetary space in every language that people spoke in concert with the listener. In those few seconds that it took to utter those words, something fundamental had changed in the human sphere. "I am here to tell you, you are not alone. The Universe is full of life, but intelligent life is another matter. It is comparatively rare." Janus smiled. "And as you yourselves have come to know, those things that are rare are precious. There is a civilization that existed before one-celled creatures on Earth evolved into multi-cell animals, and at that time they had gone to the stars. They had come to understand and revere the mysterious incarnation of physical reality in this Universe. And in so doing, they came to the realization that the emergent phenomenon of intelligent life is the Universe becoming conscious and reflecting upon itself. But each intelligent species is unique in that it is formed by its unpredictable subjective experience in the Universe. This original civilization set out to weave the community of intelligent life into a network that spans deep time and space so that the disparate parts of the conscious Universe could relay their various experiences into a meaningful whole. I am your node in this network. I can allow you to speak to your brothers and sisters through time and space so that you can find a deeper meaning in your own existence."

Janus seemed to look at the clusters of people in the theater, pausing a moment on each, trying to make a personal connection. Apparently, he had learned a lot about people during his residence in her head, Serena thought. That made her smile. Then as though he had read her mind, he found her in the crowd, held her a moment, then continued.

"Another artifact of the twentieth and twenty-first centuries is the idea that if your governments ever did contact extraterrestrial life, that fact should be kept from you. The reason given for this curious behavior was that those in charge feared that somehow the knowledge that there were others in the Universe would displace human's exalted position in the eyes of your various gods. Another reason given by many in the scientific community and by popular culture was that extraterrestrials' knowledge of Earth would be followed by a violent invasion to steal your resources or your Earth or enslave you. I can tell you that the second of these fears is completely unfounded and illogical on its face. There are vast resources in the Universe. Any culture sufficiently advanced to come to your star could easily obtain all the power and raw materials from most solar systems. Comets in the far orbits of most stars have oceans of water available, and many asteroids contain more minerals, metals, and rare earths than your civilizations have ever mined on Earth. Star-faring civilizations can terraform planets for space or construct artificial habitats like your Archipelagos. There will be no interference in your worlds by me or anyone else. It has been the experience of the Network that intelligent civilizations that continue to be aggressive and violent after a certain stage of technological development become extinct in a blaze of self-destruction. This is perhaps the source of the Fermi paradox. It is this outcome that I fear you have not fully emerged from as was demonstrated by what happened above Saturn just a few weeks ago. There is nothing to be gained and everything to be lost if you continue on this course. You have much more to fear from this than you have from me. As for the first fear that your leaders had, that of losing your exalted position, you must resolve that yourselves, I can't help you with that. I can only tell you there is a Universe out there that will welcome you if you let it."

The audience was mesmerized as Janus continued speaking, but Serena was elsewhere. The mention of Aegeus' name evoked vestiges of the past that she considered dead and thus forgotten. The vision of being on a dusty street on Earth a lifetime ago, looking up and seeing a hand outstretched. The shadow of someone masking the sun in a fluttering white shirt helping her up; kindness that she had rarely experienced on a magical day that had come and gone so fast, she often wondered if she had just imagined it all. And then she could see Aegeus growing smaller in the rear window of the autobus, standing in the middle of the street, watching the bus getting farther and farther away before disappearing into the background and in time. She slowly made her way to the door on the top level of the theater, Janus's voice growing softer and disappearing altogether as the door closed behind her. She moved to the elevator, retracing her steps as if drawn by some magnetic force. The *Preserve* echoed in her mind as she crossed the wide expanse of the plaza in front of the government center oblivious to everything else. She queried the local network and found that travel between domes involved paging an air taxi. Apparently, the drift between the islands of the Archipelago was too great to support a permanent train service. She called up directions to the port authority via the underground metro and the next thing she knew she was staring out a tube car window watching the various tube stops whisk by. She left the metro and found herself in an area with a curb and signs directing her to: *stand here, thirty seconds until your taxi arrives.*

The small craft was autopiloted and requested she download her destination, which she did. The service was free for Commonwealth citizens, which she was, as declared in the generous rights and compensation documents that Zen had sent. It was strange being a recognized part of something that required so little from her in return. The little oval car left the port on one of Aurora Prime's extended arms and zoomed into an azure sky in almost total silence. The front of the oval was completely transparent and gave her the feeling that she was just flying through the air without instrumentality. Aurora's dome shrank behind her and they headed toward a collection of dots in the distance. She was sitting in a front seat and saw the steering yoke moving by itself as the autopilot corrected its course.

"The Preserve is on our left, we'll be arriving in three minutes," the smooth feminine voice of the autopilot intoned. *"Was the ride to your satisfaction?"*

"Yes, thank you, it was very pleasant," Serena said and found herself smiling. "How do I get to the forest or green area of the Preserve once we get there?"

"The entire dome is a green area; the local directory can give you the location of whoever you are seeking if the party permits."

She emerged from The Preserve's port onto a broad reddish-brown tile trail, which circled left and right into a lush green forest. The trees and foliage stretched above and in front of her in all directions. She heard a variety of birds singing in the distance. To her left on the path was a guest lodge that looked to be made of wooden logs with a green tile roof. She'd never seen anything like it. There was the husky scent of vegetation in the humid air with a suggestion of fragrant flowers—honey suckle flashed into her mind from her implants. She pinged Aegeus and a direction icon appeared almost immediately with an attached message: *"Wait right there."*

Chapter Thirty-Six

Saturn, The Preserve, 2240 AD

The taxi stopped in front of Serena as she waited on the red-dish-brown path at the port exit of The Preserve. The little vehicle was an open-top rectangular cart on four rubber tires under modest fenders with three rows of side-by-side seats. The door opened as it came to a stop in front of her.

"*Serena Roe?*" the cart asked.

"Yes." She entered the cart, sat, and closed the door. "*Please indicate when you wish to depart,*" the cart said. When she was comfortably situated, she said, "I'm ready to go." It started and smoothly picked up speed, zipping by the lodge. They rode through the forest on a winding road, taking various turns at several intersections and forks. Light shone down from a high bright sky in dust-articulated beams that danced through the foliage as it swayed in a gentle breeze. Several times she passed hikers in the woods away from the road and occasionally saw animals rustling in the brush. She could hear the distant call of birds chirping and singing somewhere in the trees. At one point, she glided across a small suspension bridge over a large flowing stream and saw people in little canoes and kayaks paddling with the current. She found herself laughing out loud. In her wildest dreams, she'd never imagined a place like this still existed. It was as though she'd been swept back in time, before the collapse, to a world that was still thriving, something she'd only seen in books and vids. Finally, the cart came to a stop in a lot beside an archway with a horn-like body, thin at the top and broad at the base, that descended into the ground.

"Ms. Roe, we've arrived," the cart said. *"You can enter the Orchard via the archway. I hope you enjoyed the ride."*

"Yes, I did, thank you." The door opened and she got out, looked around, and walked to the Orchard's entrance. As soon as she got to the door under the arch, it slid aside revealing a wide platform. She stepped on. As soon as she did, she could feel it smoothly descending. It was a long ride that must have been at least a hundred meters straight down. As the elevator tube cleared the roof of the underground, rows of fruit trees appeared in a large area around the landing. Far to the left and right were rows of other plants that she couldn't identify; some looked like vines or hedges supported by scaffolding and dotted with purple berries and some were plants with tall stocks, and some were just green. They spread into the distance like a colorful tapestry of life.

Standing at the bottom of the elevator was Aegeus. As she descended, coming closer and closer to an apparition from the past that couldn't possibly be standing there, she felt her throat tighten and her heart start to beat faster. Her legs felt weak as she got to the bottom, and he stuck his hand out to catch her as he had so long ago. She stepped off the platform and stood before him speechless. He didn't talk, he just held her hand and led her down a row of apple trees that seemed to go on forever. They strolled down a path of rich brown dirt that lightly covered her elegant shoes, holding hands as they walked. Occasionally, she glanced at him not believing he was really there. Finally, they came to a tree and Aegeus stopped, let go of her hand, and sat cross-legged at the base of its trunk.

He looked up at a bright red apple on a low branch and said, "You can pick these, you know." Then he smiled up at her. He was still the handsome boy she remembered, although more sure of himself, more perfected. His smooth brown skin and bright dark eyes under a mane of woolly brown hair hadn't changed. He wore loose-fitting tan cotton pants and a white pullover shirt with loose sleeves and a deep vee-neck just as he had the first time she'd met him. She picked the apple and standing before him, she took a bite. She closed her eyes and concentrated on the crunchy tart taste and the memories came flooding back. She opened her eyes and held it out, regarding it, slowly turning it in her hand. "The last time I saw one of these I was thirteen years old. I've relived holding one of these for eighteen years in my dreams always wondering if it had really happened or if I'd just imagined it." She lowered the apple and looked at him in wonder.

"I waited for you to come back, you know—you never did. I even went to the Arcology, but your mother said you were gone, off-world, working for the company."

"My father died, they made me take up his contract or they'd put my mother out."

"I looked for you on the network from time to time, but eventually gave up," Aegeus remarked. "Then last month, there you were in the news vids, killer corporate soldier and something about the alien. They call him Janus now. I watched his speech just before you came." He shook his head. "You know how to make an entrance, that's for sure." Then he looked her up and down. "You don't look like a killer soldier." He rubbed his chin in mock contemplation, "More like an escapee from a cocktail party."

"I can explain," she said, still holding the half-eaten apple.

The smile left his face, replaced by a look she'd never seen on him. He was naturally casual, not given to serious overexpression. His clear eyes seemed to redden and become moist. "You don't have to explain anything. I know Zen; he told me about what's happened to you over the years, what you've been through, the terrible things you must have seen. You don't have to explain anything."

She stood there in the impossible underground garden floating high above Saturn and could feel tears running down her cheeks. She looked down at herself, smoothing her silk blouse. She stuttered a nervous laugh. "I don't always dress like this. I was at the speech at Aurora Prime, and when I got your message, I don't know, I just came." She wiped her eyes and looked at him. "It's strange, we only knew each other for a day, and…"

His eyes were clear again and he regarded her in a way that made her feel at ease, comfortable as if they'd been together for all the lost years. "I'm glad you came just as you are. You look lovely." He stuck his hand out and smiled. "Come and sit with me awhile."

She sat beside him and put her head on his shoulder. She felt his arm gently wrap around her and pull her close. She could smell his freshness just like she remembered on that day so long ago. All at once, being here became real and all that had come before seemed like a bad dream, distant and unimportant.

"Welcome home," he whispered in her ear.

The End

Author's Note

I want to give special thanks to my wife Anne Moose for her unwavering support and encouragement. Thanks to James Garnett, Tim Laughlin, and David Lerner for their comments on the manuscript. Thanks to Rose de Guzman for proof reading the manuscript.

About the Author

Peter Dingus is a physicist. He received a Ph.D. from UC Berkeley in 1988 and has had posts at Ecole Polytechnique in Paris, DESY in Hamburg, and was a collaborator at CERN in Geneva. From 1991 until it was shut down in 1993, he was a staff physicist at the Superconducting Super Collider project, in Dallas, TX.

Dr. Dingus has published sixty-five scientific papers in refereed journals (such as "Physical Review Letters"). In the mid-nineties, he left particle physics to work in the field of Speech Recognition. Since then, he has been a principal in two software startups, co-founder of a third, and co-founder of a nanotechnology company. He is currently the CTO of an R&D solar cell company in Southern California and living with his wife in Mission Viejo, California.